WARNING SIGNS

Also by Tracy Sierra

Nightwatching

WARNING SIGNS

TRACY SIERRA

PENGUIN
VIKING

VIKING

UK | USA | Canada | Ireland | Australia
India | New Zealand | South Africa

Viking is part of the Penguin Random House group of companies
whose addresses can be found at global.penguinrandomhouse.com

Penguin Random House UK,
One Embassy Gardens, 8 Viaduct Gardens, London SW11 7BW

penguin.co.uk

First published in the United States of America by Pamela Dorman Books/Viking 2026
First published in Great Britain by Viking 2026
001

Copyright © Tracy Sierra, 2026

The moral right of the author has been asserted

Penguin Random House values and supports copyright.
Copyright fuels creativity, encourages diverse voices, promotes freedom
of expression and supports a vibrant culture. Thank you for purchasing
an authorized edition of this book and for respecting intellectual property
laws by not reproducing, scanning or distributing any part of it by any
means without permission. You are supporting authors and enabling
Penguin Random House to continue to publish books for everyone.
No part of this book may be used or reproduced in any manner for the
purpose of training artificial intelligence technologies or systems. In accordance
with Article 4(3) of the DSM Directive 2019/790, Penguin Random House
expressly reserves this work from the text and data mining exception

Printed and bound in Great Britain by Clays Ltd, Elcograf S.p.A.

The authorized representative in the EEA is Penguin Random House Ireland,
Morrison Chambers, 32 Nassau Street, Dublin D02 YH68

A CIP catalogue record for this book is available from the British Library

HARDBACK ISBN: 978–0–241–76091–8
TRADE PAPERBACK ISBN: 978–0–241–76090–1

Penguin Random House is committed to a sustainable future
for our business, our readers and our planet. This book is made from
Forest Stewardship Council® certified paper.

*To my father, Robert, and his father, Louis,
who taught me not only to respect the wilderness
but that true respect is born of love*

Lord save little children! Because with every child ever born of woman's womb there is a time of running through a shadowed place, an alley with no doors, and a hunter whose footsteps ring brightly along the bricks behind him.

—Davis Grubb, *The Night of the Hunter*

CHAPTER 1

2021

"Are you scared, Mama?"

She didn't look back at the children, eyes searching the slope ahead. "Do I seem scared?"

"Yes."

"Hm. Well, in a way I am. But sometimes it's smart to be afraid. You see that?" She pointed uphill with a ski pole to where windblown snow at the mountain's ridge formed a lightly undulating overhang. "Traveling below cornices is risky. And what do you think made this clearing?"

"An avalanche," Bonnie said, then under her breath added, "*obviously.*"

"All right, little miss. Let's think it through. Does it look like it slid a long time ago? Recently?"

Zach rolled his eyes, thwacking his pole into the powder at the foot of the tree beside him again and again. He'd recognized the other car at the trailhead, the one that meant those were Jack, Sam, and their mom's tracks going straight ahead through the steep meadow. Which meant Jack and Sam were probably already at the hut, playing, eating, having fun. Not waiting like timid rabbits at the edge of the tree cover. The other mothers and their children could be on the way by now, too, might even catch up, which meant Zach wouldn't get to be one of the first to arrive at the hut, wouldn't get to choose the bunk he wanted, a spot with the bigger kids instead of with his sister and the other children who were seven, or even younger.

"I guess an old avalanche did that," Bonnie said.

"You guess?"

Zach threw an arm out toward the trail. "It's no big deal, Mom. It's safe. Look! They already crossed."

His mother's smile changed to a tense line. "When you want something to be true, Zakky, that's when it's most difficult to actually see what's there." She pressed a mittened hand slow and hard along her brow bone, the same way she did when she woke with a headache and asked for quiet, please, just a little quiet this morning.

Of course, that was almost every morning.

"Jack and Sam already tested it, Mom. You can see that literally nothing bad happened. It's not even all that deep!"

"That doesn't mean it's safe. A slide isn't always triggered by the first person on the snow. The pressure, the tension, can build, until—" She clapped her mittened hands together in a *woomph*, then scanned the meadow. "Appearances are more deceiving than anyone likes to admit. So. Look again. Tell me what you see."

"Seriously?"

"Yep. Seriously. You, me, and Bonnie? We're responsible for each other."

Their mother crossed her arms. Maybe her exasperation was genuine, maybe she was just trying to appear commanding, but to Zach the gesture seemed silly, uncoordinated, her ski poles sticking out at awkward angles. When Zach met Bonnie's eyes, his sister's dismissive shrug, the lift of her lip, said of course Zach was right, of course their mother was overreacting, wasn't an authority, not a real one, and they eased together into the familiar groove that classified her as embarrassing and illogical.

Zach's expression darkened. "You're so *dramatic*, Mom."

Grace recoiled slightly, her stern expression splintering into hurt.

He turned away as if he might be able to hide from his immediate regret over this petty cruelty. But Zach felt the strange power of the word, too, the way it pinned her, cut her down until she was so small he felt he could pluck her away, throw her aside easy as a stray hair. Why was it that his mother, the person he loved most aside from Bonnie, frustrated him more, made him lash out more, than anyone else? Even her pained softness scratched at him like a frayed wire, leaving a patch of red irritation behind in a way her anger never could.

It was her fault. She was so annoying. And she didn't fight back. Didn't stand up for herself.

Zach peeked back at her stricken face and felt his shame return. He didn't want to fight, not really. Didn't want to be another person who made his mother look that way. He forced himself to focus on the vast, open expanse of snow, peaceful and clean, touched only by the line of tracks. Although the triangular shape of the meadow meant that the space had been cracked open by an avalanche, his sister had been wrong to think it was old damage. The crunched remnants of broken trees, branches, and roots littered the bottom of the slope, their innards still yellow at the breaks. Only a few thin, young trees poked up through the meadow's cover; the ones that had been small enough to bend without breaking under the avalanche's assault. Though not even the saplings had survived intact; their uphill sides had been stripped of branches.

"There's been a slide pretty recently," Zach offered without looking at his mother. "Maybe there was even more than one avalanche with the way the little trees have their branches gone? And it looks like the wind has blown some snow. To make the cornices?"

His mother accepted this change in him with a thoughtful nod. "What does that tell you about its safety?"

Zach cleared his throat to clear away the self-reproach that rose like bile as he looked past his own impatience to see the latent threats in the cornices, the steepness, the fresh avalanche path. What had he expected? That his mother insist they were too special for the rules of nature to apply? For her to somehow change the facts of the trail ahead as if she were all powerful?

No. She was only his mother. She never pretended to be anything else.

"When we checked the avalanche report this morning, it said low risk. So that's good. And there hasn't been a bunch of freezing and thawing. No big storms lately, either. So it probably slid earlier this winter. And the snow has built up slowly."

"That's well thought out, Zakky."

He straightened at the grown-up feeling swelling through his eleven-year-old self at the acknowledgment, at her treating him like a peer.

"Bon-Bon, would you say there's a lot of snow piled up or a little?" Grace again pointed at the cornices above.

Bonnie squinted uphill. "Not so much."

"Yeah, I agree. What do you think our next steps should be?"

Zach and Bonnie looked to each other. The girl shrugged, so it was Zach who spoke.

"Well, um. There's still some danger with the cornices? And the steepness. So I guess we could dig a pit, maybe, to check on the snow layers. Then if that's okay, maybe we go one at a time?"

Their mother nodded. "Smart. Take a little peek at what the mountain might be hiding, huh? Won't take long. The snow's not deep, but you're right, Zakky, at this pitch there's always a risk. *Obviously*"—Grace winked at Bonnie as she imitated her tone, then jutted her chin toward the tangle of shattered trees downhill—"given we can see it already slid. I'll show you a trick." Grace lay a ski pole down in the snow at her feet, leaving behind its impression, then put the tip of one pole at the uphill point of the mark, the tip of the second pole at the downhill point, and brought the poles' handles together. "You see this? How it makes a triangle? Each side the same length? And you see how this downhill pole, here, leans out away from the mountain a little? That means the steepness is more than thirty degrees. And between thirty and forty-five degrees is where most avalanches happen. Not all, but most. And if I let this pole here kind of hang"—she held its handle lightly, letting gravity pull it plumb—"see how the tip goes past the mark in the snow? I'd say it's probably around . . . thirty-five degrees? So, worth doing a pit. Like Zach said. Let's find a safe spot to dig. And Bonnie, how about you try practicing the triangle trick while Zakky and I make the pit?"

Zach and his mother assembled the shovels strapped to the sides of their packs, Grace talking Bonnie through equilateral triangles, what an angle was, how the technique only gauged a small part of the slope, so it was important to make sure you chose a representative spot to measure, the difference between "degree" as in slope, and "degree" as in temperature. When they reached dirt about two feet down, Grace had Zach run his mittens over the shovel-cut side of it, polishing the snow smooth and flat to reveal the layers of different storms, which she traced with a finger, explaining the cycles of the weather, the way snowfalls could knit together peacefully, how a line of hidden weakness could grow the tension, erupt in violence, sweep everything back to begin the cycle anew.

In the pit, she tapped her shovel blade on a column of snow with the butt of her hand, compressing it.

"About as good as you could hope for," she said. "See how it's staying in place? Solid?"

"Does that mean we can cross?" Bonnie asked as their mother stepped out of the small pit.

"Yep."

Bonnie whooped, and Grace pulled the girl close in a one-armed squeeze. "I'm happy, too. But it's always best to be sure. And the very hardest thing is when it isn't okay. When it isn't safe. Or at least isn't as clearly a safe result. You have to be willing to throw away all the work you've done and walk away. And that—having to leave it all behind, all you thought you were going to do, just to be safe, without knowing if anything bad would've happened at all, that's very difficult, that's very . . . brave, that's . . ."

Words trailing off, their mother's eyes went distant, as if focused on something beyond the mountains, through them. And whatever she saw there caused her shoulders to slump, pulled down the corners of her mouth, the edges of her eyes, rounded her back, signs of a gravity Zach wasn't used to seeing in her out here.

"So we can go?" Bonnie asked. "Since you aren't afraid now?"

"I'm always afraid," Grace said, her arm tightening around Bonnie, and she wasn't speaking to her children, not really, still looking away, looking beyond them.

Bonnie squirmed. "Ugh, no more hugging, Mama."

Grace released Bonnie, dazed. "Sorry, was that too much? Sorry, I was . . . zoning out." She bit down hard on a lip, making Zach cringe, because he did the same, didn't he? Bit the inside of his cheek, tore and picked at his cuticles, pulled the fine hairs at his nape, letting his anxious mind make its mark on his skin until the hurt of it focused him away from more difficult things.

Bonnie narrowed her eyes at their mother. "Mama, can I ask you a question?"

Zach saw a familiar, resolute mischief flit through his sister, and felt an anticipatory lift. He admired it, even envied it, Bonnie's power to instantly assess a mood, her ability to diffuse things, to knock them onto an altogether unexpected track you never knew you needed.

But Bonnie's tone was serious enough that Grace's attention snapped to her daughter. "You can ask me anything. Always."

"What's the difference between broccoli and"—the girl paused to be sure her final word, heavy with earnestness, hit just right—"boogers?"

Their mother coughed out a surprised laugh, pulled back from wherever she'd gone, pulled back fully to her children. "Oh no! Do I even want to know?"

"The difference is"—Bonnie pointed to her brother—"Zach'll eat a booger."

"Eeew," he snorted, giggling, grateful. "You are *so* gross."

"*I'm* not the one in a joke about booger eating. That makes *you* the gross one."

Zach affectionately shoved Bonnie with an elbow.

"All right, all right," their mother said, smile so bright now it warmed them, both children leaning toward her like growing things tracking the sun. "Let's do a beacon check before we go."

They unzipped their coats, fished out the avalanche beacons clipped to their waists, verified that all were transmitting the signal that would allow them to be found if buried, had enough battery, before zipping back up again.

"Can I be first?" Bonnie asked, knowing you always crossed an avalanche path one by one, so that if you were taken there'd be someone left to find you.

A hitch of hesitation, but seeing the way Bonnie's need to prove herself shone in her large, pleading eyes, their mother said, "Sure, Bon. Go ahead, big kid."

Zach and Grace stood side by side in the trees, watching Bonnie's little figure steadily make her way.

"She's so small," Zach said.

His mother's brows were knit, eyes fixed on Bonnie. "Mmm. A big personality in a tiny package all right."

"You look—are you—worried?"

"A little bit."

"But we checked everything."

His mother shrugged, still watching Bonnie cross. "The guy who taught my avalanche courses way back when had a saying. 'You take the first avy course, it convinces you to do the second. You take the second, you know enough about the dangers you decide to take the third. And if you take the third, you never go into the backcountry again.'"

"Why?"

"Because by then you've learned you can do everything right, and things can still go wrong."

"But you've done all those classes. And you still come out here. With us."

"Well, that's true. But—I have to come here, Zakky." She put a gentle hand on his shoulder, as if steadying herself. "There's things you can control here, more than other places. And when it comes to what you love . . . it's worth some risk, don't you think?"

Bonnie had reached the other side, and waved a pole to signal it was Zach's turn.

Zach thought about all his mother loved, about risk. He slouched out from under her touch and said, "Maybe it'd be better. Safer. To just—not."

"Oh," she said, and he felt her eyes on him, felt her concern, heard her voice wilt. "I hope that's not what you think, Zakky. I hope—I hope that's not the lesson. Though maybe you're right. If you love someone who doesn't love you back, I mean."

He didn't answer, didn't look at her, just began skiing across the meadow. Zach tried not to focus on the cornices above, the knowledge that no matter how cautious he was, how good and right he might be, all these things he loved might fracture, might suffocate him. Might suffocate all of them.

When Zach glanced over his shoulder, his mother stared from what seemed very far away. On her beautiful face he read helpless worry, but there was pride there, too, at witnessing her children capably travel forward through a dangerous world without her.

Zach turned ahead, and kept moving.

CHAPTER 2

ONE YEAR LATER

The elk lay curled on the snow, its light brown back facing the boy. Zach stared through the haze of his frozen breath at the antlers extending above the animal's bulk. He had never seen an elk asleep before. Had never stumbled across any wild animal asleep. Though of course he knew animals must sleep. Must spend much of their time, just like he did, vulnerable.

Zach glanced over his shoulder toward the trail where his father waited just out of sight for him to do his business in private. The sun hit his eyes and he sneezed, whipping back to see the elk's response.

Nothing. It might be hurt. Or dead.

Driving over Independence Pass in the fall, his mother had spotted a distant elk herd and pulled over. They'd passed the binoculars she always kept in the car back and forth between them, watching two bull elk clash as the cows and calves they fought over either disinterestedly grazed, or were forced to hurry out of the way to protect themselves.

Thinking on that violence, Zach pictured the elk rising, tossing its head. But as he edged in front of it, what he saw was so distant from all he knew that all previous experience was whisked from his mind, useless, and he blinked slack-jawed at what lay there, trying to understand.

From shoulders to snout, there was only bone. The elk's spine lay neatly on the snow, extending out from mottled red and brown muscle where the neck had met the chest, bloodlessly cut as though cauterized. The vertebrae rested in a precise and graceful arc that ended at the animal's stripped skull. The boy's eyes tripped over the seven points on each antler, their weathered brown contrasting jarringly with the whiteness of the peeled skull. All the exposed bone— from the rungs of the spine to the inside of the head visible through the vacant cavity of the one-time nose—appeared almost antiseptically clean. Slick square teeth sat secure and yellowed in matte, pale jaws, interlocking into a tidy rictus smile.

Together with the contradiction of bright scrubbed bone protruding from intact muscle, Zach immediately saw other paradoxes that made his breath shorten, his stomach twist. There was no blood. No tracks traced around the animal's head and neck, not even its own. The body, the bones, rested as if on display. A fresh earth smell, similar to the scent of the atmosphere before an electrical storm, flared then faded as the wind blew the body's scent toward him, its appeal disorienting.

Everything about the elk was foreign and unfamiliar, except for the fact of its deadness. The absence of life was so universal in its natural unnaturalness that Zach immediately thought of his mother. The eye sockets stared so evenly past him, so reminded him of the way his mother's eyes had gazed through and beyond him, that he instinctively covered his face to hide the unsettling sight of the over-clean bones.

"Daddy?"

He cringed at the childlike word, but there was only silence. He tried again, correcting himself. "Dad?"

The angle of the wind, the odd acoustics of the winter forest, let Zach hear his father mutter low, "Son of a bitch, what now?"

For Christmas two years ago, someone had given his sister a stuffed octopus that could be flipped inside out. Flip one way, pink, fuzzy, and smiling. Flip the other way, green, slick, and glowering. As he changed the octopus back and forth, switching Outerself to Underself, Zach had thought only of his father. Impossible to know which was the true face, which was the inside-out one. Did it even matter if it usually smiled, soft and comforting, when you were aware of the furious, slippery thing forming its innards?

"What is it?" Bram called out.

"Can you come here? Please?"

Zach clenched his hands into fists in his mittens, fingernail tearing at the cuticle of his thumb.

"Just has to make me come to him," Bram said, talking to himself again.

Zach heard his father leave the trail they were following to the backcountry hut, the sound of his inexperienced wallow through the powder distinctive. He winced at Bram's stream of muttered irritations over the way Zach was interrupting his progress uphill toward his all-important goals.

Maybe the absence of elk brain, the winding away of veins, the plucked eyeballs, the vanished heft of scraggly neck mane, the evaporation of flesh and sinew and life itself, would be enough to prevent his father going to Underself, crossing arms and squinting down at the boy with an exhalation of disappointment.

"Now what is the big—"

Bram paused where Zach had first spotted the elk, not yet positioned to see the strangeness.

"Dead?"

Zach nodded.

"Did you touch it?"

Zach opened his mouth but instead of speaking he shook his head. He saw himself as a fish thrown on a bank, mouth silently opening and closing. He was sure he appeared as stupid as his classmates did when they imitated him trying to say something, anything, when he was nervous.

"You gotta be able to speak up, kid, or else people will walk all over you."

Zach kept his eyes on the elk as his father approached. The plates of its skull fit together like puzzle pieces, the thin lines between them like the rivers tracing through the topographic maps his mother had taught him to read.

He balled his hand inside his mitten, the nail of his index finger ripping the corner of the cuticle from his thumb. He folded its bloodied stickiness into his palm. Squeezed.

Bram stopped short, shocked to momentary stillness at the sight of the full body. "Holy shit," he said flatly, then moved closer.

Zach's shoulders relaxed as his father's taut irritation dissipated into interest. Bram squatted down and poked at a piece of the whitened spine with the metal tip of his ski pole, knocking a vertebrae askew, then prodding the furred body, the skull. Zach backed away at seeing the perfection of the bones' alignment set off-kilter, recoiling at his father's interference for reasons he couldn't quite assemble.

"The hell?" Bram said as he jabbed, his sharp gaze now judging and evaluating only the elk, in a way that allowed Zach to speak with no hitches or hesitation.

"What could have killed it? Done all"—Zach looked over the split body, the precision of the cut chest muscles—"this?"

Bram stood. "Maybe the back was under snow, but the head and neck got eaten by something? It's been warmer last month or so. Could've melted, I guess?"

"There's no tracks," Zach said.

Bram's gaze swept over the snow, then up to the sway of the pine branches and aspens rimming the clearing. "Birds must've picked it clean."

Zach frowned. Could birds have fished out brain and tongue and meat? No trees cast shadows across the elk that would have led to uneven melting. And how could anything, even birds, have left the snow bloodless?

"It doesn't smell bad."

"True." Bram agreed. "Probably still frozen." He jutted his chin toward the animal's tail. "The back leg's different. Something was at it for sure."

Zach had been too occupied with the bright white bones, the strangely surgical appearance of the sliced neck, to notice the leg. But as he moved next to Bram, he saw that his father was right. The back right leg lay askew, its skin and muscle torn and gnawed. Yet despite the leg's more visceral appearance, it struck Zach as somehow less disturbing, but more explicable; the expected signs of a carrion scavenger. Near the tail there were even depressions that might have been prints, windblown or melted at the edges beyond recognition.

"But the head, and the neck? It's—don't you think it's—not right?" Zach asked.

They stared down at the meticulousness of the cut chest muscles, the scrubbed vertebrae, the way even the pin-width lines between the skull's plates were scoured clean and bloodless.

"Doesn't really matter what happened," Bram said. "But it'll be a great story to tell the guys—outdoor danger and all that. And tell you what, on the way down we'll take the skull and antlers with us.

I bet someone'd pay a couple grand for it. Great find." Zach straightened with pride as Bram slapped a hand on his shoulder, gave a crooked smile. "You might not even need to ask that tightwad aunt of yours for the cash to get your sister a birthday present."

Zach acknowledged the indictment of Aunt Felicity with a noncommittal bob of his head.

"I'm kidding," Bram said. "But we'll see what we can get for it, huh?" He pointed at the body. "It all comes down to eat or be eaten. You're stronger, better, you win the game."

Zach nodded, as if his father was saying something new, something profound. But it was comforting, Bram's return to his confident baseline, the way he transformed the elk from frighteningly wonderous to a thing monetized, his neat appropriation of the scene as simply more evidence that things worked the way he already thought they did.

"Most people would be bothered, seeing this," his father said. "Don't like facing how things really are, what the meat they eat looks like before they pretty it up. Not us though."

"Not us," Zach echoed.

"Your sister, though?" Bram chuckled. "She'd probably puke."

Zach kept his face smooth. Bonnie caught the slugs and spiders that disgusted him with her bare hands, popped them into jars, sketched them before setting them free, each time a little closer to the illustrations in her favorite science books. The art teacher had even pinned to the classroom corkboard his sister's pencil drawing of a sparrow killed by striking a school window. Bonnie's labels of the bird's broken parts hung over the students like a cautionary tale: Bent wing. Soft neck. White eyes.

No, it was Zach who felt nauseous.

"Okay." Bram clapped his hands, Zach startling at the ricochet of the sound around the clearing. "Let's get this show on the road.

See if Ginny has managed to clean and prep the place. Everything's gotta be perfect for these guys—perfect! Arlo's the one to impress. Firm handshake, strong 'hello,' and then you be seen but not heard, right? Except with this Russ kid, Dave's son. Make sure he likes you. Keep him entertained and out of the way. And since Dave's the one who insisted this be a father-son thing, your line is 'Wow, Mister Dowling, this boys' trip is the best thing ever, what a great idea, so glad to be included, blah, blah, blah,' got it?"

Zach nodded enthusiastically, familiar with this lecture by now, aware of the excitement he was supposed to show. Because there were stakes his father was nervous over, but it was important to pretend his father could never be nervous about anything at all.

As Bram turned toward the trail, Zach averted his eyes from the awkward way his father's skis lapped, nearly causing him to fall before he managed to disentangle himself and move away. Despite himself Zach stared toward the elk again, then shook his head as if to shake off the influx of grotesque imaginings—yellow slit pupils, dripping teeth, surgically sharp curled claws peeling back the elk's layers.

Zach deftly oriented his own skis and hurried after Bram. Skin crawling with the sense that something watched him from the trees, gut creeping with fear over the residual presence of a predator, Zach paused to shoulder his heavy pack where he'd left it at the side of the trail. He pawed distractedly at his pockets, unable to shed the sense he'd left something important behind. Bram came into sight above, wearing his own pack and pulling the sled full of supplies he'd restrapped to his waist. His father traveled inefficiently but quickly, strength making up for his inexperience. Although the trail was obvious, well packed by previous skiers over the course of two nearly snowless months, Bram paused to look for the blue plastic diamonds nailed into trees marking the route to Pantheon Hut. Without turning to check on Zach, he went around a bend and vanished. Zach lowered his head to let the crown of his skull take the brunt of his father's indifference before following up the trail.

In motion, discomfort in his abdomen reminded him what he'd forgotten. He'd never relieved himself. But he didn't dare ask Bram to stop and wait for him again. Didn't dare pause and fall farther behind. And together with the frigid air he gulped down the elk's uncanniness, its meticulous dissection, and felt the indelible image of it lodge somewhere at the base of his throat.

CHAPTER 3

Zach stopped where the trail split at the edge of a huge, snow-covered meadow, the air over eleven thousand feet shortening his breaths. Despite being two stories high, despite its sharply sloped roof, Pantheon Hut was nearly invisible at the end of the path branching to his right, heavily buttressed on one side by blown snow. Bram had gone in the wrong direction, moving left up the trail leading to Mariah Bowl, its peak hidden behind a ridge.

It might be a test. He might fail by questioning his father. Or fail for not speaking up.

Zach scratched again at the torn cuticle of his thumb.

It didn't matter. The longer he waited, the bigger either mistake would grow.

"Dad?"

Wind whipped the word downhill. Zach knocked his ski poles together, *cling! cling! cling!* Bram turned and Zach pointed toward the hut, exaggeratedly moving in its direction. His father frowned, saw the hut, then with a lift of his pole in acknowledgment, he cut off-trail and skied downhill toward Pantheon.

Bram caught up to Zach taking off his skis at the hut's stairs. "I was so focused on mentally rehearsing my pitch, I got distracted. Eye on the prize and all. But hey, at least you inherited my sense of direction."

His father entered the door combination, and together they stepped inside. Zach felt a taut line snap when the door closed, a welcome barrier between him and the unsettling watchfulness of the forest and its unknown predators.

"Ginny?" Bram called out for his assistant. "Where are you?"

Every surface shone with varnish, giving the log walls and knotty pine floor a clean, golden glow. Tall picture windows filled the hut with winter sunlight and provided an expansive view of the Elk Range serrating a cloudless blue sky. Out the side window they could now see the pinnacle of Mount Mariah, wind spinning snow from its tip at over twelve thousand feet. A clutch of soft cobweb at the ceiling's peak some twenty feet above moved as if the hut itself exhaled delicate breaths. Under the lower ceiling opposite the stairs in back, propane burners and wood counters with an inset plastic bucket acting as a sink made up the kitchen. A massive woodstove crouched on a stone slab in the middle of the room, flanked on one side by two long picnic tables, and on the other by boxy couches and lounge chairs topped with plastic cushions. A tall metal pot with a spout at its base sat on the woodstove.

It all looked the same. Everything looked the same even though anyplace his mother had been should, ought to—shouldn't it?—look different.

"What the hell?" Bram said. "It's colder in here than outside. Where is she?" Raising his voice, he yelled, "Ginny?"

Zach stayed quiet as he hung up his coat, his hat. After removing his mittens he furtively tucked his bloodied thumb into his fist to hide the damage.

Bram stalked through the hut. Pounded up the stairs, rumbled above, then reappeared.

"Goddamn it. Goddamn it, Ginny! Takes the whole week off for some avalanche safety course. Confirmed she'd be here yesterday to set up. And look!" He flung an arm out. "No sign of her. There's a couple of packs upstairs. But I checked 'em out and it's all men's stuff. Probably a couple of the guys got here early and decided to hike up and take a run. But—she was supposed to carry up my laptop. The PowerPoint printouts explaining the offering terms! Thank God I wouldn't let her handle the checks, so at least I have those. And she said she was going to clean up, try and make it, I dunno, luxurious up here! But look!" Bram threw a derisive hand out at the hut.

Zach obediently took in the space around him. And though he saw nothing wrong, he shook his head, made a "mmm" sound, as if the state of the place offended him, too.

"At least it's a good size. Why the hell do they call them 'huts' if they're this big? More like a 'lodge.' They'd be able to charge a lot more if 'hut' didn't make it sound like you'd be crammed into a shack." Bram checked his phone. "No service. I mean, they said. But damn it."

"There was a car at the trailhead, though?" Zach offered.

"Right but, now that I think about it—that wasn't an orange Wrangler, right? A Jeep Wrangler?"

"No."

"Shit. I was so focused on getting here before the group, I didn't even think about it. But her car would've been down there if she'd come yesterday like she promised."

There was a long pause, Bram scowling as his eyes roamed the hut, Zach as still as a rabbit blending into grass. Despite his efforts to stay invisible, his father fixed on him. "We're gonna have to do it all ourselves. What did that school of yours teach you?"

Zach blinked at his father. He'd done backcountry trips with school, sure, but the huts were his mother's refuge, bundling him and his sister into the mountains as often as she was able since they were toddlers. Up rushed all those beautiful days where they had been different versions of themselves, free.

Free for a little while, anyway.

Anger fishhooked his throat. Because his dad was big, was strong, because the ski up hadn't been difficult for him, he thought he knew things. "My wife isn't your average girl," Bram would brag when it suited him. "She can handle herself in the wilderness." And yet he'd never shown any interest in coming along with his family. When no one but his wife and children was there to hear him, Bram dismissed these trips as unchallenging, frivolous wastes of time.

No, his father didn't know anything about the backcountry. Zach was vicariously embarrassed by the newness of Bram's gear; the way the stylish priciness broadcast his underlying inexperience. Up here, as everywhere else, his father looked like a man who had stepped out of an advertisement. Always the best dressed, the most casually casual, the man with the things people in the know knew. But also always a little artificial, a little off, a little much.

Maybe when the others arrived they'd see through him, too.

His father snapped his fingers in front of Zach's nose. The closeness of it, the way Bram's blue eyes were turning to the dark cold of the Underself, frightened Zach into swallowing the spark of his sullen spite to land somewhere deep and neglected.

"Anyone home? What do we need to do first?" Bram asked, as if it were a quiz, as if he knew the answer.

"Um, f-fire?"

"You sound like a little girl when everything you say comes out like a question. That what you want?"

Zach shook his head vigorously, knowing the correct answer.

When would his voice deepen and remove some of the sting of truth from this insult?

"Right. Then what's first?"

Zach forced himself to keep his eyes on his father's, to not shy away from Bram's raised eyebrow, the way his father managed to squeeze the air between them tight. Because any sign of disobedience, of falling short, might escalate his irritation.

"We need to build a fire. And melt snow in the pot for water."

"Fine. Good. I'll handle the fire, and you deal with the rest."

Zach took up the bucket sitting next to the woodstove. Outside the hut's front door he broke the snow's crust and filled the bucket from the few inches of sugary powder below, shuttling between the snow and the pot on the stove, careful to put on then remove his boots to avoid getting the floor wet.

Bram stalked through the hut, muttering to himself. "She . . . goddamn it . . . the disrespect . . . why can't anyone ever?"

Then from the kitchen Bram called out, "Come here and look at this!"

Zach went to his father's side. Crusted dishes and a pan locked together in an inch of dirty water lightly iced over at the bottom of the sink bucket. Nothing that couldn't be easily taken care of, once they had warm water.

"What a pain in the ass," Bram huffed, glaring down his nose at the mess. "I'm gonna have to fire that girl."

Things were always better when his father was focused on someone else's failings, so Zach mirrored Bram's pose, fists on hips, and shook his head to demonstrate how correct his father was; them against the world.

"Once you finish what you started and get water done we'll have to deal with this," Bram said.

Zach went back to work.

Bram loaded firewood into the woodstove. "Ginny was chomping at the bit to help when she knew Shane'd be here. Of course she was! Still deluding herself."

Shane, son of Bram's biggest investor, Arlo Oliver.

"She must've found out Pike was coming along after all."

Pike, the only one coming who didn't have a son to bring along. Pike, whose investment was less than his dad thought it should be.

Investments were never as big as his father thought they should be.

"This is exactly why I didn't tell her. Last thing I needed was her bailing if she found out Pike was tagging along. The second he heard Ginny'd be here, he was all"—Bram imitated Pike's voice in a high-pitched singsong—"'Oh a ski trip? I wouldn't miss it!' As if I'd invited him. Pathetic." Bram tossed kindling and balled-up newspaper into the woodstove. "But what was I supposed to say? 'You don't even have a kid to bring along?' Or, 'Get over it, girl thinks you're a loser, and I agree?' Hell no. He's a dunce of a trust-fund kid with money to burn. Figured if he came along, maybe he'd commit more money to impress her. Hell, maybe Shane'd invest to shut me up about Ginny in front of his dad. But now? If Ginny doesn't show, that's all ruined. Girl is impossible."

Zach tried to decipher the ins and outs of this, translating it to his own experience. Pike had a crush on Ginny so he'd wanted to come on the trip, but Ginny didn't like him. She had a crush on Shane. But Shane was embarrassed about that for some reason, and didn't want his dad, Arlo, to know. This made sense, given Zach would never want Bram to know who he had a crush on. The thought of his father finding evidence of any of Zach's soft feelings made his heart clench with anticipatory humiliation.

Bram flicked a lighter inside the stove. Swore when the paper quickly fizzled out. He went outside, returned holding a bag from the sled, and pulled out a small, red plastic container of lighter fluid.

He squirted the fluid over the wood and kindling, set a flame to it, and was forced to leap back as the thing went instantly to inferno, fire spitting out of the stove then retreating inside.

Zach's mother would never have started a fire that way. Would have thought lighter fluid not only too heavy to haul up but dangerous and unnecessary. And while that made the sudden burst of flame feel wrong and rough, Zach still watched with excited awe. The lighter fluid was not only temptingly efficient but thrilling in its showy destructiveness.

Bram gave an approving nod and slammed the stove door shut before slinging his pack over a shoulder and heading upstairs. By the time he came back down Zach had filled the enormous meltpot with snow.

"That stuff upstairs better not be the guide's. He's supposed to wait down at the trailhead to bring the others up. But"—Bram wagged a finger at Zach—"if it *is* the guide's junk and he comes back while I'm out, you tell him he's in the hallway bunk, got it?"

Zach froze, stomach knotting. There was no world in which he would be capable of telling an adult stranger to sleep in the hallway bunk, the worst spot in the hut. The Pantheon reservation had been his mother's, rolled over preferentially from year to year, and would normally house her group of up to sixteen mothers and children. This weekend there would be only nine people. More than enough room to allow the guide a better bunk.

Bram didn't seem to register his son's discomfort. If anything, the prospect of future confrontation had cheered him, and he whistled as he put on his coat and boots.

"I'm gonna head downhill and see if I can catch a signal to call Ginny," Bram said. "Don't start daydreaming like you do. Bring the rest of the stuff inside. Unpack. And remember those dishes, yeah? I don't want any disrespect."

A *woosh* of air and his father was gone, leaving behind an ominously undefined obligation to groom the hut into whatever Bram expected. Zach breathed deep. Calmed himself by counting the way his mom had taught him—*one-one-thousand, two-one-thousand.* He pulled on boots and hurried out the back door to the outhouse, at last able to use the bathroom without having to admit to his father he'd forgotten to go in the woods, or risking a lecture about how he needed to learn to hold it better, he went more often than Bonnie!

Back in the hut, the woodstove's window had gone dark. Despite his self-satisfaction at shortcutting his way to completing the fire, Bram hadn't opened the vent on the bottom of the stove, nearly suffocating it. Zach cranked the vent open and watched the flames spring up.

No, his father didn't know much about the outdoors at all.

"There's so little oxygen up here, you need to let as much air as possible sneak in," his mother said in memory, after showing him how to operate that vent. He'd laughed as she walked two sneaky, tickling fingers along his arm.

She had been like a real mother on these trips.

Don't start daydreaming like you do.

Zach shuttled the bags indoors, and added more snow to the meltpot. A brush and dustpan caught his eye and he went to his knees to sweep up the scrim of ash, bark fragments, and kindling splinters Bram had left around the stove.

He paused. Tipped his head.

Something glittered from between the pine planks of the floor.

CHAPTER 4

Zach tried to pluck the shining thing from where it was wedged, but it was stuck tight. After a moment's thought he grabbed a narrow stick from the depleted kindling pile and carefully levered it between the floorboards and underneath the bright object until it popped out onto the floor.

It was an earring, a jewel the size of his pinkie nail. Despite being dirty, it scattered oblong rainbows in the sunlight. Could it be a diamond? Zach looked furtively around the empty room, picturing a pirate's ghost snatching away this prize of buried treasure. He laid his cheek on the floor to examine the floorboard seam, then the ones flanking it. No matching earring. Nothing but grime.

What if he took the stone into one of the jewelry shops in town? Sold it for—something. Did they let kids buy plane tickets? He and Bonnie could fly to Michigan, to Aunt Felicity. Even though the last trip hadn't gone well, and Bram didn't like her, Zach found himself desperately wanting to see her; see a face that looked so much like his mother's.

He placed the earring in his palm. Wrinkled his nose, distracted from his fantasy by the crusted tangle of hairs that came up from the floorboard crack with the earring, raveled scabby through its backing and thin gold post. A small chunk of something swung from them below his upturned hand.

Zach instinctively recoiled. But as it often did, as it had at seeing the elk on the hike up, revulsion bred curiosity. He examined the dangling thing closer. What was it? Some kind of dull brown matter about the size of the diamond, thin but tightly curled, and wrinkled in a way that made it seem organic. A piece of old apple peel? A moldy wood shaving?

It all reminded Zach of a fishing lure; a sparkle of bait hiding something unknown, maybe deadly.

Ever since the world had broken, he'd skidded out of a groove he hadn't even known existed, sensing a rot lurked below things. The way the earring interlaced with something repulsive was only more proof.

He drifted into memories of that other life. His mother pulling a toddler Bonnie up the trail in a sled. His mother jumping off the hut's porch into powder screeching with joy, snow strung through her hair. Her approving nod as he switched on the hut's solar power. Her earnest expression as she and the other mothers demonstrated building a snow shelter in case of emergency, how to light a one-match fire—survival drills he and the other kids participated in with the deep seriousness universal to children who understand they are learning important, grown-up things.

But looking back now, his eyes snagged on the darkness twisting through the bright past. His mother wearing earrings that looked similar to this one, and when he asked her what a diamond cost she said, "These? They're fake. It all is. You can't tell unless you test." A rounding of her shoulders, a folding into herself. "Or at least I couldn't."

Last year, Zach sitting hidden on the stairs, those ones right over there, eavesdropping as usual, as always. One of the other mothers asking, "How do you get Bram to all those school events, Grace? Mike never'll come."

His mother spitting out, "Anything to look like a good dad."

An awkward clearing of throats, shifting in seats. His mother backtracking, voice sliding into a different tone, "Oh, ignore me. I'm cranky because we argued about how often I bring the kids up here."

Zach didn't know what price his mother had paid to take that trip, but he was sure there'd been one. Everything with Bram required an exchange, an offering.

Another mother chiming in. "Pete's the same. 'Why do you have to go, can't someone else do it?' But these trips are a godsend. So nice to get away. He's more work than my kids, I swear."

Sympathetic chuckles, then his mother again. "I mean, Bram certainly likes bragging about how I'm part of the PTA crew that does these trips." A hum from the other mothers. Mountaineering prowess and a knowledge of the outdoors held a cachet in town, the prime reason Bram didn't admit his low opinion of such things in front of others. "But he's particular. He expects the house, meals, all that kind of thing, to be a certain way. So when I'm not there?" His mother trailed off, and when she spoke again her voice had a forced lightness. "But, whatever. He has to deal with me constantly forgetting to do things. And if it's not that, I'm blubbering over something. Not to mention"—she swept a hand through the air from the top of her head to her waist, broke into a smile, and batted her eyes jokingly—"look at this body! Look at this hair. No one's ever accused me of being low maintenance."

Knowing laughter, all the women perpetually eager to put themselves down, and to cheer each other on for doing the same. All the women, too, ever ready to compare their latest surgeries, shots, laserings, things that Aunt Felicity called pricey, phony, pointless, but that his mother shrugged off as expected, even required. When Zach asked why she, why the other mothers, did such things, the only explanation she ever offered was a cryptic, "Beauty is pain."

"But you're already beautiful."

"Aren't you sweet. But every son thinks his mother's beautiful," she'd say, smiling a thin smile that showed no teeth, a smile that said he meant well, but didn't really understand her world.

But she didn't understand his world, either. Nearly every boy he knew saw mothers as useful but dull backdrops to daily life, requiring Zach to curb talking about what his own mother taught him, the things she'd done, what they did together, in order to avoid pitying looks, or being called names.

"Speaking of PTA duties," someone said, "that new avalanche path? We have to report that before they bring the kids up. It's hairy."

As the women broke down the danger, if perhaps the school outdoor education trip should be moved to a different hut altogether, Zach snuck a look around the corner to see his mother's eyes gone distant. Watched her take a long sip of wine. She wasn't part of the conversation now. She'd vanished into her glass, her head.

Zach stared down at the earring. Could it have been his mother's, one of the other mothers', lost last year? They all wore beautiful, shining things, even out here. The remote possibility this little fragment was proof of a time that existed before caused him to squeeze the earring tight.

He pictured his mother's hands holding a compass, pointing at the topo map on her GPS device, teaching him to read and understand, the pull of a needle to north an invisible magic.

It all helps you stay safe.

His teeth grit tight.

Hypocrite. How could she.

The loud bang of the door startled Zach into the present. He dropped the earring and hurried to his feet, readying an excuse for Bram about why he wasn't working.

A stubble-bearded stranger stood in the doorway.

Zach's relief at his father not finding him idle was replaced with nervousness that this might be the guide he was supposed to banish to the hallway bunk. The new man lifted his goggles to rest on his helmet. "Oh. Hey there, bud."

"Hi."

"Um, anyone else around?"

Zach shook his head. "Nah. My dad's—out."

"Shit," the man said, then grimaced. "Sorry, probably shouldn't swear, huh?" Zach saw a flash of how he must look from the outside, a boy whose huge blue eyes and light brown curls made him look younger than twelve. Even though, he thought with some pride, he was the fastest skier in his grade, almost the tallest kid, the only one who could climb the rope to the gym ceiling. He stood a little straighter, tried to look old enough to be someone it was okay to swear in front of.

"It's fine," Zach said.

"Right. It's just my buddy and I took a run down Mariah and got separated. I figured he'd come back here."

"You don't have radios?" Zach cringed. He shouldn't scold a grown-up. "I mean, um, don't you normally have radios skiing out here?"

"Yeah, but I guess Jon doesn't have his on. Idiot was pretty out of it, I told him to stop smok—" The man interrupted himself, again realizing he was talking to a boy. "You know what? Never mind. I'm Shane."

Shane. Arlo Oliver's son. Not the guide.

"I'm Zach."

"Are you—Bram's kid?"

"Yeah."

All adults fell into a vague, indeterminate state of "old" to Zach. But certainly Shane looked younger than Zach's father. His too-small eyes made him far less handsome than Bram, but they had similar dark, thick hair. Though he had to be close to six feet tall, Shane was shorter than Bram, and as he removed his coat Zach saw Shane was thinner limbed and had an obvious softness around the middle Bram would never allow himself. Zach recognized the high-end brand of Shane's coat, nodding in approval without meaning to at seeing that, unlike his father's gear, Shane's was creased and worn.

Clearly familiar with the norms of the hut, Shane hung his wet outerwear and helmet in the entry. When he took off his boots he made sure to pull their tongues wide to dry efficiently, then neatly set them next to Zach's before walking into the room.

Zach's eyes skipped over the bits of snow and ice his father had tracked along the floor, already melting, already making a mess of things, before spotting the earring next to his foot and snapping his eyes back to Shane to make sure he hadn't noticed it.

Shane peered out the window facing Mount Mariah, presumably looking for his friend. Zach grabbed the earring and hid it behind his back. Edged toward the bookshelf built into the wall of the dining area a few feet away, and surreptitiously hid the diamond and its attached mess out of sight behind a line of paperbacks.

When he turned, Shane, oblivious, was scowling down at his phone.

"There's no service," Zach said.

"Yeah. Checking just in case. Little worried about Jon."

Zach frowned. In all Bram's obsessive recital of the weekend's plans, his reminders to Zach of who was who and who was most important, he had never mentioned a "Jon."

"Is Jon the guide?"

"Nah. Buddy of mine. Great skier—a pro!" Shane's chin tipped up slightly as he added, "I'm producing his next movie."

"Oh," Zach said, then seeing Shane expected more, added, "that's really cool."

"Right?" Shane said, grinning.

If it was anyone else, an uninvited guest might be a problem. But someone Shane and his dad brought along? Bram invoked Arlo Oliver and his media fortune the way Zach's science teacher did Einstein, or the pastor did Jesus. It would be all right. Even good; a favor Bram could be magnanimous about, a mark in the ledger of things Arlo owed him.

Noticing the beads of condensation on the meltpot, Zach filled a saucepan from the kitchen with warm water and poured it into the sink. The ice cracked. He refilled the saucepan for rinse water, then began to scrub.

Shane padded over to the kitchen.

"I'm impressed your dad landed a reservation for Pan, especially on a long weekend. It's legit impossible! I heard locals have it on lock 'cause the way they run it, they give preference to whoever booked that date the year before. They don't even care if you try and offer them more. Believe me, I've tried."

"It was my mom's reservation," Zach said, rinsing a plate. "She had it since before I was born."

"Oh." Shane's eyes slid away from the boy. "That's different then."

Zach shrugged. It didn't seem different.

"Gotta say, I cannot imagine Bram up here. He's more of a"—Shane squinted at the ceiling, searching for the right word—"a country-club guy, you know?"

Zach knew.

"My dad's the same," Shane lowered his voice confidingly. "I know this was supposed to be some father-son thing, but he bailed. My dad's all talk—his idea of roughing it is the Four Seasons. Whatever, he's too old for this anyway. But Pan's legendary, so of course I still wanted to come, and Jon, too. Even though neither of us is interested in your dad's whole"—Shane searched for a word, his hand gesturing in a lazy circle—"thing."

Arlo Oliver wasn't coming.

The air squeezed from Zach's lungs. He tasted bitter panic as his imagination tumbled over the endless branching possibilities of his father's reaction to this news.

At seeing Zach's face fall, the way he swiped his palm over an eye, Shane said, "Jesus, kid. You okay?"

"Yeah, just—my dad? He'll be—disappointed. That yours isn't here."

Shane's expression relaxed into understanding. "Don't worry, kiddo. My dad's planning to re-up his investment. Obviously that's what Bram's after with this whole male bonding, father-son, return-to-nature nonsense anyway, right? So don't stress."

"Oh." Zach looked up at Shane with fervent gratefulness. "Okay! That's—thanks."

Shane sucked at his teeth and winced. "I'm not exactly supposed to tell anyone that. He still needs to look over the new offering docs and all. So keep it to yourself, okay bud?"

Zach smoothed his expression and made a grunting noise he hoped sounded like agreement.

He'd tell his father at the earliest possible opportunity.

"I heard about your mom, by the way." Shane said. "I'm sorry."

Zach pretended to care intensely about cleaning the plate in his hand. It was white with little gray scratches he thought must be from forks and knives scraping it, scarring it, bearing down too hard and indelibly marking it.

"Thanks," Zach mumbled.

He waited for Shane to prod and poke at the tender places, for morbid curiosity to curl his tongue into the hows and whys most people found irresistible. But Shane only unwrapped and chewed on an energy bar as he watched Zach slot dishes into the drying rack.

A thankfulness flared in Zach's chest at the unintrusive sympathy. He smiled at Shane, and silently offered him a dish towel. Shane held up his hands as if in surrender. "Nah, man. I'm useless with that kind of thing."

His mother's voice rang through his head. *People pretend to be stupid as an excuse to be lazy.*

Languidly comfortable in his own skin, not in the least bothered he wasn't helping, Shane's shine dulled.

He probably never had to do things for himself, or for others. Shane had probably never been pressed thin under a watchful, critical eye. And he probably didn't ask more questions about Zach's mother because he didn't actually care.

"Someone really left a mess here, huh?" Shane said. "Promise it wasn't me. We were up here crack of dawn, but we ate on the trail so we could get some runs in."

"My dad's assistant was supposed to come up and clean or whatever. But she didn't."

"Wait—like your dad's secretary? Ginny?"

"Yeah."

Shane pinched the bridge of his nose as if seized by a sudden headache. "He specifically said she wasn't coming."

"Well. Um." Zach's mind searched for a way to explain away Bram's lie. Had Zach fractured some strategy of his father's in a way Bram might find unforgivable?

"What I mean is, Ginny was supposed to come yesterday, to set up. And then, you know, leave?" Zach unconsciously pulled the fine hairs at his nape. "But she obviously didn't. So my dad went down the trail to try to call her. In case she got confused. And is coming today instead."

"Right." Shane said. "So you don't know if—"

The sound of the door swinging open interrupted him. The new arrival silhouetted there took off his helmet to reveal long blond dreadlocks, eyes ringed white and cheeks red with a goggle-shaped sunburn.

"Jon! Thought you were ass up in a snowbank, dude, what the hell?"

"Yeah, sorry, man, all good. All"—Jon looked at Zach, then back to Shane—"handled. Just tried a different line is all. Thought we'd end up in the same spot. Should've known you'd be too fast for me."

"Next time turn on your radio, man."

"Was it off? Stupid. But—check it out!" Jon jutted his chin toward the window opposite the peak, eyes alight. "Wasn't forecast, but sure smells like snow to me."

Together, the three peered out at a faraway thread of dark gray clouds, and an electric current of possibility passed through them.

"That would be perfect," Shane said. "That would be exactly what we need."

CHAPTER 5

When Bram reappeared, Zach was drying the last dish. Jon and Shane lounged in the hut's living area, loudly rehashing their morning's skiing. The fire was roaring, the kitchen clean, the hearth swept, Zach's backpack moved upstairs to the bunkroom, and the appetizers, champagne, beer, wine, and whiskey his father had pulled up in the sled were neatly lined up in a corner of the kitchen, ready to be plated or poured.

Everything in order. Every task as complete as he could get it. Though Zach could never be sure how his father would see things.

Bram entered with a gust of cold air. He took in the new arrivals, a twitch to his lip at seeing Jon instead of the much-anticipated Arlo Oliver. Zach tried to blink away the familiar sense that his father's skin had slipped to show the edge of his Underself, show its eyes, numerous as a spider's, shining dark and bubbling out of Bram's pores, *pop-pop-pop*.

"Well, well, well, Bruce Wayne finally made it, huh?" Shane said. "What's up, Bram?"

Maybe Shane did sense Bram's shadowy, well-hidden alter ego.

Though more likely Shane was only referencing his father's blue-eyed, dark-haired handsomeness, looks that drove people to stupidity and envy.

Bram gave a two-fingered salute. "Batman, reporting for duty. Great to see you, Shane! And who's this?"

"This is my buddy Jon Hensley. Amazing skier."

"The Dude, reporting for duty," Jon said, imitating Bram's salute in a way that was just mocking enough to make the muscle at the hinge of Bram's jaw clench. Jon added with a shrug, "Or El Duderino if you're not into the whole brevity thing," mystifying Zach and making Shane snort with laughter.

Bram nodded beatifically. "The Dude abides."

The words further baffled Zach, but earned an appreciative eyebrow raise from Shane, a grin from Jon. His father had clearly passed some kind of test. "Bram Fisher. Nice to meet you, Jon."

"Nice to meet you too, man, thanks for having me along." Jon rose briefly to shake Bram's extended hand, then stretched out on the couch and returned to vaping.

Smile locked tight now, in a cold sweep of his eyes Bram took in Jon's bleached-blond dreadlocks, his goatee, the knit hat sitting high on his head, his sunburn. A flicker of flinching irritation at the worn long underwear Jon lounged in, at his puffy slippers, made of sleeping-bag material pockmarked where rogue embers from numerous campfires must have melted away spots of nylon.

Zach read the invisible lash of his father's assessment: dirty, stoner, loser.

Bram cleared his throat, gaze traveling back to Shane. "So, is your dad running late?"

Shane's smile coiled in a way that made Zach think he was used to people scratching and scrounging after Arlo; had recognized and was enjoying the suppressed blaze of Bram's disappointment.

"Something came up." Shane lifted a shoulder, casually shrugging away all Bram's hopes. "He'd be no fun anyway. Old man never was exactly an athlete, no matter how much he likes bragging about his glory days." Shane's smile narrowed into something vindictive. "And I hear Ginny stood you up, too."

Fearful his father would contradict his lie, Zach, words disjointed by his nervousness, said, "I told him—I said—she was supposed to come set up yesterday? But didn't. And then she was supposed to leave today. But she didn't show at all."

Seeing Zach's nervous foot-to-foot motion, the wringing of his hands, Bram frowned and only said, "Right, yeah. I went down trail to get reception. Texted with her to see if she'd screwed up the date. But she's not coming."

"Well, that *is* what you told me. That she wouldn't be here," Shane said.

Bram's face shifted to appear convincingly mystified. "Like the kid said, she was supposed to make the place nice, and be gone by now." The tension left Zach, seeing that his father now understood the root of the lie was that Bram had lied to Shane first. "But when we got here, it was obvious she hadn't showed at all. Hell, I thought she might've gotten herself lost. But she just said—" Bram interrupted himself with the wave of a hand, whisking Ginny's excuses away as nothing, meaningless. "You know what? Never mind. Doesn't matter. Typical Ginny. Gorgeous, but flighty as hell. But"—Bram clapped his hands together, tone shifting to that of a put-upon coach making the best of players who had failed him—"who needs her? Looks great here now, right? Got it warmed up quick." Bram squinted. "Sorry, but this is bugging me. Have we met before, Jon? You look so familiar! I can't quite place it."

Zach waited for his father's line to work its usual magic, felt it pry open a space for Jon to talk about himself, to fill however he wanted.

Jon shrugged this off, but his wide grin belied his put-on modesty. Shane answered for him. "Yeah, man, I bet you recognize him! He's in ski movies. He's a big deal."

"Wait," Bram said, his expression every bit that of someone working to recall something distant but potent. "Jon, Jon—I remember now! There was one film, great music . . ."

Zach retreated into the kitchen. He knew his father didn't watch ski movies. Knew Bram had only the most general sense of what such movies were like. From the safety of the kitchen's shadows Zach's stare flicked from man to man. He hated this part, the way people gravitated to Bram as if he were the sun, warm but blinding. It was the way his mother described Bram, too, every time Zach asked her to tell the story of how she and his father had met. When he was little, that story had been a balm, proof that everything was all right, would be all right, because of how it began.

She'd seen her whole future in a flash the very first time she saw Bram at a party. Handsome, more handsome than any man she'd seen. His dark hair. Those blue eyes.

"It was a perfect, whirlwind romance. He seemed so together, not like the guys my age. Confident. He loved that I worked with Mountain Rescue. And unlike most people in town, he didn't look down on me because I'd dropped out of college for a bit to live here, just to take a break and try being a ski bum. He didn't judge my odd jobs, said housesitting, modeling, Mountain Rescue, doing whatever I could scrape together, made me a 'free spirit.' And when he found out my parents had died when I was eighteen, that Felicity and I had been on our own since then? Well, that's when he said he understood I was different from other girls. His family, they're not like him. His father was . . . well. Cruel. Physically cruel, I mean. And the whole family was very strict and religious, and they were estranged, you know? Then of course he'd lost his little boy, and

Serena. So he knew what it was not to have much family in your life. To lose people. It was us against the whole world. And that felt—it all felt—right. I never did go back to college. We got married six months after we met. He was thirty-seven. I thought I was so grown up. Seems silly now. I'm still not as old as he was when we met. But it was—it felt—special. Being loved so intensely."

But more and more often over the years, after telling the story her eyes would slide away and she'd end it with a new moral, saying something like, "Your father's very charming. He's like a horoscope. Vague, flattering, and tells you exactly what you want to hear."

". . . and the movie had this sequence where you did this massive, massive jump!" Bram said.

"You're probably thinking of *Mountain High*," Jon grinned. "It was a big hit."

Bram snapped his fingers and pointed at Jon, face alight. "That was it! Great show, Jon, really great." Bram slapped a hand on Shane's shoulder. "Thanks for bringing this guy, man. Wait until Dave gets here. He's got a teenager. They're going to lose it over this. A celebrity!"

Zach imagined iridescent, spike-tipped legs extending from the Underself's spine. Watched them hinge at the joints as they spun soft silk around Jon and Shane.

"I'm producing Jon's next movie," Shane offered.

A serious nod from Bram. "'Course you are. You're a savvy investor. Smart move."

Shane nodded back at Bram, earlier signs of irritation swept away. Jon was sitting up now, beaming into Bram's light as he demurred, "I wouldn't say I'm a celebrity."

"You're too modest, man. I can't wait to see what you two do with this movie. Fantastic."

As Bram turned away from Shane and Jon, Zach grabbed a

towel and wiped the counter, trying to look busy as his father approached.

"You guys hungry?" Bram called out, cheerful tone at odds with his gritted teeth, the tautness of his face. "I've got a few things to snack on before the guide gets here with the rest of the group. Beer, wine, whiskey, whatever, too, if you're interested."

"I could eat. And you got any IPA?" Shane asked.

"Sure."

Bram pointed from Zach to the cheese on the counter, and Zach sprung over to start preparing food.

"I'll take a beer, too," Jon said.

"'Course."

Bram rattled through the alcohol; brought two beers to the living room. "Want some ice?"

"Nah, I'm good."

"Smart choice." Bram sidled to the door, opened it, and snapped a large icicle from the sill above. He wagged it toward the younger men before sweeping the icicle up to point at a sign above the door:

WHAT IF EVERYONE DID THAT?

RESPECT OTHER VISITORS

PROTECT YOUR DRINKING WATER

USE THE OUTHOUSE AND DON'T URINATE OUT THE WINDOWS

Bram tap-tap-tapped the icicle on the word "urinate." "Best avoid the ice. Because who knows *what's* in it."

"Oh, no, man," Jon wheezed, chuckling with Shane. "Oh, no."

Bram tossed the icicle outside, and shook his head as he closed the door. "You gotta think that sign only encourages guys to use the windows, you know?"

"Men," one of the other mothers had muttered, disgusted over the polluted ice tracing from the bunk windows down the back of the hut the year before. At the memory, Zach felt the same bite of shame the word had triggered, the same simultaneous rise of indignation.

Because it was too gross. He would never.

Zach peeled the fancy labels and shrink wrap from the cheese and set the wedges on a cutting board, jumping slightly when from close behind him, Bram's voice came sharp and cold, "Isn't there something nicer to put this stuff on?"

There might be. Zach might have missed something. But he only shook his head no.

Bram prowled through the kitchen for serving dishes that would better meet his expectations, his mirth vaporized, unnecessary now that his back was to the others.

He put a bowl on the counter. "Crackers in here." Bram eyed his son carefully cutting the salami. "Give me that knife. You'll never finish going that slow."

Zach filled the bowl with crackers and stepped away, fingernail preying on his wounded thumb as he tried to think of something else to show he was contributing. With relief he remembered the water filter. He brought it downstairs from his pack, filled it, then hung its bags on the wall hooks he remembered his mother using to let gravity pull dirty water through the filter. It was the first time he'd set it up by himself, and his pride at managing the heavy awkwardness of the device distracted him until Bram said, "You're only doing drinking water *now*? How long will this thing take?"

"Oh—only a minute. Or two. It's quick."

"Fine." Bram jutted his chin in the direction of the living room. "Bring the food out."

Zach set the plates in front of the men. It was a relief to be the one serving them. Bram fetching them drinks, cutting and plating meat and cheese, was destabilizing. His mother had been the one to do all that, always in motion, smoothing their house to a perfection that was never sufficiently perfect.

All that was Ximena's job now. The nanny before Ximena quit after two weeks. But those had been two good weeks, Bram focused elsewhere, Zach and Bonnie nodding along that he was right, so right, that she wasn't good enough, that she was lazy, entitled, disrespectful.

Ximena told Zach and Bonnie about her own children, waiting for her in a far-off place. She never argued with Bram, only nodded and said, "Yes, Mr. Fisher, I'm sorry, won't happen again."

Ximena had so much to lose.

Zach set the food down in front of Shane and Jon, Shane penciling something on a piece of paper as Jon leaned close to look. "See, if we film the jump like this—"

Jon nodded. "Yeah, man, that would be sick!"

Seeing an opening in the way the younger men were occupied, Zach returned to the kitchen and motioned to Bram with an eager hand, a finger light against his lips for silence.

CHAPTER 6

Bram frowned but followed Zach into the short hallway that led to the hut's back door.

"What?"

"Shane," Zach whispered, "before you got here, he said his dad was going to invest. Mr. Oliver wants to look over documents first? But that's why he's not here. Because he'd already made up his mind."

"Arlo's going to invest? Shane said that?"

"Yes."

Bram's expression changed as he rubbed a hand over his face, as if all his anger and worry had condensed there and he was pulling off the shroud of it. He smiled broadly, genuinely. "Of course that's it! Great news. Great news, kid. Did he say how much Arlo's putting in?"

Zach wilted. Even being the bearer of this coveted information hadn't led to Bram saying his name. He was still only 'kid,' just 'my son.' Months had passed since Bram's hands had gripped Zach's shoulders tight, face so close the boy had felt its furious heat.

"*Stop. Crying. Now. Zach.*"

And Zach had obeyed.

"I don't think Shane knows," Zach told his father. "I don't think he meant to say anything at all. He asked me not to tell you."

"Of course you told me. Thinks a kid'll keep something from his dad. But we're better than that, aren't we?" Zach nodded, breathing easier, mood lifting in the rarefied air of his father's approval, the two of them a team, better than other people, whether Bram used his name or not.

His father stared past him. "Arlo believes in me. He's always liked me. He knows a good investment. Recognizes business instinct."

In the glassy blue of Bram's eyes, Zach read the vision of how his father wanted Arlo Oliver to see him. Special. Deserving. A great man acknowledging a great man.

A noise outside interrupted his father's reverie. Bram moved toward the door, gave an enthused "Look who's here!" and embraced the man who entered. He was older than Bram; tanned a dark brown that was unnatural to the place and season but somehow suited him, contrasted as it was with a head of thick silver hair. Behind him stood a teenage boy, red-cheeked, pimpled, slouching, and wearing thick glasses.

Zach saw Bram's attention dart to the teenager, expression going flat for a flicker of a second that let Zach read the Underself's sneer.

Nerd. Fat. Why doesn't he wash his face?

"This must be Russ!" Bram said, all smiles as he gave the teenager a rough pat on the back that knocked Russ's glasses to the tip of his nose. Russ scowled as he pushed them back to their proper place with an index finger.

"Great to meet you, Russ, I'm Bram. Your dad has told me all about you. Come in, come in, welcome. How was your trip up, Dave?"

Dave closed his eyes for a beat, giving him a reverent, moony look. "Gorgeous, gorgeous. What a fantastic hike. What a spot! God's country."

"Absolutely," Bram nodded. "Real wilderness out here. You know Shane, of course, but let me introduce you—Jon, this is Dave Dowling, and this is his son, Russ. Jon here is a professional skier. In movies and everything!"

Dave's face transitioned to awe. "Wait—you were in, whatsitcalled—*Mountain High*? Weren't you?" Dave asked.

"Yeah, man, nice to meet you."

"Big fan, big fan!" Dave strode over to pump Jon's hand, beaming at this brush with fame, Russ's nose crinkling in embarrassment even as he snuck interested looks at Jon.

"Russ, Dave, this is my son," Bram said, prompting Zach to dutifully shake Dave's hand.

"Nice to meet you, Mister Dowling. I'm Zach. My dad said it was your idea to have the kids—the sons—come. Thank you, I'm so happy to be here."

"Well, aren't you welcome Zach!" Dave gripped Zach's hand hard as he shook it, then said to Bram, "Look at these manners, huh? Have to teach me your secret, Bram, I can't even get Russ to make eye contact with an adult, let alone give a firm handshake."

Bram lit up at this even as Zach felt his insides flutter over the way Dave had been taken in by the scripted lines. When Zach offered a hand to Russ, the teenager didn't take it, only looked at him with pity, as if Zach was a performing monkey.

"See what I mean?" Dave chuckled.

Russ snorted. "Whatever," he said to his father. He jutted his chin at Zach. "Hey."

"Hey," Zach echoed, marveling at Russ's clear disdain for everyone in the room and sensing that a vast, indescribable country sprawled between twelve and sixteen.

Bram peered around as if only just noticing something. "Didn't the guide bring you up?"

"He's outside," Dave said. "Stowing food in the outdoor pantry."

"Did Pike come up with you?"

"Nah. The guide texted him. He said he was running late." Dave looked around the room. "Your old man around here somewhere, Shane?"

"Couldn't make it."

Dave snorted. "Can't say I'm surprised."

"Right? You know how he is," Shane said.

"Is he still coming to Sun Valley in July?"

"Yeah, I mean, how long have the two of you been going to that?"

"You're making me admit my age here, Shane, but probably since . . . when did Buffett start going? Just before that. So the early nineties? You had to be in diapers first time I met your dad there. Even though"—Dave shot Shane a heavy look—"it's as bad as Davos now. They let anyone come."

Shane rolled his eyes. "You sound just like my dad. I think he pretty much keeps going for sentimental reasons. Though he'd rather die than admit that."

A ripple of insecurity at being outside this inner circle manifested in the way Bram's jaw clenched, the way his eyes darted between Shane and Dave as they laughed over this. "You guys see the weather rolling in?" Bram said. "Maybe we'll get lucky, huh?" He smiled, then, contented at the way the men refocused on this trip, discussing the likelihood of snowfall and comparing their gear. Bram excused himself to check on the guide.

As the others chatted, ate cheese, Zach edged to the window. Outside, Bram stared the guide down stony-faced as he itemized things on his fingers, one and two and three, inaudible through the glass. The guide was younger than Bram, and more rugged—lighter skin around his eyes where his goggles had protected him from years of sun exposure, long, unkempt brown hair, a knit cap.

Zach was guiltily grateful that the guide was the one now forced to meet Bram's expectations for fixing whatever unfathomable, unending things were still less than perfect.

A bag over his shoulder, the guide trailed Bram inside. Held up a hand in greeting to the group, eyes going wide and mouth dropping open when he was introduced to Jon, but staying professional as he said, "I'm Steve, guys, nice to meet you." He passed around what looked like silicone watch bands with no watch attached, each emblazoned with the name of the guiding company.

"Ski straps," he explained. "Super useful in the backcountry," he side-eyed Jon, "as some of you I'm sure already know. Can hold together a broken boot or binding in an emergency, or you can use it to attach gear to your pack or whatever. Just a little gift from us to you."

After the group ate a lunch of premade chili and cornbread Steve warmed for them, the men lounged on the couches while Russ stayed at the dining table playing a game on his phone as Steve cleaned up. Electing to stay on Russ's side of the room, Zach retreated to the window seat in the corner, close to the bookcase where the earring was hidden. He rested his head against the window frame, trying to keep his eyes open.

These days, it was easier for him to fall asleep when it was daylight. His bladder plagued him at night, keeping him from sleep, or waking him and forcing him up.

"Tell you what," Shane said, leaning back on the couch and rubbing his forehead, "drinking sure hits harder and faster at high altitude."

"This elevation—doesn't matter how many times I do it, I get over eleven thousand feet and everything goes haywire," Dave agreed.

"The sleep's what gets me," Jon said. "I've got pills I take or else I just cannot fall asleep after a big altitude change."

"So do I," Dave said. "Though of course up here's nothing like when I did Kilimanjaro or Denali, but still."

"You trying for the seven summits?" Jon asked.

"Nah. Maybe we'll do Everest once Russ is a little older." Dave looked over his shoulder toward his son. "Right, bud?"

Russ gave a halfhearted shrug, eyes fixed on his phone.

"Though maybe not," Dave said. "It's so busy nowadays. Have you seen those pictures? Bunch of guys sucking down oxygen, waiting in line."

"The problem is, it's too cheap," Shane said. "Those countries should contract with someone to take it private. Or let people own a piece. No more crowds, better-paid jobs, plenty of taxes, happy investors."

"It's working in Montana. You can finally hunt in peace." Dave eyed Jon with interest. "Your line of work, Jon, I bet you never deal with crowds. Heli ski everywhere, huh? This trip is probably just another day at the office for you."

"Nah, man. I mean—Mariah was great this morning, but the stuff I do is generally more extreme. Steeper, hairier. But it's a lot of pressure, you know? To deliver the shot. So this is vacation, for sure. Quiet. Off-grid place on the mountain, get here under your own steam. None of the bull. You get to, like, chill. Enjoy the wildness and all."

"It's something special, being up here, isn't it?" Dave's face took on the unfixed, quixotic expression he'd had on arrival. "The peace, the distance, the—sweat. You have to earn it. Like the pioneers coming West. All alone in untouched country."

Russ scoffed, still not looking away from his game. "I mean it wasn't untouched. There were already people here."

The group ignored him.

"Frontiersmen," Bram wagged an instructive finger at Dave.

"There's a lesson in that—they didn't ask who would let them. They asked who would stop them."

"Donner Party sure stopped," Russ snarked.

Dave and Bram each shot the teenager an irritated over-the-shoulder glance.

"Those guys must've been fearless," Jon said after a draw on his vape, oblivious to Russ. "Now that's freedom right there. No rules at all."

"Totally," Shane chimed in. "Man against nature, carving out a place in the world."

The men nodded, each saying "yes, yes," all going dreamy-eyed, imagining themselves as those long-gone pioneers, as miners, craggy and tough, coring through rock, striking it rich.

But Zach only thought of the old wooden sign driven into the ground about a thirty-minute ski above the hut, just below the miner's cabin he and his mother had discovered a year ago. The message carved into the sign's grayed, grooved pine was a stark check on the nostalgic sentimentality of the men's ideas.

HERE LIES

THE SWEDE

FALLEN PAST RESCUE

"FOR THE LOVE OF MONEY IS THE ROOT OF ALL EVIL"

AUG 1881

"Don't get too close, Zakky," his mother had cautioned, pointing to a three-foot-wide hole not quite in the middle of the large clearing the sign faced. "That's a mine shaft. Abandoned mines—the air can turn to poison. The ground weakens around them. It can collapse. It's probably why this marker is all the way over here instead of near the opening."

"Do you think," Zach asked, taking in the void of the mine's mouth, "that's where he fell? That he's still down there?"

What he really wanted to ask was what his mother thought "Fallen past rescue" meant. Had this Swede, presumably the prospector who had dug this mine, been alive but unreachable when found? Did she think the Swede's friends, the ones who had carved the sign, had left him down there to die? Legs broken, arms straining up at the unreachable light? Did she think they'd come back with ropes, ladders, only to find him dead, or worse, still alive and too deep—past rescue?

"The sign says 'Here lies,' so yes, he's probably still down there." His mother's voice was a reverent whisper. "Poor man."

"How could he make the mine, but then not be able to get out?"

"It could have caved in. Or he might have fallen into a buried crevasse." A long pause. "When you're older you'll see there's plenty of ways to dig yourself into a hole before you realize you can't escape."

CHAPTER 7

A lull in the men's conversation before Dave, who Zach began to think was the type of person who got uncomfortable during even a friendly silence, asked, "Did Mariah seem solid this morning, Shane? We passed over a bunch of slide paths on the way up."

A flicker of confusion surfaced and then vanished from Bram. Of course his father hadn't recognized these. Hadn't realized Zach purposefully lagged behind, watching Bram traverse alone where the trail crossed treeless terrain. Zach had fantasized about his father being torn away in a slide, Zach searching and heroically uncovering him, Bram grateful, so very grateful.

But he'd also felt a dark quiver of longing at picturing the alternative—Bram snapped into pieces like the trees tangled at the base, gone blue as ice, powerless and dead. As Zach picked his own way across the avalanche path, the appeal of that vision cascaded into a superstition that because he'd indulged in such awful thoughts, he'd be caught in a vindictive, righteous slide that would hurdle him down the mountain.

What would Bram do then? Would he search?

"No signs of avalanche activity on the Bowl. But it was completely skied out," Shane told the group. "Other than a few spots here and there in the trees, everything was shaved off and hard-packed."

As an experienced inbounds resort skier, even Bram understood that while the lack of avalanche risk was ideal, the state of the snow Shane described was bad news. He and Dave nodded stoically, their eyes drawn toward the windows and the better conditions that the black clouds hovering on the horizon might promise.

The men drank and snacked on a steady stream of bread, cheese, and cookies that Steve dutifully shuttled in and out from the kitchen. Zach let himself sink into a kind of half sleep as Dave interrogated Jon over why he preferred his fan-fueled backpack airbag over Dave's canister type, both designed to deploy and float you to the surface or create an air pocket if caught in an avalanche; what Jon's favorite ski touring setup was; if he used the plastic ribbons called ski traces that might let you more easily find a ski lost in powder; the best outdoor smartwatch, GPS, radio, beacon, shovel.

Zach puzzled sleepily over how Jon could so adeptly answer these questions, debate all the gear, so clearly speak the language of danger—yet have left his radio off. Have ditched his friend. Done the opposite of everything Zach's mother had taught him.

The day they'd found the cabin and its mine, Zach and Grace had hiked up Mariah Bowl with a group of four other mothers and their older children, Bonnie back at the hut with some of the moms supervising the littler kids. About six inches of snow had fallen the night before, and Mariah Bowl had gleamed with promise. Zach was the youngest included, had never been allowed to ski Mariah before, and knew that being part of this contingent meant his mom thought he was ready, responsible, accomplished enough to handle it.

At the summit, the women dug an avalanche pit and identified a worrying layer of sugary snow under a dense slab, new powder on top of that. Each of the mothers inspected this suspicious layer, the way it ran grainy through their fingers, impossible to pack.

"Hoarfrost," the mothers said. "Not a good sign," they agreed.

They cut a column of snow within the pit, placed a shovel on top, firmly tapped its blade, and the snow peeled away, collapsing at their feet.

"Not bad," said one.

"Not good, either," said another.

The mothers bent heads together to discuss. And discuss.

In Zach's memory Bram rolled his eyes and pointed at his mother chatting with a group of PTA mothers after a meeting. *"Blah, blah, blah.* The bigger the mouth, the smaller the mind, kid."

The children, seduced by the accomplishment of reaching the peak, by the steep plane of open powder below, by the knowledge that they had no real responsibility, impatient with the *blah, blah, blah*, repeated, "Let's go, let's go, let's go."

But no, the mothers said, breaking from their huddle. In the face of protestations, they explained to the children things they'd already been taught, but never had to put into practice. Had them find the layer of loose, crumbling snow. Had the children sift its stiff crystals through their mittened hands as the mothers explained the way it might act like ball bearings, allowing a broken slab to roll and unleash the snow's potential energy into annihilation. The call was close, agonizingly close, but—retreat was safest.

The group skied down the gentle slope of the ridge they'd hiked up, the other children sullen and resentful as Zach. All that work, all that climbing, for nothing. Zach felt knowledge of his mother's failings seep from deep in his bones to blend seamlessly with his blood, like truth.

His father was right. In his mother's face he saw an irritating self-righteousness, a pride in ruining everything, so dramatic.

Zach moved slowly, complaining, clinging to the possibility that his mother might listen, that she might see reason. See past the uselessness of all that *blah, blah, blah.*

Grace interrupted Zach's griping to snap, "I taught you better than this, Zakky. I thought you understood the hardest, bravest thing to do is make the tough call of giving up what you've worked for, what you want, so that you stay safe."

At recalling this Zach's eyes burned.

She was such a coward. Such a liar. She couldn't even give up drinking, so she hadn't stayed safe.

A rush of frigid air yanked Zach from his drifting, half-awake state, and he looked up to see that a short, stocky man had opened the hut's door.

"Pike, finally!" Bram boomed.

It had grown far colder, and the chill had drained Pike's face of color but for a bright red nose above his close-trimmed beard. Bram, a head taller, embraced him with a firm arm. Pike didn't return the hug, just gave a stiff nod.

As Pike took off his coat, his snowpants, Zach gawked, wondering how much work it took to get muscles like Pike had, each arm bigger than Zach's thigh. Pike's arms stuck out wide from his body in a way that reminded Zach of a toddler in a too-thick snow suit, unable to rest his hands by his sides.

"Sorry I'm late." Pike's voice was a deep, scratchy rumble. "Car trouble."

"Let me introduce you," Bram said. "Everyone? This is Pike Whitlock. Pike, I think you know Shane? And Dave. And this is Dave's son, Russ, and Shane's buddy Jon."

Pike bobbed his head to acknowledge each new name as he hung up his things, removed his boots. And though Zach filed away that Bram hadn't introduced him, he knew what his father expected. He stood to shake Pike's hand, trying to tamp down the heat of embarrassment flushing his cheeks at having to perform again in front of Russ.

"You look like I feel, Pike," Dave said. "Exhausted. Quite the hike up, isn't it?"

Dave was right. Despite his bodybuilder's frame, Pike's breathing was short, his thin, light hair was plastered dark with sweat, and his shirt clung to him, wet along the collar and underarms.

"Yeah," Pike said. "Hustled like hell to get up here before dark. And you know, had to deal with the damn car."

"Arlo couldn't make it," Bram said. "Ginny either. That's probably for the best, though, huh?"

Pike's eyes narrowed. "Whatever." He rubbed at a thin, angry red cut on his huge neck.

"Right," Bram said brightly. "Ancient history. Have a seat. Want a drink? Plenty to choose from."

Pike poured himself a whiskey in the kitchen, downed it, refilled it, then carried the glass and a can of beer into the living area.

Shane watched this with amusement. "Good to see you, man." He lifted his chin at the two drinks Pike set on the table. "Trying to catch up to the rest of us?"

Pike's eyes narrowed. "Not all of us are lightweights."

Shane good-naturedly patted his belly. "Certainly not me."

"How's married life?" Pike asked. "It's been, what—a year?"

"Almost two."

"Right." Pike didn't blink, nose wrinkling as if a bad smell hit him as he said, "Guess that's easy to forget, huh?"

Shane's laugh sounded empty. "Sure, man."

Into the silence that followed, Bram said, "So guys—you mind if

I get my business spiel out of the way? It's gonna be low tech. By which I mean no tech. But hey, that suits the place."

"No death by PowerPoint?" Dave asked. "Be still my heart."

Bram didn't mention how Ginny was supposed to bring up his computer, his papers. If Zach hadn't heard his father's fury earlier, wasn't attuned to the subtleties of when Bram's enthusiasm was feigned, he never would have realized anything at all had gone wrong.

"How about you boys go play outside?" Bram looked at his watch. "Over an hour until it gets really dark."

Zach's stomach tightened at the idea of going back outdoors; at being exposed to hungry eyes, dissecting claws, especially given that the descending sun already stretched shadows from the trees. But in his father's stony face he recognized a command. Zach stood, then froze at hearing Russ jeer, "*Play?*"

Bram's Underself eyes stared at the teenager as if he might pierce him, drain him.

"Don't be rude," Dave sounded amused despite the scolding words. "Go on with Zach. Leave the phone here. And *be nice*."

Russ rolled his eyes. Got up as though it took a great effort to stand, to walk, to set his phone on the table. "My game was boring anyway," he mumbled.

Zach shot Russ a pained smile that the teenager ignored.

"All right." Bram clapped his hands. "Let's get this done so we can enjoy ourselves. I'll start with something I think you'll all *appreciate*"—he winked—"pun intended, because you better expect some dad jokes on a father-son trip." Dave guffawed at this, and with a flourish Bram held up an envelope. "Your returns!" He opened the envelope, took out a clutch of checks, and walked from man to man, handing them over face down. Shane and Dave each peeked at their checks, smiles flitting then fading as if trying to maintain a poker face. A quiver of annoyance traveled through Bram when Pike ignored his payment, letting the check sit untouched on the coffee table as he sipped his drink. Jon, who wasn't an investor, feigned disinterest and began to vape again, causing an overly sweet candy smell to drift through the room.

Bram pointed a finger at the guide, then his thumb at the door. The guide gave a two-fingered salute, message received, and like the boys went to the entry to dress for the outdoors.

As Zach left the hut with Russ, as the guide closed the door behind them, Zach heard his father lying with the comfort and ease of a man lounging under the sun, full-bellied, content, cold drink in hand.

"Despite the larger market's absolutely abysmal performance over the last six months, Ajax Property Tech's software is operational, and the properties we identified and sold have brought in record returns . . ."

His father sounded so confident. Maybe that meant everything he'd overheard his mother accuse Bram of was wrong.

CHAPTER 8

"What losers." Russ kicked at a dome of blue ice below a dripping icicle. "'Oooh, we're explorers, oooh we're so tough!' When really they're, like"—Russ pretended to hold and sip at a teacup, gloved pinkie stuck prissily heavenward before rolling his eyes. "Please."

Zach gaped at Russ. Yes, the door had closed. Bram couldn't have overheard.

Steve chuckled. "I've got a daughter about your age. You remind me of her."

"I mean come on," Russ said. "Comparing themselves to, like, pioneers or whatever? When they've got you here doing everything for them?"

The guide gave Russ a good-natured fist to the shoulder. "Eh, give your old man a break. And—Jon Hensley? Dude's a legend. What's he like?"

Russ shrugged. "Met him when you did."

"The guys were freaking out about Arlo Oliver being on this trip, but Hensley? They're going to lose their minds." Steve shook his head, amazed.

"My dad and Arlo are friends," Russ said. "Believe me, you're not missing anything. He's ancient, and so boring. Always going on about how sometimes he wants to get off the treadmill, be a normal person or whatever—exactly those words, every time—as if being a billionaire is some horrible burden, like he's so special and his life is so tough no one can possibly understand, boo-hoo. But it's all so that everyone is like, 'Oh, Arlo, you're so humble, your company couldn't do it without you, everyone needs you!' " Russ mimed vomiting. "It's gross."

"Well," Steve said, "it's gotta be pretty isolating, all that money. You'd always think people want something from you."

Russ scoffed and gestured behind them toward the hut. "Please. You think they care if people like them for their money? That's all they care about, so it's all that makes sense to them."

Zach nodded, respect for Russ, a kinship, ballooning in him at hearing this truth spoken aloud. Everything in Bram's life was tallied, compared, a record burned into his brain that scored each favor, every act and gesture, big or small, good or bad, and all of it, ultimately, measured in possible dollar outcome. Because all things in their house came from Bram, Zach, Bonnie, and their mother were required to perform absolute appreciation and intense gratefulness, yet could never pay Bram back using the only metric he valued.

It all transformed anything bought and paid for into a hollow burden, until the very idea of toys, trips, gifts knotted Zach's stomach. He knew his mother felt the same, careful with what little cash Bram allowed her, trying to carve out pockets of her own money here and there to avoid the devotions he expected.

Yet Zach's friends, their parents, his father, appeared to have an insatiable thirst for things and more things. He watched as Bram, as other grown-ups, marveled at anyone whose numbers were uncountable, as if by hoarding and devouring such vastness these others had gained the sheen of gods. So many adults seemed to believe, like his father, that if they got close enough to people like Arlo Oliver, their nervous worship might cause some of that money to rub off; might even grant them some edge of immortality.

Steve shrugged. "Hey, not my world and all. But they seem like good-enough guys."

"Right, sure. Super nice, cool guys who care about other people." Russ sighed. "This is so stupid. What are we even supposed to do out here?"

"Build a snowman?" Steve offered.

"We're not *five*," Russ said.

Steve grinned. "Hey, why was the snowman looking through the bag of carrots?"

Both boys stared at him.

"He was picking his nose," Steve said, deadpan.

Zach giggled, covering his mouth with a hand to hide it. A flicker of a smile played across Russ before he rolled his eyes.

"What'd the snowman say after losing an arm?" Steve asked.

Russ shook his head down at his feet, as if embarrassed on Steve's behalf.

"I'm never playing fetch again."

"Ugh, stop," Russ said, but fully smiling now, his ever-present eye roll turned good-natured.

"I got a million of 'em. You let me know whenever you want more awesome, not at all old-man jokes, okay?" Steve glanced at his watch. "It's already four. Want something to snack on? I'm going to hit up the outdoor pantry before splitting some wood."

The boys shook their heads.

"All right. I brought s'mores, brownies, like, three different types of chips if you're more of a salt-type guy. So. Think about it. Be back here by five thirty. And yell if you need anything."

"Sure, man," Russ said.

Zach said nothing, distractedly wondering how much dessert he'd be able to have. Bram didn't like enforcing his "no-sugar" rule in front of other people, preferring to appear beneficent, even indulgent, so long as he didn't deem Zach too publicly greedy. His mother, though, had frequently found ways to sneak Zach and Bonnie treats. "How about we go to the bank?" she'd say with a wink. They'd walk from where they'd parked at the grocery store, and all three would suck on free lollipops from the teller's desk as their mother pulled cash from her pocket, counted it out, deposited it. The last time they'd been, and the last time Zach had eaten candy, was close to Halloween. The teller had let them take handfuls of mini chocolate bars and candy corn from an enormous bowl, so much they'd had to throw some in the trash because they wouldn't be able to eat it before arriving home.

"What a nerd," Russ said affectionately as the boys watched Steve walk away. "Ugh, like an hour to kill? This sucks."

Zach recalled his father's admonition that it was his job to entertain Russ. "We could play Gray Rabbit?"

"What's that?"

"It's like hide-and-seek combined with tag? Someone's the Wolf, and he, like, looks for the person who hides? The person who hides is the Rabbit. But if the Wolf finds the Rabbit, the Rabbit can run away and hide again, if the Wolf doesn't tag him. We play it—played it—on hut trips sometimes."

"How can you even hide in the snow? There's tracks."

Zach, excited to share what he'd learned over the course of endless rounds of the game, explained, "If your boots are waterproof you can walk up a stream. Or if the snow's deep, you can double back in your own tracks, then jump away far enough the person doesn't realize? If you can jump off, like, a little ledge, or get under a tree? That's the best. Or like, out here, there's so many tracks already, you can hide your tracks kind of in others."

Russ gave him a glazed look. "Sounds like it would be better with a big group."

"Oh. Yeah. I guess we did always play it in teams." Zach's mind ran over past hut activities with other kids. "We could, um, build a snow fort?" Cringing over the childishness of the words, he edited himself. "I mean, not a fort, more like a snow shelter. My mom showed me how. It's an outdoor survival thing. There's a tree over there we used to build under. It gets a big tree well around it." At Russ's blank look, Zach said, "That's basically when the tree branches catch the snow, so the snow's kind of hollowed out underneath. They can be dangerous if you're skiing or whatever and fall in, because the snow around the hollow part can collapse on you. People even die and stuff, falling in." At this Russ began to look interested. "But if you know it's there, tree wells make it pretty easy to dig for a shelter because the hole's kind of already started. You can even light a fire in there? If you do it right."

Russ shrugged. "I guess we can try. Not like there's anything else to do."

Large shovels for digging paths to the outhouse or clearing the stairs after big snows leaned against the hut's exterior. The boys each took one and put on skis. Zach led Russ across the heavily tracked field toward the enormous blue spruce about two hundred feet from the hut, scanning the newly wakened menace of the woods. But as they moved away from the windowed gaze of the hut Zach's back straightened, his body lifted. Maybe because every step took him farther away from his father's watchfulness. Maybe because

Russ was beside him prattling about video games, about how much he hated high school at his mom's in Florida, about how he wished his dad would move to his place here in town full time instead of Russ having to visit him in Denver, Billings, or Houston, which were boring.

"You like skiing?" Zach asked.

"I like it better when I can take a lift up. All this skiing uphill sucks. I'm sure I'll be the worst one tomorrow by a lot." Russ assessed Zach as if only just realizing that might not be the case, given Zach's age. "How about you? Living here and all I bet you're pretty good. And you're, like, almost as tall as me."

Zach shrugged, dismissing his twice-weekly ski team practices, his weekends in the backcountry or spent competing in ski races and competitions. Shrugged away his work and sweat and training and euphoria, his podiums, the way his mother had driven him and Bonnie hours away, sometimes into other states to compete in Downhill, Super G, Slalom, Moguls, Big Mountain, leaving him spent by the time school started Monday. Dismissed it all because he was probably falling behind now that Bram didn't want to pay for the travel, and he was only going to the local races. And because he was good, but not good enough.

Not the best, which was all that really mattered.

"It'd be so cool to be like that Jon guy, you know?" Russ said. "Ski for a job? Instead of sitting on your butt at a desk, like my dad."

They stopped at the tree, surveying it. Zach pushed branches aside. Showed Russ the protected, hollow area underneath.

"Okay, okay, this could be cool." Russ wiped the fog from his glasses with his sleeve.

Together, they dug. Russ's chatter slowed then stopped, both boys breathing heavily as they worked to core a space around the trunk.

At last they clambered in, verified the line of the snow was over their heads, then dragged broken boughs overhead to further disguise the pit.

Sitting in semidarkness, they grinned at each other.

"This is actually all right," Russ said. "Hidden. We could, like, sleep in here if we needed to! I think it's warmer than outside."

It was not at all warmer.

"My mom says you have to be careful not to get too warm and sweaty if you're actually lost and have to build something. Because of hypothermia? Sweat can make you get cold really quick once you aren't moving."

Russ tilted his head. "So, your mom was pretty into this stuff, huh?"

How many times had he mentioned his mother?

Baby. Mama's boy.

"Yeah."

"Sounds like she was cool," Russ put his hands behind his head, leaning back against the wall of the pit and staring up at the canopy of pine boughs. "Was she a good skier?"

Was, was, was.

"Yeah. She like, worked for Mountain Rescue? Before she met my dad, I mean. She quit once they got married. He thought it was too dangerous or whatever. And then she had me, so."

"That's how she knew all this stuff?"

"Yeah. We'd come up here a lot. Or to other huts. And she volunteers at school, teaching avalanche safety and rescue things." Zach looked away from Russ. "Or, she did, I mean. She used to."

"See, that is so sick. *My* mom is completely useless. She won't leave Miami from, like, September until June she hates the cold so bad. And my new stepmom can't even ski. She just rides the gondola and prances around at the top of Ajax with her friends, or like, takes the lift to drink at Cloud 9. They literally tan at the Sundeck in bikinis. It's embarrassing, all of them like, 'Look at me, look at me,' you know?" Russ made a mocking, mincing motion with his hands, as if he were holding up an imaginary petticoat that he then dropped in disgust. "Even though they're old. Like almost thirty."

When kids Zach's age talked about their families, it was always to brag about whose dad was taller, whose brother was star of the hockey team. Zach tried to imagine spreading out his family's inner workings under the light, under the eyes of a stranger the way Russ had just done, and had to clear his throat to stop the sense he was choking.

"My old stepmom was okay, I guess," Russ went on. "She'd go skiing with me. She was even kind of good at the terrain park." Russ's voice had lost its scorn, turning wistful.

"Do you still hang out?"

Russ wiped his glasses with his sleeve again, purposefully focusing on the task and avoiding Zach's gaze. "Nah. She got tired of smiling and nodding, smiling and nodding. That's all my dad wants, you know? A, like, bobblehead. My dad goes on and on about how this stepmom is a model, like she's a new car or something."

"My mom was a model, too," Zach said, "For a little while. Before she got married."

Russ waved this off. "They all are, man. I mean, maybe your mom really was? But this one just puts pictures of herself online. My other stepmom was a doctor, and I swear my dad was, like, jealous. He pretended it was his idea to divorce her, but no way. She's in LA now. With my half brother. He's only three. But he's awesome." Russ put his glasses back on, eyes going to middle distance as if his old life hovered there, projected against the blank, snowy wall of the shelter.

Wanting to show he was a member of Russ's club, the complicated family club, Zach heard himself blurt, "My dad was married before, too. Before I was born."

"Divorced," Russ said knowingly.

Now it was Zach's turn to look askance at nothing as he muttered, "Nah. She died."

CHAPTER 9

Russ's gawped at him. "Died? How?"

Zach traced a figure eight with his mitten in the snow. "A fire."

"Whoa! Really?"

"Yeah. At their house."

"Holy shit. But your dad got out?"

"He wasn't home. My—my half brother died, too. He was eight."

Russ's face went long with horror, Zach feeling a pressing need to fill the silence as he watched Russ picturing his own little brother, and what it would be like to lose him. "I mean, it was a long time ago. And it's not like I knew them."

"Yeah, I mean, that sucks for your dad."

"He doesn't really talk about it."

Why had he told this lie? Maybe jealousy over how often Bram described how Serena, his first wife, had been the most beautiful woman he'd ever known. Charming, modest, the food she made the best he'd ever eaten, their home tasteful, pristine. How Zach's never-brother had been well behaved, tough, gifted at sports, at math, the kind of strong, silent type of child, Bram said pointedly, that you don't see anymore. Every time his dad spoke about this half brother, this other wife, Zach felt himself, his mother, fade into a dim echo of the vivid, superior family Bram had lost. Only Bonnie, the sole daughter, stood outside this, incomparable and special.

But that was all right. Because Bonnie was special.

"He'll never admit it, but all *this* is because of Serena." His mother's voice slurred as she flung an arm out to encompass their house, their life. "I didn't know for years. Years! All he's done is spend and lose what she left him."

The fire was the first thing Zach looked up online by himself. Though Bram frequently watched television while simultaneously swiping at his iPad or phone, he would go cold and self-righteous at seeing his wife or children looking at a screen.

You're rotting your brains, you're staring at that when the house looks like this?

The evening whine of Bram's garage door led to a Pavlovian response, screens off, make yourself showily busy. Until one day, Underself contorting his expression, Bram came home clutching printouts, lists of television hours, internet hours, each text and search and call logged, the data pulled from some mysterious surveillance software.

Seven-year-old Zach had cowered at this evidence of his father's all-knowingness, and screens were black when Bram wasn't home.

When Grace asked Bram if she could take the children on a hike, sign them up for ski team, go on hut trips, she would end with, *After all, we want them active! Don't want them to be iPad kids, like everyone else's children.* Bram, appeased by her submission to his ideas and to the concept that they were, as a family, superior, allowed their mother to shift the axis of daily life and expand their world. They could only venture into spaces he didn't value, of course, and only into places where he had little interest in going. But this gave them the vastness of the wilderness.

Belly down on a mountaintop, Grace identified tundra plants. "The book says it's called *pedicularis groenlandica*, or elephant's head. Can you guess why?"

"The flowers look like little elephants!" said Bonnie, Zach blowing a puff of air to set miniature ears and trunks dancing.

They'd cross-country ski through ghost towns up Hunter and Castle Creek. Pull caddisfly larvae from clear pools, eyeing the tiny, protective shells the insects built themselves.

"Look how this one shines! It must've used mica," his mother marveled.

She'd dig a pit to prevent wind whipping out a fire in the snow. "Snap the dead stuff right off the tree. And any branches of orange pine needles—those are ideal fire starters, they're dead and dried out, very flammable, so they'll flare even if wet."

When sunset forced them home, Grace cooked as the children finished their homework or played, Bonnie's narrow face breaking into a smile whenever she beat Zach in a board game in a way that made losing almost worth it.

They waited for Bram to return from work before they ate dinner. At the table his voice would boom through them, and they'd nod, make sympathetic noises, talk about their own days only if asked. Their mother vanished into her wine as she ate, nodded, made those required sounds. Her hand curled loose around her glass by the time Bram left the table to watch TV or use his computer. Her eyes would have a blurriness to them by the time she finished cleaning the kitchen and went to fold laundry. And after Zach and Bonnie brushed their teeth, after Zach read his sister a story, if their mother came to tuck them in her words would slur; her voice gone wrong and strange, and each breath a cloud of awful, oversweet scent.

The only digital space beyond Bram's reach was the library,

where Bonnie paged through books of wildlife identification while Zach read graphic novels and their mother browsed on the public computers through bloodshot eyes.

By the time he began using iPads in school, Zach couldn't remember when he'd last held a screen of his own. He'd immediately searched "Bram Fisher fire Palm Beach."

Under a 2008 headline, HEIRESS AND SON KILLED IN FIRE, Bram said his loss was unimaginable, that Serena had been in treatment but her demons had been too strong. In a linked follow-up, Serena's siblings denied she'd had any substance problems, and asked why, if she did have issues, hadn't Bram taken Abraham Jr. with him when he went to stay at a nearby hotel that night after he and Serena argued?

The classroom around Zach faded to a dull hum. In all his bragging about Zach's never-brother, Zach realized Bram had never once uttered the boy's name, let alone mentioned he'd named this lost son after himself. The words "substance problems" made Serena and his mother overlap in his mind, an unsettling feeling compounded by the photo next to the article of a blond woman with a wide smile, different from his mother, yes, but with similar hair, makeup, and wearing a necklace he'd seen on his mother many times before.

Even now as he sat in the snow shelter, Zach felt a pang of pity for Serena's family. Aunt Felicity had been the same as Serena's family was in the article, refusing to believe Grace had an alcohol problem. But Zach had lived with his mother. Loved her. Tended to her when she went fumbling and sleepy and sick—peeled down to a different type of Underself. Not a looming, threatening thing, but a hidden, frightening self nonetheless.

The article with the most recent date was the longest. Serena had both "prescription sleeping pills" and "controlled substances" in her blood at the time the fire took hold at almost midnight. The signs of smoke in the lungs of mother and son proved they'd been alive as the fire burned. This and the source of the flames being traced back to a cigarette at Serena's bedside ruled out foul play. Serena had been curled up in her bed and hadn't woken, authorities surmised, because of the drugs they'd found in her system—things meant to treat pain, depression, sleeplessness, but not used at such high dosages. Abraham Jr.'s remains had been discovered beside the closed door of his room. He'd been wheelchair bound since birth, the article said, so had been unable to escape fast enough without it, the chair charred to almost nothing in his mother's room. Zach felt a sickening tightness in his stomach over the way the article seemed to revel in gruesome speculation about the sheer terror and helplessness of the boy's last moments as he succumbed to smoke inhalation. The reporter closed with a quote from Bram, who requested that in lieu of flowers donations be made to a memorial fund he'd established to help opioid addicts.

Zach tried to match Bram's description of his first son—tough, strong, sporty—with the grainy newspaper photo of the small, smiling boy in a wheelchair, his mother's arm tight around his narrow shoulders. But then again—a smile like that with difficulties like those? A boy who so obviously had made a valiant attempt to save himself despite all odds?

Yes, tough and strong sounded correct after all.

Russ fiddled with a loose thread on his glove, and Zach struggled to come up with something to make Russ forget about fire and death. He didn't want Russ to avoid him like his classmates, who lately acted like Zach's misfortune might be contagious.

"What's with the birds?" Russ asked as a loud cacophony echoed from somewhere nearby.

"Dunno. Sounds like crows." Recalling that crows were carrion feeders, Zach's mind leapt to the elk. "We saw the weirdest thing on the way here. A dead elk?" He cringed, death again, why had he brought this up? "But it was . . . super strange. Maybe the crows found something like that? My dad thought birds had done it."

"He thought birds *killed* it?"

Zach shook his head. Described the whitewashed bones, the exposed muscle, the petrichor scent. Russ peppered him with questions, until finally he sat back in exaggerated astonishment. "So gross," he said approvingly. "So, so gross! Let's go look. Maybe the birds found something cool like that."

Zach pictured a coil of razor-wire teeth suspended over the elk. A face bristling with eyes. Thick hair, clotted and tangled, shrouding a dripping snout.

But Russ was already scrambling out of the shelter, putting on his skis. Zach hurried out behind him and did the same.

"Where the hell are they?" Russ asked, the crows' calls seeming to come from everywhere and nowhere, noises always so difficult to locate when they came from above.

Zach spotted a flurry of skybound motion. "There," he said, and skied toward the birds, Russ following.

Only a minute from the shelter, Zach paused. There was something on the snow ahead. He shielded his eyes from the early evening light cutting low through the trees.

About seventy-five feet away, below a swirl of a dozen shrieking crows, a figure bounded over the snow, long and dark and low. As it wove through the trees it somehow remained vague even in patches of sun, reminding Zach of a sea monster drawn on an old map, serpentine and only half visible. Its progress was too smooth to be the lumbering gait of a bear or a coyote's trot, too undulating to be the feline advance of a mountain lion. Too large to be a raccoon or pine marten.

The creature went brown to black to gold, slinking into the light, out of it, yet always indistinct as it floated swiftly atop the snow, growing ever more distant. It stretched tall and—where was it? Had it really gone up, could anything climb a tree so swiftly, or had it flown, lifted into the sky, the—

"What's up?" Russ said from behind, startling him.

"I thought I saw something. A . . . porcupine maybe? Only bigger. Faster. I dunno. I'm not sure. But I can't see it now."

Russ's head tipped up to where the crows now roosted in the top of a tall pine. "You think whatever you saw spooked the birds?"

"Maybe. Or the birds spooked it?" The hairs on the back of Zach's neck itched with sensitive certainty there were eyes on him, that the creature watched from the trees.

"Check it out!" Russ pointed a pole. "Tracks."

A line of prints led through the snow in the direction Zach had seen the creature. He squatted down. Each stretched nearly two inches beyond Zach's mittened hand, oddly elongated. Five short, knobbed, and tapering fingers extended, crowned by puncture marks left behind by what had to have been thick, pointed claws.

"Looks like hands, kind of." Russ's eyes searched the forest. "Weird. What could've made these?"

On their hikes, camping trips, hut trips, even looking down at animal tracks from chairlifts, Zach's mother had familiarized him with the signs left by Rocky Mountain animals. But he'd never seen anything like these. The shape, the way the claws must have curved up above the snow before penetrating it, traced a creeping quiver up his spine.

"I don't know," Zach said.

Russ spread a hand next to a paw print. "They're pretty big, bro. I bet it was a bear."

"They're hibernating. And bear tracks are bigger than this. Wider? And rounder. And whatever I saw? It wasn't a bear."

"How do you know? It could've been a little bear. Like a baby one."

"It moved . . . differently. Smoother. And the color was different."

"You've seen a bear before?"

"Of course!"

Russ's laugh sounded nervous. "You know that's not, like, normal?"

Zach shrugged. Everyone he knew had seen bears. They stalked through town regularly searching for food and garbage, lolled on haunches along mountain trails stripping sarvisberries from bushes.

"Bears are everywhere here in the summer."

"Are they mean?"

"Mostly, no? Like one time a bear fell asleep in a tree right on Main Street! Everyone was down below taking selfies all day. She looked more scared than any of us. But, yeah, sometimes they can be scary? Like last summer, my sister was ahead of us on the trail and surprised a bear."

"Whoa! What happened?"

As Zach described the scene, described the bear, he breathed deep to try to still his heart as the memory of Bonnie's scream pierced him.

He'd been teasing Bonnie, calling her a puppy because she kept sprinting up the trail then back down to let them know what lay in store before taking off again, whole body wiggling like she was wagging a tail.

And then that scream. His mother moving so fast uphill it was as if she simply vaporized from beside him. Zach turning the bend to find Bonnie in her arms and slowly backing away, eyes on an enormous bear ten feet ahead that swiped a pigeon-toed paw at the ground before charging toward mother and daughter.

Existence chiseled down to a pinpoint that was Bonnie, their mother, and that charging bear, Zach certain he was about to witness the bloody annihilation of everything that mattered to him.

His own impotence to arrest the scene, to help, opened a chasm of hopelessness.

But the bear stopped a few feet short, then strained its neck toward his mother and sister and released a disorienting yawn-like yowl.

His mother carefully picked her way backward down the trail, repeating in a low, loud voice: "I am human. My name is Grace. I am a person."

Bonnie wrapped around their mother so tight the two melded into a larger being. The bear's dark eyes, gone tiny and vicious, tracked them. The paw swatted up more dust, and the thing made a snuffling, huffing sound as the group disappeared around the bend.

Grace kept Bonnie in her arms, checking over her shoulder as they descended to be sure the bear didn't change its mind and come after them.

Finally safe enough to think, Bonnie wept when her mother at last set her down. "I'm sorry, Mama! I didn't do it right. I didn't do the rules."

Generally, Zach knew, bears were skittish or indifferent toward humans, preferring to avoid them altogether. But if you surprised one, came upon it close and unaware, it might lash out. If you surprised a bear, you were supposed to back away, speak deep but loud. Make yourself big by lifting your arms, especially if you were little. You didn't scream, collapse, or run. Those things, when it came to a black bear, were most likely to provoke it.

Grace kneeled on the dirt and pulled Bonnie into a hug. "It's okay, Bon-Bon." Her fingers were white at the knuckles where her hands gripped Bonnie, eyes vacant as if picturing what could have happened. "Sometimes when we're scared our bodies just react. Think of this as practice. Now you've practiced. So if there's a next time, you'll do better, I promise. And there are worse reactions than calling for your mama, little one."

"A mountain lion would've been even scarier," Bonnie snuffled, as if reassuring herself that it all could have been worse.

"Yes." Grace released Bonnie and they continued toward home. "Or a moose. Moose hurt more people than bears and mountain lions combined."

"Moose don't *look* as scary," Zach said, his breathing at last beginning to slow, the world around him finally beginning to expand again.

Their mother shrugged. "You can't judge anything by looks."

"Was that the scariest animal you've ever seen, Mama?" Bonnie asked.

"No."

"What was?"

"People," Grace said flatly.

Zach laughed. "People don't count!"

"Sure they do."

Zach and Bonnie exchanged an eye roll, and catching it, their mother said, "I'm serious. We talk about nature being cruel, but it isn't, not really, because nature isn't aware. Animals are driven by instinct. People, though? We make choices. Which means there's nothing as scary as people."

CHAPTER 10

"Soon after moving here," Grace said, "I was backpacking with one of my girlfriends from town to Crested Butte. We passed a pair of men going the opposite way. They stopped us, kind of quizzed us about if we knew how to set a fire, if we had enough food, that kind of thing. They seemed annoyed, like we should have been grateful even though they were criticizing us. It took awhile to kind of politely keep moving. But once they were out of sight, my friend and I both admitted we felt . . . weird. About the way the guys had acted. Their anger, it felt disproportionate—that means too big, they had too big a reaction, offended over nothing. And I didn't say it, but I didn't like how they'd looked at us. Kind of like that bear, the way its eyes were?"

Bonnie's face went tight, picturing, Zach supposed, the promise of grievous harm in the beady fierceness of the bear's eyes.

"We decided to make camp early, and we hiked maybe a hundred feet off trail. Pitched our tent where it was hidden in the trees, not at any official campsite or anything. Didn't light a fire. Just ate granola bars for dinner. Kind of laughing about how silly we were being, making a fuss over something that was probably nothing."

Grace shook her head ruefully, as if wishing the story went

another way at this point, a line drawn between what was and what could have been.

"My friend woke me in the middle of the night. There were men's voices. Arguing. When we looked out the tent's little screened window we could see their flashlights through the trees. They were on the trail, talking about how far 'those girls' might have gotten, how it was impossible we could just disappear. They were loud. And using bad words."

"They were looking for you?" Zach whispered, wide-eyed.

"Yes. But we stayed quiet. Watched. Saw their lights disappear down the trail. Which meant we hadn't woken up when they'd passed by going uphill." Grace shivered. "I didn't like that, knowing while we'd been asleep they were sneaking around. We got dressed and put our shoes on, in case we had to run."

Zach nodded, thinking of a game of Gray Rabbit, the way a Rabbit-child didn't just hide, but could run if a Wolf found him.

"They came past again. Still looking. Then near dawn we heard them go down the trail. No voices, no flashlights. But we knew it was them. We'd learned their sounds. The sun came up. We were still too afraid to do anything. Finally we heard people talking. Women. I sprinted to the trail and found two couples backpacking. They were nice, when I explained. Waited for us to pack, and we hiked with them the whole rest of the way to Crested Butte. But. They hadn't seen the men going down the trail, which they should have, given the timing. They asked a lot of questions that made it clear they thought we were paranoid. Or exaggerating. But for my friend and me? It felt like those men might jump out any second. Like they were watching us from the trees. Because they had to have hidden so that group wouldn't see them."

"Did you tell the police?" Zach asked.

"We did. But the other group couldn't identify them, or back us up. You're supposed to sign a register at the trailhead, but lots of people don't do that. I'm not even sure the police ended up checking on the people who had signed."

"Didn't you record a video or something? On your phone?"

"This was before most people had smartphones. We sure didn't have them. So there was no proof. And to the police—nothing really happened. When we told them about the men questioning us on the trail, the cops said it sounded like they were concerned for our safety. Were trying to help. Cops are a little like teachers. If they don't see a kid's bad behavior, they don't really believe it. Especially if no one's hurt."

This was true enough of teachers in Zach's experience, but he frowned at the idea the police might be the same, waving off the flurry of back-and-forth accusations, not really caring who was at fault. Unless the hurt was very bad. And for name-calling, or threats? No one ever got in trouble for that, no matter how frightening, sometimes not even when a teacher overheard.

"Let's rest a second, huh?"

Their mother sat on a downed tree by the side of the trail, both children snuggling next to her, needing her reassuring closeness after the bear. Head resting on his mother's shoulder, Zach heard her voice as a soft rumble through her body. "For a long time after those men, maybe because I'd been right about them, I thought I had good instincts. Good intuition. But"— her voice strained thin, more than it had when she went toe-to-toe with the bear—"I don't think that anymore. It's not always as easy as it was that time."

Seeing Zach's and Bonnie's puzzled faces, Grace, rubbing a temple, translated for them into the language of childhood. "I guess what I mean is bad guys aren't like in the movies. You can't just— see badness on most of them. They don't say their plans out loud. And they're not always strangers. They're more like bullies. Bullies look like normal kids, right? Sometimes they can even be nice, which is confusing. Then they'll say something that hurts your feelings, but if you show you're hurt they say they're just being honest, or that you're being a baby, or that it was a joke. Bullies say give me your toy, and when you don't, they might hit you, then say that's your fault because you didn't share. A bad guy thinks if people obeyed him, everything would be better, and that they should obey him because he's better than everyone else. Most of the time, a bully believes what he's saying. Sometimes he believes it so much it convinces you, too. So you wonder if maybe he *was* just joking, or if you're the one who is actually the bad guy. And he'll say whatever he has to, to avoid getting in trouble, because he's sure he's right, and whatever he did was really your fault."

Recalling taunts, playground violence, the indignation of even the kids who hit and harmed, Bonnie and Zach nodded.

"An animal like that bear, though? He doesn't think like that. Doesn't act like that. He doesn't know what's right or wrong. He was just . . . scared."

Standing in the woods staring down at the clawed tracks left by whatever had gone slinking into the trees, Zach shivered, desperately needing to take the sting out of his fear, push down the darkness of his memories. He nudged Russ with an elbow. "One time? Over the summer? A bear broke into my school. It went in the teacher's lounge and tore the door of their fridge right off. And it pooped"—he paused for dramatic effect—"*aaaaaaall* over their couch."

"What?" Russ grinned wide.

"Yeah! Like this big." Zach held up his hands to outline a circle about the size of a dinner plate. "Bears have *huge* poops." He frowned at his hands, then widened the space between them to beach-ball size for good measure.

"No way. Is that true?"

"That's what everyone said. And when school started the teachers had a new couch, a new fridge, and"—Zach wrinkled his nose—"it did *not* smell good in there."

Russ guffawed. "That is amazing! I have a couple of teachers I wouldn't mind if a bear took a giant—"

Dave's voice reverberated through the trees, making both boys jump. "Russ! Zach! Time to come in!"

They looked at each other. They'd forgotten the hut, the adults.

"Boys?"

"We should stay out here," Russ grumbled. His eyes darted up to the crows, still cawing from the treetop. "Go see what those birds are yelling about. See if there's another dead elk!"

Zach felt an almost physical pull toward the hut.

"Russ? Zach?" Dave called again. "Time for dinner!"

Russ crossed his arms and stuck out a petulant lower lip.

Zach squirmed, needing to obey, wanting to flee the trees, the tracks, the creature, the birds. He feigned casualness. "I mean, it's getting dark anyway."

Russ gave a put-upon sigh. "I guess. But tomorrow, we'll come search around, right? And you'll show me that elk on the way down?"

"Sure!"

"Bear crapping in the teacher's lounge," Russ said with a cackle as they skied back, snow beginning to fall lightly around them. "Classic."

Inside, the hut felt overwarm, even stifling.

"You boys have fun?" Bram asked.

"Yep," Russ said. "Zach knows a ton about outdoor stuff."

Zach covered his smile with a hand. Maybe Russ liked him after all.

Darkness swallowed the mountains and the storm thickened. When Steve switched on the porch light, the men cheered at seeing snowflakes the size of quarters dancing unpredictably down a path slanted by wind.

"Already almost two inches, wouldn't you say?"

"Could be a big dump."

"Don't jinx it, man!"

"A bear-size dump," Russ whispered, nudging Zach, and they both snorted with laughter.

As the group ate dinner, Zach felt the power of the snowstorm knit the group together in anticipation, the hut becoming ever more the bright center of a snowy world creating itself just for them. He relaxed into his new friendship, into the comfort of his father's smile, which said the storm was a benediction; proof that this trip, his trip, was right and good.

"Dude, Zach," Russ said wide-eyed, "this is gonna cover those tracks! We'll probably never get to see whatever those crows were after. Or that dead elk."

"What? A dead what?" Pike's slurred, overloud voice made Zach recoil.

Russ's cheeks went red at being thrust into the spotlight. "Oh, it's—we saw some tracks out there. With claw marks! A whole bunch of crows were freaking out, too. So we figured the crows and whatever left the tracks were feeding on a dead animal or something."

"Where?" Pike asked, squinting out the window into the night as if he'd somehow be able to spot crows circling in the darkness.

"Way back in the trees, kind of near where the trail comes out of the forest. We're gonna check it out tomorrow, right, Zach? We can show you guys where it is. We thought maybe it's an elk, because Zach saw a dead one on the way up."

"Can't believe I forgot!" Bram interjected with a slap on his forehead. "We saw a dead buck all right—huge, just off-trail. Strangest damn thing. The neck and skull were stripped to bare bone. But the body"—Bram sliced a hand across his neck then gestured toward his feet—"from here on down, it was totally intact. Except for a little gnawing on a leg."

Steve frowned, then forced a neutral expression as if trying to hide his skepticism. "I've only ever come across a few bones. Scavengers generally make quick work of things. And they don't eat just one part of something."

"It was pretty unusual, all right," Bram said. "Maybe we can poke around after skiing tomorrow, see if the boys found something similar."

Pike pressed three fingers to his lips as if he were physically forcing in his nausea before saying, "I'm not gonna go looking for some dead thing."

"So the skull, the spine, those bones were exposed?" Dave asked.

"Yep. Maybe birds had been at it, like the boys saw," Bram said.

"What about the privates?"

A confused look from Bram and sardonic chuckles around the table from the others.

"Yeah, didn't exactly check the state of those," Bram said with a half smile.

Undeterred, Dave asked, "Was there any blood? Around the head and neck?"

Bram's eyebrows shot up. "Nope. Did you see it? On the way here?"

"No, but I've seen that before," Dave intoned, voice heavy but with a lilt that held the promise of a campfire story. The others unconsciously leaned toward him in anticipation. "I grew up on ranches." The group nodded, already aware that the Dowling name had been stamped on beef products in stores across the country for nearly one hundred years. "On our place in central Colorado, we had a bull show up like that in the seventies, when I was about Zach's age. It happened—still happens—all over. And no one knows why.

My dad, he was convinced it was the federal government intimidating ranchers—taking out breeding stock while testing bioweapons or the like. Some of our neighbors thought it was satanists doing rituals. But most people thought it was aliens."

Jon, who had just taken a long inhale, choked on his vape. "You mean, like, little green men?"

Dave settled back into his chair at the head of the table, framed by the soft chaos of the snow out the window behind him. "Yep. Plenty of folks saw what looked like black helicopters flying silently at night. Next day they'd find an eviscerated animal, looking like Bram described—head and neck nothing but bone. And the privates cored right out." Dave's hand made a scooping, snapping motion that caused a simultaneous flinch around the table. "Our veterinarian at the time checked out the bull killed on our place. Said he couldn't've made it look like that with a full set of tools. Too perfect. And no blood."

Though on the way up Bram had rationalized the elk down to a simple case of bird bait, he now leaned toward Dave conspiratorially. "The cuts on the elk looked surgical. Creepy as hell."

"There you go." Dave nodded. "Ranchers started shooting at anything that crossed the sky, guys like my dad made all kinds of stink about government conspiracies, born-agains were praying over cow remains, and the hippies ran all over trying to offer themselves up to alien invaders. Got bad enough the feds investigated. We're talking the FBI."

"Seriously? What'd they say?" Shane asked.

"Nothing that satisfied anyone, that's what. Blamed flies. Like a certain type of fly that preys on the soft tissue first, so works from the mucus membranes, the anus, that kind of thing. But flies don't show up in one state for a few months, then vanish and move to another. If it was flies, every rotten cow, every dead animal left exposed would look like that. And they didn't. They don't. Years'll go by with nothing like it, then all at once—a bunch of things like this elk. Make fun of me if you want," Dave said with a portentous look around the table, "but seeing what I saw, I know a man couldn't've done it. So if someday a monster crawls out from somewhere, I'd say, 'Well, that explains it. They've been watching us all along.'"

Russ and Zach exchanged a nervous look, and Zach knew that like him, Russ was remembering the elongated, claw-crowned tracks curling through the woods, and the mysterious creature Zach couldn't describe.

"I can say one thing for sure." Dave held up a finger for emphasis, the rapt eyes of the group on him, awaiting their final lesson. "It showed me there's evil in this world you can't explain. All you can do is hope it leaves you alone."

CHAPTER 11

Zach pulled the tattered stuffed fox from where he'd concealed it in the foot of his sleeping bag. He rubbed Mr. Fantastic's threadbare cheek against his own, hoping it would help clear his mind of aliens, monsters, the horrible body of the elk, the unidentifiable creature in the woods, his mother's blurred eyes.

The orange fur and well-worn nose were a comfort, but didn't prevent him opening his eyes to stare at the ceiling.

He needed to use the bathroom. He pinched his thigh to try to convince his traitorous body it didn't actually need to go.

Holding him back after class one day, his teacher gently suggested dozing at his desk was interrupting his learning and that perhaps he needed to talk with someone, since this issue had so clearly started after what she obliquely referred to as his "loss." Zach had assumed the teacher meant he'd get to miss class to visit the school counselor, a soft-eyed woman who had fed him cookies after Geoff had punched him on the playground, and who had somehow ably cut off Geoff's aggression after a similar meeting with him.

Instead, Bram intercepted Zach at the door when Ximena

brought the children home from ski team dryland training that evening.

"They think you need therapy. Therapy! But what you're going to do is you're going to go to sleep and be bright-eyed and bushy-tailed in class, problem solved. Got it?"

"Yes."

A pat on the back. "Of course you do."

So Zach forced his eyes open at school, biting the inside of his cheek to stay awake. At home he'd put on his coat and claim to be playing outside, then curl up and doze in the plastic shelter atop the play structure. When he woke to see Ximena balancing on the ladder to peek inside, he asked if she'd tattle. Ximena told him to nap inside when he needed, and she'd wake him before his father got home.

"Mister Bram thinks obedience and respect are the same, but they are not, little one. You need sleep."

Yes, Ximena was nice so far. She was probably taking good care of Bonnie. Maybe despite Bram's marching orders she'd let Bonnie watch television on her phone, eat mac 'n' cheese, even have dessert. Had Bonnie been able to go to sleep without him? Before, she'd sought refuge whenever their parents argued, but his sister snuck into Zach's room every night now. He'd sing her to sleep; stroke her hair when nightmares made her cry out.

Zach inhaled the familiar comfort of Mr. Fantastic. If Bram saw the fox he would probably take it away like he had Blankie. How long ago was that? The beginning of third grade, so he must have been eight, like Bonnie was now.

You should've tossed that disgusting thing years ago, Grace, avoided all this fuss. My father would've kicked my ass if I acted like this at his age.

A pang of loss traveled through him, and he tightened his grip on Mr. Fantastic. But the fox was a necessary risk. Without him, sleep was impossible. Zach could always say Bonnie had hidden the stuffed animal in his bag. That was the kind of nurturing act Bram approved of when it came to his little girl.

Zach rolled over. He tried to soothe himself by picturing Bonnie at her happiest; running wild, muddy and scraped, grinning as she caught garter snakes, beetles, and crawdads, making them laugh with what his mom called "potty humor."

Despite being Bram's favorite, his golden child, Bonnie and their mother hid this side of the little girl's personality so that Bonnie could deftly navigate his moods. When Bram was there she'd learned to change into her despised dresses, put bows in her hair, and generally make sure her entire appearance was frilled and softened. But that was all right. If Zach could be like Bonnie, if he or his mother could understand their father's expectations for him so that he could conform, he'd do the same.

He sighed. Even now, despite knowing what his father expected, he wasn't able to just fall asleep, couldn't just order his body to hold it. He didn't want to walk to the outhouse, either, picturing the trip through the storm, the new snow, the dark. Where the monster could see him. Snatch him, tear away his skin, his tongue, his—

Zach squeezed his eyes shut and told himself he was already asleep. But late autumn flies swarmed in the darkness behind his eyelids, the greedy threads of their forelegs rubbing together over the eviscerated elk.

It might be a dead fly dangling from the diamond earring. Squished and blackened.

Zach sighed. There was no more fighting it. He had to go, and his dark thoughts wouldn't let him rest until he did. Russ, Dave, and his father were all asleep and had been for some time, which at least reassured him they probably wouldn't wake up as he snuck out. He tucked Mr. Fantastic into his shirt, the rub of soft fur a warm bolt of courage. Slowly, careful not to disturb the others, he crawled out of his sleeping bag, grabbed his headlamp, and put on his slippers.

Downstairs the fading woodstove fire painted everything orange and black.

He could avoid going to the outhouse if he went out one of the windows. But the memory of the mothers' reaction to men having done just that rippled through Zach. And anyway, there was nothing to be afraid of. He put on his coat, his boots, switched on his headlamp, and plunged outside.

The wind sliced through him. The darkness was so complete, the snowfall so thick, that his headlamp illuminated a windblown vortex of thousands of white flakes but little else. The snow was already a foot deep, slipping into his boots and clinging to his long underwear pants as he bounded to the outhouse. He shut the door and the wind instantly cut. After he used the pit toilet he turned to leave, then paused with his hand hovering over the door latch.

Something felt out of place. Had he dropped something, left something behind?

No. His mind had somehow registered before he could process it that there was movement outside.

Zach clicked off his headlamp, heart lapping at his ribs. He backed away from the closed door, feeling as though a string had cut behind his knees. When he felt the back of his legs bump into the rim of the toilet, he sat down even though his pants were on. Had he turned his light off soon enough for it to go unnoticed by whatever stalked on the other side of the wall?

A soft crush. A dragging, punctuated by a squelching—feet or ski poles, paws or hooves, plunging through snow.

The sounds slipped liquid-like through even the smallest crevices of the outhouse, and Zach tried his best to blindly track them. No headlamp or flashlight shone through the uninsulated walls. And it couldn't be another member of the group trudging out to use the toilet. The noises came from the wrong direction, filling his imagination until it overflowed with images of black helicopters beating silently overhead. A monster slicing flesh to scapula. Precious things eaten raw. Licked clean.

Zach's body stiffened then dissolved into a quiver at the sound of an inhuman howl. He knew instinctively that the sound had traveled through sharp teeth. It was too similar to the tiger he'd heard at the zoo last year—its discontent simmering in the throat before spreading into a snarl—to think anything else. Though this sound was lower. Different. And inexplicably, it had come from far away, from some unknowable distance in front of the hut the outhouse sat behind, completely separate from whatever moved nearby. And the thing dragging through the snow had gone silent, as if it, too, had been frightened by the creature's cry.

Zach waited, each bit of him focused solely on trying to hear through the wind and the awful pulse of his terror.

Finally, the slippery noises resumed. The thing was moving again, past him and uphill. Slowly, torturously slowly, its dragging softened. Maybe it was gone. Or maybe it waited, crouched in the trees, nocturnal eyes fixed on the outhouse door.

Snow that had caught in the scrunch of Zach's pants above his boots painfully iced his ankles. He could hardly feel his toes. How long had he been outside? Ten minutes? Twenty?

The wind swelled, its shriek worsening the chill and obscuring any noises the thing might still be leaving in its wake.

Zach partially unzipped his coat and crossed his arms over where Mr. Fantastic snuggled in his shirt, warming his bare hands under his armpits. He stood, shifting his weight to bring his cold feet back to life. But he couldn't stop the trembling that came from deep in his chest, the still freeze of the small room combining with visions of red eyes, peeled and waiting, the dry rasp of a long tongue against the wood of his shelter.

He waited. Nothing came through the whistle of wind, the ragged scratch of his own breath, the *pat-pat-pat* of his heart.

Nothing wicked dragging its prey through snow.

It had only been the wind. A blown branch skidding across the snow. A mountain lion. A porcupine.

And he was going to freeze out here, hiding.

Wimp. Scaredy-cat.

Zach used the toilet again, and his shame over how much he needed to go again, how little his body seemed to understand itself, cut slightly through his fear. He needed to take care of himself, because no one else would, no one else was here, and the pain of the uncontrollable shaking, his frozen ankles and toes, was veering into territory that was becoming more real, more palpable, more dangerous, than whatever might stalk outside.

"Okay. All right," he whispered.

Zach flung the door open and stumbled through the snow toward the warm glow of Pantheon Hut.

CHAPTER 12

Within seconds Zach twisted the hut's lock behind him. He pressed his face against the door's window. No signs of life. The only sound the wet surge of his own blood.

At some point the snow had stopped falling. In the slice of the outdoors visible through the glass, the smooth sheet of white was only marred by his own tracks, curlicues of blowing snow already softening them.

Nothing. There was nothing at all.

Zach rolled the soft hairs at the nape of his neck around a finger and pulled. It calmed him; satisfyingly painful. He peered out the window for one minute, two, until he was sure there was nothing to see, that no creature hunted there.

He set his wet boots next to the woodstove to dry, put another log on the fire, and held grateful hands up to the stove's renewed heat. His damp socks steamed and he wavered, drained.

Everything he knew standing there feeling himself begin to thaw, the spread of warmth dissolving his fear, told him his mother had been right when she said fire was the most important ingredient for surviving in the winter wilderness. The primordial draw of it made it impossible to go upstairs. The intensity of his trembling slowed, then stopped.

Someone had left the red bottle of lighter fluid only a few inches from the stove. He frowned at this and moved it beside the woodpile, the plastic hot to the touch.

Braver now that the strange sounds were a memory, Zach trotted to the hut's front door to peek out in the direction the creature's yowl had seemed to come from. No new tracks had been left behind by any living thing. The bolt of the keypad lock was firmly in place, the group's footprints on the porch transformed to uneven depressions by the wind and the new snowfall. There was the dim silhouette of the woods where the crows had circled over the strange creature, and on the horizon hovered a yellow, diffused brightness. Though Zach knew it had to be the distant lights of town, in that moment he saw it as warmth radiating from the place where Bonnie lay sleeping and safe.

Zach counted the boots paired neatly by the door, one through six, a reassuring reminder he wasn't alone. Bram's boots lay on their side in a pool of snowmelt. Zach moved them next to his own by the stove, standing them proud and bending the tongues out so that they would dry by morning.

Zach curled up on a couch, pulling his coat over himself like a blanket, Mr. Fantastic tucked under his chin, and a hand gripping the lump of survival essentials his mother had secreted in an inner pocket of his jacket, things she said everyone should always have in the backcountry. A small box that contained a folding knife, compass, water purification tablets, and of course, matches. The satisfying camping kind where the orange flaming part took up most of the stick.

There was no bloodthirsty monster in the woods. The men would be happy. Bram would be happy. Things would be okay.

As okay as they could be.

Zach closed his eyes, drifting. No matter how he fought it, every night he traveled back in time as he traversed the space between waking and sleeping.

Because no matter how his mind scratched at it, he knew he didn't fully understand what his parents had said. And because he couldn't help returning again and again to the night that had been the last time before the worst time.

His father's thundered criticisms had woken Zach when his parents had returned from their night out. Grace had laughed when she shouldn't have, talked too much, drank too much, smiled too little, interrupted, hadn't listened. She embarrassed him. Why couldn't she ever? Why couldn't she just?

But when his mother finally spoke, it wasn't her normal sputtering defenses or weepy, slurred apologies. Instead, her voice trickled exhausted through Zach's bedroom wall. "I need—quiet. I'd—I'd like it—I'd like you to sleep somewhere else tonight. Please."

Bram's voice had the gravelly righteousness of the Underself. "So you humiliate me, and now you want me to leave? No."

Bonnie squeezed Zach's hand. He'd been asleep when she'd snuck into his room, already anticipating trouble. Like him, Bonnie was attuned to the patterns of the house. She knew when their parents dressed up, went out, it meant that when they returned there was a good chance there would be a reckoning, their father furious over whatever he had decided their mother was and wasn't.

And Bonnie didn't like to be alone when that happened.

"I didn't say leave—I just need quiet—I can stay in the guest bedroom, or you—"

"Please. Would've been nice if you'd needed quiet at dinner tonight, instead of interrupting me every time I brought up the business. You knew the whole point was getting Jim to invest. It's like dealing with a child."

His mother didn't respond. Zach heard something inside him whisper, "At least it isn't me. At least he's not mad at me." He squeezed his sister close to fight off his shame at this thought.

"I needed him to sign on, but instead we got the Grace show, everyone pretending you're so hilarious, so clever. That's pity, them laughing, you know that? Laughing at a drunk. You think he's going to invest now? After that?"

"Maybe it's better he doesn't."

"What?" Bram snapped, the sound a menacing curl that made Bonnie bury her head into Zach's chest. "What did you say?"

"Nothing. Nothing! It's just maybe—with the business the way it is . . ."

The children waited for Bram's voice to fracture walls, cull their mother to a shadow, turn her raw and repentant then quiet as a stone.

That was all necessary before there'd be peace. And tomorrow they'd all pretend nothing happened.

"What do you know about my business?"

"Nothing, I just mean with the, uh, economy—"

"The economy! Christ, you're a joke."

"Just let me—let me—I'll sleep in the guest bedroom. For tonight. How's—"

"You want me out of my own bedroom, in the house I own, and you're giving me that face, pretending you're some victim? Poor you. Why do you do this to me? I give you everything. What more do you want?"

Zach flinched. When his father held the scales, if on one side sat honesty and on the other saying whatever his father wanted to hear—which was always "sorry, I'm so sorry, I'm the problem here, you're right"—compliance without question was the only way to bring things to balance.

"I want a—a separation," his mother said, voice so low Zach barely heard her.

The children exchanged a wide-eyed stare. In the ensuing silence, Zach pictured his father's expression, just as surprised at this unprecedented turn as his children. Just as shocked that their mother had stood up to him. Quietly, stutteringly, but even so.

Already Zach floated into another life, another house, where he and Bonnie came home only to their mother, and she was a real mother, the mother who took them into the mountains rather than whatever she became in the house, his heart beating with a *yes, yes, yes* drum of hope even as his gut roiled with hot fear of Bram somehow intuiting his disloyalty. What journey might lay between this moment and that dream? And would there be anything left of Bram at the end of it if he was no longer their leader, commander, dictator?

When his father finally spoke, the edges of his anger were softened by a kind of curiosity. "What's your end game here?"

"There's no game."

"Is this some kind of sick joke? A divorce?"

Bonnie hugged her brother tighter. He rubbed the spot between her birdlike shoulder blades the way that had soothed her since she was a baby.

"I—I didn't say that, I said I just needed quiet, to be—to have space. A separation. Only for a little bit, just to—"

The Underself leaned into the injustice, a blameless victim. "You would be that cruel? Rip our family apart like that?"

"You're their father, you—"

"I know that, Grace," Bram interrupted. "But what are you? A mother? No woman would drink like you and dare to think of herself as a mother. I've sheltered you. Protected you. Provided for you. At your age, you think you're going back to that so-called modeling career? Or that they're going to let you pretend to keep up with the guys at Mountain Rescue? And we have a prenup. You divorce me, you'll have nothing."

Their mother laughed. Laughed! An icy, rueful laugh Zach had never heard before. Her audacity filled him with horrified wonder.

"There's nothing to *have*, Bram," she said. "You don't *have* anything."

In response, a sudden smashing noise made the children jolt, the muffled words and sounds that followed unintelligible. Into Zach's head sprung the image of his father slapping a jar over his miniaturized mother, the Underself sealing that jar, lifting it, his mother captured like an insect, running on the infinite, uphill plane of glass Bram spun ever faster.

Their mother's voice shook. "You stay right there."

"Everything in this house is mine to break." A pause. Another crashing sound, Bonnie's grip tightening. "I don't have anything, huh? Then what was that? Looked like 'something' to me."

"There's nothing. It's all lies."

His mother kept talking when she should be going small and smooth and unresponsive. And she knew that. She knew better than anyone. She was the one who'd told Zach, *If you're attacked by an animal, you fight back. Unless you're fighting with a grizzly bear or your father. Then you play dead.*

"You're crazy, Grace. We live in a goddamn mansion. What's your Range Rover, some fantasy? What is so wrong with you that you always try to ruin everything, even yourself?"

Their mother's voice cracked, ruptured by what sounded like grief. "You. You're the one who—breaks things. You're a bully."

"You want to break vows, and you talk to me about breaking things? No." Their father's voice reverberated through the house, infused with the conviction of a true believer. "I see through this, Grace. You provoke me with insults, then say I'm a bully. You lie, so you call me a liar. Every accusation out of your mouth is a confession." Zach felt the rapid drum of Bonnie's heart. "The truth is all I do is for you. Private school for *your* children, I pay for *your* vacations, your endless clothes and bags and—"

"None of this is for us. And all that's nothing, compared to what—"

"The disrespect! After all I've done for you?"

"You don't want respect. From me, the kids? You just want obedience."

"Are you on something? On top of the drinking, I mean. Because—"

"It's fraud, Bram!" their mother interrupted, an act so forbidden that Zach and Bonnie gasped.

"You *are* insane," their father said, sounding so calm now, as if this revelation explained it all. And their mother did sound strange. Shrill, out of pitch, her voice breaking in the middle whenever she spoke. "You want to find fraud? Look at our neighborhood here, huh? You've got oil and gas execs, a diamond mine heiress, a server farm billionaire. All the money in this world is blood money, and guess what? No one gives a shit, not even you. Those are your friends. Yet I build a business from the dirt up, and you act like I'm some kind of, of—fraud? No. I'm the only one who works hard, who deserves any of it."

"I don't want to hear about other people, Bram. I care what *you've* done. You think everyone's below you, hate that you're not the best, the richest, and—you haven't thought of what it will mean for the kids, and they said you've taken risks your investors didn't agree—"

"What 'they'? Who's 'they'?" There was a new and unprecedented hitch in his words, an urgency, and Zach imagined the Underself crouching, spider legs pinning his mother, eyes examining every twitch in her expression.

Bonnie started to cry. Zach leaned close and whispered, "It's okay, it's okay. She'll stop. She'll stop making him angry."

"What 'they,' Grace?"

"No one." Their mother's voice had transformed to a thin, transparent husk.

"This is—you've been planning this. After all these years you've decided I'm not rich enough so you—what? Stole some account information? And showed someone. Of course you did. That's what gold diggers do." The Underself's darkness seemed to soak through the walls, coating the children in a membrane of cold, ominous threat. "Probably showed them the prenup, too, which is why you're lying, trying to blackmail me. That's what this is. Who'd you show, Grace? What did you bring them?"

"Stay there. Stay right there." Their mother's voice was a desperate plea to something wild, over which she knew she had no control.

"You're so *dramatic*," Bram said, but the familiar assessment, familiar insult, was fissured with an unfamiliar, hissing insidiousness. "I can't believe you, playing innocent when you want to destroy my family, my business. Who are *they*? What did you show them?"

A long beat before Grace capitulated, voice trembling at the edge of something. "Just—the life insurance trusts. I wanted to understand how they worked. So I talked to a lawyer, who talked to an accountant."

"What else? They wouldn't say anything about Ajax Prop if all you handed over was the trust agreements."

"Only—Alpine Bank. And a—taxes folder. From your office."

"Which office, home or downtown?"

"Here. But"—their mother's words tripped over each other in a rapid waterfall of reassurance—"I didn't let them keep anything, and it's all confidential, lawyers can't say anything and the accountant, that was all anonymous, so they can't say anything to anyone, so it doesn't matter."

"What exactly did they say?"

"No-nothing."

"What did the lawyer say, Grace."

"Just that—they thought—you might not have software at all. That even if you did, you haven't used it to buy undervalued properties, because the business doesn't own any real estate at all. And that instead the investor money is in risky things. Shorting stocks. Crypto. And it did well. For a long time. But now, that's changed. And it's gone. Or almost gone."

During the long quiet that followed, Bonnie squeezed Zach's hand until it hurt. He didn't shake her off, consumed by trying to understand. What was a trust? A short stock? Things his father had to think about. Things that had made him pause. When Bram finally spoke, his straightforward, unemotional precision frightened Zach more than anything that had come before.

"Think it through, Grace. They couldn't know what every subsidiary holds. Not with only those files. Sure, there have been some losses. But every sector in the world is in free fall right now. Did you ask how the business was doing compared to everyone else? Because I'm fine, Grace. And it'll bounce back. Only a matter of time. Look at who my investors are—those are the real businessmen, and they chose me."

"They said without investor knowledge, it's criminal, tha—"

Bram cut her off, a man whose patience was being tested. "You're buying into some lawyer's incompetence. After all I've done. Taking some stranger's word over mine, over the father of your children. The only person who truly knows you, and still loves you."

In her hurt voice, the same one she used when she came back from the hospital after breaking her fingers in the slamming door, she said, "I don't think you ever did. Love us. I don't think you can."

Another potent lull before Bram's bitter judgment: "If I didn't love you, you couldn't hurt me this way."

"I'm sorry," she said at last. Too late, because what she'd spilled couldn't be put back, the unforgivableness of it clear in their father's voice. "I'm sorry, Bram."

Silence. Stillness. Bonnie breathing beside him, waiting.

"I'm going," Bram said, "just like you wanted. I can't be anywhere near you right now. You're disturbed. Heartless. You need help."

Bram's footsteps down the hall, his mother's muted weeping, then the distant grind of the garage opening. Grace cracked Zach's bedroom door, Bonnie snoring beside him by then. Through the knit of his lashes as he pretended to be asleep he saw his mother had a bottle of wine in one hand, a glass in the other.

"It'll all be better. He's gone now. It'll all be okay."

Zach stayed still, breathing evenly so that she'd leave, so that he wouldn't have to talk about what he'd overheard.

The wind outside shrieked, and it was his mother calling for him across the open expanse of the avalanche path she'd watched him cross last year. It was his mother, shrieking, desperate, searching.

"*Zakky?*"

He shot up, disoriented, dry-mouthed, and unsure of where he was in space and time.

CHAPTER 13

Zach paced, trying to slough off the residue of the recurring nightmare that was the past.

Moonlight shone in white columns through the hut. The fire had dimmed. Zach rested his forehead against the glass of a window, its coolness helping settle him. In the distance loomed Mount Mariah, so pale after the storm that it had a bluish, antiseptic quality.

Zach frowned. Stepped back from the window to better see out of it.

There was something moving in the distance above the tree line, above where the miner's cabin hid in the forest. A black, wavering form, cast into high relief against the snow by moonlight, headed uphill toward the ridge that rimmed Mariah Bowl.

The monster.

It had to be—what—half a mile away? It was so difficult to assess distance in the mountains even in daylight, let alone to try to guess how far away something moving up a slope in the dark might be. But Zach comforted himself with the knowledge that it was too far from the hut to carve things away from him, to leave behind bone, stripped muscle, an absence of blood.

The way the thing shifted reminded Zach of the way his own hand's shadow grew and shrank when he used a flashlight to create a bunny or a duck on the wall to make Bonnie smile. Its shape was humanlike, yet not. Animallike, yet not. It bent and swayed, an arm going long, a leg suddenly short. Three limbs, then five, then none; a columned shadow. A cape, a wing, extended behind the figure before whipping back. The distorted, night-traveling unknown stretched to immense proportions, then a moment later metamorphosed into a black marble.

It had to be whatever he'd heard dragging through the snow while he stood frozen with fear in the outhouse.

Zach ducked below the window frame at the sudden realization that he was visible, too, with the firelight at his back. Squatting on the floor, his mind spun out awful possibilities. The creature might have seen him outlined in the glass. If he looked back through the window he could find himself face-to-face with twisted teeth.

But when Zach snuck a cautious look outside, he saw that the thing was continuing its climb. The longer he watched, the more at ease he felt. Being inside where it was warm, where fire burned, where Mr. Fantastic lay nearby, allowed Zach to feel protected and curious. Only babies believed in monsters. There had to be a rational, grown-up explanation.

A person, looking funny because of the distance and the way the moonlight shifted through the clouds. A wandering coyote. A weather balloon? Though he'd heard those last words before, Zach didn't know what they meant. He pictured a drifting Mylar party balloon, its ribbon tied to a drone.

Up the thing went into thinner air and darker night. It didn't hug close to the ground the way a four-legged animal would; the way the thing in the trees had.

Could someone be lost?

No. With the hut's fire lit, anyone lost would have seen its glow, would have headed toward its promise of warmth and safety. Would be able to see it even now, from up there. And the hut was a five-hour ski from the trailhead; the trailhead a two-hour drive from town. No one would start such a trip late enough to reach this point in the middle of the night.

The figure vanished from sight. Instantly, as though plucked off the mountain. Was it hiding? Or it might have reached the top of the ridge, its silhouette erased against the darkness of the sky—still there, just invisible. Zach waited, searching for any sign of the fluid figure along the rim of the Bowl above. The sky resumed spilling huge flakes. The wind redoubled its howling, blowing that snow into an endless white array of crisscrossing fireworks.

Should he wake everyone up? Tell them what he'd seen?

Zach pictured his father's reaction to any hint of something wrong on this trip, his trip. The long fingers would wrap around Zach's upper arm, a *pop-pop-pop* of all-seeing eyes emerging from skin. Zach's breath tightened and he shook his head no.

And anyway, the thing was gone now. Probably some animal, his imagination filling in the scary parts. He realized he was chewing on the cuticle of his thumb and forced himself to stop. Why should he think that his eyes were more governable than the rest of his body?

Zach lay down, this time choosing a couch that had its tall back between him and the window out to Mount Mariah; a kind of shield against watchful eyes. He pulled his coat over himself, letting the pocket with the folding knife, the tablets, the compass, the matches, press against him like a good-luck charm. He hugged Mr. Fantastic. His eyes closed and saw a wandering ghost, drenched white as the storm. A flesh-hungry, darkened monster. Claws and flies and water and the whitened elk skull, a dirtied diamond earring dangling from its eye socket.

All you can do is hope it leaves you alone.

The smell of bacon woke him. Seeing the room filled with the light of an overcast morning, Zach understood he'd had one of those sleeps where time vanishes to a blink.

He startled at finding Pike staring at him from the couch opposite.

"Oh! Uh, hi," Zach said.

Pike's drawn face, the familiar squinty, bloodshot look of his light brown eyes, confirmed he'd had far too much to drink the day before.

Steve hummed as he cooked breakfast in the kitchen, his back to them both.

"Were you down here all night?" Pike sounded irritable, as if Zach's potential restlessness offended him.

"Not really? I came down and it was warm, so I guess I fell asleep."

"Doesn't look comfortable." Pike jutted his chin at Zach's couch. "You couldn't've slept much."

Zach shrugged. "It was okay."

"I slept terribly. Could've sworn I heard a window or door banging around."

Zach stiffened. The dragging claws of an alien. An amorphous creature in the moonlight searching the mountains for marrow and blood and—

But in daylight, the memories of things seen and unseen the night before melded with past nightmares, and all of it took on the sheen of the imagined.

Pike had likely heard Zach slamming the hut's door behind him after returning from the outhouse. No wonder he seemed annoyed.

"There were a lot of noises with the storm and all." Zach gestured to the accumulated powder outside, hoping this offering of a different offender would distract Pike from the possibility of Zach himself.

Pike rubbed his knuckles hard against his eyes, a childlike gesture at odds with the muscularity of his thick arms. "Tell you what, I think Dave's story got to me. Kept thinking about aliens. I even thought I heard something screech out there."

"Me too!"

At this Pike leaned toward Zach, a posture that Zach realized mirrored his own, equally excited to share in the strangeness.

"What did you hear?" Pike asked.

"An animal, maybe? But I couldn't tell what."

"From where?"

Zach gestured toward the snowbound meadow out the hut's windows. "It sounded like that way, but it was hard to tell."

"Did you investigate?"

"You mean, go outside to see?"

"Yeah."

Zach shook his head vehemently. "No way."

"Smart kid," Pike said, relaxing back now onto his couch, "because it sounded weird as hell. I was more than happy to stay in bed, too."

Zach let Pike think the cry had woken him the way it had Pike. It would be humiliating to admit the way he'd fled from the outhouse, then been glued to the windows, eyes searching the meadow below, the slopes above.

Though if Pike had heard the monstrous howl, that meant it had been real. Which would mean the strange figure moving up Mariah, the dragging sounds by the outhouse, might also have been real.

Zach shivered.

"You believe in that aliens and monsters stuff? From Dave's story?" Zach asked.

"Nah." At seeing Zach sag, look disappointed, Pike added, "Though, I mean, we don't, like, know everything. And there's something about the dark, you know? It makes that stuff seem more real. Makes everything seem scarier."

Despite Zach's suspicion that Pike was saying this only out of pity, Pike did look oddly haunted, staring out the windows as if he, too, feared something waited outside. It all made Zach feel lighter. If an adult like Pike didn't like the dark, if a man as broad-shouldered and physically imposing as Pike had been bothered enough to bring up what he'd heard, it meant it was normal to be disturbed by a frightening story, to imagine things at night, to do a thing like tremble in the outhouse before sprinting to the hut in fear.

"Who's that?" Pike pointed at Mr. Fantastic, who had slipped onto the floor sometime overnight. Zach hurriedly secreted the fox in his coat.

"Oh, my, uh, sister—she must've hidden him in my bag."

"That's sweet." Pike cocked his head slightly. "You two must miss your mom, huh?"

Zach shrugged, eyes skittering away from Pike's face to fix on nothingness, on a spot beyond Pike's shoulder.

"My ex liked her." Pike slumped back on the couch. "Said she and your mom had a lot in common. Putting up with your dad and all."

"Oh," Zach said, fidgeting with the torn spot on his thumb, still looking elsewhere, nothing quite distinct. "Wait, who?"

"Virginia George. Ginny." Pike made a dismissive, snorting sound. "Though I hope for your dad's sake that's all they had in common. Ginny was a piece of work."

Zach blinked at him, confused. Bram had said Pike had a crush on Ginny. Yet it didn't sound as though Pike liked Ginny at all.

"Yeah. I mean, I guess they look alike too?" Zach said, remembering Ginny's blond hair, her smile from behind the reception desk in the little room outside Bram's office.

"I guess." Pike rubbed the bridge of his nose as he said, "I know this whole trip's about the skiing, but honestly the last thing I want to do is hike up another mountain. It's gonna be an absolute slog in this much snow." His hand moved to massage a temple as he asked Zach, "Which way's Mariah?"

Zach pointed.

"Really?" Pike's eyebrows shot up. "I could've sworn it was there." He thumbed over his shoulder toward the bookcase. "What's that direction?"

Zach shrugged. "Just like, the woods? Nothing fun."

"Huh." Pike scowled at the steep slopes above as the clouds pulled away, a slow lift of a veil. "I got turned around."

Trepidation rose in Zach's belly as Pike's words pushed forward the previous night's idea that the thing up the mountain might have simply been someone lost, bereft, in need of aid. Zach crossed his arms over his chest as if that might suppress the unsettling feeling he might have done something wrong.

"Yeah," he said. "That really can happen easy out here."

CHAPTER 14

Steve and Jon took turns breaking trail through the new powder. Russ, red-faced and sweaty, took up the rear, Dave regularly giving his son a thumbs-up, shouting, "You got this, Russ! You're doing awesome."

Zach was grateful for Russ, because otherwise he'd be the slowest. Jon and the guide made the climb seem simple, the gap between them and the rest of the group ever wider as they tore through the untracked snow like paper. Dave gave up on encouraging Russ in favor of trying to keep up with Jon and Steve. Shane and Bram chatted some twenty feet ahead of Zach with little apparent interest in exerting themselves the way the other men were.

"It's at least two feet, don't you think?" Bram said. "And getting deeper as we climb!"

"Can't pay for luck like this," Shane replied affably.

"Right, right. Look, I don't want to make this weird? But I've gotta tell you something, Shane. About Ginny."

Zach, who had been focused on staring down at his own skis, lost in wondering who had first come up with the idea of attaching the stiff, angled hair of synthetic skins to the bottom of skis to prevent downhill sliding, shook himself out of his reverie to eavesdrop in earnest.

Shane's smile vanished. He glanced downhill at Zach, then, seemingly reassured by the boy's distance, by the way Zach immediately looked out at the view as if it had all his attention, asked, "What about her?"

"When I texted her yesterday, she told me about your—relationship. I would never've asked her up here if I'd known."

This was a lie, wasn't it? Because before going downhill to text Ginny, Bram had said something about Ginny liking Shane, how Shane would want to keep that crush secret from Arlo. And Bram had wanted her to come on the trip because of all that, not in spite of it.

"What'd she say exactly?" Shane's voice was neutral, but his shoulders rose, tense.

"She texted she wasn't coming because of your . . . past. Said it ended badly, and recently. What worries me, why I'm bringing it to you, is if she's telling me, who else is she talking to? I'm her boss. She knows how highly I think of you, that we're friends, and she still told me. In writing no less. You know she and Pike dated? I told her that was unprofessional as hell. I was gonna fire her. She said it wouldn't happen again, that it was over. But she still pursued you. I'm not sure, maybe it's better I keep her close, keep an eye on her for you, if she's acting that way. Bit crazy and vindictive, I mean. Because if it got back to your wife? I just—I hate being the messenger here. But I respect you too much not to bring this to you directly, and privately."

Shane turned to face Bram. "I appreciate that, man, you know how it goes. And yeah, absolutely, probably best you keep an eye on her, though I wouldn't worry much—" He cut himself off, seeing how close Zach had gotten behind them, and Zach felt heat come to his face over the way he'd unconsciously drawn closer to hear better.

"Hey kiddo," Bram called out with feigned sunniness, "wait here for your buddy Russ, huh? Make sure he's doing okay?"

Zach stayed put, resentful over the way it hurt that Bram easily said Russ's name given how long it had been since he'd uttered Zach's. The *drip-drip-drip* of the unsaid felt like a kind of water torture slowly drilling an emptiness through him.

Shane and Bram skied all the way past the tree line before they paused and spoke animatedly, this time well out of earshot. Shane threw his arms out. Bram shook his head as if it were heavy. Yet the initial seriousness faded quickly into nodding agreement, and by the time Russ caught up to Zach with a "This *sucks*, bro," Shane was chucking Bram affectionately on an arm, both men smiling.

With Russ at his heels now, Zach continued uphill, reassured that things were all right, that his dad had managed the strange weave of these adult relationships in a way that pleased both him and Shane. Zach snuck a glance downhill at the fallen pine marking the spot where if they were to veer into the woods, continue straight for less than ten minutes, they would come to the abandoned miner's cabin. He quickly looked away, as if any attention might alert the others that something secret, something sacrosanct, hid there.

Seven people ahead and behind, not including him. Seven more people passing by the cabin unknowing. He felt the place tug at him.

There was much less snow the day Zach and his mother had discovered the small, squat cabin, but when Grace lifted the door's wooden latch, pushed it open, they had still had to step down from the snowpack into the cabin's single room. The sunlight spilling in from the doorway illuminated a list of names on the wall opposite; some carved, some written in marker. The earliest were dated 1881, presumably the four men who had erected the memorial to the fallen Swede after finding him "past rescue." Above the list an etched admonition:

KEEP THIS GROUND

FROM FURTHER MORTAL GREED AND PERIL

Including the 1881 visitors, there were twelve names on the list. Some had returned, adding a new date for each trip. In large block letters between "Jim Gerbaz 1956, 1968, 1972" and "P. Popish 1981, 1985" someone had carved "DON'T TELL OR ELSE." Drawn next to this warning in the same black marker used to write "M. Cerise, 1998," was a cartoon ghost, its word bubble reading, "OoooOOOooh!"

"Kidding on the square," his mother said.

"Huh?"

"It's when you pretend you're joking, but really mean it. You'd have to be thinking about a ghost to draw one, you know?"

He understood. Kidding on the square, like when he and his mother and Bonnie would say, "Let's stay up here forever."

The cabin's wood plank floor was intact, though Zach felt some softness under his feet here and there. Despite the creak of the potbelly stove's hinges, his mother easily opened its door. She assessed the stove's tidy interior, its flue.

"Probably still usable. Incredible! Someone, maybe a couple of someones, did a lot of work here, keeping this up. Look at the walls! They filled in all those gaps. Hardly even feel the wind."

The narrow bed lay half collapsed, its mattress askew to reveal the remains of the strapping that had once held it up. The ticking of the lumpy mattress had largely been spirited away by mice. There was only one window in the place, its glass whole. A chair listed in a corner with a pair of boots underneath it, leather a crackle of dry rot. On a small table next to the stove, a fork and knife rested in a tin cup with a rusted-through bottom that had left a misshapen blotch of burnt orange on the wood top. Although the cabin's single room, about ten feet by ten feet, was remarkably dustless, it nevertheless exhaled a smell unique to things untouched and old, the fused scent of rotting fabric, crisp metal, rodent activity, and turned mushrooms.

As though they were archaeologists investigating a dig, Zach and his mother circled inside, then around the building's perimeter, noting repairs by later visitors. Corrugated sheeting patchworked the roof's exterior—clearly a more modern addition. The spaces between the outside logs had been filled with a muddy-looking mortar. Inside, part of a floorboard had been cut and replaced, shiny Phillips-head screws securing it. Bits of faded beans, peaches, and corn printed on wood—old fruit and vegetable crates, they agreed—had been used to patch chinks along the doorframe, brown streaks of rust dripping dry from the nails that secured these makeshift fixes to the walls. Yes, these were probably older repairs than the metal of the roof, the screws in the floor.

It all gave the cabin a potency, a magic, as if it had slipped through a crack in time. Such a contrast to the mortal, fall-down remnants of the mining days on Independence Pass, where cabins visible from the road were chewed nearly to oblivion by the elements and the souvenir taking of those passing through, or else had been restored into new things altogether. Mysteries seeped from the miner's cabin walls to fill Zach and his mother with a kind of reverence. A sense of responsibility.

They took turns scratching their names with the small folding knife from Zach's survival kit, the fresh cut of "Zach + Grace, 2021" looking oddly at home on the wall. They counted it out and realized they were the thirteenth set of visitors, an inauspicious number that made them exchange nervous glances. Each promised the other to obey the cabin's orders not to tell, to keep it theirs, this new membership in a secret order. Who would want to tempt fate by taking a memento? Who wanted to risk disturbing a ghost? Such an action, such blasphemy, might cling to them the way the cabin's smell had after they left it.

This feeling was redoubled by the discovery of the mine just downhill from the cabin in the clearing by the cliffs. Zach and Grace paid their silent respects to whatever parts of himself the miner might have left behind at the bottom of that pit.

Climbing up toward Mariah's peak behind the men, Zach wondered if he'd ever understand why the world folded over some things, some lives, while inexplicably preserving others.

Halfway up the wide ridge that made up the edge of Mariah Bowl, the group stopped for a break. Tiny ice crystals spun in the wind, set alight by sunbeams. Everyone breathed deep, drank water, and took in the view.

Zach oriented himself among the layers of mountains that sawtoothed the horizon, his internal map pinpointing the angles of things, the knowns and unknowns.

Above and ahead loomed Mount Mariah. The ridge they stood on ringed its bowl in a gentle ruffle. The only break in the snow was the rocky outcropping at the top that marked the mountain's summit. The untouched white of Mariah Bowl's skirt funneled below. Groups of pines appeared about halfway down, clustered in designs like those made by water flowing through sand, each grove spaced and shaped by old avalanches.

As though he was exhaling a prayer, Dave whispered, "Gorgeous."

"Perfect," Jon agreed.

Bram pointed toward town. "See all the jets circling? Everyone trying to land for a powder day."

"Too many people can fly private these days," Shane said. He lifted his chin toward Mariah Bowl with a smile. "But we've got something they don't."

A muffled blast. Another. The group flinched as one. Ski patrol was bombing at the resort.

Back in second grade, Zach's friend Alex had told him that the bombs made to safely trigger avalanches looked like soup cans with a string out of one end. Alex said the ski patrol duct-taped one of these bomb cans to a cafeteria tray, held on to the end of the detonator string, slid the tray down the mountain like a tiny sled, string whip-whip-whipping out until it hit its maximum distance and then—*BOOM!*—an explosion that caused an avalanche.

Zach didn't know if any of this was accurate—in fact, he was sure it couldn't be, because wouldn't cafeteria trays veer off course into trees or rocky ledges?—but he didn't care. He liked thinking of Alex's soup can taped to a bright red lunch tray rushing bravely down the steepest, most dangerous parts of the mountain. Liked imagining the little can's hidden power, the *ka-boom!* of can and string and plastic, the fragments exploding ever outward, fracturing snow until *woosh*, down came the avalanche, tearing away all the loose and dangerous layers to leave behind safe terrain.

If there was any other idea that so indulged Zach's need for the thrill of explosive destruction and his conflicting desire to heroically protect, he'd yet to find it.

But standing at the foot of the powder-laden Mariah Bowl, the faraway *hawumph* of the controlled explosions had a gnawing insidiousness.

Pike asked aloud what they were all thinking. "Do you think it's safe? If ski patrol's bombing, I mean."

"I'm sure it's fine." Bram turned to Steve. "Right?"

The guide shrugged and opened his mouth to speak, but Jon preempted him. "It's a totally different area. You never know if they have a wind slab, say, which doesn't look like it has here. And conditions can vary peak to peak. We won't know until we summit."

"Right," Bram said seriously. "That's right. But it looks great so far, doesn't it?"

"Absolutely," Shane huffed.

"We'll get to the top and assess," Steve said, causing them all to tip their eyes toward the summit.

At the sight of the untouched purity of those slopes, Zach felt something blaze in his chest. A deep-rooted longing to make a mark. To mar that beauty. To cut through that whiteness, look back, and be able to say, "That was me, I did that."

"Who's gonna get first tracks?" Shane asked, as if he, too, was thinking of the satisfaction of being first, that plunge of possession.

"Everyone gets first tracks today," Bram said. "Plenty to go around."

A pained flicker crossed each face. Because the point was first. The point was the joy of ruin. Ownership of something unownable.

Zach returned his water to his backpack, sliding it below the specialized airbag pocket. Even with the greed he felt at picturing the snow sliced open behind him, his airbag folded and tucked there, ready for deployment in an avalanche emergency, unsettled him. He pushed the airbag from his mind as though dwelling on it might summon disaster.

Shouldering his pack, Zach realized they were stopped right about where the figure had vanished the night before.

From this spot it was easy to see the hut below them; its windows unnatural and obvious.

Yes, anyone hiking here in the dark would have seen firelight.

Which meant it couldn't have been a lost person. Just an animal, its tracks covered by wind and snowfall. Nothing intelligent or cruel, which would have known to seek out their shelter.

The sunshine further blotted out any dark ideas, the mountains radiant with a sublime eternity. In Zach's head his mother sang, "Oh what a beautiful morning!" the way she always did in the outdoors, off-key, beaming, eyes bright at being free, free, free. "Oh what a beautiful day . . ."

Ascending, he hummed along with her. His father always complained she didn't smile enough, wasn't cheerful enough.

But she was nearly always smiling. Almost always cheerful. Up here.

CHAPTER 15

Clouds darkened distant on the midmorning horizon as Jon, Steve, and Bram stood in the newly dug avalanche pit, examining the snow's layers. With optimistic eagerness Jon noted there had been no collapsing crust or cracks in the snowpack as they climbed or as they dug. Steve frowned, poking at the base of the pit's wall.

Bram shooed Zach away to sit with the rest of the group on the sheltered side of Mount Mariah's rocky summit. They ate the sandwiches Steve had made that morning and pretended they weren't listening in, eyes sliding covetously down the cup of Mariah Bowl.

Steve stood and laid the blade of his shovel flat on a pillar of snow he'd isolated in the pit, handle facing his chest. *Thwap, thwap, thwap.* He hit the shovel almost gently with his hand, first swinging from only his wrist before hinging at the elbow, all while counting aloud. When he hit fourteen, the column of snow peeled toward him, slid forward, and collapsed.

Zach's chest tightened. A year ago the mothers had gotten a similar result, hadn't they? He tried to remember how quickly the column had failed during their test, their discussion after, but the memory of his own disappointment drowned out everything else.

Steve knit his brows and shook his head, staring at the floor of the pit.

"I mean—that's pretty great," Jon said. "No way we'll trigger anything with the loose stuff buried so far down. Look how deep it split off! And it didn't propagate all the way across."

Steve muttered low as if he didn't want the rest of the group to hear. Zach made out something about depth hoar, dry slab.

"Come on," Shane said. "It's *fine*."

Jon nodded. "Up here is gonna be the most windswept, exposed like it is, you know? So maybe it's slightly iffy here, but it'll only get safer the lower we go. And yesterday the Bowl was skied out—packed solid. Makes for a great base."

Again Steve squatted down, running a gloved finger horizontally along the snow near the pit's bottom where the column had fractured. Crystals shot out around his hand. "I don't know, guys." He stirred a handful of the loose snow. "I gotta say I don't like the way the split propagated, you see here? How it carried off some of the column? The avalanche report this morning said we're looking at level two conditions. Which is to be expected after a big snow, but—it's not nothing. Means that maybe an avy won't happen on its own. But human triggered—more likely. And we've got Zach and Russ. Something to consider."

Bram crossed his arms, eyes gone to glassy Underself at facing anything other than immediate compliance. "What we need here is a game plan. This can't be the first time you're seeing similar conditions. I mean—it's your job to figure this out."

"Exactly," Shane said.

"I hear you." Steve's voice shifted to a lower register. "But maybe the boys should go down a different way."

Bram rubbed heavily at his chin. "What I want to know is what's a safe way down the Bowl. In these conditions."

"Russ can handle it," Dave chimed in.

"Right," Bram said. "If that's what you're worried about—my kid can manage the skiing fine."

Zach insides went alight. His father believed in him. Maybe Zach should just ask why Bram hadn't used his name in so long. Maybe that was the point of Bram avoiding it, a kind of test. And maybe, similar to the column test Steve had just done, it was to see if he held together by speaking up. Or if he broke apart.

"It's just—there's—or there should be—a different risk calculation when there's kids involved. Want to make sure I put that out there. That we're still in the green, but not as green as I'd like. And I need to make sure we're all on the same page about that." Steve paused, leaving space for either father to speak. Bram and Dave stayed silent. "Right," Steve said. "If we're going to do this," he pointed, "we ski down over that way, and we stop in those trees halfway down. I've skied Mariah enough to know where to find a more forgiving degree. But down below and over here on skier's left it's far steeper. Not saying it's a hundred percent safe if we do that. But it's safest."

"Nothing in life's a hundred percent safe," Bram said.

Across Jon's face stretched a strained smile. "Look, I don't think that's necessary. But yeah, that area's less steep. It's gotta be under thirty degrees, even. So there's, like, not enough steepness to have a slide, basically."

Zach watched his father reevaluate Jon in real time, sweeping away his judgment over the younger man's dreadlocks, his casual entitlement, his vaping, his worn clothes. Jon grew the special shine of a man of action who was smart and reasonable. Which for Bram meant agreeing with Bram.

But hadn't this same conversation happened before? The mothers had said things were right at the edge, but tipped too far into unsafe. What had made the difference between then and now? Zach's hands itched, gripping his poles tight as if he might set them up for the triangle test to verify Steve's and Jon's assessment the way his mother had taught him. He tried to imagine rising and instructing the group, and felt his voice stopped up in his throat behind a kind of brittle mesh slowly, painstakingly installed there to prevent defiance. No. It was impossible to even picture. And anyway, they were the adults. Steve and Jon were both experts. Even if Bram didn't know things about the backcountry, they did.

What Zach could see easily, what did feel simple, natural, was imagining the powder opening beneath his skis, the speed and joy of it. Fantasy after fantasy jumped up unbidden. Bram patting him on the back after the run, impressed. Zach telling his classmates he'd bagged Mariah Bowl, their faces finally shifting from fear and pity to respect, even jealousy.

"We can regroup in those trees for extra protection to wait before we hike back up." Steve pointed again at a large group of mature pines downhill and to the right. "That'll make the hike up safer, too, hiking through the trees."

Jon shrugged. "I don't think cutting the run short's necessary."

"We've all worked hard to get up here. Wouldn't want to overcorrect," Bram said.

Steve flinched. "I wouldn't say it's an 'overcorrection.' Again, personally, I'd rather the boys skip it altogether. And that section we're talking about skiing is close to the line, safety-wise. Meaning it's safe enough I won't say it's a no-go. But it's a different risk calculation with the boys here. For me."

"Whatever." Shane shrugged. "If Jon's good to go, so am I."

"I wouldn't've brought my kid up here if he couldn't handle it." Bram forced a smile, but his eyes were hard fire as he focused on Steve. "I know you're not implying Dave and I would do anything like that, are you?"

"Oh, no, I mean," Steve stammered, skin going red. "You're his father and all, just. No, that's not what—"

"Good," Bram cut him off coolly. "So are we agreed on the game plan?"

Jon gave a double thumbs-up. "Absolutely!"

"Sure," Pike said. "I'll defer to the experts. So I'm in."

"What do you think, Russ?" Dave asked. "You up for it, tough guy?"

"I'm not, like, going to be the only one who doesn't go," Russ grumbled.

Bram gave Russ an approving punch to the shoulder. "Way to man up."

"It's colder than hell." Pike rubbed his gloved hands together grimly. "Are we ready or what?"

"Yep." Dave agreed, smile brimming with impatience. "What's the verdict? We all in?"

Zach said nothing, waiting for Bram to ask his choice. Then Zach would say he'd ski the Bowl, too, of course he would, and then maybe his dad would turn a warm, approving light on him.

Bram glowered at the guide. "Well?"

"Yeah," Steve said. "So long as we do that route, okay. As long as you're—they're—the boys—are okay with the risk. And we all understand."

He looked pointedly at Zach, who looked to his father.

"Great, we're in! So. You're the expert, Jon." Bram slapped a palm on Jon's back, ignoring the way Steve twitched at his tacit dismissal. "Want to lay out the plan?"

Zach squared his shoulders, physically fighting off his disappointment. Once again his father had spoken for him, decided for him, as if Zach weren't even there to speak for himself.

The group peered downhill as Jon pointed out the key landmarks of the agreed route. "We'll drop in over there on skier's right, where it's a gentler slope, then we'll go down until we hit those trees there. See? About a third of the way?" Everyone assented. "We'll rally there."

Zach felt an electric rush of anticipation, a contagious confidence at the men's certainty that the mountain was on their side.

Yes, it was good he hadn't cast a shadow on this. The Bowl, the sky, the horizon, it was all so beautiful, and he'd ski beautifully, too, and Bram would be proud.

"What order'll we go in?" Russ asked.

"Why, bud, wanna go first?" Jon teased.

"No way," Russ flushed and shook his head vehemently. "I guarantee I am like, the worst skier here."

"You're going to do great." Dave shoved his son lightly with an elbow in a way that made Zach swallow down a barbed envy.

Russ side-eyed his father. "Whatever."

Bram clapped his hands to rally them. "How about this? We want to be sure we protect the boys. So Shane, you head down first. Then Jon. Then the boys. That way between the guide and Jon, we've got one expert up here, and one down there keeping an eye out. And Dave—you go next, then Pike, then me. And the guide'll take up the rear. Any issues with that?"

Zach immediately understood this hierarchy.

Shane and Jon sheltered under the wing of the absent Arlo Oliver, Bram's largest and most important investor. Shane was beaming, he and Jon exchanging smug grins at getting first tracks. Ensuring someone skilled was uphill and downhill for Russ was designed to please Dave, his father's next largest investor, who nodded and said, "Great idea, Bram, looking out for the boys." Pike, as the smallest investor, was last to all but Bram, gracious host, and Steve, paid to be there.

Pike grimaced before taming his expression and managing a flat, "Whatever. Fine."

The group busied themselves removing the skins from the bottom of their skis that had allowed them to hike uphill, carefully placing glue sides together before rolling them tight and packing them. Their heels, unfastened to make uphill travel possible, were dutifully locked into bindings for descent. They made sure their backpacks had airbag triggers accessible; flipped on avalanche beacons; radios, switched to the correct channels, sent verifying beeps and static, Steve flitting between them to make sure they were doing it all correctly.

At the chosen spot, the group paused in a lull of anticipation. Then Shane poled himself to the Bowl's edge. With a smile he said, "Here goes nothing," and dropped in.

As one, the group leaned over to watch. The initial drop was steep enough that at first they couldn't see him, but within seconds Shane was visible, arcing clean turns through the open snow.

"Yeah!" Jon pumped a fist in the air. "He's killing it."

"Beautiful," Dave agreed.

When Shane stopped at the grove of trees, he made a happy *whoop* noise and shook his poles in the air triumphantly. Without a word, Jon followed.

The group on the ridge unconsciously released an appreciative sigh at the flawlessness of Jon's run, his body at ease even at a speed so fast it veered into the impossible. Jon cut a deliberate line to his left and launched over a massive hummock of snow on a steeper area of the slope. He hovered midair, poles wheeling, the group inhaling in veneration, exhaling as he landed smoothly, deftly angling to the right and coming to a stop next to Shane with a casualness that made his daring appear all the more impressive.

"Jesus," Steve said. "Guess that's why he's who he is. But no one else cut that far left, okay?"

"What a show I lined up here, huh?" Bram grinned at Dave as if the storm, the powder, Jon's ability, were all things he'd planned. "Don't see that every day!"

Dave chuckled, nodding. "Incredible, Bram, really. Ready, Russ? It's your turn, kiddo."

Russ shook his head emphatically. "Uh-uh, no way I'm following *that*. Zach, you go."

"You sure?" Dave asked.

"One million percent."

"Go ahead, Zach, you got this!" Dave said.

Bram gave a curt nod of permission, and Zach made his way to the edge. The oncoming weather was darkening the sky, but even in the flattening light Zach could better see the pitch from his position at the top of its drop.

Yes, it was steeper than it had looked before. But a run always appeared steepest when at the top, the uphill perspective visually lengthening the vertical. And always, looking up afterward a slope transformed itself to something tamed and flattened.

Zach, poised at the cusp of that precipice, could feel his blood uptick and his back stiffen at the anticipation of weightlessness.

Blah, blah, blah, said the mothers, but what had they really been saying?

The seconds went by. Zach's fear, his reticence, his sudden intuitive certainty that something had misfired in the safety discussion, the pounding of his blood, was drowned out by the prickling, dark crawl of his father's presence at his back, that latent threat more palpable than any hypothetical danger waiting below.

In a single, fluid motion, Zach pushed himself off the edge, away from his father.

The initial drop was so sudden that for a moment Zach plunged through silence, the wrench of his stomach the only thing tying him to reality. But his freeskiing competitions, his races, his years of training, had taught him to angle himself just right, and he landed, turning in a *poof!* of powder. The snow streamed below him, behind him, around him, up onto his goggles as he flew down, down, down.

He fought centrifugal force, felt the proof of gravity and momentum through his quaking bones, grasped at the realities of his own biology as muscles raged and tears spread from the corners of his eyes with the rush of wind and speed and cold, even through goggles.

The glint of the snow, its sandy sound, the dark clouds rimmed by bright, hidden sun, the untouched slope ahead, and every mountain that pierced the horizon beyond all united into unfathomable wonder. The purity of that beauty, of the connection between body, skis, cold, snow, mountain, wiped Zach clean. All his grief, all the uncanny strangeness, all his worry and fear vanished into the everlasting brevity of the now. As Zach sank and lifted through the powder, he was no longer a thing separate but merged with the snow, the air, the speed. The mountain, his mother, Bonnie, the rocks beneath him, the immortal earth beyond, the eternally recurring yet utterly unique snowstorm above, the physics that held them, and him, and everything, coalesced into an unbounded oneness. Yet despite the drawn-out infinity of it, the whole run passed in an instant—a finger snap of ecstatic comprehension.

Zach slowed, then stopped next to Jon and Shane. They slapped him on the back, good-naturedly cuffed his shoulder. "Nice job, what a run, huh? Who knew you had it in you? Who taught you to ski like that?"

He blinked at them, coming back to himself. Immediately things began to tear apart, to revert back to their everyday distinctions, leaving Zach's mind to lap desperately at the scraps of the beautiful sublime he had just glimpsed.

CHAPTER 16

"We can swing out over there." Jon indicated the edge of the pine grove, where Steve had said the Bowl narrowed and grew steeper.

Shane and Jon, oblivious to the wonders Zach had just seen, were locked into a discussion Zach couldn't quite grasp, mind still drifting up, up, toward the slope he'd just plunged down.

"Remember the route from yesterday? It'll be amazing in these conditions."

"Totally," Shane agreed.

"I mean, it was crap snow yesterday, imagine how it is now."

"Let's do it, man, absolutely."

"Are you—but"—Zach stammered, confused, resentful at being pulled away from the beauty of his run—"Steve said we're supposed to wait here?"

"Who? You mean the guide?" Shane waved a hand as if sweeping Zach's words away. "We're paying him, not the other way around. Guy's got no balls."

"Don't worry, little man," Jon knocked affectionately on Zach's helmet. "The tests up there were great. I've skied way hairier stuff than this, like, a million times. I saw it yesterday, it's not as steep as all that. It'll be epic. Wanna come?"

What had Steve said? What had the mothers said?

Blah, blah, blah.

Jon had hiked up for another run rather than wait for Shane yesterday. He'd left his radio off. And now he wanted Zach to defy his father?

"You—we said we wouldn't."

He hated the tremor, the pitch, of his own voice. Remembered the closeness of his father's breath accusing him of sounding like a girl.

"It's cool, kiddo." Shane shrugged. "Don't come. Just tell the rest of the group we'll meet them hiking the ridge back up, okay?"

Zach flinched at the way he'd been downgraded from "little man" to "kiddo."

"I can—radio them."

"No, don't do that." Shane turned to Jon. "Ready?"

"Go get her," Jon said, then called out a loud, "Yeah, man!" as Shane went out of sight downhill.

"He's doing great, right?" Jon said. "He'll be super into doing the movie after this."

"That's not . . . all set?" Zach asked.

"Nah. Soon, he said. But not yet."

Looking at Jon's yearning face, pity tightened Zach's gut. He saw written there a mirror of his own need for approval, his own desire for a deliverance more elusive, a prize more amorphous, than the connection with Shane that Jon obviously hoped would bear profit.

"He'd better follow through, after this trip." Jon's eyes narrowed. "He owes me now, that's for damn sure."

"Because you guys are . . . friends?"

"Yeah, sure. Good friends." Jon glared toward where Shane had gone through the trees. "Doesn't mean I don't think he's an asshole."

Zach said nothing. But he knew better than most that you could grovel and scrape to someone, love someone, comply to their every whim, desperately prop them up, and simultaneously despise them. Fantasize about them evaporating.

"I'm off." Jon gave Zach a playful salute before poling downhill and slipping out of sight.

Zach sidestepped on his skis until he was close enough to a tree trunk to lean against its branchless base. It felt good to take some weight off his legs.

Movement pulled his attention up the Bowl. Russ had been correct; he wasn't particularly capable in powder. After nearly falling during his initial drop, the teenager carved a wide, clumsy turn. The Bowl's funnel shape bounced sound in unexpected directions, and Zach heard snatches of Russ talking to himself. A happy "Ah!" after a more capable turn. A muttered "You got this!" after a recovery.

The clouds eclipsed the last of the blue sky, turning the light completely flat, erasing texture and variations in the snow. Powder rainbowed behind Russ, the growing wind catching and spinning it in enormous whorls.

From below, a cheer from Jon or Shane, the sight of them blocked by the trees.

Slow and steady, Russ continued his descent, the four men watching from the top of the ridge. The last remnant of Zach's euphoria died. Although he'd felt the joy of unity, of dissolving lines, looking up toward Bram he desperately wished that he could always keep this distance, this many obstacles, between them.

The mountain groaned and Zach startled, the reverberation completely unfamiliar.

Russ slowed, head swiveling, trying to figure out the source of the noise.

A clipped, wordless shout came from downhill, followed by silence, the otherworldly vibration echoing only in Zach's memory. There were no obvious changes in the snow, in the weather, making him doubt he'd heard anything unusual at all.

Russ continued skiing. One, two, three unsteady turns.

Then the Bowl exhaled a soft, sighing, *whumph*, and Russ jerked downhill about a foot, as though he'd jumped off a stool.

The depth of this new sound, the strangeness of Russ's movement, quickened Zach's heartbeat before his mind processed what it meant, his eyes widening in horrified comprehension.

The top layer of the snowpack must have collapsed. The flat light smoothed things to deceptive evenness as Zach searched for some sign of change, some indication of whether or not the snowpack had gone unreliable. And then he spotted it.

A thin, rushing line shot from downhill, curving to cut above Russ. The break traveled so fast its sickening, ripping cardboard noise took a beat before reaching Zach's ears.

How far away? Impossible to gauge distances in the open. One hundred feet above Russ? Three hundred feet above Zach? Less?

"Avalanche!" Zach screamed. "Go, go, go!" he pointed his poles to Russ's right, gesturing frantically in the direction that was Russ's only chance of escape. And despite Zach feeling as though his voice had been sucked to a whisper by fear, Russ seemed to hear him, see him, seemed to understand, and began to pole in the direction of safety, angling his skis downhill to help carry him more quickly.

But the slope was transforming into a living, oceanic thing that shifted, rolled over in its sleep to shrug off its cover of snow. Above Russ the field of white fragmented into flat, angular pieces, some large as a bus, others small as a skull, and all of them beginning to slip downhill whole, like sheets of paper set too close to a table's edge.

Already Russ's efforts were useless, the avalanche snatching support from beneath him. Russ yelled something incoherent, his voice tipping up to a shriek as the slide peeled him away, tossed his body into its vortex. A flash of bright yellow—a deployed airbag?—before Russ was lost. The freed snow sped up, the slabs destroying themselves now, churning into their undersides, into the mountain, with a rolling motion that became the pounding hooves of an apocalypse.

Zach's mouth had gone to cotton; his body stood so rigid he had to consciously force himself to move, to shake like a wet dog, to wake his mind and muscles.

It couldn't happen. He was only little. Russ was only sixteen. Bad things happened to kids, but they weren't supposed to. They weren't supposed to happen to him. And the grown-ups weren't even here.

But it was happening. To Russ. To Zach.

His mother's voice traveled from the past. *Deploy your airbag. Keep your hands in front of your face to create an air pocket. It can give rescuers more time.*

More time before you suffocate, the snow burying you, your breath turning it to ice and sealing in the carbon dioxide until—

Zach threw his poles aside and artlessly wedged his skis perpendicular to the tree he had been leaning on and a smaller one immediately beside it. Pressing his skis' edges as close as possible to the brown, scabbed trunks of the mismatched pines, he turned his back to the avalanche and flung his head between the trees, shoulders braced against them. He wrapped one arm around each trunk, the thin, low branches on the smaller pine scratching him, fighting him. He held his hands over his mouth and squeezed his eyes closed.

The rush of frozen air pushed downhill by the mass of snow hit his back, its sound a continuous thunderclap.

The airbag.

He unwound an arm from one tree and fumbled along the shoulder strap of his backpack until he found the pull cord. He yanked, but it slipped through his mitten. He tried again. With an explosive hiss, the force of the bag inflating knocked him backward from the bracing trees, and fearing he might fall he said, "No, no, no," aloud and threw himself at the pines, wrapping arms around them and hands in front of his face again just as the avalanche hit him.

In the crosscurrents of snow, everything turned to deafening blackness. Something bashed his helmet. Something jammed into his side, and he involuntarily tried to fold toward that pain but found he couldn't move, the screaming snow pressing him brutally immobile against the bending bark.

Zach closed his eyes against the onslaught of the ice, the air, the speed. His face twisted in anticipation of lethal rocks and debris, his body trying to bear the unbearable. Something sharp struck him in the exposed place between his coat collar and helmet. He felt the mountain, his mother, Bonnie, felt the force of the suffocating snow and the physics that crushed him, condensed him, could destroy him, the barriers between him and all things again dissolving, again reminding him of his own smallness, but this time forcing the realization of his mortality; the inevitability of things ending, the universality of consequence.

He should have said something. He should have spoken up. And he'd known that. He'd known it the whole time, he could admit that to himself now. But now it was too late.

Blah, blah, blah.

For a dim moment Zach thought he saw Russ, face frozen in an open-mouthed wail, pressed against an enormous tree downhill, arms spread wide in a crucifixion. But if the older boy had ever been there at all he was instantly gone again, devoured by cold and darkness.

And amid the torrent of snow, rock, debris, ice, the trees around him snapping, straining, Zach's voice, inaudible even to himself, again and again keened into the chaos the oldest and most universal prayer—"Mama, Mama, Mommy!"

CHAPTER 17

With a low shudder, everything stilled.

Zach opened his eyes to near darkness, and in a rush of fear that he was buried he thrashed, immediately realizing that he could breathe, he could move; that he was looking out to murk only because the cloud of snow released by the avalanche so darkened everything around him.

He was still standing. His feet and skis were under about a foot of snow. His back and sides were caked such that as he moved snow fell off of him in chunks. He unhooked his stiffened arms from the pines, one leg twisting awkwardly. He tried to lift a foot, but the snow over his skis and boots wasn't the light powder he'd floated down less than ten minutes before. Instead its consistency was that of dense, plowed snow. And just like the icy curls plows forced to the edges of parking lots, the crust over his feet swirled with dirt, rocks and sticks.

With wonder, he realized it had all taken only seconds.

He was only vaguely aware of physical pain. His shoulders hurt where they'd pressed against the trees. He felt a tenderness in his left side just below his ribs. And there was a wet warmth on the back of his fleece neck gaiter he knew had to be blood, though he felt only a distant throb. His nausea, his uncontrollable shivering, were the only things that broke through his numbness.

But he was okay. He was okay. Wasn't he? He twisted frantically, trying to free his feet.

When you get upset, when you're having trouble talking, try counting and breathing slowly. We'll do it together, all right, lovebug? One-one-thousand, two-one-thousand.

He counted it out. He was alive. He could breathe. He would be okay. The snow around his feet and skis was beginning to break apart.

The avalanche shovel. How could he have forgotten? Mind turned to dirt-filled sludge, just like the snow.

Zach unshouldered his backpack. Its airbag sagged, speared by a freshly snapped stick the size of his index finger. The stick was bright with blood and he blinked at it. Traced the blood under his neck gaiter with a bare hand and only then truly felt the pain. A strip of skin the size of a dime was missing. His trembling fingers came away bloody, redoubling his nausea.

Three-one-thousand, four-one-thousand.

It wasn't that bad. It couldn't be. He was able to move his arm. It hurt, but even so.

Just a scratch.

Zach unstrapped the blade and handle of his avalanche shovel from his pack, shaky hands managing to slide the pieces together with a *click*.

He jabbed around his feet until he could reach through the snow's fissured crust, release his bindings, and step out of his skis onto the hard-packed remains of the avalanche.

Russ.

The way Zach's body had gone unlaced and sweaty with fear

had polluted all coherent thought. He should have remembered Russ right away.

Zach reattached the shovel to his pack, fumbling with the snaps. He unzipped his coat and grabbed his avalanche beacon from where it was strapped around his middle. He let it hang down from its springy, spiral cord, zipping up his coat before taking the transceiver in hand. He stared down at it dumbly.

For a moment he was looking down on himself from above, watching this separate Zach making an unnecessary fuss, putting on his pack, its airbag flapping behind him. Turning the beacon's dial from "transmit" to "search." Going through the well-remembered motions he'd learned at his mother's side as he moved toward the tree where he thought he'd seen Russ. Everything had shuddered so out of step that even in motion he drifted, lost, confused over how he had gotten to this place where a mountain had flipped to its underbelly and tried to eat him alive.

But it was all really happening. The adults were somewhere absurdly far away; useless, out of sight, out of earshot. His mother wasn't looking over his shoulder under a blue sky, patiently demonstrating what to do. But this was the point of all that playacting.

Within fifteen minutes, someone buried in an avalanche will suffocate.

"Okay," he said aloud. "Okay, Mommy."

Zach stumbled through snow marred with branches, weaving among snapped trees, chunks of compacted snow, his blood filling his ears with a rapid *woosh-woosh-woosh*.

The number ten appeared on the transceiver.

He slipped, dropped the beacon. It knocked him hard on a knee. He grabbed it up from where it bounced on its cord, hands swollen, legs loose.

Nine, eight, seven . . .

Ahead, an orange glove stuck out of the snow. A guttural

sound slipped from Zach, so strange it seemed altogether separate from him.

And then Zach was next to it, yanking off the glove to expose a pale, unmoving hand he squeezed tightly with his own. He wasn't thinking at all now, couldn't think, just tore the avalanche shovel from his pack and pounded it down and down again around that hand, pieces of snow loosening slowly, painfully slowly, the shovel scraping, rasping, and he heard himself screech in frustration at the way the displaced snow tumbled back over what he was trying to expose. But there! A shoulder, the strap of a backpack, which meant the face—the all-important mouth and nose had to be—

An inch down the shovel skidded off Russ's helmet and bright red bloomed through a scrim of snow. With his mittens Zach pawed snow off lips, mouth, a newly bloodied nose tip, and realized that all along he'd been yelling, "Russ, Russ?"

Russ didn't react, didn't flinch. Like the elk. Like his mother.

No. No, no.

Russ's cracked goggles were packed with snow. Zach pried them off, exposing closed eyes, one bruised and swollen. There was a blue tinge to Russ's lips, his skin an unnatural white that was only interrupted by a cheek gone rugburn red and the bleeding slice on the nose. Zach whiplashed back in time to see his mother's pale face before returning to himself and the emergency at hand. The strap of Russ's helmet pulled so tight under his chin that Zach thought the older boy might be choking. He flung off a mitten and used naked fingers to unsnap it, the nylon bands flying away from the neck.

Did the blueness fade a little?

"Russ? Russ?" Zach held a bare finger under Russ's nose, but felt nothing, not even the cold, as if Zach's own body had gone senseless with adrenalin and terror.

Russ coughed.

The relief was so immense Zach sat back, stunned, head washed muddy, disparate things colliding.

"Russ? Russ are you there?" Dave's tinny voice scratched through the radio.

Zach unzipped his coat pocket and pulled out his own radio. Why hadn't he contacted them right away? Such a simple, basic thing to forget. Not that the adults could have done anything but slow down his search for Russ with a bunch of talk. And the men hadn't contacted him, either. Hadn't thought to radio until now. How long had it been?

"Shane? Come in!" Bram said.

"It's Zach. I found Russ, I'm digging him out. Over."

"Russ?" Dave repeated.

"No, it's Zach. I'm digging Russ out."

"Is he okay? Is Russ okay? Where are you?"

"Where we're supposed to meet. In the trees. Russ is breathing. I'm digging him out."

"Russ, buddy, you there?"

Russ groaned.

"He can't answer. I'm still digging. At the meeting point. Over."

A swelling sob through the radio. "You dig, you just dig. We'll be right there! I'll be right there, Russ, I'll be right there, bud!"

"Where's Shane?" Bram asked again.

"Dunno. Over and out." Zach pocketed the radio, ignoring Bram saying, "Wasn't he with you? Where is he?"

The teenager's unhurt eye fluttered open and then shut again as tiny, shining pieces of broken goggle plastic, disturbed by Russ's movement, tumbled into it.

Zach blew hard to disperse these broken bits, some of the tiniest pieces lodging in and sparkling among the blood and melting snow smeared on Russ's cheek, his nose.

"Are you okay? Can you breathe okay? Does anything hurt?"

A dry, pained sound escaped Russ's open mouth.

"I'll get you out, then you'll be able to breathe easier, okay?"

As Zach dug, huge flakes drifted onto Russ's unburied skin, onto the closed eyes and smashed goggles. It wasn't the settling snow from the slide, but the start of another storm. Snow collected gently on the older boy's clotting blood, on his eyelashes.

Maybe right now Ximena was making Bonnie pancakes.

One-one-thousand, two-one-thousand.

"My side hurts," Russ wheezed. "My head."

"It's okay," Zach said, words piling on top of each other through rapid breaths, through tears that froze his cheeks. "You're okay. I'm here, Russ! You were hardly covered, I've almost got you out and then we can see—"

Voices called out from the unexpected direction of the ridge above.

"Russ? Russ?"

How were they so close already? And why up there? The men must have skied down the more forgiving path they'd taken up to the peak along the rim rather than risk skiing the steep Bowl after it had slid.

"Can you hear me? Russ?" Dave called.

"Here!" Zach yelled.

The men didn't respond.

After seeing the gloved hand, Zach hadn't needed to use his avalanche probe to locate Russ's body. But he took the folded aluminum pole from his backpack now, and banged it against the handle of his shovel.

Cling! Cling! Cling!

"Did you hear that? Boys? Russ?"

Cling! Cling! Cling!

"It's there—it's from over there."

Zach couldn't see the men through the still-hovering cloud of settling avalanche snow, through the trees and the storm, but their voices got closer. Again he called out, "Here!" And Dave and the guide materialized out of the gloom.

"Russ!"

"He's here," Zach said.

Dave popped out of his skis, rushed clumsily along the snow. "My boy—Russ! Are you okay?" Dave went to his knees and embraced his son. "My boy, my boy! My God!"

Russ winced. "Dad! That hurts."

Steve was beside them now, pale face stretched into strange lines and hollows. Behind the guide Pike slid into visibility, gaping at the scene.

"We need to—what do we need to—" Dave couldn't seem to pull his thoughts together, groping at his pockets as if answers hid in one.

"How was Russ when you found him?" Steve asked Zach.

"He was asleep, but he woke up fast."

Bram's voice came from behind him. "He's okay. Thank God." A pause. "Where are the others?"

"How do you feel?" Steve asked Russ.

"My side—it hurts. My face. I'm—kind of dizzy?"

"I'm going to check you out, okay? I'll be gentle. Just want to make sure nothing's broken."

Russ didn't respond until Steve lay hands on his left side, which made his face twist in pain.

"It hurts there?"

"Yeah. Otherwise—the eye. And my head."

"Could it be—" Dave hesitated, as if voicing his worry might manifest it, breathe life into it, then whispered, "Could he have internal injuries?"

"He may have broken a rib. Or bruised it. Cracked it. No way to know. The eye's swollen but looks okay. If he was unconscious when Zach found him, and with head pain, that black eye, he might have a concussion. We'll have to get him help."

Bram's head jerked around alert, an animal trying to locate its food. "Where's Shane? Where are the others?"

"He—" Zach had to clear his throat to choke out the words. "Shane and Jon skied down. Lower into the Bowl. Before Russ started his run." He pointed at where the two men had dropped out of sight.

"I told you. I said it!" Dave snapped. "It wasn't Russ. I saw where it started, it cut uphill, was triggered from lower down. Those arrogant little shits, I—"

"We need to find them," Bram interrupted with grim determination. "They're not responding on the radio."

Steve nodded. Stood.

"You're not—you're not just leaving my boy here?" Dave said.

"Mr. Fisher's right." Steve stepped back into his bindings. "Russ is okay. Stable. You get him warm. Give him water. Something to eat. If the others were caught, they're dying right now. There's no time to waste. You take care of your boy."

Bram was already moving out of the trees in the direction Zach had indicated, but seeing that the guide was getting something out of his bag instead of following, asked, "What are you doing? Shouldn't we hurry?"

Steve took out what appeared to be a brightly colored radio. "Sat phone," he said. "I'm gonna try again. I don't think I got through before." He dialed a number, waited. "I'm calling to report—hello?" He took the phone from his ear and looked at it with a frown, then spoke into it again. "Hello, can you hear me?" He gestured to the sky above. "Interference from the storm. Or the tree cover. Hello?

Hello? Uh, SOS, emergency? We have an emergency. There's been an avalanche at Mount Mariah above Pantheon Hut. One injured, two missing. We need immediate rescue. Hello? Acknowledge? Mariah Bowl. Immediate aid—shit." He shook his head, then redialed. "Emergency! SOS! Avalanche at Mariah Bowl above Pantheon Hut, immediate help needed. One injured, two possibly buried. Hello?" Again he took the phone away from his ear and looked at it.

"You're wasting time." Bram gestured downhill, exasperated.

"Maybe they heard," Steve said, more to himself than the group. "It's hard to tell. I'll send a message." He typed for a moment, then tucked the phone in his coat. He pulled out a smaller device Zach recognized as similar to the Garmin his mother insisted Zach have on trips in case of emergencies, and began hitting buttons.

"What now?" Bram said.

"SOS communicator," Steve said without looking up. "Anyone else has one, now's the time to use it. It won't call Mountain Rescue directly, but it will ping an emergency line that will call them."

From his pocket, Bram fished out a device Zach recognized as his own. Bram had pulled it from the neat piles of gear Zach was packing before the trip, telling him he was too young for it, that his mom should never have wasted the money on something so expensive for a child, when had she even gotten it?

"I could do it," Zach offered, "I could send a message if you—"

His father hit the SOS button, then pocketed the device. "It's done. You stay here."

Zach nodded, relieved at being commanded to rest, at being absolved of further responsibility.

"They should get the distress calls." Steve's soft voice inspired little confidence. "And we'll try calling again. Out of the trees. Ready?"

Yes, the trees closed in tight above, and the clouds brooded over them dark and dense. Zach felt a nauseating gap in his knowledge, because he hadn't known that might matter, he'd assumed such devices always functioned. But his mother, perhaps obeying Bram's 'no phones or internet for kids' edict, hadn't yet taught him how to use a sat phone, hadn't taught him anything about the functionality of the small alert device Bram had taken for himself beyond showing Zach how to send an SOS, cautioning, *If the worst happens, you call for help, but if someone in your group is buried, you search. No rescue will be there as fast as someone who already is.*

"It's been less than ten minutes. We still have a window here." Steve spoke rapidly, desperately, as if trying to convince himself of his own words. "We have to search the avalanche field. Spread out. Each of us three"—he pointed to Bram and Pike before resting a hand on his own chest—"will take a section, grid search it with the beacons, and if you get a signal you call out. I'll go down first. Get the lay of the land just in case. Then you two follow when I radio. Got it?"

His father and Pike agreed, but a blankness behind their eyes reminded Zach of Bonnie when she pretended to understand a word she didn't know.

Steve skied out of sight.

How to explain to his father and Pike the way beacons worked? What a grid search was? How because the signal arced out from a beacon in winged parabolas, there was a specific strategy to efficiently trace a signal to its source?

It was all too much, too difficult, too technical. It was a thing that had to be learned well enough to become second nature, and even then when Zach had searched for Russ he'd stumbled, been slow and messy. The stress, the fear, the awful need for speed . . . Zach could only lay out the most basic element.

"You have to turn your beacons to 'search.' Like Steve just did. Or else you won't be able to pick up a signal."

His father didn't look at him, focused downhill where Steve had gone.

"You need to switch to 'search.' Or else you'll be sending a signal instead of receiving it."

Steve radioed Bram to follow, and wordlessly Bram pushed off so fast it was as if his body had been coiled in wait.

Zach stared at the empty space Bram left behind. Had his father even heard him? Had he already switched his beacon? Maybe. Or maybe Zach should have been louder. Stronger.

Pike fumbled in his coat. "What do I switch?"

"That there? At the top? Flip it to 'search.'"

Pike frowned at his transceiver, then hit the switch. "All right. All right." He waited, shifting side to side and looking blankly at his feet.

Zach pulled a Mylar blanket, still in its packaging, from his backpack. Dave had managed to get Russ atop the snow, and he and Zach silently wrapped Russ in the blanket, tucking it over his dented helmet, around boots where part of a broken binding dangled.

Pike didn't move when Steve said it was his turn. Steve radioed again. Nothing.

"Pike?" Dave said.

"Yeah?"

"Time to go."

"I know." Pike's sigh caught and trembled. "It's just—I shouldn't be here."

Dave, cradling his injured son in his arms, Russ's lips still bluish, his face still that sickly white, the blood on his nose a browning red, said clipped and cold, "Either stay and help, or go and help."

Pike blinked at him for a moment, then turned downhill.

Dave held the cocooned Russ on his lap and rocked back and forth. He groped for, then squeezed Zach's mittened hand. "No matter what happens, Zach, I will never forget this. What you did for my Russ. Thank you, son, truly. I thought—"

Dave kissed Russ on the forehead. "We're going to get you out of here," he said, and began to weep.

Zach had never seen a grown man cry before. He stood and moved away, unmoored.

CHAPTER 18

Zach dug out his skis, still trapped next to the two pines he was sure had saved him from being swept down to be buried or broken.

A beep from the radio in his pocket, and then Steve's static-roughed voice said, "Anything?"

A pause.

"Nothing. Goddamn it," his father responded, sounding winded and far away.

Zach's skis looked okay. No binding broken, no splits. He'd even found one of his poles as he'd pulled the skis from the snow, which would make it easier to hike out. He took in the slope above.

A blue, zigzagging line marked the avalanche's crown. It was difficult to tell from his position, but the fracture looked at least two feet deep. The top of the crown maybe thirty feet wide.

The path broadened as it descended, the avalanche's remains a round-topped triangle. It was nothing, really, the mark left by the avalanche. An insignificant smudge on the open fields.

About a third of the slide had crashed against the grove of trees.

The rest, Zach saw, had charged down the chute beside the trees that led to the route Jon and Shane had taken.

In the end, Zach had only taken the brunt of the thing's edge.

"Any sign?" asked a breathless voice on the radio, followed by two curt "nos."

So Jon and Shane had been caught and buried. The others wouldn't be radioing back and forth like this if they were able to see them.

This translated the yell Zach had heard from downhill before the mountain cracked open into something grisly.

How could he help? He couldn't. He already had.

Trembling with diffused energy, Zach drank water and discovered he'd drained his bottle without meaning to.

"Signal, signal! On me!" Steve's voice crackled through the radio.

Zach shoved his torn airbag back into his pack hurriedly, unsure if he was preparing to go and help, or to flee.

Maybe he was in some kind of shock.

He didn't know what that meant, not really, but he'd heard people say it and the word sounded right. He felt shocked. His muscles spasmed intermittently, unpredictably. It was difficult to speak, his teeth clattering, his heart surging then slowing. Not so different from the experience of touching a faulty outlet years before. Only this time, the electricity kept spiraling through him. This time it felt cold; icy barbs of panic penetrating his veins, his bones.

Zach zipped the airbag away. He wouldn't be able to use it again after it had already been triggered, been punctured, but at least this way he could put the pack on without it flapping behind him. He headed back to Dave and Russ carrying his skis, pack, and ski pole.

"Did you hear?" he asked. "It sounds like they found someone."

"What?" Dave looked up from his son. Russ appeared slightly less pale, was breathing at a more normal tempo, but rested with his eyes closed.

"They radioed, they said they found a signal. They're digging someone out."

Dave didn't reply, only rubbed his son's limbs roughly through the Mylar blanket.

"Pike, where the hell are you?" Bram's fury blasted in stereo simultaneously out of Dave's and Zach's radios, both startling at the sudden noise in the utter quiet of the pines.

Russ's backpack, his radio, must have been ripped away by the snow.

"I'm—I'm coming." Pike said.

"Russ looks better," Zach assured Dave.

Dave's eyes snapped to his. "You think?"

"Yeah."

Dave's voice was shot through with despair. "I don't know—I don't know what to do. What do they say to do about a concussion?"

Again the hiss of static before Bram said, "Get over here now, Pike. Now!"

"We need to get him to the hut." Dave's gaze fixed above, toward the promise of warmth and safety.

Even through the radio there was palpable fear in Pike's strained voice. "I can't get through the debris."

"How are we supposed to get Russ back up there? How can we carry him? Do you think we should—"

"You get down here now, Pike, help dig, goddamn it—"

"Maybe we can carry him, you and me, Zach? Maybe that wouldn't be too painful for him?"

"I dunno, Mr. Dowling, he's—"

"Or you, or someone, can go back to the hut. Get a sled to pull Russ up?" Dave turned his head this way and that, as if a solution might materialize from the trees. "Or maybe we should just wait for whatsit—Mountain Rescue? How long will they take?"

"Pike, you son of a—"

"Leave it!" Steve's voice was light, distant, because it came through only in the background of Bram's radio. "Just help me dig, Mr. Fisher."

"I'm cutting across." Pike's heavy breathing was clear even through the radio. "I'm coming."

"We'll get you out of here, Russ, it's all right, it's okay, son, I'm—"

A noise pulled Zach to his feet and arrested Dave mid-sentence; a whipping crack, as though a high-tension wire had somehow, somewhere, been violently severed.

"Was that a rescue plane?" Dave asked, scanning the sky. "A helicopter?"

Zach didn't respond. His heart contracted fast and irregular, a small, frantic creature in his chest.

"What was—?"

A dim *woosh* reverberated from the edges of the Bowl, bounced off mountains near and far, and because of the way the noise traveled, because his range of vision was hemmed in by the trees, Zach couldn't locate the source, or the direction.

Dave's face contorted, head swiveling. "Where is it? Where is it? It can't—it already slid. It can't, not again it—"

Zach's tongue went sour. His stomach withered. Like Dave his eyes searched the slopes above, body stiff with panic.

And then he saw it. Pointed. Called out in a high-pitched voice he didn't recognize, "There!"

Some unknowable but short distance below the spot on the ridge where they'd paused for a water break on the hike up, a cornice sliced open so precisely it looked as though the hand of God had reached down to invisibly cut the snow with a blade. The break grew to what Zach thought must be at least forty feet. Within seconds it had doubled in size.

The awful rift began to gape, enormous chunks casually tumbling, the fracture line beginning to go critically irregular. It released a muted, sighing sound that echoed through the Bowl in a way that made Zach look in every direction, terrified of being somehow surrounded. But no, he could breathe a little easier, was able to swallow dry air over a tongue that tasted putrid with bile, because the avalanche was far away. It wasn't above the pines, wasn't a danger to him.

A slow spill, a gentle heave away from that line, and the fractured snow was fully in motion.

"Snow is frozen water vapor," Zach thought numbly as he watched, the slabs so resembling ice floes as they hovered over the liquid roil of the loose, bubbling snow beneath. Observed from his remove, the avalanche had the silken ease of a waterfall as it pulled the slabs downhill, rolled them, the motion gnawing away at their edges.

Because he'd been beneath it, the first avalanche had been a thing grotesque and monstrous. But from this new place of safety, the scope of the destruction was magnetic. A titanic rush, a broken dam releasing death itself.

And yet there was such a thin line between fear and wonder. Because as he marveled at the thing, felt the relief of the protection his position afforded him, Zach put the geography together with a bone-shuddering rush of realization.

His father. His father!

He scrabbled for his radio in his pocket.

"Avalanche, avalanche, avalanche! Above you!"

Black boulders tumbled like teeth pulled from the mountain's jaw. Billowing flakes leapt into the sky. The slide vanished out of sight behind treetops.

"Y-you think that—?" Dave stuttered, not finishing the sentence, running a gloved hand over his mouth that left behind a line of wet across his lips, his cheek.

"Yes," Zach croaked.

Russ was sitting up now, eyes wide, gawking, half turned to watch the spinning destruction of this new attack, the mountain's reawakening also rousing him.

"Did you see that?" Russ sounded dazed. "Did you?"

At the sound of his son's voice Dave turned, running his hands over Russ's body through the blanket as if the violence of this new avalanche had redoubled his worries over his son's condition, over the vulnerability of their position in the trees. "You're talking clearer, that's good, that's good! How're your ribs? Anything else hurt?"

"Stop, Dad! I'm okay. It's just"—Russ winced—"it's like I said. My chest. My eye. It hurts to breathe. And my head aches."

"Can you stand? We need to get the hell out of here."

A creaking shudder. And then silence.

Zach spoke into his radio. "Hello? Hello? Anyone there? Over."

"Just let me rest, Dad, okay? Stop—stop poking at me, jeez."

"Hello? Anyone? Over."

Dave's hands and body shook. "Maybe you can try to walk? I don't—I don't think we should stay here."

"Please—Daddy? Steve? Over."

"Calm down, Dad, all right? I'm—tired."

Silence from the radio.

"Okay. It's okay to rest. But we should go."

Zach unzipped his coat, took out his beacon, and saw it was still set to search. He shouldered his pack, took his single ski pole in hand and clipped his boots into his skis. He carefully folded his avalanche probe and tapped it into the snow, experimenting with how it might function as a makeshift ski pole, but it sunk deep and useless. He took two of the ski straps Steve had given him out of his pack. Fastened one to the top of the probe to secure it, the other to the bottom to act as a basket, and tapped again. Yes, that worked just fine.

It felt natural, doing these things. It felt easy and right, his breathing calm now. As though the first avalanche had shaken Zach apart, and the second had pressed him back together.

"What do you mean by tired? Describe it."

"Just—groggy. But—better? I dunno. It hurts to talk."

Zach moved toward the place where the men had skied down.

"What the hell?" Dave's voice wavered as he called out. "Zach, what are you doing?"

What was he doing? His skis were on. His beacon stuck out of his hip pocket, its springy wire looped under his coat to attach to his belt. His radio hung heavy in his other pocket. His avalanche probe was in one hand, ski pole in another. He felt his pack on his back, straps painful against the tender places where he'd been pinned against the trees. He was probably bruised there. Did he have water? He was so thirsty. But no, he'd drank it all. Which was stupid. Before it was gone he should have put some snow in it to melt. Without fire, you could really only melt snow effectively if you started with some water. He scooped up snow and let it melt in his mouth. Better.

"What are you doing?" Dave repeated.

The answer was so obvious Zach couldn't speak, only patted his coat with his mittens as if the words to explain might be secreted somewhere. He calmed even further at feeling the emergency kit tucked close to his heart.

"Are you going . . . ? You can't do that! You're a kid! It's not safe. Didn't you see? It could all go."

Zach smiled and shook his head at Dave, as though he'd told an embarrassing joke. Didn't he know what was happening, right now, below them?

His father was trapped under the snow. Contorted, suffocating. Dying.

Although Zach had fantasized about his father being swept away by an avalanche during the hike up, it had all been distantly theoretical, an impossible fantasy. Bram was larger than other people, stronger, filled so much of Zach's mind that he melted through Zach's every action, thought, swam through his blood; a prime biologic directive. And they were so close, so close to achieving Bram's goals. The things that would at last satisfy him and bring peace. Bram would be all right. Bram had to be all right.

"You should go too, Dad," Russ said. "Help them. They need help."

Dave shrank back, face that of a lost child. "I can't leave you. What if you have internal injuries, a punctured lung, a—"

"You can't just let them—it was—being caught like that—"

Splayed readable across Russ's face was his memory of whiplashing downhill, unable to tell which way was up or down, falling hundreds of feet in seconds and being buried alive, light through the spiderwebbed snow vanishing as it filled to the black of a tomb.

Russ rubbed hard at the line of his forehead below his helmet.

"Russ? Are you okay?"

"Stop asking, Dad, Jesus. Just—go."

Dave turned in a circle, as though unsure of where he was.

"Mr. Dowling?" Zach gestured downhill.

"Right. Right. Where are my skis?"

Dave's helplessness suffused Zach with disgust. This man, bumbling around stupefied, was supposed to be the adult. All Dave's bluster about man against nature was hollow hypocrisy, his overconfidence, like Bram's, a cover for incompetence.

It all was so obvious, what to do next, a stepping-stone path ahead. But it would take too long to explain it all. Dave would have to learn by watching Zach's example.

"I'll meet you down there, Mr. Dowling. We should go one at a time anyway."

"Wait, Zach, just—"

But Zach had gone.

CHAPTER 19

As Zach emerged from the trees into the lower reach of the Bowl, he was the only living, moving creature.

To his right, above and below, were the remains of the second, larger avalanche. Parts of the slope lay scraped nearly to dirt. Boulders studded the path. Branches scattered throughout the devastation.

Yet there was still a vast amount of untouched terrain, all of it holding the promise that more could go wrong.

To Zach's left lay the path of the first, smaller avalanche that had charged past the grove of trees. The termination point was impossible to discern because the two avalanche paths had crossed at the bottom of the Bowl; the larger swallowing the smaller.

There was so much space. So much to search. Everything quiet, obliterated, and irrevocable.

One-one-thousand, two-one-thousand.

His brain ticked through the facts he was sure of.

Shane and Jon had been buried in the first, smaller avalanche. Steve and Bram had picked up a signal and had been digging. Pike had been on his way to join them. And now no one was responding.

It was unnervingly similar to the logic problems his math teacher recently had made Zach's class do. "If Z isn't sitting next to W, X isn't next to Y, neither Y or Z are next to V, and W should be on V's left, what's the order of guests, left to right?"

In real life, with real people scattered, with the slope laid out below him, tangibly showing the way things had played out, this particular logic problem felt far more straightforward than in his classroom. The ease of his analysis, the way his mother's training rose clean and simple, unsettled him. It was as though he'd always been expecting something this horrific. Expecting the world to break apart so completely that all responsibility would be left to him. And now that it had, it was a relief that coated him in a strange kind of serenity.

Jon and Shane, caught first, could be buried anywhere in the smaller avalanche's path. But if Bram, Steve, and Pike had been searching higher in the path of the first avalanche, they would have avoided the second. Which meant the three had to have been searching where the avalanches' remains overlapped.

Yes, that all sounded correct. Where the avalanches ran together had to be where at least three, maybe even all, of the five missing men were located. Given the huge spread of the debris, this didn't narrow the search area to an easy span. But even so, it was something. The only spot where there was a breath of certainty, and therefore the location it made the most sense to prioritize.

The first avalanche's path cut near where Zach stood at the bottom of the pine grove. He decided to ski close to it as he descended, beacon on, in case Jon or Shane had been buried, undiscovered, higher up.

"Mr. Dowling," he radioed, "I'm going to go along the path of the first avalanche to see if I can find anyone. There must be at least four buried at the bottom. Please follow. Over."

WARNING SIGNS

There was a brief pause before Dave came over the radio. "Zach, do not ski down alone. I'm just—I'm getting—you wait. You wait."

Something about being told what to do, about being bossed around by a not-his-father father, caused Zach's hands to curl to fists in his mittens.

Dave was one of the adults who had done everything wrong. They hadn't protected Zach, hadn't protected Russ. What did they know? They weren't like his mother, the other mothers.

And yet, despite all her teaching, Zach knew his mother wouldn't want him to be brave like this. There was the potential to trigger another slide. There was the future difficulty of escaping the Bowl after he descended farther into it.

A melting longing, followed by indignant fire.

She wasn't there to stop him. She wasn't there to be the brave one. Wasn't there to help him. Because she hadn't taken any of her own advice about caution, responsibility, or care. He remembered her frightened expression as she watched him cross the avalanche path a year ago. And yet, she'd left Zach and Bonnie alone to go on without her.

Zach gripped his ski pole in one hand, the probe in the other, and descended. He itched with anticipation of the telltale *whumph* sound; of the ground falling, pulling, destroying.

But there was nothing. No sound of buried air pressed from the snowpack. No *ping* from his beacon, which he'd switched to its widest spread of searchable distance. Just the soft hiss of powder under his skis and the falling snow. Intermittent howls of wind.

Despite his deliberate pace, despite the awkwardness of skiing while using his folded probe in place of his missing ski pole, Zach quickly found himself standing by the stilled mayhem of the spot where both avalanches had settled in the flat bottom of the Bowl, hundreds, maybe even a thousand, feet from its summit.

Up close the wreckage had a colossal scope he hadn't been able to appreciate from above. Roots, clods of dirt clinging to them, twisted from the snowpack, presumably still attached to trees submerged under slabs. Gray boulders sat askew.

"No signal along the smaller avalanche path. I'm starting to search the"—Zach couldn't recall the term he wanted, and paused—"the messy bottom part? Of the avalanche? Avalanches, I mean. Over."

There was no response from Dave. Zach poked at the churned snow with his pole. It was the same consistency as the avalanche remains he'd been caught in; as hardpacked as if it had been condensed by a plow blade.

Debris field. That's what it was called.

Zach clicked out of his skis. Beacon in one hand, probe in the other, pack on his back, he clambered onto the frozen slag.

In his head his mother mimed a grid search, showily running about fifty feet before turning and angling in the opposite direction, her footprints marking enormous W's as she went back and forth, beacon held close to the snow.

Among the broken things, the rocks, the hard chunks of snow, it was difficult to move as precisely, as evenly, as his mother had demonstrated. It was difficult to move quickly at all, his feet slipping, catching on rocks such that he tripped, fell on his hurt side, and lay stunned for a moment before getting up again to press forward. He squinted ahead and around him through the snowfall to try to make out anything human. Synthetic. Brightly colored. His breath huffed loudly in his neck gaiter.

It had grown very cold.

A drumbeat of "Hurry, hurry, hurry" pulsed through Zach as if he could hear the silently screaming men buried somewhere beneath him, could see their legs fishhooked over backs like scorpion tails.

It had been minutes. It had been hours. Time had bent. He should have noted when he'd left Russ and Dave so he could know how much fruitless time he'd already let go by.

So little air left for the buried to breathe. So much space to search, the irregular spread of the destruction at least the size of a football field.

Zach paused. A round, humped thing protruded from the snow ahead, a bit of neon orange on its surface. Zach moved as quickly as he was able toward the unnatural color and went to his knees.

It was the curve of a black-coated back; the neon orange the cursive name of the coat's manufacturer printed between the shoulder blades.

Someone was trapped face down.

Zach threw his probe aside and unshouldered his pack. He clicked the handle onto the blade of his shovel and thrust it into the snow where the head had to be buried, judging by how the shoulders were positioned.

For a time there was only the *chip, chip, chip* of the shovel. Then a *thunk* as Zach hit helmet, rapidly digging around its bright yellow.

Dave went to his knees beside Zach, startling him with this sudden appearance. Zach's focus on the buried man, the sound of the shovel, of his heart, had drowned out everything else.

Together, they scraped at the snow. Though Dave was older than Bram, he was still stronger than Zach, and soon Dave was able to lever his shovel blade under where the face was locked until the snow broke apart around it.

Sufficiently freed, the head turned toward Zach, and a face manifested out of the boy's nightmarish visions.

Blue lips stretched wide around a frozen scream, the mouth packed tight with snow below the emptiness of reflective goggles.

Zach whipped off a mitten and hooked two bare fingers into Pike's mouth, pulling out snow, and more snow, before a tongue punctured through, jaws able to move at last to cough out the snow that had been wedged there, hard as concrete. Pike gasped. Spat. Wheezed a huge inhale of air. Again with his strange, calm clarity, Zach saw the condensation in Pike's nostrils had turned to ice, enough that it must have been incrementally thickening and suffocating him as he was forced to breathe through his nose. Zach pinched Pike's nose and snotted ice shot out. Pike heaved in air.

"Thank God," Dave said. "Thank God."

Together they shoveled until Pike was able to pull an arm loose, hand going straight to his mouth and further clearing it, clearing ice from his nose with thick exhalations and taking enormous, bronchitic breaths.

"You all right, Pike? Anything hurt?"

Pike shook his head, and when he spoke his voice was thin gravel. "I think I'm okay. I think. My God."

Zach stood. "I'm going to keep searching, Mr. Dowling, all right?"

Dave didn't respond, focused on freeing the belly-down Pike's other arm.

Only a few inches down, really. Only a few inches deep.

"Wait one second, Zach, just one."

Dave levered a chunk of snow away and Pike was able to push up, to twist into a half-sitting position, torso clear of the snow that had imprisoned him.

Dave unstrapped the avalanche shovel from Pike's pack, clicked it together, and handed it to him.

"Can you get your legs out yourself, Pike? We have to try to find the others."

Pike wordlessly took the shovel and began to stab at the snow covering his legs with frenetic violence.

"Okay, bud, how about I go this way"—Dave pointed—"and you search over there?"

Zach nodded and took to the snowpack, his beacon extended, his heart afire, now, with hope.

Because he'd found one. He'd found one. Five minus one equals four. Four more.

CHAPTER 20

eep.

Zach turned in a circle. No sign of life. He moved in the direction of the beacon's flashing arrow.

Beep-beep-beep.

There! Ahead, a bit of red against the snow. But it was gone? No, there it was.

Zach rushed toward the flicker of red. Drawing closer distilled it into a bit of fabric whipping in the wind, going in and out of visibility behind a huge snow slab.

"Mr. Dowling!" he said into the radio. "I've got something, come quick, over."

Zach kneeled. The fabric was a piece of a sagging balloon from a deployed avalanche airbag, half buried in the snow. He gripped hard, stood, braced himself, and used his body weight to pull. As the fabric unfurled, as it scattered snow cover, it exposed his father's face embedded in the debris.

Bram's voice was a rattling whisper. "Get me out."

Dave had caught up, was already digging. "We've got you, Bram. We've got you."

The snow covering his father's body, though dense, was shallow. Zach felt separate from himself now, separate from the sweat trickling from his armpits, running down his spine and temples. Separate from the hands he watched work until Bram was able to push himself up, able to kick his legs out of the snowpack and lay prone, stunned but free.

Zach's hands went slack and foreign. The dormant menace of the Bowl pressed him like a specimen between the glass slides of a microscope. An animal sound somewhere between a keening mourning and a groan of relief tore from his throat, and he involuntarily covered his mouth to block the foreignness of it, his preternatural calm whisked away by the sight of his father.

Bram's skin had gone so pale it bordered on translucent, shot through with thin blue veins. He blinked vacantly and swiped his face with fierce, violent slaps of his hand, as if he had to check that he was alive, that his physical self still existed, could feel things.

"Dad?"

Bram squinted at Zach. Looked around blankly, as if trying to grasp where he was, and how he'd arrived there, then turned to Dave. "Thanks, man. Thank you."

"You all right? You okay?" Dave asked.

"I think—I mean I'm sore as hell but"—Bram moved his limbs experimentally—"yeah, I think nothing's broken."

"Can you stand?"

Zach sat on the snow, staring at the miracle of his father rising.

Bram fixed on him. "Stop that."

Only then did Zach realize he was crying, the tears and the sweat that soaked the foam of his goggles already freezing uncomfortably at the edges. He instantly obeyed his father, biting down hard on the inside of his cheek—his old trick, drawing blood to cut off emotion with pain.

Bram staggered. His body shook. His teeth clattered. His gaze went loose in a way that made Zach think his father was staring through things to whatever he'd seen while trapped, face wrapped by the torn nylon airbag, the fabric sucking into his mouth whenever he'd tried to inhale.

Zach wondered if he'd looked the same pinned against the trees when he'd realized he was still alive. When he first understood how close he'd come to being swept away to whatever came next.

"Looking cold there, Bram, yeah?" Dave rubbed Bram's arms rapidly the way he had with Russ. "Some adrenaline, too? You need to move. Need to get the blood flowing."

"Course. Yeah," Bram said, still pale and distant, still not quite back in the world. "The others?"

"We found Pike. He's okay I think," Dave said.

"Shane?"

Dave shook his head. "No sign of him. Or Jon, or the guide."

Bram's posture changed at this, snapping straight, and his eyes went sharp as if his mind had slung back into place behind them. "Let's look. We have to look."

"Yes," Dave said. "You okay to help? Maybe each of the three of us take an area?" Again he pointed, designating the different search directions.

"What's that noise?" Bram said.

It was the *beep-beep-beep* of Dave's and Zach's beacons.

Things slid together, and Zach's jaw clenched.

"Your beacon, Dad."

Bram didn't respond. His eyes roamed the devastation around them as if he'd see Shane wandering toward him.

"You have to turn your beacon off? It's transmitting."

His father looked up at where the second slide had released, muttered, "Who the hell cares?"

The *shush-shush-shush* of Zach's pulse echoed in his ears. A ticking clock counting down the seconds wasted.

Zach's words tumbled out fast, unstoppable. "We can't search for the others unless you switch it off 'transmit.' Because your signal's interfering. If it's transmitting, it's not searching, and you won't be able to find anyone."

Bram patted his middle, then fished out his beacon.

"I told you," Zach said, hating the way his voice cracked, the high, whispery pitch of it, "I told you up there to switch it to 'search' and you ignored me and—"

A warning finger shot up to silence him, and the sight of the Underself's eyes instantly clotted Zach's words. In tandem with his obedience rose self-loathing, because even as Zach stood surrounded by what should have been greater terrors, it was so easy for Bram to spindle out a dark tether that seized Zach's mind, wrung his gut like a rag, and curdled his insides to nervous sickness.

And through it all, somehow the worst thing was that, just like always, Bram had profited from breaking a rule; had benefited from doing things wrong. Zach followed back the thread of events and knew that if his father had listened to him, if he'd switched his beacon to "search" up in the grove of trees, if his beacon had been effectively scanning for the buried men when the second avalanche hit, Zach might never have picked up the signal that led him to the red airbag that led him to his father. If Bram hadn't ignored him, hadn't made a mistake, broken rules, he may well have suffocated under just a few inches of snow and some fabric.

A hot bile of rage rose to sour Zach's tongue, his hands clenched to fists.

Things were always this way, always, consequences for everyone but his father, and for a moment the awful, urgent thoughts of the men suffocating fell away, Zach only hearing Bonnie choke out, "Daddy will be so mad" through tears.

Their mother's eyes connected with Bonnie's in the rearview mirror. "Everyone loses things, Bon-Bon. We'll get you new mittens, okay? Your dad doesn't care about little girl's mittens."

Bonnie's tiny hand squeezed Zach's so hard it hurt, and that hurt rushed through him, sharpened by the knowledge that he was powerless to help her, shield her, from the unpredictable but inevitable consequences Bram rained down for even the smallest perceived infraction.

"Even if Dad doesn't *really* care," Zach muttered, "he still cares."

Grace didn't argue this truth. "Well then." Her hands tightened around the steering wheel. "We'll make sure he never knows."

"He always knows," Bonnie whispered through gulping, snotty breaths. "He always knows everything."

Their mother drove without speaking, parked in the grocery store lot, and walked them five blocks to a shop with a sign that read: SUSIE'S CONSIGNMENT—HIGH END STREET WEAR.

The children trailed their mother through tight-packed racks of clothes to the counter, where she recited a number from memory. The woman there disappeared and returned with a paper she referenced as she counted out cash, the children gawking at seeing a $100 bill, until Grace ordered them away to find replacement mittens.

Wandering the store, Zach paused before a shelf, confused. Among others he didn't recognize sat a pair of his mother's shoes, ones he remembered because his father had brought them home from a trip as a gift, yet got annoyed if Grace wore them, saying they were too expensive, too precious, for this or that occasion.

Zach cradled the light little wing of the dangling tag and read:

> W sz 7
> In the style of Gucci
> (REPLICA)
> $40

Things folded together. The way his mother smoothed out receipts, put them in a drawer, Bram spreading them out later on the kitchen island, ticking through each item, Grace with a drink in hand as he reviewed her choices of milk, Band-Aids, fruit. Things were always ill chosen. Too expensive. Unnecessary. Their mother texting before swiping her card in a store, and if she forgot, stiffening as her phone rang, Bram's voice reduced to a tinny drone on the other end. "I'm sorry, it's for that prescription? Right, but there was a three-dollar copay . . ." Zach pretending to be asleep on Aunt Felicity's couch the year before and hearing her say, "You need to take him to court," his mother whispering, "How? With what money?"

She was selling her things. Using the money not just to buy Bonnie replacement mittens without their dad knowing, but to have money Bram didn't know about at all.

It was a stunning defiance. His imagination spun ever outward at the prospect of Bram finding out, immediately exhausted at the sheer volume and endlessness of the inevitable lectures, lessons, fury . . .

One-one-thousand, two-one-thousand.

As they walked to the car, his mother, edgy, read something in his expression and asked, "What is it, Zakky?"

He couldn't look at her. Said down to his feet, "You're gonna get him mad."

"Maybe." She sighed. "But maybe we train people how to treat us. And maybe I . . . failed at that somewhere. Or maybe it has nothing to do with me at all, I—I'm not sure. I just, I don't like . . . the treatment. Of you two. Or me. It's all"—she looked up to the sky, searching for the right words—"getting so much worse now. And I don't like secrets. I don't. But some secrets are to do good. And this secret is for the three of us. Because I don't think any of us should get in trouble for tiny nothings like lost mittens. For having a little bit of money in exchange for my old things. Do you?"

"He's mean," Bonnie spat so viciously that Zach couldn't help but laugh, not just because he laughed when he felt awkward, but because he was impressed. He told Bonnie she was right, and then Bonnie laughed, too, the sound of it a wild and bitter purge.

No, Zach didn't want Bonnie getting in trouble. And why did their father get to come home whenever he wanted, travel whenever he wanted, buy whatever he wanted, when they had to ask permission to do anything at all? When Bram took their mother to task for drinking but still brought home boxes of full, clinking bottles every week?

"We won't tell," Zach promised. Bonnie clutched his arm tight, and his mother mouthed a silent "Thank you," and in both their eyes, trust, trust, trust, and from that a rushing sense of power, of unity, because they loved him and he loved them. He felt greedy, then, for more secrets; rebellions to cling close and nurture.

Months later, after everything, Bram charged into the kitchen where Zach and Bonnie sat eating the dinner Ximena had prepared.

Bram squared up in front of Zach, eyes ablaze, face red. "Did you know your mom had a bunch of cash? In a safe-deposit box?"

A slithering impulse to betray, to obey, wrapped around Zach's ribs, but then he focused on the question. "What's a safe-deposit box?"

Bram stared at him for a beat, but reading Zach's confusion gave a curt nod before circling the kitchen as if caged, a straining tension to his hunched posture that made Zach, Bonnie, and Ximena shrink away. "She got what she deserved, that sneaky, disrespectful . . ." He paused. Straightened. A crooked smile unwound across his face, ugly and vindictive. "But you know what? As it turns out, it's convenient. She helped me out, your mom. God, she'd hate that."

Yes, even beyond the end of things his mother had still been found out, still been punished in a way Zach couldn't understand, while Bram was rewarded, always rewarded for his cruelty, his errors, as if by the universe itself.

Dave took Bram's beacon from him. Switched it to 'search.' "Your boy's right," he said. "Can't search unless you've got in on 'search,' right, man?"

Bram swiveled. "I can read, you son of a bitch."

Dave was momentarily dumbstruck at the sight of the exposed Underself, but seemed to reconcile something, voice filled with pity and expression concerned as he asked, "Are you sure you're okay, man? You've been through it, here, it's all right to take a minute."

Bram pressed a hand to his forehead. "I'm just—I don't know what I'm saying."

"I know. It's all right. Zach and I will search. You rest."

"No." Bram surveyed the expanse of debris. "We need to find Shane."

"All right. But radio us if you feel dizzy or whatever, okay? How about I search this third, you there, Zach there?"

"Right," Bram said. "Let's do it."

Zach, tongue thick with the bitter taste of an unjust world, eyes stinging and his lip bleeding, now, with the viciousness of his own bite to stop his tears, pushed down his memories, his resentment, and did as he was told.

CHAPTER 21

Searching, the practiced familiarity of it, the purposefulness of it, brought back a little bit of calm, let Zach feel his mother's skill in his own.

He moved between Dave, some fifty feet away, and his father, about thirty feet away. Bram, unsteady, held his beacon up to the sky as if trying to get cell-phone reception from the air instead of trying to pick up a low, buried beacon signal. Pike lay behind them near the edge of the debris field, completely dug out now but sprawled on his back.

Dave's voice came through the radio. "There's someone buried here!"

Zach hurried toward Dave, who was stabbing his probe into the snowpack. Was that a leg? Yes. A black-panted leg.

"He can't be far down," Dave told Zach. "I hit something here with the probe."

Zach took up his shovel, but then Bram was there, shoving his son aside.

Useless, an obstacle.

Shovel in hand, Pike limped across the snow as if the legs he'd freed were only half back to life. He went to his knees next to Bram, who shifted to give Pike space to dig. Unsure of what to do but needing to do something, anything, Zach kneeled next to Dave and dug, even though he knew it was unlikely from the leg's orientation that any part of the buried man lay beneath his shovel.

Across from Zach, ice crusted Pike's facial hair, his eyelashes. His lips were still purpled. He kept pausing, drifting, gazing uphill, around him, then would shake himself as if he'd been about to fall asleep, and return to shoveling. Bram appeared to be recovering more ably, working with a maniacal focus that was only interrupted when he coughed, a cough so deep Bram's body heaved with it, the sound enormous and dry, ricocheting around them like a live thing.

Bram's shovel skidded against something hidden, then exposed the collar of a coat; a sliver of throat skin and clavicle. Which meant the head was—

Zach waved a hand at a spot on the snowpack. "Here! His head it has to be over—"

"Yes, yes," Dave muttered, repositioning himself.

Bram moved opposite Dave and hacked away with his shovel.

Out came a flash of a silver helmet and then hands, one folded over the other. It was Shane, and he'd had the presence of mind to clap his hands over his mouth and nose to try to create an air pocket. Dave and Bram, invigorated, scraped his head free, both repeating, "Shane? Do you hear me? Shane?"

Shane's goggles sat askew, half hiding a blue eye that stared at the heavens as the falling flakes landed on it, sticking then melting.

"Shane? Shane?"

Shane didn't respond. Didn't blink.

"Let's get his chest out, so he can breathe," Bram ordered.

Zach felt as though he were floating somewhere far away. Shane was dead, even if the adults didn't realize it yet. Zach had seen an eye like that before. But he couldn't say it. Couldn't breathe that reality aloud because then he'd be the one making it true.

Together, Bram and Dave tried to sit Shane up in the snow. His hands fell away from his mouth, and he slumped black, limp.

"No." Bram gripped Shane's shoulders. Shook him. Shane's head lolled, eye still staring.

"No, no, no. This can't happen." Bram whipped off a glove, wedged his fingers into Shane's collar to feel for his pulse.

"Do either of you know CPR?"

The men shook their heads.

Zach had taken a CPR class at school. There was something about a song you could sing to remind you what to do. Zach couldn't remember it. But it didn't matter, because Shane was so obviously dead. Pike and Dave knew it, too, now, exchanging a stunned but heavy glance as they stood up, took a step back from the body.

Bram laid Shane down flat. He began chest compressions, alternating with mouth-to-mouth.

The rhythm, the pattern, the force—though Zach couldn't recall what was right he did know all of this was wrong, his father imitating things he'd seen in movies. On television.

"Shane? Wake up, Shane."

"He's gone," Dave said at last, putting a hand on Bram's shoulder. "Look at the neck. It's not—it's not right."

The force of Bram's efforts had jolted Shane side to side, pulling his neck gaiter down to reveal a discoloration; an unnatural angle.

"This can't be happening." Bram turned to Pike and Zach. "This is—he's Arlo Oliver's son!"

Bram eyes moved rapidly, frantically, as if tracking specters and invisibles that would allow him to rewind time.

"We should keep searching," Dave said, unable to look at Shane's body, already turning his back.

"I can't." Pike shook his head. "I think—I'm in bad shape, here. I was buried. And he's dead! He's dead."

Bram stood and tightly paced beside the body, his hands in fists.

"Goddamn it! He just couldn't do what he was told. How could he do this to me? That selfish little—"

Pike retched into the snow, and though nothing came up the sound of it made Zach nauseous.

"Did he—Shane didn't have a satellite phone, did he?" Zach asked.

Something seemed to click back together in Bram at the mention of technological aid. He shed his dazed desperation and began searching his own coat, and Zach recalled Bram sliding his SOS device in a pocket up in the trees before the second slide. Not as helpful as a phone that would allow them to talk to someone, but at least something they could use in another attempt to summon help, to hit a button and send a distress signal out into the void. But at finding he'd failed to zip his pockets, Bram's eyes widened. The device was gone. Noticing Zach watching, his father glowered and pressed a quick finger to his lips to demand silence.

"Wait, yes! Shane told me yesterday he had his own sat phone," Dave said.

At this Bram unzipped Shane's coat, pawed through the pockets, then sat back. "There's nothing. And his pack was ripped off him. Sat phone had to be in there."

"Jon had one too. And the guide of course. But he already called, right? So they should be coming. Christ." Dave swiped a hand across his forehead. "I should've just paid the five hundred for the thing they tried to sell me, paid for the stupid phone plan . . ."

There was no way to know if Steve's distress calls had been received. No way to call for help. No way to call for rescue. Not without finding Steve or Jon, or Shane's pack. But what did it matter?

"They probably can't get here, anyway." Zach pointed to the sky. "Not with a storm."

"We can't know that," Bram insisted. "The guide called again from down here. Texted or something? Though maybe the bastard was lying and the damn thing wasn't even working."

Snow had collected at the edges of Shane's nostrils now. In the soft cartilage of his ears. A flake stuck to a blue iris and this time it didn't melt. Dave closed Shane's eyes with his gloved fingers. When he lifted his hand the eyes opened a sliver. Dave turned off his beacon, which Bram had tossed in the snow as he searched the body. "Poor kid. Jesus."

Zach ached where his body had pressed against the trees, where the stick had cut him. He didn't dare speak up again, but his mother had told him about people Mountain Rescue hadn't been able to reach for days because rescuers couldn't fly through bad weather, couldn't safely hike up under slopes loaded with new-fallen snow. But he didn't know everything. Maybe far away in town things were happening. Vehicles moving. Snowmobiles and helicopters deployed. Maps laid out on tables, discussed among a tight band of experts. Somewhere under the snow, Steve's satellite phone might be ringing. Did satellite phones ring? Above them, miles and miles away in even greater cold, Zach pictured a spinning satellite, shiny as Russ's emergency blanket, rotating through the heavens and glossily informing the world that they were here. That they needed help.

Steve had been the only one to hesitate. To suggest Russ and Zach stay behind. They needed to keep searching, because right now as they sat around feeling sorry for themselves Steve might be rebreathing his own exhalations, slowly suffocating on his own polluting breath.

Zach gave voice to an awful possibility that struggled to the surface of his disconnected thoughts. "Before the second slide, Steve radioed that he'd found a signal. So that—doesn't that have to mean his beacon isn't transmitting?"

"Sorry, but, what? What do you mean?" Pike asked.

Dave's defeated voice answered, "It means our beacons won't be able to pick up any signal from the guide, because his beacon won't be sending a signal. His beacon is set to search, not transmit."

Barely louder than a whisper, Pike asked, "What do we do?"

"Keep searching," Bram said, tired but matter-of-fact. "We might pick up Jon's signal. Have to keep our eyes up. We could get lucky and see one of them near the surface."

"Right," Dave said. "Pike, you over there, me here, Bram, Zach, okay? And if your beacon starts beeping, call everyone over to search. That's—that's what we learned in my avalanche class anyway. Does—does anyone have any other input?"

"Walk in zigzags. And keep your beacon low," Zach swept his beacon below his waist to demonstrate.

"Right, right," Dave agreed. "Anything else?"

There was plenty more, all so clear in Zach's head, the way the transceiver emitted electromagnetic flux lines, the way they curved out so that their center, the spot where a buried person would be, was the cross-point of a giant figure eight. But he said nothing, because until they got a signal, none of the rest mattered.

They resumed searching. Plodding, this time, the hope sucked away from them by Shane's broken body.

CHAPTER 22

As the group paced the debris, Zach tried to remind himself that the results of the rescue so far were a twisted kind of miracle. Two avalanches, everyone except Dave caught—and yet his father, Pike, and Russ only inches down, even Shane, though fatally swept away, had been hardly covered. Which meant, and Zach felt a pang of guilt at the thought, they'd wasted minimal time uncovering Shane. All had had something visible above the debris. Zach himself had been trapped only to his knees. Russ seemed to be the only member of the group injured enough that he might not be able to hike out of the Bowl under his own steam.

Yet Zach's optimism faded each time he scanned the mottled snow without any sight of cloth or hair or boot, and all their beacons stubbornly quiet.

In his mind, that faraway satellite spun farther into the void, ever more unreachable.

The group's paths began to overlap as each hit the edges of their search areas, and at last Bram gathered them together in a small circle. Eyes lowered, he said, "I don't think we're going to find anyone. I think it's too late even if we do."

Dave cleared his throat. "I hit a timer on my watch after Zach and I found Pike. It's been"—he consulted his watch—"an hour and sixteen minutes since then."

They took this in. Registered the afternoon tilt of the sun. Then nodded and stared elsewhere, unable to meet one another's eyes.

"We need to get to Russ. Then get him the hell out of here before dark," Dave said.

"Shouldn't we wait?" Pike asked. "Mountain Rescue might be here any minute."

"I think we should assume no one's coming and try to get back to the hut on our own," Bram said. "Russ is in no shape to be waiting around. We need to think about Russ now."

Zach's face burned. Now they were thinking of Russ. Now? When at the top of the mountain both fathers had used that quiet look of theirs, that stare, to ask Zach and Russ, "Are you one of us, or are you something else? Are you going to embarrass yourself, embarrass me, and stay behind, or are you going to obey and receive my benediction?"

Dave teared up. "Yes. Let's get Russ. Let's get out of here."

Pike nodded, silently concurring. Zach swallowed deep, trying to accept this new reality in which Steve and Jon were dead. In which they were about to leave Shane's body abandoned on the snow.

Bram directed a shuffling of equipment while Dave radioed Russ, who assured his dad that he was all right, that he was keeping warm. Dave kept his own skis. Pike had one of his own skis and one of Bram's they'd found while searching, the top third broken off. This left Bram with the final ski they'd pulled from the snow, his other foot loose. Bram and Pike each received a pair of ski poles. Dave and Zach each were allotted one pole, but created makeshift ski poles to substitute by folding their avalanche probes and wrapping ski straps at the bottom to prevent the probes plunging deep and useless into the snow.

No one protested, nodding stoically at their lot and dutifully applying skins to the bottom of their ski or skis for the trip uphill. Discovering that the binding on the ski he'd assigned himself didn't match any of their boots, Bram used two more of Steve's promotional ski straps to hold his boot in place. All agreed they'd shift gear as needed.

Zach again recognized the hierarchy his father imposed. Bram was still trying to eke out some success. He gave the best things to Dave as the wealthiest living investor present and gave himself the worst, likely hoping Pike and Dave would appreciate his actions under pressure rather than blame him for his choices, their choices, on the mountaintop.

Grateful his own skis were too small to be of use to the adults, Zach ate snow to slake his thirst and looked at the slopes above as he waited for the men to be ready.

How would this work? Because always, in every scenario he'd learned, the way to evacuate after an avalanche was downhill. But to get to the hut, they had to go uphill.

"What's the safest way?"

"What was that, kiddo?" Dave asked.

Zach hadn't realized he'd spoken aloud. "Oh, just—I'm not sure—is it safer to go up in the avalanche path? Or safer out of it?"

The men, bewildered, seemed to see their still-precarious position anew.

"Shit," Pike muttered.

Bram scowled, eyes darting between Pike and Dave, calculating, Zach guessed, not the risk of the options for ascent, but the risk of not being first to speak, and the risks of speaking.

"It's gotta be safest in the avalanche path," Bram said. "Not like it can slide again."

This was obviously false. The broken cornice loomed hundreds of feet above them like a wave frozen at its crest, still laden with enough snow to do damage.

"I mean heading where it's cleared would be easier." Pike tapped his broken ski, shooting a resentful look around the group. "Especially using less than great equipment. But"—he pointed up at the cornices—"I don't like the look of those."

"Dave, any thoughts?"

"Honestly? I think there's no safe way to get out of here."

Zach nodded. There was plenty more snow that could funnel down the areas that had already slid. But the open snow had twice proven unstable.

No good choices. No good options.

"Are we absolutely sure Mountain Rescue isn't on the way? How long does it take them to respond?" Pike asked, clearly rattled by Dave's cold assessment of the danger.

Dave shouldered his pack. "Who cares? We have to get to Russ, I'm not waiting around here."

Zach eyed Bram, who said nothing. How could Bram not know, with all his mother's stories about her days in Mountain Rescue?

"My mom—my mom said the timing varies a lot." Seeing Dave's and Pike's blank looks, Zach added, "She worked for Mountain Rescue. Before I was born. They have to get a team. A helicopter. But with the weather today? It might take awhile. Sometimes it's days before they can even try for a rescue."

Dave squared his shoulders. "We need to help Russ *now*. We need to move *now*. With the storm last night, and again today? The kid's right. They probably won't be able to get here even if they're trying.

We need to get to Russ. And get out of"—he spun a finger to indicate the vast, ominous slopes above—"this whole area."

"Agreed." Bram pointed to the second, larger, avalanche path. "Let's go up that way. Should be easiest."

"I don't like it," Pike said, again eyeing the heavy cornices.

"What's your idea then, Pike?" Dave asked sharply. "Because every other option looks a hell of a lot worse to me."

Pike's eyes narrowed. "Fine. But I'm not carrying your kid back to the hut."

Dave shot Pike a withering look before beginning to trek uphill. Over a shoulder he shouted, "Stay here and wait then if you're so scared."

But Pike joined, taking up the rear of their line behind Dave, fastest because of his superior equipment, because he hadn't been bashed, bruised, buried. In motion Zach felt himself thaw a little. His fingertips had been going numb, a thing he realized only now that he felt the pain of them coming alive. He'd have to keep moving or risk the cold burrowing into his bones before he was aware of the danger. He tried not to think about the break above, the way the cornices were still pillowed heavy with snow that could spill over, could—

"I've got something here!" Dave yelled from uphill. He stood already assembling his shovel next to a jagged accumulation of displaced ice at the avalanche path's edge, his backpack thrown aside. The group pressed forward, surrounded him.

A silver ski boot protruded from between two large chunks of snow.

Zach blinked, trying to orient space, time, facts. It didn't make sense. Jon had been caught in the first avalanche. Steve had been searching for him. Neither could be uphill, lodged in the path of the second slide.

Maybe he didn't understand because the avalanche had softened his skull. Maybe the cold had already trickled so deep in his brain things had gone funny there.

Dave lanced his avalanche probe around the ski boot to try to pinpoint the orientation of the hidden body. "I think—I hit something. I did. But far down. Like four feet down? Maybe the head or chest? Given where the foot is?"

Bram shot his own probe down. "Right. I'm hitting it, too. How about you and me dig here, Dave, my kid digs around the foot there, and Pike between us?"

Zach unshouldered his pack and assembled his shovel.

"Do we—really need to get him out?" Pike's skin was waxen and his voice thin.

"What?" Dave spat.

"Just, another body—I don't know if I can. There's no chance, you said? That someone could be alive?"

"We're digging him out." Dave's voice was commanding, his eyes alight. His obvious disgust at Pike's squeamishness embarrassed Zach, because he didn't want to see another body, either. Was already dreading the eyes, the brokenness, the color of the skin, the face. But Dave was right. There were stories of air pockets made with hands or by airbags, of people who happened to get stuck beneath boulders that allowed for more oxygen, or under a slab that created space to breathe. Of people being pulled out alive after forty minutes, after an hour.

It was possible. Or at least not impossible.

"We want a sat phone," Bram hissed low and quiet.

Zach's eyes darted to Dave. Had he understood Bram only cared about the phone? Had they seen his father's carefully applied mask go askew again?

But Dave was already digging. If he'd heard, if he'd noticed something wrong, he ignored it. Or maybe Dave's silence was a kind of agreement.

Because if they had a phone, they would at least know if help was coming. Part of the reason Zach's heart strained with anticipation was because he could picture the device buried there, ready to call out to its shining satellite.

Zach reached in his coat, checked his beacon.

"There's no signal," he said. "No signal on my beacon. Which means—it has to be Steve, doesn't it? Because Jon would be transmitting."

A look of confusion fluttered over Bram's face. "Steve?"

"The guide?" Zach said.

"Right," Dave agreed. "It has to be him."

"I don't—maybe I could just rest a—" Pike muttered.

"Dig, Pike," Dave ordered. "We've got to get him out fast. Not just for him, but so we can get back to Russ."

At this Dave again got on the radio to check on Russ, their brief conversation drowned out by the sound of digging. Zach could only penetrate the frozen, compressed snow next to the boot a half inch at a time, slowly exposing a bit of black ski pant. Radio back in his pocket, Dave settled into a back-and-forth rhythm with Bram. Pike jabbed grudgingly and ineffectually between Zach and the two other men.

With the way the leg vanished straight into the snow, whoever it was might be trapped upside down.

How awful to be so deep.

Maybe they'd uncover injuries that were crude and quick. That would be much better than suffocation. Much better than hope slowly dying with each breath, being unable to move, to see, cold and alone and bent under snow. And worst of all, being aware of what was happening, tortured by the scream of your own thoughts at being buried alive.

Zach sliced his shovel in beside the boot and felt it skitter off of something.

Was the body positioned so that he'd hit an arm? The other leg? Probably just a rock.

He pried out a crust of snow with his shovel, then pawed with his mittens to sweep the crystals off whatever he'd struck.

What was it? Zach took off a mitten the better to brush the flakes aside with his bare fingers. Tipped his head and examined the pale, matte strangeness in the snow. Then his lungs tore out a quick, unnatural shriek, and he fell backward, hands and feet windmilling him away, away, away, his body a foreign thing that propelled crablike across the snow to distance itself from what lay exposed there.

"Shit, kid, what the hell?" Pike's voice was venom, displacing his anger at being scolded onto Zach.

"You okay, bud?" Dave asked.

Zach couldn't speak. He wrapped his arms around his legs to hug himself tight and put his head between his knees.

The men turned toward where he'd been digging. They hesitated, realizing what might be there but not yet ready to confront the brutality of another shattered man who could have been them.

Embedded in the snow, a face stared toward the sky. Its eyes were open but blistered with ice crystals. The point of Zach's shovel had cut into a cheek, had bloodlessly drawn up a flap of skin the size and shape of a clipped thumbnail.

But what it had taken Zach a moment to absorb, to truly see, was that it was a woman's face. He felt the sight branding itself deep inside him, looping and tangling with other memories to become the same memory, the same wound, and the face in the snow became his mother's.

The sound of his scream when he'd found her submerged in the bathtub was the same as the shrill, shocked wail of denial he'd just released. And just like before, the longer he looked the more the reality of death dovetailed and locked together, unchangeable.

It was too late. He'd failed her. His mother was gone for always, body sloughed off, only the husk left behind. In Zach's throat swelled the same panic over the same nearness to pale, still-hovering death. His fingers had touched the same cold skin. He felt the chill of the water as he'd tried to pull his mother out of the tub. The chill of the snow he'd just scraped away from her face.

The same blond hair. Same open eyes staring through and past all things. The same smoothness of cheekbones, nose, chin. He felt the same fierce need to yank his mother out from the suffocating dimension where she was trapped and the same conflicting terror at the idea of touching her again.

He looked up at the men. "Get her out."

When none of them moved, Zach crawled toward the hole he'd made on hands and knees and began digging out his mother, one hand still bare.

Would she sit slumped, like she had before, blond hair going dark over her face when she was taken from the water? The frozen water? Would she still be naked? Would the same small, thin line of pink slip from her mouth and coil upward like a plume of smoke?

"Out," Zach whispered to himself, hands widening the hole; a scrim of snow slipping back over the face. "It's too cold. It's too cold. She can't breathe."

The men spoke, voices distant, muted. Someone put a hand on his shoulder and he shrugged it off. After a pause, arms threaded under his armpits and lifted him away, dropped him, and he sat, stunned, a few feet away from where his mother was buried.

Would they find a bottle under there, the shards of a broken wineglass scattered? Mess and disarray his mother would have never left behind, never ever, no matter what condition she was in. Because she knew how Bram would react.

But maybe she hadn't been expecting Bram up here, because he never came with them. Or maybe just like the day she'd decided to die, or decided to risk dying, she'd simply stopped caring, hadn't hid what she'd had to drink because she knew she'd never have to face her husband's wrath again.

"It's not the guide," Dave said. "That's a woman."

"Get her out. Get her out." But no one seemed to hear Zach, their backs to him as they faced the spot where his mother was trapped.

"A woman?" Bram said. "That's impossible."

"She's wearing jewelry, for God's sake, look!"

"She needs air," Zach said. "She can't breathe."

"We don't know what this is." Pike threw out an arm in the direction of the buried body, as he paced back and forth. "Should we be doing this? I told you we shouldn't do this. We should leave it. If it's not the guide we should leave it. Isn't it the guide?"

Bram pressed his face close to the snow. His mouth went small and his eyes wild, voice cracking in the middle as he said, "It's Ginny. It's Ginny!"

CHAPTER 23

Pike froze, body and expression gone wooden as he asked, "My Ginny?"

Bram nodded. "It's her. It's Ginny."

Zach had only met Bram's secretary once, when his father showed Grace, Zach, and Bonnie around his new office near the base of Ajax. "You see? If you're smarter, if you work harder, you might earn something like this," Bram had said as they all dutifully acted impressed and pretended to care as he highlighted the gaudy, gold-edged desk. The antique rug. The size of the place.

There was a snapping sound somewhere in Zach's head, as if a gear had audibly clicked into place, and the buried face metamorphosed; no longer his mother.

"It's not her." Zach rocked back and forth where he sat on the snow, repeating the words to make them true. "It's not her, it's not her, it's not her."

Ginny had given him and Bonnie candy out of her desk drawer in the anteroom of Bram's office. Held a finger to her lips. "Our little secret, okay?"

Zach had long ago recognized that his mother conformed to a sameness. It was as though she'd tuned into a channel that issued undeniable orders regarding appearance; messages Ginny also received and complied with, as did almost all the other mothers. Which meant that both Ginny and his mother had sun-kissed skin in all seasons. Both their faces were lineless, despite his mother, Zach guessed, being about a decade older. They had the same fine, straight nose. The same long hair (in both Ginny's and his mother's case, blond, though a glossy brown also seemed permitted). Similar dark brows on polished foreheads. Bodies that curved thin to not thin. Lips that stayed full even as they smiled down at him.

Not that Ginny, not that these other women, were as beautiful as his mother. Other than Bonnie, no one was as beautiful as his mother. That would be impossible.

Ginny's rimed hair had platinum streaks. Her frozen lips were larger. The whole shape of her face different, nothing at all like his mother's now.

He should have realized. Was he already forgetting her? He closed his eyes tight against this possibility, head echoing with ocean sounds as if submerged, too soggy to think.

Bram and Dave worked with shovels to widen the hole Zach had created, slowly exposing Ginny to the sky.

"*You* said she wasn't coming. *You* said she texted she wasn't coming," Pike said from his remove, punctuating each "you" by pointing an accusatory finger at Bram.

"Who is it?" Dave asked Bram.

"Virginia George," Bram said low. "My secretary. The one who was supposed to come help set up yesterday, but canceled."

"You're sure it's her?"

"Yup."

"It can't be her." Pike slammed his probe into the snow and released it, the metal vibrating with a *twang*, then began stalking back and forth, still refusing to approach but muttering to himself, thick arms crossed and eyes fixed on the snow.

"Did he know her?" Dave asked Bram in a low voice.

"They dated for a couple of months last year," Bram said, then grimaced in a way that silently communicated he thought that Pike was overreacting, overemotional.

Dave pursed his lips tight and nodded in silent agreement with Bram's disapproval.

But Pike's anger, his denial, didn't appear unreasonable to Zach. Zach's heart beat so hard it pained him. He couldn't breathe quite right, as if he were sipping air through a narrow straw.

He blinked back tears. He'd never see his mother again, even dead. It was as if she'd somehow been snatched away yet again.

"You think she might've had a sat phone?" Dave asked as he continued digging.

"No idea, but we need to check."

"Don't dig it out," Pike said. "It's not our responsibility."

"Wait." Dave paused his work. "If she had a sat phone, had anything that could help, wouldn't she have used it yesterday?"

Bram's shovel hesitated in midair. "What do you mean?"

"I mean—she had to've have gotten lost yesterday, right? She probably changed her mind after texting you. Hell, even if she tried to get in touch to let you know she'd changed her mind, how would you have known? You wouldn't have had a signal. So she'd have tried to hike up alone, maybe thinking you knew she was on the way. Had to've gotten off the trail somehow, or else she accidentally overshot the hut, got lost, and ended up here."

The weight of the scraping, dragging noise outside the outhouse. The figure whipping like a blackened flag in the wind, too malleable, too loose, to be human.

Had it been Ginny? Ginny lost in last night's storm, too frightened or disoriented to notice or understand or see the lure of the hut's light, trekking uphill until she tripped, wallowed, got hurt, or until she became so exhausted that she collapsed and—

His silence in the outhouse, the way he'd watched that dark outline travel through the bitter cold while he'd been safe and warm in the firelight, imbued his blood with a slug trail of guilt and horror.

You gotta be able to speak up, kid.

It was his fault. It had to be. And Ginny had been punished for his mistakes, as if there was no fairness to the world at all.

Zach slouched into himself as if his very core had been culled out. Would the men be able to read the awful mistake on his face? Somehow intuit that he could have helped Ginny, could have called out to her from the outhouse?

It was his fault. A nauseating urge to confess washed over him.

One-one-thousand, two-one-thousand.

"You're right," Bram said. "It would've been easy enough to accidentally take the Mariah trail. I nearly did it myself yesterday. From the angle the trail's at, Pan was so snow covered you could barely see it. And that was *before* the storm."

A deep, pained moan caused Zach to look up. Pike leaned over the place where Ginny was trapped, hands steepled over his mouth and nose. He fell to his knees, whipped off a glove, and stroked Ginny's cheek, her hair, with his bare hand. He leaned down, and his lips brushed her frozen skin in a way that made the others flinch.

Pike looked up at them, face stretched strange and pained. "I don't understand. This can't happen. How could she do this?"

"She must've gotten lost, Pike. She's been out here awhile." Dave turned to Bram, tapped at his own eye to indicate the way Ginny's eyes were iced over, and added quietly, "Did you see?"

His fault. All his fault.

"How could she do this?" Pike asked everyone and no one.

Dave put a hand on Pike's shoulder. "She must have come up yesterday and gotten disoriented. Confused in that storm, maybe. And then the avalanche—brought her down. I'm so sorry, Pike."

A crazed, overstretched smile flashed across Pike's face before vanishing. He stood. Stared down at his hands and turned them palms up, then palms down as if trying to figure out what to do with them before meeting Dave's eyes. "I can help you dig."

"Sure," Dave said. "But it's okay if not. It's obvious she . . . meant something to you."

Pike nodded rapidly, unable to look at any of them now. He chewed on his lower lip, and seeing Pike draw blood, Zach wondered if hurting himself like that helped Pike repress tears the same way it did Zach.

"I think we should still check," Bram said. "Still dig her out. Just in case she has some way to call for help on her."

Dave gave a curt nod. "As long as we move fast. I don't want Russ waiting."

The men redoubled their efforts digging. It didn't occur to Zach to offer to help or even to move. He could only stare.

All his fault.

Ginny's profile was visible, her long hair lacing in and out of the snow, and as the men exposed more of her body it became obvious the avalanche had folded her in half, leg next to her neck, boot extended out of the snow at a slight angle. That was why Zach had exposed her face despite digging next to her foot.

Glimpses of something bright pink and knit. A turtleneck sweater.

The surge of questions provided a momentary distraction from the sickening chew of Zach's guilt. How was it possible? Had the avalanche torn off her helmet? Her goggles? Her coat and pack?

Out came an arm twisted over her breasts, the spot between

elbow and wrist bent as if a new joint had been created there. Zach winced. The bone had obviously snapped, though the break was hidden in the sleeve of her sweater. Maybe Ginny had taken her coat off to assess it. Or maybe it had happened when the avalanche had tumbled her dead body down, down—

"What the—? What's that?" Dave dropped his shovel and its scoop of snow, his voice gone high-pitched. The hand he pointed with trembled. "Is that—what is that?"

Zach had to know. Had to bear witness to all he'd done. He stood up to see better.

In removing a shovelful of snow, Dave had exposed a thick, curving stick, crusted an icy red.

"The hell?" Bram muttered. He levered his shovel beneath the block of compacted snow where the strange object was stuck, and hoisted it away.

Bram stumbled backward. "Holy shit. Holy shit."

Ginny's ribs reached out toward the sky like curled fingers. The blood that remained on the bones, the webbing of muscle that was left, burned bright in the flat light, the vivid red of it preserved by ice and cold.

Snow packed Ginny's abdomen. Snow dotted the bloodied bones. The pink sweater wrapped around her belly torn, raveled, stained, and did nothing to cover where skin was missing, where seemingly all the muscle and viscera of Ginny's stomach and lower chest was simply gone.

One of the exposed ribs was broken, its jagged edge an eggy white.

The viciousness of the sight felt like the puncture of a previously unknown part of Zach's brain. And yet the grotesqueness of it all had a gnawing, insidious familiarity.

The elk. It was like the elk.

CHAPTER 24

At some point had the elk looked like this? Before the creature that stalked the mountains eviscerating living things had scraped its bones tidy?

Maybe the avalanche had interrupted the predator. Maybe it was watching them, red-toothed and furious that Ginny had been snatched away by the rush of snow.

Or maybe it had been buried, too.

The things that might be under the snow beneath him manifested ghoulishly in Zach's imagination. Knotty blue intestine and ragged cartilage, stiff with ice. Clean, cauterized cuts like the elk. Bulging, fly-covered, side-of-the-highway carrion things.

Zach scanned the destroyed mountain around him. Nothing moved but the flakes still falling from the sky. The snow fell on Ginny, too, drifting down on the exposed cavity of her middle as if trying to hide it again, reclaim her.

The gruesomeness of the body, the carnage of the blood and missing skin and the pain it all spoke to made Zach cover his mouth with his hands.

His fault. His fault.

He shouldn't have hid like a baby in the outhouse. He'd heard the faraway yowl of the creature as he trembled in the cold and the thing passing by had paused at that sound, too. Because it had been Ginny, and Ginny had been pursued by the monster. Instead of calling out, helping her, rescuing her from the cold, from the awful thing that had destroyed the elk, he'd stayed silent. Too scared of the monster. Scared of his father. Of getting in trouble. In trouble! That was nothing, compared to this.

And because he'd been a coward, the monster had caught her. Killed her. Torn her apart.

A pained moan squeezed from Zach's lungs.

Pike—drawn close again by the way Bram and Dave had turned from Ginny, by the stretch of their horrified expressions, drawn by the way Dave retched now, into the snow—peered down at the body.

He spoke in a whisper. "Who did that?"

Dave only spat into the snow. Bram dropped his shovel. He shook out the hand that had held it as if whatever had destroyed Ginny might have crept up its handle to penetrate his glove with a contagion that would unseam his stomach, crack his ribs.

The men had gone almost unrecognizable, eyes overbig, mouths agape, their expressions twisted as if their skin had been pulled taut and puckered by strange things sprouting or cratering underneath it.

Did Zach look like that, too?

He stroked his own face. Everything moved so very slowly around him, each snowflake separate from the others, and the trees, the rocks, Ginny's body, seemed cast into a bizarre high definition.

Maybe they were all losing their minds. Maybe this was what it felt like. Looked like. Madness seemed a reasonable response to the madness of the bones clawing up at them, here, in this impossible place, from this impossible body.

"How did this happen?" Pike asked, and he was in slow motion, too, voice muddy, vowels long.

The monster, Zach thought, and with instant regret he realized he'd whispered it aloud. He clapped a hand to his mouth as if he could snatch the word "monster" from the air, stuff it back into his lungs.

"The monster, a monster?" Something uncoupled behind Pike's eyes. He lunged at Zach, swung a fist. Zach felt the ghost of the punch as a breeze on his cheek. Pike had swung from an awkward, sideways angle, too far away to connect, then tripped forward, barely managing to stay standing, his immense fist still tight on a loose arm by his side.

It was as if Pike's mind couldn't gauge distances quite right. As if his muscles weren't taking cues.

Bram roared and came at Pike chest first, like some enormous, strutting bird. Zach sealed his mouth even tighter with his mitten, trying not to let loose the frantic laugh that bubbled so inappropriately in his throat.

Pike reeled backward, and fell.

"A monster, he said, like this is all some joke! You think this is funny you stupid little—"

"My son!" Bram said. "Mine. You get that? You don't touch him."

Zach roused himself, scrambled behind the wall that was his father.

"He's just a kid." Dave stepped between Bram and Pike, held his palms out, nervous but trying to soothe. "He isn't laughing, Pike. You can see he's scared. And it's my fault—the story I told about the bull and all. Zach saw that elk and now this? Of course he's scared! We're all scared, okay? And he saved your life! He dug you out. Don't forget that."

"You have no right," Bram spat down at Pike. "No right."

Pike's face creased into a tearless expression of hurt. He drew his knees to his chest, laced his fingers behind his head and put his head between his knees, muttering incomprehensibly and rocking back and forth.

Bram whipped around to face Zach, who beamed up at him.

His father had intervened on Zach's behalf; had protected him. No matter how he cast his mind back Zach could remember no precedent for it.

Bram seized his son's chin and wrenched Zach's eyes to his. "Not another word out of you." Zach held his expression hard and smooth so as not to betray his feelings, focused instead on the stale heat of Bram's breath. "No more of that nonsense."

The roughness of his father's touch, the cold cruelty of those Underself eyes, killed the grateful worship that had surged through Zach. By the time Bram released him Zach was soaked in cold fear and frantic hate, his eyes flying to the others to see if they'd witnessed his humiliation.

Pike still rocked on the ground. Dave stared uphill, pulled out his radio and said, "Russ, you okay?"

A staticky "Yup."

"This is going to sound weird, but I think there's maybe an animal out here? Something big. A mountain lion or a bear or—"

"Bears hibernate, Dad. It's *winter*."

Dave closed his eyes at Russ's know-it-all tone as if to remind himself to be patient. "Just, listen, okay, Russ? Keep an eye out for any animals, all right? Keep your radio close. Make a lot of noise if you see movement."

Silence.

"Okay?"

"Okay." Even through the radio, Russ sounded as though he was rolling his eyes.

"We need to get Russ back to the hut. This"—Dave gestured in Ginny's direction—"we don't need to be doing this. She doesn't even have a pack on. If she had a way to call for help she would've used it when she got lost. We're just wasting energy. And time."

Bram frowned. "I'm gonna—I'll check her pockets. Just in case."

He kneeled beside Ginny and gingerly patted the area below the carnage of her ribs, searching. "Let me just—let me see—"

Dave turned his back on Bram. Hands shaking, he struggled to break down his shovel, and swore quietly to himself.

Bram fumbled, averting his eyes from the places he patted down. When he sat back he held a pink-cased phone. "This is it. This is all she had on her."

Dave glanced back. "So let's go."

Bram hesitated, then slid Ginny's phone into his own pocket. "Yeah."

"Pike? Time to get a move on."

As they strapped shovels to packs, stepped into skis, Pike joined them, quiet now and unprotesting, but his eyes darting furiously around the group as he put his gear back on and readied to leave.

Zach, giving Pike a wide berth, went to retrieve his own shovel from where he'd dropped it beside the body. He checked over a shoulder to be sure no one was watching before pausing to stand solemnly over Ginny, one hand holding the other tight.

The men's digging had freed the platinum sheath of Ginny's hair so that it no longer partially hid her face the way it had when Zach first uncovered her. He focused on that face, trying to remember it as it was, mentally erase the icy crust, the way the whites of the frozen eyes had gone red. Maybe Ginny, the real Ginny, not this left-behind shell, was still nearby, and if he formed his thoughts very carefully and deliberately she might hear them. Might take his words with her wherever she was headed next.

I'm sorry, I'm sorry, I'm sorry. It's my fault. I'm so sorry.

But his repetition skidded. Stopped.

There was a diamond earring in Ginny's right ear.

Zach started to reach for the jewel, mind briefly short-circuiting into the assumption that somehow he'd brought along and then dropped the diamond he'd found between the hut's floorboards. Before his fingers grazed it he recoiled, clutching his hand against his chest as if he'd been burned.

Because Ginny's other earlobe was ripped and bloodied, its earring missing. Because above it, a brown patch the size of a dime showed that a piece of her scalp and hair had been torn away.

Because whoever, whatever, had ripped that earring, that hair and skin, away from her, had been inside the hut, and had left the matching earring behind.

CHAPTER 25

Zach trailed behind the silent line of men, every bit of him taut and his mind reverberating with a humming swarm of dark thoughts.

The diamonds were the same size. The same shape. They were a set. A matching set. There was no way around it.

The curling thing dangling from the hairs had to be that missing piece of scalp. That's why the hairs wouldn't release it. They were rooted there. It explained why all of it was dark and flaky. Blood.

The irreconcilability of the facts detached Zach from his exertions, and he floated instead of hiked up, up, up over deadly terrain toward the spot Russ waited.

His fingertips swelled with the urge to wash his hands, scrub his nails. Yesterday he'd touched the earring, the scalp, the hair, the calcified blood and dust.

The earring in the hut. But Ginny buried in the snow, broken by the avalanche, her stomach opened. The monster had consumed her to hollowness; had left behind that wrecked hull of ribs.

What had Dave said?

She must have come up yesterday and gotten lost. Confused in that storm, maybe. And then the avalanche—brought her down.

But the earring had been in the hut before Zach and Bram arrived.

The group stopped, startling Zach out of his grim reverie. Russ sat with the Mylar blanket cowled over his head and Zach tried to accept that they were already here. Time could stretch long during bad things, tight during good. And now? It contorted into bendy, unknowable shapes because things were at their very worst. Their least comprehensible.

"How you feeling, Russ?" Dave helped his son stand and rubbed his arms through the crinkle of the blanket.

"Great. No animal attacks," Russ said with a crooked smile. Seeing his father's stricken expression, Russ grew serious. "I'm better, Dad. I can walk okay. But breathing still hurts." Russ took in the assembled group. A realization bloomed and he went as sickly as when Zach had first dug him from the snow.

"Where's—where's the others?" Russ stammered.

Dave cleared his throat. "We found Shane. He—didn't make it. We couldn't find anyone else. And—and we found Virginia."

"Who?"

Dave leaned close to whisper, to protect Pike from the words. But Zach could still hear what Dave said, and he supposed Pike could, too. "Bram's secretary. Pike's ex-girlfriend. Ginny. The one who was supposed to join but didn't? She must have decided to come after all. Got lost. And . . . something happened to her. An animal had been at her. Either killed her? Or got to her after she got hurt. We found her. Her body."

Russ shook his head, the Mylar blanket falling down to reveal his dented helmet. "What? What do you—"

Dave cut him off. "The point is, we need to get out of here. Between the avalanches and whatever . . . happened . . . to Virginia, we need to get back to the hut as quick as we can, all right?"

"Won't there be a helicopter or whatever?"

"It's been about"—Dave glanced at his watch—"three hours since the guide called. They could still come, but with the storm, who knows. We've got to do what we can for ourselves."

Russ's shoulders slumped, but he nodded. "Okay. It's just—how am I supposed to hike out? There's so much snow. It hurts and . . . my skis, my pack? They're gone."

"How do we do this?" Dave asked the group.

"He can take my kid's skis," Bram said. "His poles."

Zach's head whipped to his father so quickly pain shot through his hurt shoulder. But Bram focused only on Dave.

"Zach, I'll give you one of my skis," Dave offered. "It's big, but it'll do."

They reshuffled equipment and began to climb uphill toward the ridge following the softened tracks the men had made searching for Russ and Zach hours before.

The bruises, cuts, and aches of whiplash were starting to show themselves as the group's adrenaline faded. Bram shrugged off his coat, lifted his sweater to have them assess a dark purple bruise along his neck, shoulder, and back, like a folded wing. Pike complained of a pulled thigh muscle, sharp, incoherent jabs of pain in his midsection, a high-pitched humming noise. He rolled up a sleeve to inspect an elbow gone deep blue-black.

Zach floundered through the powder. Though his feet were large for his age, the adult ski binding didn't fit right, the leg without a ski plunging down deep and useless. Even so, he was faster than Russ and Dave. Whatever was wrong in Russ's chest turned the teenager's breathing to a wheezing rattle when his heart rate ticked up. Though Russ's face went tight with pain at each step, he pressed forward with a persistence that kept Zach moving, too. They'd ascended less than fifty feet up the steep pitch when Dave declared the situation untenable.

Someone needed to get to the hut and bring back a sled so that they could pull Russ uphill.

It reminded Zach of a riddle: How to get a fox, a cabbage, and a rabbit across a river without anything being eaten, and only one at a time fitting in the boat?

"Dave, you agree you and I are in the best"—Bram's eyes rested on then shot away from Pike before he continued speaking—"uh . . . condition? To pull Russ up?"

Dave nodded. "Yeah. But I'd like to stay with my boy. You okay with getting the sled and coming back? Then I'll be rested, and can pull Russ up."

A barely perceptible grimace passed over Bram's face, but his response was quick. "Of course." He gestured at Pike and Zach. "The three of us will head to the hut. Then I'll come back here with the skis Pike used, the kid-size skis, and the sled. That way you, me, and Russ will each have a pair of skis, just in case there's any trouble pulling him."

They redistributed equipment. No longer in motion, the sweat on Zach's spine went icy and a deep tremor snared him, looping all the way into his stomach to pull at the snow he kept eating to stave off dehydration.

He needed to get back to the hut. Needed to strip off his soaked base layer and get himself dry and warm as soon as possible.

"Stay safe," Bram said to Dave and Russ. "And keep your radios on."

Bram silently took the lead, breaking trail as Pike and Zach fell into line behind him.

Though Zach's muscles burned, though his neck and shoulders ached, the warmth of exertion was a relief and his mind returned to its confused churn.

Ginny's coat, backpack, mittens, goggles, skis, and poles—missing. But she was wearing her ski boots. Her snow pants. Could the avalanche have ripped all that off her? It had torn skis and poles from the others; ripped away Shane's and Russ's packs. It was possible.

But her coat? And the avalanche couldn't explain the missing earring. Couldn't explain her stomach; the way her sweater had been torn to reveal chewed ribs.

An animal had been at her. Either killed her? Or got to her after.

No matter how logical it was, he couldn't picture a coyote or mountain lion destroying Ginny. The violence of it spoke to needled teeth, scabrous skin, switchblade claws.

One-one-thousand, two-one-thousand.

Only Shane and Jon had arrived at the hut before Zach and Bram. Maybe one of them hid an Underself, a cold-blooded viciousness that could rip away earring, scalp, and belly. Maybe behind the closed door of the hut, Shane or Jon had shown his true self to Ginny.

It seemed impossible that Jon's lazy affability could turn to violence. But Shane knew Ginny. On the way up Mariah, Bram had mentioned a relationship, said Ginny was acting crazy and talking too much. That Ginny might tattle about something to Shane's wife. Then out of Zach's earshot Shane and Bram had come to some kind of understanding, and after that Shane hadn't seemed bothered at all.

It was difficult to picture Shane doing anything messy, anything difficult. But no one liked a tattletale. Especially a bully. If the secret Ginny had was big enough, if she was really going to tell Arlo, would Shane have hurt her?

Zach's head pounded at trying to untangle the knots of the grown-ups' cares and worries. He'd lay out the chain of events, the order of things. That would be more straightforward.

Ginny had to have arrived at the hut earlier than Bram and Zach, because her earring had been waiting there. No way to know if Shane and Jon arrived before or after Ginny, but they had already left the hut by the time Zach and his father got there. Bram had gone downhill to get service and call Ginny. Shane had returned soon after Bram left, complaining he'd lost track of Jon. And Jon hadn't had his radio on, or at least hadn't responded. Jon had come back to the hut before Bram. At some point Bram had gotten reception, texted with Ginny, then headed back uphill.

But that didn't make sense. Ginny couldn't have arrived at the hut before Zach and his father, the earring torn from her, scalp ripped, then later on been low enough on the trail to have reception, and whole enough, alive enough, to text with Bram.

Unless his father had lied. Or unless someone else had used her phone.

And Ginny's car. Her Jeep hadn't been at the trailhead when Bram and Zach began their ascent. There had only been one other car when they arrived, presumably the one Shane and Jon had driven in together.

Steve, Dave, and Russ had come up next. Pike soon after. And they hadn't seen Ginny.

Maybe Ginny had driven with Jon and Shane. They'd all gone to the hut. Jon or Shane or both had done—that—to Ginny, unknowingly leaving the earring behind.

The memory of the earring spindled ever upward in Zach's throat like something that needed to be spat out. Purged.

It was possible Jon hadn't been out skiing at all, that he'd been downhill texting Bram using Ginny's phone. Had hurried up to arrive before Bram returned. He was faster than Bram, more skilled. It was possible. Then in the dark he or Shane might have dragged Ginny's body up the mountain, just like Dave planned to drag the injured Russ up on a sled.

Already Zach saw fissures open in these theories. Bram had said Shane didn't know Ginny was even coming, so why would Shane, Jon, and Ginny have driven up together? How could Jon have avoided Bram if they'd both descended to get reception? And more than anything, why? Why would they have done it? How big could a secret really be if Shane had hardly seemed to care about it earlier that day when he spoke with Bram?

He'd tell his father about the earring. Who else was there to tell? Bram knew things about Shane and Ginny Zach didn't fully understand. And though Zach had no idea what to do, Bram always had strong opinions, as if what he thought should be done was always the most obvious thing, the most correct.

A *woosh* noise startled Zach, who looked ahead to see the source. Bram was about thirty feet ahead, and had grabbed a branch that had released a rush of powder. He coughed deep and rough.

Again Zach was struck by his father's strength. Despite being hampered by his injuries and a lack of technique, Bram still managed to break trail and stay ahead of Zach and Pike.

The slope tipped to its most vertical as they neared the Bowl's rim, forcing them to sidestep uphill until they broke out onto the open ridgeline and stood catching their breath, each looking instinctively toward the break that had released the second avalanche some impossible-to-measure distance away. Though obscured by the falling snow, the line that had cut free all that death seemed to pulse with power and warning.

"You know what they say," Bram said with a tight smile. "It's all downhill from here."

The ski down the gentle slope to the hut was so pleasant, so easy after the difficult climb, after the whiplashing terrors of the day, that despite the cold, as he skimmed through the powder Zach laughed. At hearing it he sputtered, choked. It sounded so foreign.

Like a child's laugh.

CHAPTER 26

By the time Zach entered the hut, Bram was already shooting a stream of lighter fluid to drench the firewood shoved in the stove. Ready for the leap of flames this time, he stood back as he tossed the match in, igniting the wood with a satisfying *woosh*.

The quiet of the hut, its familiarity, the everydayness of the mess they'd left behind that morning, dizzied Zach. Zach glugged water until he no longer felt the awful dryness of his tongue and altitude-wicked throat. The chill of the wet fabric against his skin soaked through to his marrow, and he hurried upstairs and extracted the extra set of long underwear from his backpack. His hands were thick with cold; difficult to uncurl. His damp base layer clung to him, the fabric balling up uncomfortably at his ankles and wrists as he peeled it off. For a torturous moment Zach stood trembling naked before putting on dry pants and shirt, skin still too clammy to allow him to dress easily. New socks, a dry sweater, and he went downstairs cradling his wet things.

Pike and Bram ignored him, busy pulling at their noses and ears as if to bring them back to life in the low heat now emanating from the cast iron. Zach dragged a chair from the head of the table to sit next to the woodstove and hung his clothes to dry on the back of the chair, then sat, rubbing his thighs, his arms. His sit-bones rattled against the wood of the seat.

"I can't believe I have to head back out there," Bram groaned.

"Yeah," Pike said lightly enough to come across smug. "It's gonna be a bitch getting the kid up that last part. He's not exactly a lightweight."

Bram stalked to the kitchen and grabbed two bananas, a bag of walnuts, and a container of dried cranberries before returning to the woodstove. His face was etched with a deep frown as he handed Pike a banana, took the other for himself, and set the dried berries and nuts on the table.

"Maybe it would be smarter for me to ski down and call for help," Bram said.

"Work smarter, not harder," Bram regularly scolded, but Zach had learned that "smarter" meant whatever Bram wanted it to, and this time his father was clearly longing for the easier thing, so was labeling it the smart thing.

A self-satisfied smile crept across Pike's face. "I dunno. You were pretty insistent that kid not be out there in the dark. It's already two twenty. It took us an hour and a half to get back here. That means it'll take you at least—what—an hour to get there? More? And maybe even three to get back? Given you'll be pulling the kid and all? It'll be dark by then, even if you left right now. If you go down instead? They'd be stuck out there alone."

Bram's scowl deepened, and Zach's neck crawled as his father's eyes turned to him.

"While I go back for them, you head down," Bram said. "See if you can get a signal."

Zach shriveled, shoulders hunching. But before he could think how to protest without punishment, Pike said, "Is that a joke? He's just a kid!"

"Yeah. *My* kid. And don't pretend you care—I don't know if you should even be alone with him after that stunt you pulled. Trying to hit a scared little boy."

A scared little boy? Was that what he was?

Pike's grin vanished, his glare matching Bram's as he leaned forward, a challenge in his muscle-bound frame, the way even his thick neck seemed to flex.

Something rippled under Bram's skin. An uncertainty.

"The trail'll be snowed over," Zach said quietly into the tense silence.

Bram broke his stare. "I guess. Last thing we need is another person getting lost. And Pike—you touch a hair on his head, I'll—"

"Whatever," Pike interrupted with a roll of his eyes. "If I'd actually wanted to hit him, I could've."

Bram stalked upstairs.

Pike flopped on the couch and stared at the ceiling. Tearing at a cuticle, Zach forced himself to say, "I'm sorry. About the . . . 'monster' thing."

Pike rubbed the bridge of his nose. "It's fine. I shouldn't have reacted that way. It was just—Ginny and all."

"Yeah," Zach said. "Okay." He stood and went up the stairs, hoping it wouldn't be obvious he was following his father to talk in private.

Bram had changed clothes, was exiting the bunkroom as Zach reached its door.

"I need to tell you something."

"Tell me by the fire. It's freezing in here."

Zach shook his head. "Pike's there. I don't want him to hear."

Bram's brows knit, but he gestured for Zach to follow him into the bunk room, then closed the door behind them.

"What?"

Zach's heart fluttered, his voice breathy. "Um, yes-yesterday? When you were getting firewood? I was sweeping up all the junk around the woodstove. And I found an earring. A diamond earring. All crusty and gross with hair and like—stuff—stuck to it."

Bram exhaled an irritated sigh and said, "And?"

Zach wiped a hand across his mouth, trying to figure out how to make sense, to refocus his mind from its exhausted reeling over blood and hair and bone.

"What I mean is—there was only one earring. And when we found Ginny? She was wearing the other one. The matching one. And her other ear was all torn. That earring—the torn-out one? That's the one I found. Here, in the hut. When we first arrived."

Bram's blue eyes burned cold and intense. "Walk me through exactly what happened."

Zach stumbled through where he'd found and hidden the earring, the way he'd thought someone must have lost it, or that it was junk. Lied and said he'd forgotten all about it until he'd recognized its match on Ginny's body, saw her torn scalp. Bram went downstairs to verify the earring's existence, then burst back into the room, a finger waving just above Zach's nose.

"You're not messing with me, right? You didn't yank that out of her ear today to try to steal it or something."

Zach shook his head. "No, no!"

Bram stalked back and forth through the room, body thrumming with intensity. "It's Ginny's all right, I'd recognize it anywhere. Blood and hair and—she wore those earrings constantly, bragging how they were a gift. Always name-dropping. 'Harry Winston this,' 'just like Natalie Portman wore to that.' So vain. Acting like she'd earned them."

Zach's mother, twirling a green jeweled bracelet on her wrist, said, *Do you think any of it was ever real? Or was it all fake from the beginning?*

Bram stopped pacing. Looked at Zach as if he'd lost the thread of things somewhere during his rant and was only now grasping it again. "And you're sure. You're sure about *when* you found it."

Zach nodded.

"You notice how the whites of her eyes were bloody?" Bram tapped at a corner of his eye. "I figured that was just from exposure, or being bashed around in the avalanche. But if someone's strangled?" He wrapped his hands around a phantom neck and shook so violently Zach shrugged his shoulders to his ears. "That's what happens to the eyes, if you choke someone. Blood in the whites."

This was a thing his father knew.

"'Ginny got lost and fell off a cliff' my ass." Bram straightened. "Wait. Wait! I've got her phone."

He pulled Ginny's bright pink phone from a pocket, tapped at it, and held it up triumphantly so Zach could see its lit screen. "Ha! Wasn't working up there, but it's fine now. Must've just been too cold." He began swiping.

Zach's heart tightened. Bram regularly picked up his mom's phone from wherever she'd let it rest and scrolled through it, and if he couldn't he'd hold it up and ask, "Why do you need a password?"

"Oh," she'd demur, "that must have gotten put on during the software update. You know I'm useless with tech stuff. How do I get rid of it?"

But his father had a password. On his phone. On his computer. Even on the television.

And Ginny's phone didn't.

"Okay. Here she is texting with me. I'm sorry, blah blah blah, decided not to come because Shane's going to be there." Bram shook his head. "Such bullshit! As if I didn't know she was obsessed with the guy. Let's see . . . I wrote her back, asked where the hell she was, no response." Bram scrolled, tapped at the phone before saying, "Looks like those were her only texts and incoming calls yesterday, the ones from me." He frowned. "But it's weird. There aren't any texts at all from the day before that. But that girl was always on her phone. Always." A long pause as Bram swiped at the screen before he looked up, a baffled expression on his face. "No texts or calls in her history from Shane. Nothing from Pike, either, even from months ago when they were dating. And the recently deleted folder's completely empty. Which means everything from both Pike and Shane was deleted, then the 'deleted' file was emptied. It doesn't make sense." Bram muttered to himself as he began pacing again, then asked, "What time did we get up here yesterday?"

"Eleven? Maybe a little earlier?"

Without looking at Zach, without interrupting his frenetic back-and-forth through the room, Bram said, "Yeah, that sounds right. Because my first text to her landed about eleven thirty. And I skied for at least an hour before I found reception. Maybe more. So we must've arrived ten thirty or so. And the earring was already here. Jon and Shane were out. That was two hours after the trailhead meet time, so everyone else would've been hiking up by then. Even Pike; he got here more than an hour after Dave."

Zach remembered his mother's unattended phone lighting up, his father reaching for it, responding to whatever text had come through and tossing it back on the couch.

"She didn't have a password," Zach said, "so anyone—"

"You think I'm an idiot?" Zach didn't move, hardly breathed as his father turned on him. "She obviously wasn't the one texting me. She wouldn't have had an earring ripped out of her head up here, claimed she'd never come up at all, then ended up on a goddamn mountaintop. No. She was probably already dead when someone sent those texts. Just who, and how the hell'd he manage it? Either killed her in the hut, or accidentally dropped the earring here before we arrived after doing it somewhere else. Either way, he had to get downhill low enough to have reception, then somehow dump her all the way up on Mariah, with her phone back in her pocket. That's what doesn't make sense. All that uphill and downhill and none of us saw anything? It's like someone else is up here."

Zach released a panicked whimper. Bram winced, irritated at his train of thought being interrupted. "Jesus kid, what?"

"Last night? I did see—I saw something? On the trail up to the Bowl?"

"What do you mean?"

"I went to use the outhouse, and I heard something moving outside. I thought it was"—a monster, a beast, a creature born from nightmare—"an animal, or the wind."

"What time?"

"I don't know. But the fire was still going pretty good when I came down, so probably not too long after bed. Maybe an hour or two? When I came back into the hut, I looked outside and saw—like something was going up toward the ridge? Kind of outlined in the moonlight. But then—"

Bram clapped his hands on Zach's shoulder as if to physically press information from him. "Who'd you actually see upstairs before you went to the outhouse?"

"You, Russ, and Dave were all in our room. And Steve was in the hall bunk."

"You didn't see into the other room?"

"I think the door was closed?"

"And outside, where did you see this person exactly?"

"I—I couldn't tell that it was a person, so I didn't wake you up, I—"

"I don't care," Bram snapped. "Where was he?"

"On the trail going up to the Bowl. But then the storm started up again and I couldn't see where they went."

Bram released his son, and massaged his jaw in thought.

"You didn't see anyone come back in?"

"I sat down to warm up. I must have fallen asleep on the couch. That was all I saw."

Expressions flitted and faded across Bram's face too fast for Zach to read. "No one could've survived out there without some kind of shelter. It had to be one of these guys. Had to be."

"Shane and Jon were here before us," Zach offered. "Ginny's car wasn't at the trailhead. Maybe they drove up with her, and something . . . happened. Because while you were gone, Shane came back to the hut without Jon, maybe Jon—"

"Wait, Shane came back here alone, while I was trying to reach Ginny?"

"Yeah. He said Jon had ditched him skiing the Bowl."

"When did Jon come in?"

"I guess, thirty minutes before you? Thirty minutes after Shane?"

Bram resumed his pacing. "Thirty minutes. Thirty minutes. Would he have been able to get downhill far enough to get reception and get back here before me? Without me seeing him?"

Zach knew better than to offer a guess, and stayed quiet.

"It could be. It could be. I dunno that Shane would ever have the balls to get his own hands dirty. If you push a man far enough. . . . But that stoned hippie? It's tough to picture. Though people will sacrifice anything for money. And Pike." Bram shook his head, expression contorted with disgust. "He had it bad for that girl. Even after she ended it, he kept coming by the office. Ginny started sneaking out the back when she saw him pop up on the security camera.

Number of times I pretended not to see him idling in that midlife crisis of a Porsche outside . . ."

"Pike got here way after us, though?" Zach said.

"Right," Bram acknowledged without looking at Zach. "It probably wasn't Pike. But Shane didn't have much of a reason to kill her, you know? He didn't seem to care that Ginny was blabbing about their affair. What'd he say to me?" Bram looked toward the ceiling, searching his memory. "It was something like, 'No one ever believes these women, not when you have my kind of money.' So, yeah, I thought I had something on him, but he was right. Women lie, especially to extort a man as rich as Shane, and everyone knows it. Even if Ginny had proof, who would care? In business it's an asset to never be satisfied, to always go for the next, better thing. He's supposed to turn that off? People understand *that*. But *this*?" Bram cracked his knuckles with grim, energized satisfaction. "A dead girl? Hell, would people think he needed a reason? Everyone knows a woman can drive anyone to the brink. I have to see what I can shake out of Pike. Make him pay through the nose if he lets something slip. And if there's any chance Shane was involved, I bet Arlo'd be willing to make a deal to shut me up." Bram's eyes met Zach's. The look of optimistic ruthlessness on his father's face daggered deep into Zach's gut, making him shrink back, making his mouth go sour.

"It could work," Bram said. "This could be the answer. Because people love a dead girl."

CHAPTER 27

In the days after his mother's broken fingers, she'd repeated, "I can't believe I let it happen." Bram, unnaturally tolerant, tears in the corners of his eyes that never fell, doled out tense, one-armed embraces to Zach and Bonnie, a thing so foreign they went as still and stiff as cornered rabbits.

Aunt Felicity listened over speakerphone while their mother cooked dinner, breezily recounting how she'd fractured all four fingers on her right hand. "My reflexes are terrible, Fee. Seriously, I watched it happen and didn't even move."

"Grace," his aunt said at last, "stop with this passive voice BS. This didn't just 'happen.' *He* did this. *He* shut the door while your hand was there. You and the kids need to get away from him. He's not—right, you know?"

His mother's face hardened, and she took her sister off speakerphone.

"He's complicated. But he's a good man. My kids have a good life, better than you and I had. And you know how I feel about this, how I hate the way he bosses me around, and then you go ahead and do the same?" Zach rarely heard his mother angry. Watched with interest as her expression sharpened. "You're just like him, Fee, think you know better than stupid little Grace."

What his mother didn't tell his aunt but weepily confessed to the children was that she'd been drunk. Too drunk to do the obvious thing, which was to move her hand when she saw Bram closing the door. Her drinking was why she and Bram had been arguing in the first place. If she hadn't been so out of it, so slow to respond, hadn't been holding on to the doorframe to pull herself up from the floor, her fingers would never have been crushed one-two-three-four in an even line as she gripped above the door hinge.

With the way she swayed, caught her feet, tipped over so easily in the evenings, the children didn't ask why she had been on the floor in the first place.

Months later, after their mother was gone, Bram had handed Zach the phone to talk to his aunt. "Tell me the truth, Zach." He'd instantly known the thickness in Aunt Fee's voice meant she'd been crying over the report that had listed Grace's blood alcohol level; the one that said she'd had some kind of medication in her bloodstream, too. "Do you think they're right? That she'd been drinking? Do you think your dad's right that your mom had a problem? With drinking?"

When he'd said yes, Aunt Fee had gone quiet. "You aren't just saying that because your dad's there?"

"No! I'd never."

"I know you wouldn't. I know what she means to you." Then, hesitant, as if unsure she should ask a child the question at all, "She'd taken some pills, too, Zach. Did she do that a lot? Or do you think . . ." Here Felicity had to gather herself, audibly breathing deep, exhaling, before continuing. "Do you think she could've done it on purpose?"

"I don't know." Zach bit hard on the inside of his cheek, but despite the distraction the pain offered, his voice still cracked in the middle as he said, "Maybe? She was . . . sad a lot."

Aunt Fee had sobbed, then, seeming at last to accept it. Or accept it enough that she stopped questioning Bram whenever she called, got rid of the lawyer she'd hired to press the police to investigate further, stopped withholding the money for Zach's and Bonnie's tuition. Even so, the fact that their mother had left Aunt Felicity in control of money at all, money, Bram said, that should have gone directly to Zach and Bonnie, enraged their father. After Felicity refused to hand over these funds and quietly paid their school directly instead of sending Bram a check, he'd refused to let Aunt Fee speak to Bonnie and Zach. It had been more than a month since either of them had been in contact with their aunt.

"What does she think? That I don't know where you go to school?"

When his mother had hurt her fingers, Zach asked if they'd stay with Aunt Felicity again so she could tend to their mother, help her feel better, recalling the time two years before when Grace had packed them all off to Michigan. Their mother had worn sunglasses indoors because the bright lights of the airport, the sunlight through the plane window, made her wince. He and Bonnie had shared the couch, Aunt Fee on an air mattress beside them, and their mother in Felicity's bedroom because it was darker in there.

That first night as they fell asleep on the couch, Bonnie asked Zach what he thought had happened. "She probably drank so much," he said with authority, "that now she's hungover for days and days and needs Aunt Felicity to take care of her."

Bonnie had nodded in disappointed agreement.

Whenever their mother emerged from the darkened bedroom she'd put on a tense smile. "Such a fun vacation, right?" And despite their mother being cloistered away, the constant murmur of her voice through the wall either arguing with her sister in person or her husband on the phone about how long, exactly, the three of them would stay in Michigan—Bram wanting the visit cut short and Aunt Fee wanting them to stay for always—for Zach and Bonnie the trip had been fun.

Felicity laughed loud, easy, and often, wrinkling her nose whenever the children told her something she'd suggested doing was against Bram's orders, winking as she said, "Let's do it anyway." She took them to see movies in the theater where she bought them candy and popcorn. Showed them the wonders of the local arcade. "That's 'cause hoity-toity places like where you live look down on cheap thrills," she said when they told her their town didn't have an arcade at all.

Sometimes Zach still dreamed about Skee-Ball, the *ka-thunk* of a shot dead center into the 300, the *thwip-thwip* of the machine rolling out an orange tongue of tickets.

There'd be no trip to Michigan this time, Grace said. But things would change. She would change. She'd be better. For all of them.

Alight with self-reproach and bolstered by Bram's repentance, she'd managed a few months of sobriety. But by the time her hand was out of its cast, Bram's awkward affections were a thing of the past, and her promises to Zach and Bonnie were soaked with the rotting smell of alcohol-sweetened breath as she repeated that things would be better, that she'd be better, tomorrow, and tomorrow, and tomorrow . . .

There in the hut Zach hung his head, feeling the words *People love a dead girl* as a personal indictment. Because it did sometimes feel like he loved his mother more now than he had when she was alive. Alive she'd so often been a source of irritation, so imperfect, so flawed beneath her flawless beauty. But dead, he missed her in a way so painful it made it difficult to be alive. Now that she was dead, when fury sliced through him over her weakness, that she'd left him behind, the knife was always edged with Zach's own self-blame.

"What's crazy is that whoever it was, they might have gotten away with it," Bram said. "If it hadn't been for that avalanche Ginny might not have been found for months. Might not have ever been found."

Zach's voice came out as a pale squeak as he recalled Ginny's ribs. "Maybe it was a stranger? She was so . . . torn up."

His father waved this off. "Just some scavenger like got at the elk, probably. Unless whoever did it went really psycho. Which"— Bram snorted—"is possible. Maybe he wanted to make her suffer. I know they sell you that bullshit in school, stranger danger and all that, but these things are almost never random. No one can piss you off like someone you know. And out here? In a storm? There would've been nowhere to find shelter but this hut." Bram sighed deeply and shook his head. "What an unlucky damn break with Shane. As long as I get Dave's kid back here and he gets home safe, Dave, at least, will owe me big time. But after today, you can bet Pike's not putting in another dollar unless I find a way to force him. Arlo would've made all the difference. But the only way I'll get more from him now is if he thinks he needs to shut me up."

Bram moved in so close his pant legs touched Zach's knees. He leaned down, breath smelling sickeningly of banana, and pressed a finger under Zach's chin, tipping Zach's eyes up to his. "Don't you even think about telling anyone about that earring. I'll deal with this. Your job is to zip it. Understand?"

"Yes."

At this, Bram stepped back. Stared at Zach in a way so quiet and strange it was impenetrable.

"We better hope I find out," Bram said at last. "We better hope I can use it."

His father swept from the room, leaving behind air gone tight with the residue of a threat Zach couldn't grasp. Sitting on the hut's bunk and rubbing his knuckles into his temples, Zach recalled his father's mimed strangulation. In his imagination, Ginny's turtleneck now hid the bruised imprints of cruel hands. Zach's mind slipped somewhere safer. What was Bonnie doing? Maybe eating dinner, watching a movie on Ximena's phone. Ximena reading to her in the pink glow of the bedside lamp. Bonnie falling asleep the way she always did, wrists and hands twisted funny to tuck under her chin.

But it was still light out. Bonnie wouldn't be in bed. Why had he thought that? No, she'd probably just gotten home from school.

Today was Sunday. No school.

He couldn't think right. Something dark and buzzing floated over cleaned bones and tidy eviscerations, moved over Ginny's body before leaving their work half done. No blood around the elk. No blood here in the hut. Again Bram's strangling hands leapt forward. There might not have been blood at all, just the earring left behind as Ginny struggled.

The dishes. He'd forgotten the dishes. Those had been left behind, too. One pan, a spatula, one fork, one knife, one plate. Breadcrumbs that had frozen but still looked somehow soggy suspended in ice. The pan had been difficult to clean, something burned on it. A single meal cooked for a single person.

How long would that much water take to freeze? Longer than a few hours. Had Ginny made that meal?

Maybe Ximena and Bonnie were waiting in line at Paradise Bakery with all the tourists to get a ginger molasses cookie, Bonnie's favorite. Or maybe Bonnie was pouring Goldfish crackers into her applesauce. "Fish and apple soup," she sang, "kind of tastes like poop." But maybe she didn't sing like that when Zach wasn't there. Maybe without him to gross out she didn't enjoy that at all.

Who knows what people do when you aren't there?

Zach sucked at his bleeding cuticle. All the bonds he'd felt knotting the men together the night before, the threads of friendship that had seemed to interweave so seamlessly, had been snipped, untethering him among the remains of connection and hope.

He let tears come. He wanted to go home. He wanted Bonnie.

Bram had been so angry, said such mean things about Ginny being late. But Ginny must have been dutifully hiking long before dawn, long before he and his father. Or maybe, and yes, as the thought occurred it was at once obvious, she'd done exactly as she'd promised and come to the hut the day before them.

"Get down here!" Bram yelled up the stairs and Zach leapt to his feet, wiping tears away with a sleeve.

At seeing Bram packing, Zach didn't wait for instructions. He bagged food, added ibuprofen from the first-aid kit, and filled water bottles for his father to bring to Russ and Dave. Pike still lay on the couch, a half-empty glass of brown liquid now sitting on the table beside him.

"Keep your radios on. I'll call if there's an emergency."

"Use a different channel for emergencies," Pike said without looking at Bram. "Don't want you and Dave radioing back and forth waking me up."

Pike didn't see the knife-edged look Bram shot him.

"Right. Channel two will be emergency use only."

"Should I—should I look in their packs? For dry clothes you could bring them?" Zach asked.

"They aren't going to be changing clothes out there."

They probably should. Might even need to. But Zach only nodded.

Bram shuttled everything to his sled, already loaded with Zach's skis, and the skis and poles Pike had used.

"I'm outta here, guys. Rest up, I guess."

"Good luck," Pike said.

"Thanks. And look, man. Tensions were high. I get it. I'm not proud of how I acted. No grudges from me, okay?"

Pike sat up at this. Nodded. "I appreciate that. Same here. Same to you."

Zach had never seen his father come so close to an apology. As Bram reached the hut's threshold, Zach went to him, encouraged by this openness. The people who loved Ginny had to know she hadn't left them by mistake, by weakness, or on purpose, the way his mother had. They had to know there was someone to hold responsible. Someone other than God to point to and say, "See? It's his fault. Punish him."

"When we get home, we'll tell the police, right?" Zach whispered. "Give them the earring?"

The waning daylight around Bram shimmered, his face utterly still but for the slow, forced stretch of his lips into the facsimile of a smile. Zach recoiled, took a step back from the unsettling discordance of it as Bram said, "Sure, kid. Of course we will."

CHAPTER 28

For the first time in months, Zach fell asleep so swiftly he failed to relive his parents' final argument.

He woke in the dark bunkroom with no idea of how long he'd slept.

But no—no!

He'd actually done it. He'd wet himself. Zach explored his body with his fingertips. His long underwear was soaked from mid-belly to mid-thigh. The nylon of his sleeping bag was slick.

A groan of shame stopped short in his throat as he remembered where he was. He held still as possible, eyes darting rapidly.

He was alone. The others must not have returned yet. Mr. Fantastic, wound close to his neck, had stayed clean. He set the fox aside. But the smell. He balled his fists and squeezed his eyes shut to fight the rolling humiliation of it.

The hut was silent. With relief Zach realized that he could simply replace his sleeping bag with Steve's in the hall, dark blue just like Zach's. There'd be no reason for anyone to notice. But Zach's relief went to guilt at the gutting memory of Steve saying he had a daughter, a teenage girl who right now didn't know her father was dead.

All Zach's efforts to avoid getting his legs and feet wet as he crawled out of the sleeping bag were useless. Shivering, he stripped off his clothing and stashed it in his sleeping bag, the cold so tight against his wet, naked body it felt as though it were constricting his organs, biting his bones.

Zach tiptoed naked down the stairs past the closed door of the other bunkroom, exposed and trembling under the black gaze of the hut's windows. After sneaking a look around the corner to be sure Pike wasn't downstairs, he worked by firelight, a wary eye searching for any movement, any hint of someone approaching the hut or coming downstairs. He wet paper towels using the snowmelt pot on the stove and wiped himself down until he could no longer smell the low odor of ammonia. He patted dry, then stuffed the used paper towels in the woodstove with two fire starters and a new log. The flames leapt up and blackened the wet paper.

Zach slid into the long underwear he'd hung to dry by the fire. Though the clothes smelled lightly of sweat, they were reassuringly warm and stiff. Standing by the stove the cold drained from his thin bones and he stood sleepily, gratefully, in the orange firelight.

Men's voices outside brought immediate panic. Zach fled to the stairs and froze out of sight on the first step. The outside light switched on, illuminating the porch, visible from where Zach stood in the stairwell because the image of it reflected in the window of the hut's back door a few feet from him.

His father stood under the light talking to Pike, who was smoking.

Pike must've been outside all along. Had he seen Zach, shivering and naked, change by the woodstove?

The muffled voices grew louder. The liquid outline of Pike's reflection gestured emphatically with an arm, the ember on the tiny nub of whatever he'd gone outside to smoke leaving an orange trail behind it through the darkness.

Bram opened the hut's front door.

"That's not what I meant, Pike, not at all."

His father's tone aimed for soothing, but came out tense.

"Of course it is!" Pike bellowed.

"Shh, my kid could be awake, Dave's right—"

"What do I care?"

But Pike did seem to care, because he lowered his voice to a harsh whisper. Zach, plastered against the wall of the dark stairwell, was sure they would hear the loud suck of his breaths, the *rat-a-tat* of his startled heart. The men stood unmoving in the entry, their heads tipped, listening, assessing if anyone was awake, then looking over shoulders to see if Dave and Russ were in earshot.

One-one-thousand, two-one-thousand.

Zach didn't dare move.

"They can't be that far behind," Bram said quietly.

"Who cares, who cares?" Pike hissed wildly, but still at low volume. "Can you throw that shit outside? It'll stink up the whole place."

"That's what you're worried about?"

Pike tossed whatever he'd been smoking into the snow, then slammed the door shut with such force Zach was sure he felt a vibration. Pike's wide, muscled body seemed to expand and contract.

"Hey, now, man," Bram said. "Let's take a minute. Think this through."

A short, shrill burst of laughter. "You're crazy."

Bram spoke slowly, enunciating each word. "If I wasn't sure, if I didn't have proof, you think I would've confronted you?"

"You didn't find anything"—Pike's pitch edged higher—"because there's nothing to find."

"Look." Bram pointed outside. "I can see their headlamps. So how about we talk later, when they're asleep, all right?"

"You show me this 'proof' you found. Now."

"Just—shit, there's Dave. We'll—we should get out there to see if he needs help. I won't say anything, all right? For now."

A dismissive huff from Pike.

"We'll talk later. I'm gonna go help Dave."

Pike sat and took off his boots, a showy refusal to assist. When Bram slipped outside, Pike's dark, runny image put head in hands.

Zach moved up one step, then drew his neck into his shoulders in anticipation of some noise, some squeak or twitch of the boards that might give him away. But there was nothing.

In the upstairs hall he took Steve's sleeping bag off the bunk and replaced it with his own, the quiet slither of nylon making him cringe. He cradled the clean sleeping bag in his arms, tiptoed down the hall, and laid it out on his own bunk.

It looked all right. No one would notice.

The loud slam of a door and a flood of overlapping voices traveled from downstairs.

Should he get into Steve's sleeping bag? Pretend to be asleep?

No, exhausted as he was after the day's events, it still wouldn't be believable that he'd slept through this much noise.

Dave spotted him first as he hesitated at the base of the stairs. "Zach! How you doing, bud?"

Zach padded toward them.

"Okay, Mr. Dowling, how're you?"

Russ listed slightly to one side as he sat at the dining table eating beef jerky. Dave put his hand on his son's shoulder. "We're better now. And you see this tough guy here? Needed help on the way up, but made it downhill on his own steam. Your skis did the trick, bud."

"How do you feel?" Zach asked Russ. The teenager looked more like himself somehow, and Zach realized it was because Russ was wearing his glasses again, his prescription goggles left broken in the Bowl.

"I'm okay. I mean, it hurts, you know?" Russ put a palm to his chest, then his head, to indicate the places that pained him, and a new, vulnerable sincerity crept into his voice as he added, "But I'm like, pretty glad to be back here."

"That's right, that's right!" Dave said. "We did it. You did it! We'll warm up. Rest. Then tomorrow someone will head down, get a cell signal, and call Mountain Rescue so we can be sure once and for all they're coming. And we'll be none the worse for wear, right?" Dave grinned around the little circle, but as his eyes reached Pike his smile vanished. "Shit, I'm sorry, I don't mean to make light of—anything. I mean Shane, his dad, and I are close, it's going to be . . ."

Bram cleared his throat. "If Pike's up for it, he and I can head down in the morning. Russ is in no shape, and I know you'll want to stay with him, Dave. Could be Mountain Rescue's here by morning anyway, after the guide doesn't check in with his bosses tonight. He said he was required to call in and update them twice a day."

"Sure," Pike said, "we can talk about it in the morning."

Zach sat at the table with them, hungry again. As the group tore open bags of chips, hacked off slices of frozen salami and cheese, he snuck a glance at Pike, then unwittingly began to stare.

If Pike had killed Ginny, it hadn't marked him, hadn't twisted him to anything recognizable as evil. Zach's head ached with the effort of trying to pick out a shadowy Underself that might be hiding in his belly. His skull.

Dave helped Russ upstairs to bed before returning to eat more. Pike went up to his bunkroom next, shooting Bram a heavy look that Zach knew meant, *This is pretend. I'm coming back down to talk, and you better be here.*

Fearful of another accident, Zach used the outhouse before going upstairs, pulling hard at the fine hairs on his neck as he planned what to do.

"Russ?" Zach whispered into the dark bunkroom. "Are you awake?"

"Yeah."

"I was thinking, tomorrow, when they go down to try to get a cell signal to call for help? I was thinking I'd go with them. Do you mind if I take your phone?"

A long pause before Russ answered, "I don't think you should go, Zach."

"I want to help."

"Don't be stupid," Russ snapped.

Zach stayed silent, unsure if he should confide his real plans to Russ. Deciding against it, he said, "Maybe I won't go? I just—it'd be good to have the option is all."

An exasperated sigh in the darkness before Russ responded, "You can have it. But it's beyond dumb to go, man."

"Are you sure? You don't want to play games or whatever?"

"I tried using it and the light hurts my head kind of?" Russ shifted in the darkness. The rectangle of the phone lit up, and he handed it to Zach. "Here. Just—don't say anything about my head. To my dad."

"Okay. What's the password?"

"Oh, it's stupid. It's just nine, like, repeated."

"Is there a charger?"

"Yeah, it's plugged in by the couch. There's hardly any outlets in this place."

"Thank you! And maybe, would you not tell the grown-ups? That I have your phone, I mean. My dad, he doesn't think kids should have a phone."

"It doesn't even have reception, dude."

"I know, but still. He wouldn't like it."

The darkness provided a kind of anonymity, and into its blackness Russ's voice poured a desperate earnestness free of his usual eye-rolling, sarcastic self-consciousness. "Don't go with them, Zach. Use the phone to play games, whatever, but stay here, okay? None of them know what they're doing. You see that, right?"

"Yeah," Zach whispered.

"My dad, yours? They're selfish—they nearly got us killed! And for what? Steve said you and me shouldn't have skied it, and they ignored him, because God forbid they don't get to do exactly what they want all the time. And you watch, they'll blame Steve for everything, but if he'd been louder about it they still would've ignored him. Threatened him. You know I'm right. Our dads? They never, ever see themselves as the problem. And I saw you up there, Zach, you knew more than all of them combined, and not one of them listened, not one . . ."

Russ's words echoed Zach's own thoughts in the grove of trees and during the awful hours of the search for the buried. Yet remembering Dave's indulgent smiles at his son, his stricken face in the glade after the avalanche, Zach said, "Your dad seems okay, though, he cares, he's—"

"I'm just, like, a busted, I dunno, car, that he can't get rid of. So he's stuck trying to fix me up the way he wants." Russ was becoming more difficult to understand, voice growing sleepily slurred the longer he talked. "He only brought me here because he thinks a trip like this'll toughen me up, make me different, someone different, so he can brag, but he's not tough, no matter what he thinks. You saw it. He woulda let your dad die out there, wouldna searched, wouldna . . ."

Zach waited, but Russ had faded out and didn't continue. "Are you okay, Russ? You sound kind of strange."

"Just tired. I'm, like, already asleeping. Asleep."

"I'll let you rest. Thank you for the phone, Russ."

As Zach opened the door Russ roused himself, said, "Zach?"

"Yeah?"

"Thank you? For finding me. Digging me out. I know you were the one. Who saved me. And don't go with them, okay? That's me saving you this time. Okay?"

Zach felt his face flush hot. "All right," he said as he closed the door behind him. "It's all right."

In the hallway he entered Russ's passcode. He swiped until a search bar came up, then searched the word "record." Nothing. Searched the word "voice." An app called Voice Memos appeared. He hit the red record circle, clicked the power button to make the screen go black, then whispered into it, "Testing, testing." He touched the screen to wake the phone, hit stop on the recording, then entered Russ's password and played it back, flinching in embarrassment at the unsteady sound of his own voice.

But it worked. Even with the screen dark, even if it was locked, the phone would record a conversation.

And if someone picked up the phone while it was recording? Would they be able to tell?

He hit record again. Turned the phone's screen off, then woke it. A red icon showed on the bottom of the screen, making it obvious the phone was recording.

Zach's stomach lurched, but he didn't allow himself time to think about the choice he was making. He hit record, clicked the phone's screen to black, and went downstairs.

"We were blessed, if you really think about it," Dave said to Bram. After checking neither man was looking in his direction,

Zach plugged in the phone and tucked it out of sight under the couch. "Found nearly everyone so close to the surface, even with two slides. It could have been much worse. God looked out for us today."

Zach frowned. Because if God had been there, didn't that mean he'd buried Steve, Jon, and Shane? Allowed Ginny to be murdered? Torn apart?

"Here, kid," Bram said, shoving a water bottle at Zach. "You need to drink this. May not feel like it, but you're dehydrated after today."

Zach took the bottle, cast adrift by Bram showing signs of care, and trotted toward the stairs.

"I'm serious," Bram called after him. "Have that finished by the time I come up."

The humiliation of the wet sleeping bag loomed large, and Zach didn't dare drink more water. Yet touched by his father's attempt to tend to him, he feigned obedience by pressing his lips to the bottle, blocking the opening with his tongue, and pretending to sip as he went upstairs.

"Good boy," Bram called after him.

In the bunkroom, Zach emptied the water out the window and set the bottle where his father would be able to see it. As he crawled into Steve's sleeping bag he listened to Russ's loud snores, and tucked Mr. Fantastic into his shirt, close but hidden. He tried not to think of the phone recording downstairs. Tried to force away the reeling, intrusive thoughts of all the horrible ways Bram would react if he discovered that Zach was spying on him.

CHAPTER 29

Zach's bruises had settled deep and made whole patches of him tender. Opening his eyes in the dark, only the sudden memory of the phone recording downstairs, his knowledge that every minute increased the risk of it being discovered, drew him out of the warm sleeping bag, sore and exhausted. He kept Mr. Fantastic in his shirt, slipped past Dave, Russ, and his father sleeping, and went downstairs. He cupped his hands around his face and peered out a window toward Mount Mariah.

No light. No tracks. No sign of anyone—animal, man, woman, or monster.

He unplugged the phone and hit stop on the recording. The screen read 4:41 a.m. Zach placed another log on the low fire, sat next to the stove, hit play, and clicked the volume down low.

First came a scraping sound that had to be Zach himself setting down the phone. Then Bram ordering him to drink water. The *clunk-clunk* of Zach heading upstairs.

"Lemme get you a drink, too, Dave. Something a little stronger than water, maybe?"

"I shouldn't, but after today . . ."

"I hear you, man."

"It's almost like—like we were chosen," Dave had the same dreamy, self-important tone Zach remembered him using the first day as he'd fantasized about being an early Western settler. "Chosen to survive."

"Everything happens for a reason," Bram said.

The recording was silent for a time, as if both men were contemplating how special they must be, what a grand purpose they must have compared to those who had died.

Impatient to know what his father had said to Pike, Zach skipped ahead, paused, heard Dave say goodnight, then skipped ahead again until he heard Pike's voice. Zach rewound carefully to the precise point his father and Pike began speaking.

Bram's voice. "Want a drink?"

"Whatever."

Shuffling sounds. Shifting sounds.

When he next spoke, Bram's voice came through louder and clearer. The men must have settled on the couches near the phone.

"First off, I don't think bad of you, Pike. It's not like that."

"You accuse me of something so—so—awful? I didn't do anything. I didn't do anything wrong."

"I didn't say you did anything wrong, bud. Any man who says he can't understand is lying to himself. Women—they can make you do things you never would otherwise."

A hesitation before Pike spoke. "She must have gotten hurt coming up here. Alone. Lost. Like Dave said." Pike transitioned to a hoarse whisper. "They might wake up, one of them is going to come down and hear you saying—"

"They're not."

"You can't know that for sure, you—"

"I swiped some sleeping pills from Jon's pack. Dissolved them in their drinks. The kids'll probably be out until noon. Dave, too, the way he was hitting the whiskey on top of it. So we can talk without worrying."

Zach's mind immediately sprang to Russ, and he pulled at his hair hard with worry. *It's like I'm already asleep*, Russ had said. Were pills even safe if Russ had a concussion? But no, it was all right, Russ had been breathing just fine, snoring as Zach left the bunkroom only a few minutes ago.

And wait, *kids*, his father had said, which meant Zach, too. But he'd poured his water bottle out the window. A flare of outrage kindled in Zach's chest at the violation of it, at the way his father had disguised deception as a parent's nurturing care.

Pike must have appeared shocked by Bram's admission that he'd drugged Zach, Russ, and Dave, because Bram scoffed, said, "Please. Don't pretend it's some big thing. My wives both used that stuff like it was candy. I know how it works. And I needed to talk to you, man to man, without having to think about them. Because—this is some bad business. I mean, Ginny's stomach alone—"

"I didn't do that! That was animals, like Dave said. None of it—none of it was me."

"A sight like that," Bram marveled, "it sticks, yeah? Makes for a story. It all does. A billionaire's son and a D-list ski-movie star dead? A beautiful girl's body found mutilated in the same slide? Add that to who your family is, who Dave is . . . this group—it's going to be a story. A big one. And let's say into all that mess I whisper the word 'murder.' All her faults, Ginny was a knockout. Young, blond, white, surrounded by money. How do you think people would react?"

A sound of outraged, wordless denial from Pike, but Bram pressed on, slippery and relentless. "There's evidence, Pike. We're talking DNA, airtight proof that Ginny died right here. Right here in this room."

"You're lying."

"Am I? You did it right over there."

Zach pictured his dad pointing toward the woodstove.

"I wasn't even here," Pike insisted, gaining better hold of himself now, strident. "You got here before me. Maybe *you* did something."

A rumble of smug pleasure from Bram. "Let's see, huh? Let's see how much I know. Ginny got here when she said she would, a whole day before the rest of us. You knew she'd be up here early. I'm the one who told you that, and I remember, Pike, because you lit up when you heard it, got so excited you invited yourself on a father-son trip with a father too old come and with no son at all. You asked me not to tell Ginny you'd be there, remember? Said you didn't want things to be awkward. But that was obviously bullshit. You didn't want her to know because she wouldn't have showed. She told me all about it, how after she ended things she blocked you, avoided you, and that pissed you off. You think I didn't see you lurking outside the office whenever you were in town? Didn't notice how often you dropped by for no reason? Hid in your car outside? They call that stalking, buddy. She'd sneak out the back to avoid you, you know. The disrespect of it, Pike, no wonder you figured 'Hey, this is my opportunity to get her to listen. Get her somewhere she can't run off, somewhere she'll be forced to hear me out.'"

Bram paused, waiting for what Zach wasn't sure. In the silence Zach bit the inside of his cheek and pictured the size of Pike's arms. His ropy neck. Zach's knee-jerk concern for his father sickened him after the revelation of the sleeping pills, and he tried to slough it off, his love or need or whatever it was that kept his body and mind tied to Bram a dried skin needing to be peeled away to clean him.

"After she was killed," Bram went on, "killed right over . . . there . . . you tidied up. Packed up. Hauled her and her stuff outside, way off-trail and out of sight. Then, well, you did a hell of a lot of cardio, bud. No wonder you looked so wrecked when you showed up yesterday. Figured you'd leave the body in the woods, maybe pile some snow on it. But you had to make it like she was never even here, yeah? You had to get rid of her car. Had to text me her excuses. So you grabbed her car keys and her phone, and you headed back to the trailhead. Drove her car and parked it out of sight or pushed it off the edge of the road. Plenty of spots to do that. Had to hike all the way *back* to the trailhead and get your own car and move that, too. I'm guessing you parked up the last road that split off before the Pantheon parking lot. Then you stayed there in your car, maybe got some sleep. Waited past the guide's meet time so you could come up last, look as innocent as possible." Bram snorted. "Right off I knew her texts were weird. But it all makes sense now, because of course when you were using her phone, pretending to be Ginny, you couldn't resist taking a dig at Shane. What was it, again? That she wasn't coming to Pan because she hated him? Then back up the trail you came. No wonder you were downing drinks. That's a stressful twenty-four hours."

Pike's voice had a shaky thinness. "No. You don't know. You're guessing."

Bram continued as if Pike hadn't spoken. "Now why the hell haul her all the way up Mariah? I'm thinking once those boys came in jabbering about how they saw a bunch of circling crows, once Dave got us all fired up about going to see if some alien had been munching on a dead elk, you thought, 'those birds found her,' and decided to get her as far from here as you could, yeah? So you waited until we were all asleep, fetched her, put her phone and keys back in her pocket, dragged her up there on your pack sled, and dumped her over the ridge. Probably thought the storm was perfect, huh? Would cover her up? But of all the places you could've tossed her, man—miles of woods and mountain in every direction—you chose the spot that slid. What are the chances? That's some bad luck." His father's scornful, artificial laugh faded out and there was a beat of quiet before he asked, "You still think I don't have any evidence? Because that hangs together pretty well, Pike. No way I could know all that without evidence."

Yes, his father lied so fluidly, so convincingly, that even for Zach it was difficult to believe he didn't have more evidence than a few texts and a crusted diamond. Bram must've filled in these blanks on his way to and from where Dave and Russ waited on Mariah. But it did fit, made any other suspect sound impossible, each little puzzle piece assembled into a frame; the only missing piece the question of what had destroyed the elk, had ravaged Ginny's middle.

"Why are you saying these things? What are you after?"

Bram didn't hesitate. "You need to invest more in Ajax Prop."

Now it was Pike's turn to laugh, bitter and still unsteady. "Boy, are you barking up the wrong tree."

A sigh from Bram. "Look, this is what it is. You want me quiet, you put more in."

"Nope. I need to cash out, actually."

In an uncharacteristic loss for words, Bram stammered, "I—I don't think—you're not fully appreciating—you're not getting your situation here, Pike."

"No, Bram, *you're* not getting it. I'm cut off, man. Like, fully. The whole angel investing thing? My dad let me run it, as a kind of . . . test. And according to him, I failed. And now he's not giving me a penny more. His words. I'm living in a house that isn't mine. I have to beg my dad for any dollar I need to live. Ajax Prop was the one investment I had that's in the black. The one investment that made me think *maybe* I'd pull my fund out from underwater at some point down the line. But given you're sitting here trying to blackmail me, I'm gonna take a shot in the dark and say AP's a failure, too."

When his father didn't respond with outraged defenses, Zach only heard his mother's voice.

There's nothing to have.

"But, there's got to be . . ." his father came through strained as if speaking from far away. "Wait, you mentioned your place in LA? And you fly private. A trust fund, or—"

"I'm thinking you know a bit about how to look like you have money when you've got nothing, Bram. The banks are all over me. That check you gave me, that's going straight to them, whether I like it or not."

A tapping noise. Bram pacing?

"Your dad wouldn't want this coming out," Bram said. "Maybe if you tell him about Ginny, he'd—"

Pike interrupted with a scoff that ended in a kind of sob. "Please. He'll throw a damn party over this." Pike collected himself. "In his mind, it'll prove he was right, and that's all he really cares about. He couldn't stand that the rest of the family was on my side, on and on about how he worked his way up from nothing. How I'm a spoiled brat. The same old tired nonsense. The man inherited a quarter-of-a-billion-dollar empire at twenty-two that's worth less now than it was in the seventies, and *I'm* the entitled one? *I'm* the bad investor? But he believes it. He believes every word of his own bullshit. Once he cut me out of the will, the rest of the family shut up. The cowards are too scared he'll do the same to them if they don't get in line."

"So there's nothing? Really nothing?"

"Technically, less than nothing." Pike sounded perversely pleased at being able to rub his failure in Bram's face. "I owe around five hundred grand." He paused, then added, "It makes sense now, though. What Ginny said."

"Ginny?"

"You know her family cut her off, too? When she was in college, they found out her brother was gay, wanted to send him to one of those reeducation camps. But Ginny came and got him, and that was it. She had to figure out how to support herself, pay for her school, her brother's, all of it. After we broke up she wouldn't even talk to me. But when my dad cut me off, I knew she'd see we were the same. I just had to get her to listen, you know?" Pike took a long breath, shedding his sad desperation as he continued, words a release of pressurized spite. "But when I came up here early, when I tried to explain, she refused to hear me. So self-righteous. So smug. Said her being cut off was nothing like me *pissing away millions of dollars*. Those were the words she used. Vulgar, you know? She whined about stuff that didn't even matter from when we were dating, like how I wouldn't let her see her friends, told her to close her social media accounts or whatever, when obviously all that was me trying to protect her. And *then*," Pike paused for dramatic effect. "She said my dad was right to cut me off. Because I was an idiot who fell for your scam with Ajax Prop."

Bram didn't respond.

"I thought maybe she was in on it, but looking at you now I can see you didn't know she was onto you. But yeah, even Ginny figured out you were a fraud. Even Ginny, who was stupid enough to kick a nice guy to the curb for no reason, then go gold-digging after a married man. And she called me stupid, because of *you*. It was—humiliating. It was all like—like I had no say in any of it. Why should *she* get to decide? Why should *she* get to look down on me?" A wistful tone crept into Pike's voice. "I loved her. If I didn't love her so much, none of this would've happened."

"Brought it on herself," Bram murmured almost automatically, as if his mind was elsewhere.

Annoyed by Bram's apparent detachment, Pike snapped, "If *you* hadn't cheated me, things wouldn't have gone this way. This is on *you*. Who knows how she would've used what she knew. She was probably trying to figure out how to drain you of every damn dime. I mean, that's what she tried with me, with Shane. Money's all they care about." A mirthless laugh. "You think if I tell them you're running some scam they'll reduce my time, Bram?"

At this the two men went quiet, and Zach wondered if they were trying to figure out, the way he was, what might be next. What each man wanted, and what he would do to get it.

Bram's voice punctured the quiet, calm and even. "It's not just me who knows what happened to Ginny, Pike. My son knows, too."

A cold thing slithered around Zach's heart. Squeezed.

CHAPTER 30

Pike's furied disbelief was palpable as he spat out, "You told your *kid?*"

"He's the one who told me, Pike." Bram sighed. "He saw you hiking up Mariah in the middle of the night. He's the one who found other things, too. The proof of what happened to Ginny. He didn't understand any of it until he saw the body. But then he put two and two together. That's how clear it all is. A child figured it out." A forced casualness as Bram added, "Honestly, I'm surprised he only blabbed to me. He gossips. His mother's son, you know? Weak. I've tried to explain to him how life works, but she sheltered him; wouldn't let me teach him consequences the way my father taught me."

Zach's hand went sweaty. He set the phone on his lap and wiped his palms on his pants. He checked the room around him, as if Pike's newly exposed Underself might be snaking toward his neck.

The betrayal of it. The danger. And though Bram had berated Zach countless times for weakness, for showing any emotion but anger, hearing his father say such things behind his back was a new and deeper humiliation.

Pike's voice was threaded through with tension. "So you were trying to blackmail me even knowing full well you couldn't keep your kid quiet."

"No. That always had to be another . . . obstacle. That we need to solve." Bram paused. "You heard about my wife passing?"

"Yeah."

"I had a couple of life insurance policies on her. One was a key person policy. Through the business."

"What? For your *wife*? Those type of policies are only for like, major executives, aren't they, so the business isn't kneecapped if they die and there's turmoil or whatever. Did she even work . . ." Pike's protests faded out, probably recalling, the way Zach was, that Ajax Property Tech was as counterfeit as one of those false-fronted buildings dotting old Colorado towns and the sets of Western movies. From the street it might appear to have an imposing number of stories, but another angle shattered the illusion to reveal an overly tall facade slapped on one sad, squat level. "The checks you handed out—that money is from the key person insurance payout?"

"Yep."

"So there's—you said there's a few policies? Is there more money?"

"Enough to cash you out. Enough to tide me over long enough to let crypto rebound. Let my shorts have time to succeed."

"Christ, man." Pike's outrage still held, but now it was tinged with exhaustion. "You were out there using my money to speculate on crypto and short stocks? Isn't crypto at, like, prepandemic lows? And what'd you short?"

A cold edge to his father's voice. "Doesn't matter."

"Fine, whatever. But if you've got these insurance payouts, why are you even bothering trying to get money from me?"

"There's a . . . wrinkle, I guess you could say. My wife didn't know about the key person policy. But her standard policy? She changed it. So that I'm not the beneficiary."

"Okay. And who is?"

"My kids. Each gets half the payout."

"You can't—can you even do that? Give that kind of money to a kid?"

"Sure. Just have to put it in a trust. Designate a manager."

A sardonic laugh from Pike. "Sounds like she had your number. Sounds like she outsmarted you."

A hot acidity crept into his father's carefully controlled voice. "Please. She didn't understand any of it. She never understood how life works. Didn't understand the . . . implications. I set up the trusts so I was manager for both, which would've meant carte blanche, basically. But that stupid—she changed the trustee to her sister. And her sister? Nasty woman. Hates me for no reason. Always has. But it was a double payout, Pike. Massive! Because they ruled it an accidental death. And under the trust, I get paid if something were to—happen."

Pike went quiet, as if absorbing this, sorting through it, before asking, "What does this have to do with me?"

During the long silence that ensued, Zach imagined that Pike, like Zach himself, was waiting for Bram to explain what all this actually meant. There had been something his mother said about a trust during that final argument, something about how her own lawyer had been worried by it, but Zach hadn't understood it then, and the words remained impenetrably adult now.

"Wait, wait." Pike said at last. "Are you saying you'll keep quiet if . . . two kids? Oh, no. No way. I'm not—Ginny—that was a—that was different—"

"Don't be ridiculous," Bram snapped. "The policy paid out into separate trusts for each kid."

"But your sister-in-law—"

"What can she do? Nothing. It's not her money. It's mine. I was the one—my payments, my loans!—who set it up, who paid the premiums. The trusts are clear on what happens."

"No way. No."

"Man up, Pike. Don't pretend you're some innocent. You murdered Ginny and tossed her over a cliff because she didn't want you. You don't even feel bad—and why should you? What did she expect? And now, here you are, outraged? Give me a break!"

A strange, heaving sound was met instantly by Bram's voice, brimming with the arching lash of his Underself. "Don't think for one second you can intimidate me, Pike. I'm not some woman half your size. And you're not stupid. You know that even if you get rid of me, you *still* would have to get rid of the kid. And you have to know you could never explain two of us. But if something . . . changes . . . with my insurance situation, I'll cut you in. Fully cash you out. Plus, say, twenty percent? That'll more than cover your debt. You can rub your dad's face in your success, because you'll have money to build with. And you'll have dirt on me, too. Which is your guarantee I won't be back with my hand out."

"He's just a—Jesus."

Bram gave a snorting laugh. "Jesus is right. God didn't hesitate, with his son."

"You're God now?"

"When it comes to my family I am. That's how it is. But what I am, really, Pike, is a businessman. And when I see an opportunity, I take it."

Pike's voice, cutting but quiet. "You remind me of him. My father."

"And you remind me of my kid, handed everything and still whining about your mean dad. You've got no clue. *My* dad kicked my ass every day of my life. Didn't give me a penny to cut me off from. And I hated him for it. But guess what? Because of him I'm a fighter. I know how things really work. I've always known. It's time to toughen up, Pike. It's time to do something for yourself."

Zach pressed Mr. Fantastic against his chest, mind flooded with ink-black terror over the righteous, vindictive voice of the Underself.

"We'd never get away with it," Pike said.

"Somewhere up there are four dead bodies. Two avalanches. And the snow's still falling. Conditions are hell. Dave's already convinced Ginny got lost, that a bear or something chewed on her. Probably one did. Tomorrow, three of us head down the trail to try to get help. And two come back telling a story about more bad luck."

A scoffing sound from Pike before he said, "Why wait? Just grab the kid now, drag him down the mountain."

But Bram responded matter-of-factly, as if Pike's suggestion was reasonable, as if sarcasm hadn't drenched every word. "The storm's still going. It's dark. If rescue's coming at all, it won't be until the weather clears and it's light out. I bet when you dumped Ginny you kept the hut in sight, because you knew you'd never find your way back otherwise. But to make *this* believable we need to head down the trail through the woods, make it look like I told Dave, and we're just going to find a cell signal to call Mountain Rescue. But the trail's snowed over. The trail markers are far apart. To try in the dark? It's stupid to think we'd manage to do anything but get lost, and fast. And the way I dosed them? They won't wake up just from us talking down here, and they would be real out of it if they did wake up, but a loud noise, or being jostled? Someone could wake up all right. How the hell would we explain that to Dave, if he or Russ sees us grabbing the kid in the middle of the night? No, I'll set an alarm on vibrate so it'll only wake me. Wake him quietly when it's light. Tell him we need his help. He'll buy that. All the attitude he's been giving everyone, his snide looks? Kid thinks we're all idiots about the backcountry compared to him. So in the morning, down we go.

Come back with a sob story for Dave. You think anyone would blink? You think they'd call it anything but tragedy?"

"Your wife dies, leaves your kid money, and then something happens to him, too? The avalanches, four dead, and then another accident? Of course there'll be questions."

"That's the thing." Bram sounded eager, even excited. "The conditions, the mistakes, four dead already? It'll all just be the same event, really, and so much to sort through, so much to dig out and try to find. And all the way up here. With no witnesses. With the snow still falling. And an arrogant kid who made stupid choices. It just has to happen so it looks like an act of God. Looks as accidental as the rest. Though—where's Ginny's car?"

A pause before Pike responded, "At another lot. Close."

"Good. It was shoved off the road or something. There might be a problem. That might be impossible to explain. But that's good."

"The cops, they'll have to investigate. The sheriff or whatever."

"Let them. They'll find blunt force and suffocation, right? That's what's to be expected after all we've been through. Avalanches, snowstorms, everyone out of their depth. Sure, a few people might make a fuss. Ginny's brother, maybe. My sister-in-law. But Arlo most of all. You have to know he'll pull all the focus. Even with what happened to Shane clear as day, the media, search and rescue, law enforcement, you name it, they'll all be absolutely salivating over Shane. That'll only help us. I'll be devastated. Beside myself. You and me'll tell the same stories, and Dave won't know better than to join in. Who would think, who would really believe, that this was somehow planned? Especially if the evidence I told you about doesn't . . . appear." Bram's voice lowered into a soothing, instructive tone. "People want to believe these things happen for a reason. Think about it. Ginny was unprepared. She got lost. Kids are disobedient. Fragile. Jon and Shane made fatal mistakes. The guide nearly got us all killed. They'll blame the snow, the conditions, bad luck. But they'll mostly blame whoever doesn't come back."

The sound of footsteps grew and faded, grew and faded, and Zach imagined one of the men pacing back and forth. At last Pike said, "You want it done, you do it. And I'll say whatever you want."

A long silence. "I can't rely on myself to do it. Not . . . close up. Like it'll need to happen."

"So this is all just you talking tough, basically. You can't even stomach doing it yourself, but you expect me to?"

"I'm not arrogant enough to think I'm reliable to do it. You have more . . . distance. Even if I've got no choices, even if I've been pushed to these extremes, I'm still a father. But I can accept it. And you've already shown you've got what it takes. It's a problem you can solve for us both. This gets us each what we need."

Bram's voice had a familiar curl, his tone a soothing manipulation. He was trying to sound human, ready to admit weaknesses in a way that hid the ruthlessness of his Underself. It all made Zach instantly sure that the only reason Bram had enlisted Pike was so that he'd have someone to blame. Zach pictured Bram cornered, holding up clean hands, and saying, "You see? I didn't do anything at all." The idea he would stay silent for Pike, a man he ridiculed, a man who had already admitted his uselessness to Bram because he didn't have enough money to buy him off, was, to Zach, utterly absurd. What seemed likely was that his father would let Pike take the fall if he needed to, and he'd use the threat of the earring's evidence to wring Pike dry for the rest of his living days.

But Pike didn't know Bram the way Zach did.

"I—I can't, it's different it—"

"After Ginny, you know how it is. How simple it is. The first time you think it, picture it? In a way—it's already done." Bram sounded soft, almost dreamy. "The rest is just waiting for the moment. That moment when everything comes together. A new life, right there, for you to step into. Isn't that how it was? With Ginny?"

A long pause.

"I remember—her makeup. Too much mascara. For who? It was like that. Already done. Once I saw that."

"Yes. Neither of us have a choice here, Pike. But both of us can face things. And you know as well as I do what needs to be done."

Another pause. The sound of a wood knot popping in the fire.

"How much money is it, exactly?"

CHAPTER 31

Bram and Pike rattled through numbers on the recording. Zach half listened, spreading his fingers around his skull to try to keep himself whole as his mind cleaved apart, bifurcating into two entirely different understandings of reality.

One side of himself whispered that he knew nothing about stocks, insurance, trusts, beneficiaries. That the vagueness of that grown-up language, its dullness, its benignity, only meant that his father was taking care of important things; taking care of him.

The other side throbbed with a single word that grew so loud it drowned out everything else: "Run."

Sounds still slipped from the phone, but Zach heard only the men's panting hunger; a ravening for a satisfaction just there, just beyond their line of sight.

He hit stop on the recording. The phone read 5:12 a.m. It would be light within an hour and a half.

Descending the snowed-over trail in the dark would be dangerous. Not just because of the possibility of slides, but the likelihood of getting lost. His mother's lessons had included stories of stranded groups, and invariably the physically strongest, the ones too impatient to wait for the snow to stop, to stay put for rescue, were the people who ended up wandering the woods, injured or even killed because they underestimated the indifference of a winter wilderness.

He felt the menacing darkness of the wilds roll through him.

Zach stood, his decision made for reasons that were still too slippery to cobble together, reasons distilled into his mother's voice, frantic in a way it had never been when she'd said the words in real life:

Sometimes it's smart to be afraid.

He would run. He would take Russ's phone downhill. He would send the police the recording the moment he got reception and let the grown-ups figure it all out.

And after that, he'd keep going. Half the insurance his dad had talked about was his sister's, and he felt a desperate urgency to reach her, to physically cup his body around Bonnie's like a shield.

As he packed water, food, fire starters, Zach tried to ignore the hum of his heart. Had to work to breathe through the weight of the ceiling pressing down heavy from above, laden with the threat of his father, of Pike.

A 50 percent charge on his beacon. His radio at 72 percent. He'd be traveling alone, no one to communicate with, but if he got hurt? It might be his only lifeline. His avalanche probe leaned against the entry wall, still modified to substitute for his lost ski pole.

He placed a matchbook among the growing pile of items, nervous that the matches from his mother's emergency kit might be insufficient if he was forced to stay outdoors for any extended period. After a moment's thought he took Mr. Fantastic out of his shirt and set him atop the pile to be packed, too.

As he worked, Zach deliberately avoided the area where he'd found the earring. He couldn't bear the idea of stepping where Ginny had taken her last breath. Didn't want to pass through the air where some residue of her, some gossamer bit of soul or shard of her final pain might adhere to him like a fresh-spun spiderweb on a morning trail.

He hadn't been back in his mother's bathroom, either, since the day she died.

What was the list of things required for outdoor survival?

Fire, water, shelter, food.

A whisper stroked prickly through his brain. His plans didn't fully hold together. Nothing he'd overheard quite interlocked in a way that let him truly understand. Maybe he was being rash, foolish, shortsighted.

Or maybe Pike was waiting in the shadows, ready to strangle him.

Zach ascended the stairs and went down the hall one cautious foot at a time. Pushed the mercifully quiet bunkroom door open. The wheeze of the sleepers was punctuated now and then with snores. Zach acclimated to the blackness until he could discern the outlines of things; until the signs of human life within—the exhalations, the occasional twitch of a sleeping lump—took on a reassuring regularity.

His backpack sat at the foot of his bunk. He lifted it two-handed and crept back into the hall, resting it near the top of the stairs. Then he tiptoed back into the room and began to pull the sleeping bag he'd appropriated from Steve off the plastic mattress.

The slither of it cut through the quiet to force Zach's hands still. He waited, listening, blinking at the sleeping figures around him. He resumed drawing it toward him more slowly to mute its sound, the painstaking gradualness of it a torture that forced him to suppress a jittery impulse to whisk the bag off the bed in a single motion.

One-one-thousand, two-one-thousand.

At last he held the sleeping bag in his arms. He waited for any hitch of breath, any atmospheric change or eddy in the cold black that might indicate his father had been disturbed. Should he try to wake Dave, play him the recording?

The pills loomed large in Zach's head. He'd be far more likely to wake Bram than rouse a drugged Dave, a possibility that forced Zach to back tentatively out of the room, the sleeping bag swishing.

In the hall, Zach shouldered his pack and grabbed the sleeping bag storage sack flopped on Steve's bunk. After a moment's thought, he put the guide's backpack on his other shoulder and descended the stairs, forcing himself not to run, not to make any noise.

Downstairs, he stuffed Steve's sleeping bag into its sack, then quietly emptied his and Steve's backpacks onto the kitchen counter, shoving unnecessary items—a bulky sweater, a book—aside. He was about to fill two empty water bottles next to the sink when he recalled the sleeping pills Bram had used to dose the others. Could there be residue, some little bit of the drug that might make him sleepy? Zach scrubbed the bottles just in case, then rinsed, filled, and packed them. He decided to take Steve's small first-aid kit, emergency blanket, clean long underwear, and a pair of his socks. The clothing was too big, but given that Zach's extra base layer now sat soaked in the bottom of his wet sleeping bag, at least it was a backup.

Rooting through the side pockets of Steve's pack, Zach discovered a palm-size orange device with a small screen. The screen lit up green, and he toggled through the options.

It was a handheld GPS. His mother's had been a newer model, but similar. Like hers this one had topographic maps preloaded. Like her Steve had uploaded the trails to, from, and around the hut.

But unlike with his mother's GPS, there was no way to use this device to call for aid.

Even so, the invisible bands around Zach's chest loosened. He'd be able to find the route down to the parking lot, down the mountain, even if he lost sight of the blue plastic trail markers nailed into trees. Why hadn't Steve taken it along yesterday? It didn't matter. He squeezed the device in his hand like a talisman, feeling its protection from disorientation, from directionless wandering.

It was 5:38 a.m. Out the hut's windows, the edge of the world was glowing blue through the falling snow. The sun would be up in about an hour.

The thought of coming light made his hands go shaky and stupid, a countdown to something unidentifiable but horrific. Zach, frustrated by his own nervous inefficiency, by the way he couldn't move as fast or coordinated as his mind told him was necessary, packed and dressed, grateful that though his neck gaiter, mittens, coat, and snow pants all reeked of sweat, saliva, or both, they'd dried overnight. He put his beacon around his waist and set it to transmit. The flip of that switch both silly and responsible, given he was preparing for disaster knowing there'd be no one to receive any signal of distress.

Once bundled, Zach immediately felt a rising creep of perspiration on his neck. He was about to plunge outside when he paused.

The earring. What should he do about the earring?

He went to the bookshelf. The diamond was still behind the books, its trailings looking like the dried-out remains of a tiny jellyfish.

He couldn't leave it where it was. His father might destroy it, or Pike might find it. Maybe he should take it with him?

But the crust on the thing, the hairs? What if he somehow destroyed DNA by having it in his pocket, or it got wet, or he dropped it? He didn't know how it all worked, but the risk of ruin was too high. He'd hide it in the hut, dry, safe, and waiting, somewhere his father and Pike would never look.

Zach scanned the room. On a shelf in the kitchen sat a line of extra paper towel rolls, still in plastic. There was a nearly full roll already open by the sink.

If he hid it inside the packaging of the last in the row, someone would be guaranteed to find it. Not right away, but soon. Because there was no way that in the next day, even two days, their group would use enough paper towels they'd open multiple rolls.

And cleaning supplies struck Zach as a special kind of safe haven. He'd never seen Bram tidy anything but his own car. Pike, Dave, even Russ, they had certainly acted the whole trip like that kind of thing was below them, letting Steve bustle around with no offers to help.

Zach punctured the plastic covering the hollow cardboard tube with his thumb. He tore a blank page out of a paperback, fished a pen from a drawer, and scrawled, "This belongs to Ginny George, murdered in this hut by Pike Whitlock. Her body is on Mt. Mariah. It is DNA EVIDENCE. My dad Bram Fisher is lying about his business and there is something about insurance please tell the police." Zach printed his name and the date, then after a moment below his name wrote, "I love you, Bonnie." He slid the paper under the earring and its mess so as to avoid disturbing whatever clues it held, folded the paper around it, then slotted the tiny, makeshift package through the hole in the plastic. Before putting the roll back, he smoothed the torn packaging so that the note wouldn't fall out.

Ginny must have been so scared. What would it be like, to look into the face of death and see someone who claimed to love you?

Zach wiped away tears with a sleeve. Forced away thoughts of Ginny's last moments.

He had to go. Had to go down the mountain toward town, toward a cell-phone signal. Toward Bonnie.

A bead of sweat dripped down Zach's spine. He put on his backpack and rushed outside, only remembering the creature that might be waiting there as the door clicked shut behind him.

CHAPTER 32

Each sound was his father and Pike in pursuit, or the monster cracking its knuckles. Every time the storm combed through branches to whistle Zach heard his father's fury, heard the breath of a beast. Because Bram and Pike might soon be behind him. Because whatever had been in that clearing, whatever had killed the elk, had torn Ginny's middle, had to be out here.

One-one-thousand, two-one-thousand.

Zach knew life hid under the deep drifts. Pictured snakes, chipmunks, marmots, bears, all sleeping, all warm and full and safe. And right now Bonnie was sleeping, too, tucked into her bed.

He compulsively checked the GPS to confirm the route and Russ's cell phone to see if he'd descended far enough to get a signal.

About a half hour after leaving the hut, the slow creep of the coming sunlight allowed Zach to pick out a few blue plastic diamonds that showed where the trail undulated ahead along distant slopes. Within an hour he had enough light to spot a refuge under the ground-skimming skirts of an immense pine. Leaving his skis and poles on the trail, he parted the branches and scrambled beneath it, limbs closing behind him like a curtain. Sitting against the pine's trunk on a dry bed of needles, he ate a snack and glugged water, glad for the brief respite from the wind and falling snow, eyes closing at the relief of it.

But they must be awake by now. They might already be following his tracks down the trail. They'd be faster because they were bigger, stronger, could follow in his wake rather than having to figure out the route themselves.

Why had he stopped, why had he risked resting? Zach shook off his lethargy and reemerged into the storm, flakes spinning into his collar and melting along his neck. A half hour of skiing later and he stood at the edge of the same steep, almost treeless expanse he'd crossed the year before with Bonnie and his mother.

He hadn't thought ahead to this part of the trail. On the way up the snow cover had been so thin patches of dirt peeked through, the slope made completely powerless and forgettable. But the sight of it snowed under thickened his throat. Zach squinted across to where his mother had waited, watching, hollowed by the memory of how even then, with so much less snow, they'd dug a pit to test the dangers.

The wind whipped over the open space, made visible in twirling coils of flakes that skittered along the snow's crust. Above, the cornices were immense, weighed down with the new powder.

To cross this treeless zone, to keep moving toward help despite clear signs of avalanche danger, would be both courageous and completely idiotic. Zach slid a few steps backward, the reality of his situation making him feel faint.

He lifted Russ's phone, moving it up, down, around to try to catch the gauzy tip of a signal at a just-right angle. But there was nothing. No reception. No way forward. And he couldn't go back.

What now? The meadow was an impassable river. Zach dazedly checked the GPS as if the earth might have somehow shifted in the seconds since he'd last looked, and traced the steep contours reflected there. Hiking up the slope to cross above or skiing down to traverse below were exhausting, risky prospects. Not only was the terrain steep but there was no guarantee he could safely pass.

The GPS read two below zero. Even getting his feet wet at these temperatures could mean hypothermia. Frostbite. And without aid and comfort, either of those might mean death. Something as simple as a twisted ankle and he might be lost forever.

Zach acknowledged the limits of his own ability to think, to plan, frightened as he was. He'd forgotten the meadow. What else might be slipping through the gaps? The memory of Ginny's body was a cruel reminder that there might not just be dangers he was failing to assess but evils waiting that he had never even conceived of.

Half of the money Bram had talked about was Bonnie's. He needed to get to her. Needed to run. But even the longing that screamed at him to reach his sister, protect her, couldn't shove him onto that meadow. Not with all his mother's careful consideration of the trail here the year before. Not when Shane's loosely broken body twisted in his past.

He'd be no good to Bonnie if he let himself be swept away.

Yesterday Zach had lulled himself into thinking he'd had no choice. No responsibility. That it was safe to ski the Bowl because others said it was safe. Because they said it was logical. But there was no such illusion now. No diffusion of responsibility. It was an impossible traverse because he'd done the mental math and simply couldn't accept the risk.

There was no way through. No way around.

He closed his eyes. Tried not to cry.

He had to go back. He had to hope Russ or Dave would emerge from their drugged state and he could corner one of them alone and play the recording. At some point one of them would go outside to get food from the outdoor pantry or to use the outhouse. Zach could hide easily enough along the tree line, watching and waiting.

It wasn't a good plan, wasn't a totally thought-out plan, but it was the only option he could see. And it felt physically impossible to simply wait, trapped with his back against a clearing of impenetrable snow.

He took another drink from his water bottle, then packed it. Took his skins out of his bag and hurriedly attached them to the bottom of his skis for ascent. Then he followed his own tracks up the trail, faster now despite his uphill direction because he didn't need to use the GPS and markers to locate the path. Faster because he'd already broken trail.

Before each bend Zach paused, listened, his skin tingling with animal terror over the possibility that Bram and Pike might be around the next corner, or the next, following him, chasing him.

He had to get off the trail. Had to figure out a way to get back to the hut without risking running right into his pursuers.

Again he looked at the GPS. On the downhill side, a precipitous drop. A granite outcropping on its uphill flank. No, he couldn't travel off-trail here. But, yes, there! The terrain leveled off ahead in a way that should allow him to cut up off the trail, travel parallel to it in the woods, out of sight, toward the hut.

He put away the GPS and resumed moving uphill.

How to hide his tracks leaving the trail? Only the day before yesterday he'd described the options to Russ as he'd told him about Gray Rabbit: walk in a stream, travel where the snow was already heavily tracked, hide your tracks in someone else's, backtrack, jump far enough off-trail your tracks weren't noticeable, hide somewhere so close to the trail your tracks would go unnoticed.

He'd have to be observant. Find an opportunity.

And he'd forgotten about the shelter. He could hide in the shelter he'd dug out with Russ. Was it close enough to the trail that Bram might not notice the curve of his tracks toward the tree?

A distant noise, and Zach froze, head ticking around as though it was the second hand on a clock, trying to ascertain the source. A light, crunching sound, its direction impossible to discern, which at first seemed to come from behind him, then above, then ahead, as if he were being circled.

The monster.

No, noise could travel strangely outside, move unpredictably in the snow. It wasn't that he was being hunted, it was that his senses weren't reliable when it came to pinpointing a sound through wind, weather, and distance.

Which wasn't particularly comforting.

A voice reverberated through him, far away but distinct, and so recognizable Zach felt acid rise in his throat.

It was his father. And if he was talking, it meant he wasn't alone.

Zach felt fully prey now. More than he'd ever felt playing Gray Rabbit. He trembled, dropping his poles then scrambling to pick them up. Where to hide that they wouldn't find him? How to hide so they wouldn't see his tracks? The question, so theoretical only a moment ago, now constricted his chest, his lungs. He spun through the list of strategies he'd listed for Russ, but there was nowhere to jump, no tracks to hide his own in, no stream to wade through.

His mind leapt to the spot a few minutes back—or how far back? He wasn't sure, with the way his thoughts tumbled, the way his body shook—the spot where he'd looked at the GPS, with that drop on the downhill side. Could he leap over it in a way that left no sign? Hide out of view?

Again a voice rang out and at the sound of it Zach changed direction and rushed downhill, scanning for the place he remembered thinking was too dangerous to go off-trail.

Was he really going to jump off there now?

Behind him voices echoed through the trees, still unintelligible but louder. Closer?

He went around one bend, another, and then, yes—on the long, straight stretch of trail ahead, there it was. He leaned, trying to look over the ledge, careful not to step out of his own tracks.

The drop was so sheer Zach couldn't see where he would land. A dark gray boulder next to the trail vanished out of sight along that drop, reassuring evidence that something, at least, had found earth below. It might work. But it wasn't without risk. There had to be powder down there next to wherever the boulder rested, but there might also be a felled tree. He cowered at the idea of impaling himself on a jutting branch. Or it might be so steep he rolled uncontrollably.

And yet, in the thick weave of trees it was unlikely to slide, and if he did jump far enough without marking the snow, if he did land safely—anyone skiing by, anyone not expecting a person to fling himself bodily over an unknown edge, would only see tracks pointing ahead, and trackless snow to either side.

Zach hurriedly released his bindings, throwing one then the other ski carefully over but to the right of where he wanted to end up. His poles followed. After a moment's thought he threw his backpack as well, hoping that none of the items slid downhill, or would be buried too deep to recover.

That was everything. It was his turn. Zach planted his feet, swung his arms and leapt across the untouched snow and over the edge.

CHAPTER 33

Zach plunged into powder, a gray rock face rushing toward him. His arm shot up reflexively to protect his face, and his elbow and helmet struck the boulder as he landed. He righted himself. Tentatively stretched his arm. It seemed okay. He took in his surroundings. The powder came almost to his waist; had compacted around him when he landed. He removed his helmet. A new divot. Not bad. But his helmet was bright green—too obvious. He partially unzipped his jacket, clutched the helmet to his chest, and zipped his coat over it, then shook his hood free of snow and put it over his head.

At least his coat and pants were black, a kind of camouflage against the rocks and dark trees.

Zach looked up. He'd dropped about four feet onto a small lift of ground that leveled briefly before plunging lower. Lucky. So lucky he closed his eyes in a kind of silent prayer of thanks to the mountain. His eyes were at trail height. He saw with pride that he hadn't made any other marks in the snow as he'd jumped.

A voice echoed through the trees, and Zach crouched, powder sifting onto and around him as he hugged himself tight and tiny. The boulder blocked any uphill view, but when he looked downhill among the weave of aspens and pines he saw snatches of his tracks where they curved around one slope and reappeared at the next, stopping alongside the meadow he'd failed to cross.

If whoever it was passed by him, continued down the trail, he'd be easy to see if they happened to look back.

Startling, he unzipped his coat. Turned off his beacon. Just in case the men had thought to set their own to search in hopes it helped them find him.

A swishing sound and Zach balled tighter and closed his eyes.

It was awful to try to still his shaking and fail. It was awful not to look; not to check the progress of what pursued him. To hear the thunderous beat of his blood and fear others could, too. The voices shifted close, behind him, far away, indistinct and windblown.

Then the men were above him on the trail.

"You don't know, you don't know what he's up to, why the hell would he come out here alone? You said we'd wake up before—"

"Shut up." Bram's voice sounded forced through gritted teeth.

"Don't tell me what to do, you don't tell me—"

Then the voices went vague, muted by the men turning a corner on the trail.

Zach risked opening his eyes. He tentatively raised himself until he could see the trail. Pike and his father had gone out of sight.

Zach made his way through the snow around the boulder, hoping to hide behind it from any chance Bram and Pike might see him if they looked uphill from where the trail curved below. But the far side of the rock was buttressed tight with dirt and snow.

He couldn't get out of sight, the slope he stood on easily visible from the open, dangerous meadow where Zach's tracks ended and Pike and Bram would inevitably stop.

Zach flailed to the divots that indicated where his possessions had landed in the snow. His backpack was simple to find, the other items more challenging, and as he searched for a ski the men came into view. He froze, averting his eyes so as not to make their necks creep.

One-one-thousand, two-one-thousand.

When Zach finally snuck a look they'd gone around another turn in the trail. One ski out, two, a pole. He almost gave up on finding the avalanche probe but at last wrapped a mitten around its thin frame.

He propped his things against the rock. What to do? The snow was falling lighter now, the spot below where the trail met the meadow growing more visible and making him easier to spot, too. How far away was it? Five hundred feet popped into his mind, but he didn't know what that meant, not really, and distances were so difficult for him to gauge looking downhill, around curves of trail and boulders. But it had taken him perhaps fifteen minutes to climb from the meadow to the spot he now stood. That meant that in a few minutes the men would arrive there, see his tracks end, realize he must have somehow evaded them, and look uphill to see if they could spot where he'd gone.

The implications dizzied him. They were too close. He'd never make it back onto the trail and all the way to the hut before they caught up with him.

Maybe he could talk to them? Reassure them. They didn't know he'd recorded their conversation. He could insist he'd only left the hut to go for help. That he was trying to be the hero. He could say he'd figured it all out, and it had all been Shane, and Shane was dead. Which meant nature had taken care of justice, and there was no need to tell the police at all. Because that would only cause Ginny's family pain, Shane's family pain.

You know how it is. How simple it is. The first time you think it, picture it? In a way—it's already done.

Zach's hope chilled. Because although Bram berated Zach, Bonnie, and their mother if they didn't complete a task promptly, precisely, fully, he regularly preached that in the real world everyone took shortcuts, everyone cheated, that anyone who didn't understand perception was reality, didn't know how to bend the rules, was, at the end of the day, a sucker. Bram prided himself on being able to draw the start of the high wire and its end together without ever having to traverse the perilous middle—the place where the actual work was done.

This time, Pike would do that work. This time, Pike was the shortcut. And it would be Pike Bram blamed as he walked away with what he wanted.

No, Zach couldn't stay here. He had nothing to offer up as a substitute for those dull words—trust, inheritance, insurance—that all meant "money." He gritted his teeth in frustration with his ungovernable heart, which even now beat longingly with the hope that Zach was wrong about everything.

But the truth was that what mattered most to his father wasn't him, Bonnie, their mother. It was the admiration of other men. And to Bram, nothing gained the admiration of other men as effectively, as irrevocably, as money.

One-one-thousand, two-one-thousand.

How to scramble back up? He took his helmet out of his coat, clipped it to his backpack, then lifted his pack over his head. Zach nearly fell backward as he pushed the pack onto the flat of the trail. He threw his skis and poles up beside it. Experimentally, he kicked the hard toe of his ski boot into the snowy slope to try for a foothold, but the loose powder gave no purchase. He swiped at the snow clinging to the drop and quickly brought it to dirt and roots. Jammed shallow into the frozen earth, the plastic toes of his ski boots gave him just enough leverage to climb. He clutched roots to use as handholds until he threw himself onto the trail, panting. Powder tumbled down his neck, onto the exposed skin of his ankles and wrists.

He sat up. Movement caught his eye.

Bram and Pike had reached the clearing, their backs to him.

Zach plunged to his stomach and wiggled down into the snow the way he'd seen fish do in ocean sand in nature videos. He waited. Carefully lifted his eyes.

His father was staring back up the trail, pointing uphill with a ski pole.

Zach flattened, feeling as though his ribs vibrated with the speed of his breath and blood.

Bram was probably saying, "He must have turned around." He was probably saying, "He must've retraced his steps."

Or maybe he was saying, "I saw him! He's right there."

Unable to resist the urge to know, to see, Zach tentatively lifted his head. His father and Pike hadn't moved. They stared across the field, then looked back at the trail, gesturing this way and that. They must not have spotted him. Though they were out of earshot, it was clear they were trying to decide what to do.

While Zach's face was somewhat protected by his neck gaiter and hood, the surrounding snow still siphoned the warmth from him, the sweat that slicked down the channel of his spine going cold. He couldn't stay hidden this way for long.

But where could he go? Because if—when—they turned around to find him, he knew they'd overtake him quickly. They were bigger, stronger. There was no conceivable way he could make it back to the hut before them. Again his mind leapt through his Gray Rabbit strategies: hide tracks in other tracks. Backtrack and jump. Walk up a stream. Hide.

Zach recalled the tree he'd paused to eat under on the way down the trail. When he'd scrambled out of its protective branches he'd noticed how low they hung over the trail. Best of all, the tree was uphill, away from Bram and Pike and closer to the hut.

He was already partway there.

Again Zach risked looking in the men's direction. They stood maybe the length of the soccer field at school away, still facing the clearing.

Zach stood, body hunched as if his muscles thought that might better disguise him. He had to clear ice from his bindings with the tip of a pole before he was able to click his boots into his skis, but as soon as he felt them attach he put on his pack and skied up the trail, forcing himself not to look back.

Yet as he reached the curve that would take him out of sight of his father and Pike, he felt the hot breath of a pursuer on his neck; heard the snap of jaws. Awful anticipation drew his eyes irresistibly over his shoulder.

From this new vantage he could see them more clearly. Pike pointed at something downhill. The snow-covered avalanche debris? Bram leaned over to look with apparent interest, Pike behind him.

Then, with a rush of motion, Pike's huge right arm circled to lock around Bram's neck.

Bram's arms flailed, his poles flinging wide and awkward, still looped around his wrists, hands tearing at Pike's forearm, pounding it uselessly. Zach couldn't see either man's face, only the scramble of Bram's legs, the swing of his arms and poles. Bram paused, found his footing, and flung himself backward, his greater height working to his advantage. Off balance, Pike stumbled, releasing his chokehold on Bram, and together they fell, ski poles whipping out stiff from wrists and arms wheeling. Their ski tips shot toward the heavens before landing tangled, still attached to feet. A wordless roar traveled uphill toward Zach. The clumsiness, the splay of the men's skis as they fell, the way Zach couldn't quite see their faces or hear their words at this distance, the powder shooting up around them like a puff of smoke, all gave the assault, the fall to the ground, a kind of cartoonish unreality.

Pike's huge arm rose from the snow to try to wrap around Bram's neck again. But Pike must not have been able to see well from where he lay in the powder underneath Bram, because he couldn't seem to differentiate neck from joint from waist, and as he ineffectively tried to find purchase, Bram, frenzied, managed to roll off and away, kicking hard to free his skis from where they were crossed with Pike's. On his stomach beside his attacker, Bram pushed up to arms and knees, back rounding and falling as he inhaled huge breaths. Had Pike damaged his windpipe, crushed his throat? Pike was a knot of thrashing limbs, the rest of him invisible to Zach in the snow. Bram, hampered by his skis in his attempts at a hands-and-knees scramble to put more distance between him and Pike, twisted stiffly and pawed at his bindings until he was able to release them. He crawled away from Pike on all fours.

It couldn't be real. It couldn't be happening.

Pike sat up then, covered in packed snow that fell away in pieces, one ski still stuck vertically in the snow, and Zach was reminded of how Pike had been buried, the way he'd been coated white then, too.

Both men were yelling, but their words were made indistinct by their fury, by the distance they traveled to reach Zach. Bram hadn't stopped moving, and his arms swept in circles through the snow as though he was searching for something.

Pike managed to reach his ski, release it, and it fell. He leaned over his other leg, frantically digging with his hands, presumably to reach his other boot where it was buried so that he could escape the ski binding, ensure he wasn't trapped there at Bram's mercy.

Bram staggered to his feet some ten feet away from Pike. Then turned and tipped his head at Pike, assessing the situation. The angle of Bram's head as seen from Zach's remove made his father look like a curious child. Despite this, despite being unable to see his father's expression, Zach was sure Bram's face showed a furious resolve, the vengeful grimace of the wronged Underself. Bram moved toward Pike now, feet plunging deep without skis to hold him atop the snow, each step requiring him to pull one leg from it, then the other, and after three repetitions of this Bram unceremoniously belly flopped onto the snow and began crawling again, fast and animal-like, able to move more efficiently with his weight distributed widely.

When he was within reach of the scattered, thrashing Pike, Bram raised onto his knees. Circled his arm back, up, then forward in a way that reminded Zach of a baseball pitcher's arcing rotation, the similarity growing all the stronger and stranger when he realized that his father was clutching an object in his hand. At the apex of that motion there was a quiver, the thinnest of hitches, before Bram's arm continued down, down, down toward Pike, and the thing in his father's hand connected with Pike's face. A thin howl reached Zach uphill before Pike's arm rounded out at Bram, fist connecting with cheekbone. Bram fell backward, and Pike sideways.

A wild upkick of snow as both men scrambled, Pike's ski removed at some point without Zach realizing. The men faced each other, heavy breaths creating a wraith of white mist between them, and Zach had no fear of them noticing him at all, not now when they were only able to see each other.

As if obeying some unspoken command, they fell upon each other, trying to land punches while unstable in the snow, swatting, ski poles still dangling from Pike's wrists to catch and interrupt his movements. They toppled, flailed, sprang up again, swung wide. Their helmets crashed together with a dim thud.

Zach watched, confused, disoriented, the entire scene too darkly ridiculous to be real, the violence so awkward, so unpracticed, so utterly different from anything he could have expected.

In the chaos, his father's gloves had vanished and Pike's helmet had gone off-kilter. Bram knocked the helmet from Pike's head with the butt of his bare hand, Pike's goggles flying away with it.

For a moment the blood trickling down bright red from Pike's cheek in the midst of an all-gray world was the only thing Zach could see.

This time Bram showed no hesitation as his right arm flew through the air and down, striking the top of Pike's skull. From where Zach stood the vicious impact of the round, gray object Bram held in a bare hand was silent, and Zach only heard it as the hard grit of his own teeth as he reacted to his father hitting Pike's skull again, and again, and—

Pike flung out his arms and wrapped them around Bram's waist in a desperate, suffocating hug, both of them stumbling, tripping on the snow, their knees going soft, and then they fell together out of sight off the trail's edge and down the wooded slope that Zach thought had been too steep to descend to go around the avalanche path.

Zach couldn't make himself move. He felt separate from things, as if he'd watched a poorly staged play.

But the unreality of it all was punctured by the awful spray of red left behind on the snow. By the object Bram had held, which Zach was pretty sure was what he now stared at, laying like a dark smear on the spot where the men had fought.

Was it a rock?

At that moment an arm clawed over the trail's edge. Then another. His father's face reared up. His eyes met Zach's across the distance. And all at once, Zach was part of things again.

Bram, blank-faced, lifted his hand in a wave.

CHAPTER 34

Father and son were still, each seer and seen. Zach stared at Bram's raised hand. A hand that had done irrevocable things. A hand that had ripped a line between a before and an after.

Despite knowing that Bram hadn't been first to strike, the idea of being near his father, being anywhere in reach of that raised hand, caused a cold, rough tongue of fear to drag across Zach's insides.

He turned his back on Bram and fled uphill.

His father yelled something, words drowned by the remove, by the blood thundering through Zach's ears. A turn in the path and Bram's voice faded. Another and it was gone altogether.

Zach's breathing was ragged, uneven, and he realized he was crying. But he pressed upward, his muscles, his gut, his heart raging with the physical need to go to ground.

With no sense whatsoever of how far he'd traveled or for how long, he spotted the tree he'd eaten under. It grew straight and even from the slope of the path's uphill side. Its downhill limbs extended partially over the trail. The tracks that passed it swung slightly wide to avoid these branches.

As Zach approached, he couldn't see signs he'd previously taken refuge there. Any earlier markings made when he'd ducked under the tree had been disguised by the messy arcs the lowest limbs traced along the powder as they blew in the wind.

He popped out of his skis. Without them distributing his weight, his boots sunk into the snow. If his father looked closely he'd see these footprints, these deep holes in the ski tracks and get suspicious, wouldn't he?

But there was nothing Zach could do about that.

Zach shoved one ski, then the other, then his poles through the boughs to land on the protected ground below the tree. They were satisfyingly difficult to see draped in the shadows.

He left his backpack on, took down his hood, clipped on his helmet, and put on his goggles to protect his eyes from the scrape of pine boughs. Then he parted the branches and took an enormous step over the tree-scratched powder and through the limbs. Unsteadied by the shift in weight and the resistance of the branches, he nearly fell, but managed to seize a limb tight and lever himself forward until he crashed through.

He lay on the ground under the skirts of the tree, resting a beat as the dry pine smell surrounded him.

One-one-thousand, two-one-thousand.

He sat up. A hot line of pain let him know he'd scraped his cheek. He touched it lightly as he peered through the branches toward the trail. His back foot must have dragged along the powder, leaving a shallow line in the snow from the ski tracks to where he now hid.

Zach took hold of a branch and moved it experimentally back and forth. As it swept through the snow, its markings obscured part of the line.

More confident now, he did the same with another branch, then another after that. Snow fell from the tree to pockmark the powder, and the branches' tips roughed the signs he'd left behind.

He paused. If someone was paying enough attention, they might find the number of half circles traced by the branches odd. But if his father was rushing? It looked okay. Okay enough he probably shouldn't do any more.

Zach dragged his things to the opposite side of the tree's shelter to avoid their colors catching his father's eye. He wedged his backpack against the tree trunk as a kind of pillow and rested against it.

No longer in motion, Zach's shivering intensified. The snow that had worked its way into his collar and cuffs as he hid in the powder had left both pain and numbness behind. And his mind clamored, now that he was still, with the unendurable reality he'd deferred fully facing.

His father was planning to kill him.

The tears sprang up again, the vicious answer to the unanswerable "why" of it throbbing painfully through his mind. Why? Because Zach had never been and could never be good enough. He'd failed to earn his father's love. Failed to prove a worth greater than whatever Bram could trade him for. Which meant Bram would toss Zach's body like an offering into the fathomless maw of his greed. His chest strained with the immensity of his shortcomings, with fear for his sister if he wasn't there to take the brunt of Bram's disappointment.

If Zach had only done things right, better, gotten a little closer to perfect?

I don't think you ever did. Love us. I don't think you can.

His heart stuttered at the thought of his mother. Was something broken in Bram? And if so, did that mean there was nothing broken in Zach?

Maybe it was as simple as Russ had said. Bram was selfish. So selfish he'd do anything to get exactly what he wanted.

Zach wrapped his arms tight around his knees and closed his eyes. In his head the hut filled with the chattering mothers, the chaos of children. He groaned aloud at the longing that rolled through him. For fire, warmth, affection. To be by Russ in the hut. To be near his mother. He'd never had to worry about earning her love, yet she hadn't loved him enough to stay. She'd trained them to survive but had chosen to die. Or else she hadn't cared enough to fight her addiction, allowing herself to go unconscious, slip under, and leave them behind.

Adults burned the world down, threw their children into that fire, and as they warmed themselves they told each other it couldn't be helped, it wasn't their fault, it had all been necessary, that there had never been any other way.

Zach's balled fists wiped away his tears. He wouldn't obediently allow himself to be used for ends and sacrificed to things he couldn't see, couldn't name, didn't understand. He'd done that his whole life, but never again. Not when his sister was at stake.

He would do as his mother said but not as she did. He'd survive, he'd never willingly leave Bonnie behind. Never leave Bonnie to remember him the way he had to remember their mother, tousling his hair at the hut, *Good morning, Zakky,* because she knew he got embarrassed if she hugged him in front of other kids. Why had he ever been embarrassed? His mother's grin, her cheering as he finished a race. Her expression of wonder as they'd found the miner's cabin.

Zach straightened, eyes snapping open. The cabin.

It instantly became the den that would protect him from all things. He'd been stupid to think he could get back to the hut and hide without his father catching up to him, finding him, spotting his tracks. And after what Zach had just witnessed he saw a new unpredictability, new stakes. Even if he played Dave the recording, even if Dave believed him, there might be violence.

But in the cabin? No one could reach him in that fairy-tale, unfindable place. Almost no one had ever found it, hidden among overhanging trees, buttressed by the steep cliff that ran behind it, wrapped in mysterious spells and magic. Zach had the inexplicable certainty that even the miner's ghost would watch over him, happy to be needed after more than a hundred years.

It was far away. It would be cold. But it had solid walls and a potbelly woodstove his mom had thought looked functional. If he could light a fire there, he could survive. He wouldn't put himself, Dave, and Russ in any danger. He could avoid his father altogether and simply wait out the time until rescue. From the cabin he'd be able to hear any helicopter, any snowmobile coming to find them; he'd be close enough to quickly head downhill toward the hut. He could even watch the hut, hidden along the tree line near the cabin.

And help would come. It would come because Steve hadn't checked in with his team. Because Shane and Jon wouldn't arrive home. Because Dave and Russ wouldn't return to Russ's new stepmother. When help came he'd be safe, a wall of strangers between him and his father, the phone pressed into the hands of someone in charge.

Now he understood why in scary movies people always did such stupid things. It was impossible to focus when you were listening for the huff of a scenting beast; for the exhale of a man so much stronger than you. The cabin was the obvious choice, and he should've settled on it earlier.

A cold blade of wind shrieked through the forest, yet another reminder of all the things that wanted to lay claim to his body.

And through it, a crunching sound.

Zach forced himself still. He'd seen a snowshoe hare from a ski lift once, only spotting it because the animal had suddenly bounded across the open snow. In motion, it became a rabbit. When motionless, it transformed into a single black eye.

And here he was, a skittish rabbit, dressed in black, hiding in shadows from a predator. Zach squeezed his eyes shut.

The sound drew closer, pulling deep at the place behind Zach's temple the same way the noise of a rusty hinge did.

Behind his eyelids a monster's talons ripped flesh and brought it to a lipless mouth; a dull rock began to glisten with blood as it rose and fell.

A wheezing, a creaking. It had to be his father, yet all Zach could imagine was a whip-tailed creature sniffing the air, searching for him. It parted the branches, razor teeth luxuriating with anticipation as they hovered, about to sink into his neck.

A *pock-pock* of poles or hooves puncturing the windblown crust of snow. A *woosh* of skis or of dank, clotted fur skimming over powder.

Zach squinted through one eye, which instinctually fixed on motion.

It was not his father.

A shadow, close to the ground, detached then fused with the gloom of the trees on the opposite side of the trail. It floated above the snow, low and fast but still indistinct between the branches, size impossible to gauge from Zach's vantage. Was that a thick switch of brown fur? A flash of golden skin? A bristled, spiny back? Zach closed his eyes against the sight of it, a whimper slipping from him, body pushed hard against the tree trunk to hide from the thing, make himself invisible. Could it smell him, was it even now doubling back to strip his eye sockets, crush his chest?

Zach listened to the crack of trees, the strange instrumentals of the wind through the woods, until at last he forced his body to break its clenching tension. Opened an eye.

Nothing but hibernating forest. Nothing to hear but the rapid thrash of his heart.

But there, along the trail lay hollows that the thing's feet, its hands, had left behind.

Zach didn't dare emerge from his hiding place to check if they were the same clawed tracks he and Russ had seen in the woods.

The idea of waiting here relying on nothing but hope and a scrim of branches to protect him as his father passed by or the monster doubled back was utterly unbearable.

With a shaking hand, Zach clicked through the GPS options, and assigned an "X" to where he thought the cabin sat, just above a flat area that had to be the meadow with its mine, backed by the tight topographic lines indicating the cliff behind it. Two miles and change away.

Not as far as he'd assumed. But with the obstacles, the grade of the slope, and the way he'd have to turn the climb into easier to manage switchbacks, very far. But he craved action and movement so desperately it was almost a compulsion. He'd escape, hide his tracks, by crawling out from the back of the tree. He could begin his trek uphill there. Neither Bram or the creature should be able to see his tracks that far away from the trail.

How much time did he have? Why hadn't his father passed by yet? He had to be drawing a curtain over the horror he'd left behind. Pike stiffening, pushed downhill where the cold water of a hidden stream ran over him, his blood irrigating it red.

Zach forced himself through the branches out into the snow. In motion again, in possession of a plan, a wing of hope beat through him.

CHAPTER 35

The light was low through the storm by the time Zach found himself face-to-face with the carved board memorializing the Swede. The steep and onerous climb over felled trees, around rocks, had been further slowed by Zach needing to constantly adjust his route to avoid small cliff faces and areas too vertical to make progress, and the aches from his injuries and exertions the day before had increased with every step, although his slow progress largely kept him from getting short of breath. The GPS read just after 3:00 p.m. How long had he been hiking? Zach had been so focused on navigating he couldn't recall when he'd started uphill. But it was later than he'd expected, given that Pantheon Hut now lay only a half-hour's ski below him, and his trip downhill this morning had taken maybe an hour and a half.

It didn't matter. All that mattered was that he was here before it got dark. Before it got really cold.

Zach ran a hand over the sign, knocking snow from the words, trying to confirm it was real, to accept that the cabin was close, that he'd get to rest soon.

He scanned the area where he remembered the mine shaft

waited, a sneering, dangerous emptiness. The heavy snowdrifts had reduced its mouth to a small, benign puddle.

Zach shivered. There were so many unknowable, unseeable dangers in the world. He pressed uphill and in minutes stood in front of the cabin, only a sliver of it visible between the snow on the ground and the feet of powder on the roof.

He sagged in relief. He was safe.

Though could anywhere really be safe?

Zach swung the door inward and peered through the gloom.

He bit his lip hard at seeing "Zach + Grace, 2021" written on the wall opposite the door. The words had gone as gray as all the other carved names and dates. He'd scratched his name in the wood yesterday. He'd done it a million years ago. He'd written it in a different life entirely.

But he'd made it. His mom would have been proud.

And the creature wouldn't find him here. It had become ever less a monster as he climbed, put distance between himself and whatever stalked the mountain. It was an animal. Just some animal. Not one he could identify, but what did he know? He'd thought human lives couldn't be exchanged for money. He'd thought his father and Pike were normal men.

He didn't know anything.

After the exertion of his climb, every touch of wind brought pain. But if he lit a fire would it give away his position? If it stayed cloudy, smoke would be hard to see. And once it got dark?

Zach was so unbearably cold that it didn't matter. Fire was a necessity.

The frozen air, the ache of his punctured neck and bruised side, all his misery latched so deep he felt sure he'd never heal or be warm again. And the knowledge of everything he had to do before he could rest, could sleep, made tears eke out.

It had been such a grueling climb.

He had to focus on the fire. On the possibility of warming up. Sleeping.

One-one-thousand, two-one-thousand.

Because one side of the cabin was encased in a drift, Zach was able to simply ski up onto the roof. He knocked snow off the chimney with a mitten, then poked inside the pipe with his unfolded avalanche probe. It slid in easily, then hit something. Zach stirred the probe around with a *clink, clink, clink* of metal on metal until he heard and felt something dislodge and fall into the woodstove below with a soft *whumph*.

A chipmunk's winter food cache, dead leaves?

He fed the probe farther down the chimney until he hit the stove's bottom. He rattled it around, up, down, but there was only the shiny clang of metal.

It was as cleared as he could get it. It might be safe.

Zach folded the probe and skied to the edge of the glade, looking for any dead branches he could snap off, any dry wood that might be hiding under canopies or beneath fallen trees. The pickings were thin; most of the wood wet, moldy, or alive, all of which would create little heat and cause billows of smoke. He had no way to cut any large pieces smaller so they might fit into the stove. Every time he found wood he thought might be burnable, might light, Zach threw it inside the cabin, growing less and less selective as the sun lowered and the world grew ever more frigid around him.

At last he admitted he was too cold to keep searching. He relieved himself, hoping that his bladder wouldn't force him outside again, took off his skis and poles and leaned them against the wall, then sat on the snow and dropped off its ledge into the cabin, shutting the door behind him.

Though it was only four o'clock now and still light outside, the cabin was almost completely black, illuminated only by the beam of his headlamp and a sliver of dim, fading sunlight that cut through the one tiny window. Zach stomped his wet boots. Knocked snow from his coat and mittens.

Everything looked the same. The half-broken bed, the miner's boots leaning beneath a chair. The rusted cup with its rusted utensils. The smell of mushrooms, metal, and faraway rot. The same sense of being tucked into a spellbound refuge. And though the door didn't lock, though he knew his tracks led straight to this place, though he could feel the air whistle through the unpatched chinks studding the place, he felt lighter. Felt a safety that was unfamiliar, new, wrapped tight by his aloneness, by the low ceilings and close cabin walls.

Zach opened the stove. His stirrings above had dislodged a mouse nest. An old one, because among bits of stolen quilt and a mass of leaf fragments were skulls the size of his pinkie nail. Bones tiny as pins.

What had happened to the mother mouse that they'd been left behind this way?

Zach decided to leave the remains where they were, not wanting to touch them. But also because what was left of that nest was dry, and might make decent kindling.

He inspected the chimney pipe. No rusted-through holes visible. No openings along its seams. Zach removed his mittens and ran his hands around it, the metal a new level of bitter cold, but his fear of smoke, of dying the way his never-known half brother had, was more intense than his need even for warmth. He felt no thin spots or punctures. He'd have to watch closely, see if any smoke escaped into the room. Tried not to think about what he'd do if smoke did slip out, and he was forced to sleep here with no fire to avoid suffocation.

The room was so still, so frozen and silent, it felt as though he'd been swallowed by a creature that now cruised ocean depths.

Zach stacked the wood in the stove, adding all but two of the fire starters he'd packed due to the wood's wet condition. With a grind of metal he forced open the stove's intake vent, using the blade of his emergency kit folding knife as a lever. For a moment, the orange flare of the camping match blinded him to all else. He touched the match to the fire starters and with a *woosh* light traveled over the starters, the branches, and the dead things in the mouse nest. It all released a noxious, moldering smoke Zach closed the iron door against. He scanned the potbelly stove's chimney with his headlamp. No signs of leaking smoke. A slow but growing heat. A creep of firelight through the vent at the stove's bottom.

Zach warmed his hands. The cloud cover, the snowfall, should disguise any billowing smoke. And his father was probably back inside the hut for the night, where the lights were on and the fire going and brightness made it difficult to see anything outside at all. He'd be tending to Dave's worries, explaining what happened to Pike. Pretending to be concerned about Zach.

In all the stories in school, the stories in church, the bad people lost. But in real life, the cruelest people always seemed to get exactly what they wanted.

Zach rubbed his eyes. He needed to sleep. Needed to lie down and erase himself from things for a little while.

He unpacked Steve's sleeping bag. Although the cabin's damaged bed still had bits of mattress and old quilt on it, he could smell the fabric's corrosion, its oddly chemical-scented decay, and so unrolled the sleeping bag on the floor.

Within the growing perimeter of the stove's warmth Zach changed clothes, his base layer soaked through with sweat and snowmelt yet again. He put on Steve's too-big dry things and hung his own long underwear to dry. With the fire going well now, he filled the stove with as much wood as could fit inside so that it could burn as long as possible, warming him as he slept.

Zach slid into the cold nylon of Steve's sleeping bag. He tightened into a ball around Mr. Fantastic and gazed up at the outline of where his long underwear hung on the back of the old miner's chair. His mother always said staying dry and hydrated were paramount in the outdoors. When Bram had raged at Pike after he'd swung at Zach, the boy had seen it as protection. But now Bram's actions were recast as territorial, and the small, boring tendings his mother had taught him shone with the light of true love, true protection.

Tomorrow morning he'd hide to watch the hut from the edge of the forest, so he wouldn't be forgotten by rescuers. Behind Zach's closed eyes, a helicopter landed and he popped out of the forest, *Surprise!* His father's jaw dropped, eyes bugging to say *How could it be?* as Dave and Russ celebrated his resurrection. A mustachioed Mountain Rescue man wearing a badge like an old-timey sheriff patted him on the back as he said, *Here's a recording of everything, sir, and there's DNA proof hidden in the hut.*

He wasn't quite sure how DNA worked, but he'd seen television so knew it was important. Incontrovertible. Came from blood and nails and . . .

Zach rolled over in the sleeping bag, uncomfortable. The chill of his body kept him awake despite the exhaustion that pressed his bones. He eyed the half-broken chair, the bed in pieces.

That all might make good firewood. Why hadn't he thought of that? Nervous over these signs of his own errors, Zach switched his headlamp on and swung its beam over the stovepipe and around the body of the potbelly stove. No leaking tendrils of smoke.

Unlike his classmates, unlike the other children on his mother's

PTA trips, he'd never liked the fire-building part of outdoor education. He'd dutifully learned how to efficiently light a fire in bad conditions (rain, snow, ice) and good (in a fireplace, in a stove), but that instruction had always come with ghosts. Because although neither he nor his mother ever said it, Zach knew they both felt haunted by his father's other, better family every time they lit a fire. Watched it lick wood black.

But here there were no leaks. No smoke. It should be okay.

He switched off his headlamp.

It would all be okay.

CHAPTER 36

Agust of wind swept over Zach's face. Was that what had woken him? Had the cabin's door blown open? The fire had nearly gone out. Zach was about to draw out his hand to grope for the headlamp when a low, creaking sound stilled him.

There was something in the room with him.

His hands clutched around Mr. Fantastic as he strained to listen, to convince himself that he'd only heard the wind, the creak of the cabin straining against the weather.

But the even, sandy hiss of it was unmistakably the in and out of breathing lungs.

Zach couldn't move, even as his mind screamed that if cornered, to survive a predator you were supposed to make yourself look big, and just as his mother had done with the bear on the trail, talk loud and low to let the beast know you were human; that you weren't its normal prey.

Zach repressed a shudder. Did those rules even apply for whatever thing had killed and stripped the elk? Gnawed Ginny to bone? Left those humanlike handprints behind in the snow? Maybe a predator like that, something that materialized out of dark skies, silent black airships, maybe a beast like that could see in the dark. Was right now extending a long, thin claw.

Or maybe it was his father, ready to wipe him from the world in exchange for riches and the admiration that would come with them. Maybe it was Pike, not dead at all, preparing to take vengeance on the boy who had discovered his evil.

Body still as a rabbit, Zach's eyes sought a route for flight. And as he stared, as the blotches of firelight faded from his pupils, he saw that the door was open, a wedge of dark blue against the cabin's black, and that this small bit of moonlight was broken by the inky shape of an amorphous silhouette moving slightly side to side, unsteady on its feet.

Zach pressed a hand over his lips to stifle any sound. Seen from his spot on the floor, the thing's height appeared unnatural, its head skimming the roof. It undulated in the cold, a darkness on a darkness.

Immediately Zach thought of the shape-shifting creature he'd seen climbing Mount Mariah. The formless, changeable monster he'd spotted twice now in the woods.

A light swishing noise as Zach unconsciously shrugged himself deeper into his sleeping bag. The thing went still at the sound, then lurched, its approach exploding Zach's heart into panic.

A wordless yelp tore from him, and then to his surprise, his own voice, high and clear, sounded through the room. "My—my name is Zach. I am human. I am a person. I am not prey. My name is Zach."

The thing paused.

Hope inflated in him at the way the creature had halted, at the way his mother's instructions were working. Louder and lower now he said, "My name is Zach Fisher. I am a person."

A guttural roar ripped through the cabin, tilting Zach's world into the unknowable. The thing leapt and Zach folded around the sudden pain of violent contact with his middle—a hoof, a cloven foot, a densely furred hand crusted with dried blood—something had hit him in the stomach, taken the air from him, had crushed a rib, or stabbed him or—

Then the thing went low, was all around him, the darkness of it obliterating everything else as Zach writhed, tried to breathe around the pain, a stuck worm. The violence was so unprecedented, the intensity of the hurt so sudden and new, that his mind couldn't accept it, even as his body absorbed it. Zach inhaled the sweet, sweaty reek of the monster as it lifted the head of the sleeping bag into the air. Separate from himself now, he felt his body rolling, tumbling into the tight, narrow bottom of the sarcophagus-shaped bag. The nylon, the soft fill of it, pressed against Zach's mouth so tight that he was suffocating, suffocating in complete darkness before the thing released the bag, released him to slam to the floor, his nose hitting the floorboards through the fabric and synthetic fill with an awful *crick* sound that was somehow both sharp and muted, the blood stopping up his nostrils, the pain punctuating his vision with white splotches. Zach turned his head and gasped, open-mouthed, only able to get the smallest sip of air because the press of the fabric, the hurt of his middle, the blood flowing from his nose blocked everything but asphyxiation. He groped at his face and the blood wet his fingers. He pushed those fingertips against the nylon to gain a wisp of distance between mouth and fabric, pressed a palm to the bag's inside trying to find where he could stick his head out, breathe cool air again, unrestricted, every movement pulling deep at the new, stabbing pains in his side, his nose.

He couldn't speak. Couldn't even moan.

And yet his mind rebelled against the idea of his own impotence, his own vulnerability, hands still making space to breathe and searching, scratching, for the bag's opening.

In every direction there was only slick fabric, the newly bloodied fur of Mr. Fantastic, the helplessness of his own small body.

There was so little air.

Above his head a tight gathering of fabric. The opening? He pushed against it, against the nylon around him, frantically, wildly, crazed by the need to breathe.

And then he understood. He was trapped. The monster, Pike, his father, had somehow cinched the top of the sleeping bag closed, sealing him in like trash in a tied plastic bag. An enormous, venomous spider had wound him in sticky silk so tight he could barely breathe. It would puncture him with its fangs. Suck him dry as its needled legs forced him still and utterly helpless in this awful, suffocating trap where his breath condensed the fabric to wetness, where his blood washed things slippery, where—

One-one-thousand, two-one-thousand.

He cupped his hands in front of his face to create an air pocket, as if those hands could generate oxygen between mouth, nose, and the sticky sleeping bag.

A dragging noise, right by his head. Something big but an oddly soft sound. A tail tracing along the ground? A clicking. Steps? Two or four legs? It was impossible to tell, everything muffled. Zach strained to listen, his skin, pained breath, his tender hurt places, all torturous reminders of how trapped he was, how exposed, that hurt could come at any moment, anywhere, from any direction.

A metallic creak. The stove door? The thing cracking its knuckles? Taking out a weapon?

A grunt, deep and rough. Another sound like a voice, but also not, came through unintelligible, stifled by the stagnant cocoon of the sleeping bag.

Utter blackness surrounded him. Zach tentatively rubbed his

nose, hoping to clear it so he might breathe a little easier, then recoiled from the bitter pain of his own touch.

A rotting, sulfurous smoke scent forced what little air there was to noxiousness. Zach tucked his face into his underarm, but even through his damaged nose the smell crawled over him, inescapable, choking. A screech from what had to be his attacker, whatever language it might be using, whatever animal instinct it exhaled, transformed by the layers of the sleeping bag into a sound of primal anger.

At once Zach was weightless. The shock of being swept into the air again emptied his lungs, stole away all thought, the vicious damage to his ribs the only pinpoint of reality in the whole world.

The thing shook the bag, as if checking for signs of life, then dropped him. This time Zach landed on his back and felt strangely grateful to the creature for not slamming his nose again, not further damaging him in this second plunge to earth.

It would be hard for Bonnie, him dying. He felt sure, there in the suffocating darkness, in the hot misery of the bloodied bag, that it would be more difficult for Bonnie if she lost him than it would be for Zach himself if he died, because dying couldn't be much different from what he felt now. Buried, sightless, twisted, desperate for breath. The rest had to be more of the same, and then the bliss of no more pain. And it wasn't so bad. It wasn't so terrible, for him, because it was inconceivable this suffering could continue much longer.

But for Bonnie? Bonnie without Zach there as Bram's scapegoat. Bonnie, whose longing for their mother had made her go sunken around the eyes. Bonnie, who had so much trouble sleeping she had to snuggle next to him to find any kind of peace. Bonnie, Bram stalking around her, picking away at her, waiting for his opportunity to wash her from existence.

Zach couldn't make himself move or utter a sound, could only listen for how things would end. How relief might come. He was sorry only for his sister, and the ways he'd failed her. Surely the bag would open before things finished, and at least then he'd get a last breath of pure, cold air.

Silence. Stillness.

He wiggled. Pushed against the confines of the bag. Listened.

No response. No sound.

Had the creature left him? His father would never leave a task undone this way. It had to be Pike, the monster, who had attacked. Was it stalking outside now, looking for—what? A place to lay him out on the snow like the elk, like Ginny?

He could still only manage tiny breaths of the fetid air, nose and mouth filled with blood, sweat, the decayed smoke scent. It was too hot, the bag too filled with his own exhalations.

Zach saw Shane, broken, pale, hands gripped over his mouth, and this vision of asphyxiation came on so viscerally he went wild, thrashing uselessly, mind screaming, hopeless sobs cut short only because the deep sucking motion of crying pulled the nylon tight as a plastic bag around his mouth.

One-one-thousand, two-one-thousand.

It wasn't like being trapped under ice and snow. Some air had to get through the fabric, the zipper. Maybe he could undo whatever the thing had done to trap him?

Hampered by his hurt ribs, Zach groped above and around his head. Again he found where the fabric gathered into a cinched knot above the crown of his skull. It was tight. He couldn't even wedge a pinkie finger through. How was that possible?

He felt for the zipper, found the interlocked line of its teeth and followed it with a fingertip, hoping to hit the zipper back so that he could try to force it down; unzip the bag from the inside.

The hard plastic line vanished into where the bag was secured at the top. Zach whimpered. The zipper's pull had to be trapped outside where the bag had been sealed—useless. Unlike his mother's sleeping bag, which also had a zipper pull at the bottom so that it was easier to control temperature, to stick out a foot or leg if you were overwarm, his child's sleeping bag only zipped from the top down.

But this wasn't his bag. It was Steve's.

Zach's fingers traced the zipper down to his hip and could reach no farther. He squeezed his eyes tight against the pain as he shuffled his body down farther into the bag. The zipper still continued past his reach. He winced. He was going to have to bend to reach farther down.

The possibility that his search would result in all hope of freedom being lost made him retch in fear, the hot claustrophobia so complete that again he kicked out, only stopping because of the pain.

One-one-thousand, two-one-thousand.

He shifted bit by agonizing bit, ribs a torture, nose a throb. It was only possible to bend into the narrowest section at all because the sleeping bag was made for an adult. He paused frequently to push the fabric from his face, to try to breathe through the panic as the air grew ever tighter.

Zach's thumb and forefinger gripped the zipper's tab for several seconds before he fully absorbed what he'd found, and then he cried out in relief, body shuddering with gratefulness that this was real, that it was in his hand, that he might, just might, escape.

There was no pull on the inside of the bag, forcing Zach to use his fingernails to drag the small, flat piece of plastic along the zipper. As difficult as that was he still pulled too quickly, snagging nylon in the mechanism an inch down, immobilizing it, forcing him to carefully, so carefully, undo his progress and zip the bag back up, the pressure on his fingernail as he worked to free it of the nylon pure frustration. Once he managed to undo the catch of fabric, he unzipped tooth by tooth, an agonizing slowness.

At five inches, he felt frozen air flood in. Salvation. Zach wrestled a hand out and pulled the zipper from the outside, awkward but infinitely easier, until he rolled out of the sleeping bag onto the dusty floor.

Sweat plastered his hair to his skull; his long underwear clung wet to his body. Blood spilled over his mouth and chin. He gulped in deep breaths. Blinked out at the room as if seeing the world for the first time.

He made out his headlamp close by on the floor, so fastened it to his head and switched it on. Immediately he saw and snatched up his water bottle. Drained it. Set it beside him. He wiped the blood from his face with the back of his hand, avoiding touching his nose. Already feeling the way the air crept icy at his skin, Zach cocooned the unzipped sleeping bag around him as he took in the room.

Mayhem surrounded him. The thing had emptied his backpack, flinging his belongings in every direction. The tattered, rodent-gnawed miner's blanket lay partly on the floor, but a section of it had landed in the potbelly stove, tendrils of smoke rising.

That explained the toxic smell. The old wool, saturated with mouse-leavings, had smothered whatever fire had remained.

Light fell on the end of the sleeping bag blanketed over him. The sight of how he'd been trapped redoubled his trembling, a deep nausea rolling from his belly and the room's disarray instantly taking on a human menace.

Someone had tied the sleeping bag closed with a silicone ski strap.

CHAPTER 37

Zach drew a finger along the band as if to verify its existence. Yes, it was one of the promotional straps Steve had handed out to the group that first day. It might even be the extra strap that had been in Zach's own pack.

It had to have been Bram who attacked him, bruised his middle, broke his nose. His father who cinched him tight to smother him, suffocate him.

Yet Zach was still alive. Would his father have left him that way? Half broken yet still breathing, Zach provided no benefit to Bram whatsoever. Maybe Pike had clambered up that cliff and pursued Zach.

Maybe he simply didn't understand the monster.

Zach thought back to his paralysis, his inability to speak, as he'd been dropped to the ground.

Maybe his father did think he was dead.

He closed his eyes, disoriented. Every beat of his heart hurt his nose. Every breath felt like a kick to his hurt side.

Bram, Pike, the monster—why had it pulled the blanket through the room and left a corner stinking and smoking in the extinguished stove? What had it been searching for as it dumped Zach's things on the floor? Maybe Bram had realized the earring was gone and thought Zach had taken it. Maybe Russ had tattled that Zach had his phone, and his father or Pike realized he might have recorded them.

His thoughts buzzed and dropped like a radio station gone out of range. Did he have a concussion? He needed to focus. Because none of the strangeness of the scattered things, the blanket in the stove, really mattered. Not when his attacker might come back, bringing more pain. Worse pain.

A hand to his middle, Zach stood and limped to the door. He tried to shut it against the wind and the approaching dawn, but as he pushed it swept up the snow that must have tumbled inside when the thing entered, making it difficult to fully close. Zach leaned his back on the door, let his weight fall against it, until he could fasten the simple wooden latch. The immediate cut in the wind clawing its way through the cabin, the sense that something, at least, lay between him and the menace of whatever had only just left, allowed him to think, to assess.

His shirt was stiffening, the blood on it already beginning to freeze. His teeth clattered.

The pants he'd hung to dry had landed halfway under the bed. The shirt was still over the chair where he'd left it. He gathered them up.

How many times in the last forty-eight hours had he been forced to remove wet clothing from wet skin, put on a dry but dirty base layer? Zach sagged with exhaustion over the endless cycle of self-preservation he'd somehow fallen into, an inescapable loop.

His pants were easy to remove, turning inside out as he flopped them off his feet. The shirt was far more difficult, and Zach let himself weep with the agony of pulling the bloodied shirt over his head and putting on the dry one.

Maybe the monster had broken his rib. Cracked him. Like it had done to Ginny.

The clothes didn't feel fully dry. Not really. But they were in far better condition than what he'd removed, and he felt warmer almost immediately.

A hard coughing seized him, slicing through his muscles, his lungs, his face. The smoke from the smoldering blanket was irritating, the stench growing denser now that the door was closed. The whole cabin creeped with the potential return of the beast, with the awful burned rot.

Where could he go? There was nowhere at all that was warm. He'd have to hide in the tree line, watch the hut, wait for rescuers to show. Try for the hideout he and Russ had dug under the tree, the only possibility for safe shelter he could think of.

Zach picked up his coat from where it lay twisted on the floor, and as he gingerly put it on his headlamp reflected off an object almost completely hidden by the wool blanket. Russ's phone. His attacker must not have noticed the phone falling from Zach's coat pocket during the crazed search through the cabin, or hadn't cared enough about the phone to take it. The screen lit as Zach picked it up: 5:51 in the morning, 10 percent battery left.

The absence of the familiar lump in his coat alerted him that his emergency kit was gone, too. It had been zipped in. Had his father or Pike taken it, searched it for the earring there? An awful longing for the kit constricted his heart, because it had been a gift from his mother. A quick swipe of his headlamp around the room, and he saw it open next to the woodstove, contents spilling out. While shoving them back in he frowned. The camping matches were missing. In his exhaustion had he used them the night before?

But he didn't need them. And he was wasting time.

His shaky fingers struggled to slip the kit, the phone, into a pocket. His whole body felt somehow distant yet its pain so very present, the cold daggering through him, every creak of wind the creature's frozen claw down his spine. He picked his way through the room, toeing things aside rather than bending over to sort through them to find what he needed, because any movement of his torso triggered searing bands that lapped deep and cruel around his bones. Zach bent at his knees, keeping stiff as he could, to pick up a mitten. His goggles. He found and gingerly pulled on socks, snow pants, his helmet. His boots stood by the door where he'd left them. There was his other mitten. There was no sign of the GPS.

But he didn't need it. The cabin was so close to the hut, and the hut would be easily visible from the trees.

Zach cracked the door and peered out, queasy over heading into the nighttime wilds so unprepared. The skies had cleared. Dawn was dimly visible at the edges of the forest. Zach eyed the dark circle of trees warily. Were yellow eyes watching? Did reddened teeth wait, just there, just out of sight?

He put a hand to his damaged head as if to still the spin of his imagination. There was no monster. A monster hadn't wrapped that ski strap around the sleeping bag. A monster hadn't looted his bag searching for something. What he needed to fear was his father. Maybe Pike.

The fumes rising from the blanket went intensely bitter in his throat and painful to his eyes, as if to remind him of the urgency of fleeing.

He'd have to rely on the wind he heard howling outside to obscure his tracks as he headed toward the tree well shelter.

Zach scrambled out onto the snow, not powder now by the door but pressed more solid by the intruder's slither into the cabin. His skis and poles had been knocked over, either by the wind or the attacker. His boots wouldn't latch, the bindings iced over. Zach lifted each ski, his side a livid burning, his face all a throbbing pain as he jabbed the pointed end of his pole into the locking mechanism to knock out any obstruction. At last he was able to secure his boots to his skis.

He tried to ignore the rattle of branches in the forest around him, each sound the creature plunging through the woods to attack; the Underself weaving like a ghost through the trees. His headlamp picked up large indentations in the snow that had to be tracks, already so windblown they were unidentifiable. Which hopefully meant his tracks would vanish, too, even though the sky was clear and snow no longer fell.

The pain forced Zach to move slowly and to take breaths as small as he could make them. He traveled down the gentle slope through the trees in the direction of the mine, planning to cut along the edge of the clearing for easier travel where branches wouldn't snatch at him. His headlamp bore a dim hole ahead. Was his light making predatory things invisible in the darkness outside its circle? Was something, someone, even now softly, smoothly approaching as his headlamp blinded him to anything outside its reach?

He switched off his light. The seethe of wind through trees hollowed him with loneliness. Against the immensity of the mountains, against the unforgiving chill of the air, he felt keenly his smallness, his vulnerability, how easy it would be for jaws to swallow him. He waited to let his eyes adjust a little.

It was better, only having the coming dawn and the fading moonlight to guide him. Branches, fallen logs, rocks, stood out black and distinct against the snow without the headlamp, making obstacles easier to avoid. Even better, he had a wider range of vision, which lessened his sense of being followed, his fear of something slipping through the darkness unseen to finish its brutal work.

As the ground leveled and the trees opened into meadow, Zach stopped to orient himself, looking for the sign memorializing the Swede.

The wind whipped the snow into frenzied whorls in the openness of the clearing, clouds of it veiling things then snapping back to reveal what they'd hidden. Yes, there was the big rock—so close! Only ten feet from him. Which meant the sign was—yes, there it was against the rock face. Sure of where he was and where he was going, he followed the line of trees ringing the clearing in the direction of Mariah Trail.

The exertion, the deep breathing required now that he was no longer headed downhill, squeezed Zach's ribs so horribly that he paused to rest after moving only about fifty feet.

His injuries made all of it so much more difficult than he'd expected, not letting him move with enough rigor to warm himself. Maybe he should head back, at least the cabin had walls, maybe—

Zach stiffened at a noise. Tipped an ear toward whatever rippled through the air.

A flash of light caused a seizing fear, Zach's chest going painfully tender.

The light grew, stroking tree trunks, branches, seeming to come from everywhere and nowhere all at once. Zach recalled Dave's story of alien creatures descending from night skies to obliterate cattle and leave behind bloodless mystery, but he forced the idea away as childlike fantasy. No silent black ship hung over the meadow. Nothing but fading stars met his eyes when he looked up.

It came from almost exactly the spot he had planned to plunge into the woods to head in the direction of the trail.

Panic momentarily overcame pain and Zach dove into the trees to hide himself, a ski catching under a branch that took him a moment to free, a whip of pine across a cheek that made him gasp. But the second the shroud of a pine's thick branches lay between him and where the light was growing he squatted low, willing himself to disappear, to be absorbed. Maybe his black coat, pants, the way he was balled tight and near to the ground might keep him out of the thing's sight, indistinguishable from a rock or log poking through the powder.

He tucked his head between his knees, forcing himself not to look, to stare straight down into the snow, to avoid triggering the sixth sense of whatever approached that it was being watched; that its prey was eyeing it from the woods.

The light washed over him. There was silence. And then a voice.

"Come on out."

Zach didn't move. Didn't breathe.

"I can see you. I can see your tracks. Come out."

Zach obeyed his father.

CHAPTER 38

Zach lifted a hand to shield his eyes from the blinding brightness of the light Bram trained on his face.

"I've been looking for you."

Zach said nothing. Neither of them moved.

Bram cleared his throat. "I hope you know, what you saw—Pike attacked me. I was only defending myself."

Zach still couldn't see Bram's face, only the star of his headlamp, steady and fixed some thirty feet away.

"He must've picked up on something you did or said," Bram continued, "because he knew you'd figured out what he did to Ginny. Went after me same as he went after you, back in the Bowl. But I won." His father's voice softened, crinkled into kindness, and though Zach knew every word was a lie, that Bram himself had told Pike what Zach knew, he still wanted to swallow the sound of his father's affection deep, let it warm him, wash him clean.

The light didn't allow Zach to read his father's expression, to evaluate the changes on the familiar face.

"Is he—is Pike dead?" Zach asked, voice humiliatingly high, excruciatingly hesitant.

"He didn't leave me any other option."

Zach fiddled with his coat, feeling naked under the light, patting himself as if to check that he hadn't somehow been stripped and exposed.

"Come on," Bram said. "We'll go back to the hut together."

"I can't see. Because of your headlamp."

The light danced down as Bram aimed it toward Zach's feet, transforming its beam into an elongated oval that stretched from father to son.

Zach squinted at the dark shape that was his father. "What about the money?"

A pause. He pictured Bram's face going furrowed.

"What money?"

Yes, what money? The money his father had stolen from investors? Or the money Bram had held out to Pike like bait, only attainable if Zach was snatched from the world's reach?

"The insurance money," Zach whispered.

The light wobbled. "Can't hear you, buddy," Bram said. Zach slid slightly backward on his skis, unsettled by his father's bright tone, his lack of irritation.

Bram was hiding his Underself.

Zach could pretend he'd said nothing at all. Despite the way his hairs prickled, the way his eyes scanned the meadow around him for some escape, his exhaustion kept him from fleeing. Yet he couldn't force himself to move toward his father. Not without knowing who Bram really was.

This time when he spoke he was louder, but a tremble still fissured his voice, betraying his fear at questioning his father. "What about the insurance?"

A hesitation, as if sound in this place took an unusually long time to traverse the space between them. "I don't know what you mean." Bram remained so calm, his words so even, that Zach found himself hoping he'd been wrong, that his own memory, his own understanding, had been as dim and fragmented as the blowing snow made his father's light.

"I'm glad I found you. I've been worried, Zakky."

The sound of the nickname his mother had used ripped through him, sucking air from his lungs as sudden and cruel as the kick to the ribs in the sleeping bag.

Months of being "you," or "kid" or nothing at all. Months of being a thing summoned, dismissed, criticized, commanded, but not fully human. Not worthy. And now Bram was uttering the endearing diminutive only his mother and sister had ever used.

"Are you—are you crying? Stop that." Bram's disgust, his instantaneous anger, seethed through the darkness bare, as if masquerading as a loving, concerned father for so brief a time had been burdensome enough it made Bram all the more disdainful of Zach's show of emotion. "Sonofabitch," he muttered. "Just—let's get a move on."

Zach switched on his headlamp. It cast Bram's shadow to enormous proportions on the wall of trees behind him. Against the deep black of that shadow, his father's face was bloodless wax. A sneer carved across the Underself, teeth clenched. Zach shook, weightless and adrift.

"You didn't ask, Dad," Zach said, voice small.

Bram held up a hand to shield his eyes.

"What?"

"You didn't ask. How I got hurt."

Bram had no patience for other people's pain. Only when Bram was hurt or sick did pain and sickness truly matter, so unjust and awful, his family expected to bear witness and tend to him like a suffering saint. But even Bram, under normal circumstances, would've commented on what Zach could feel; his nose swollen huge and bent, blood curling down his face to flake on his skin like drying rust.

His father paused. Did he hear the challenge in the words? Yes, he had to, because his anger dissipated into a dismissive shrug, a matter-of-fact tone. "Assumed you'd fallen. You're always getting yourself hurt. Lemme take a look."

Bram slid a few feet closer before Zach called out, "No. You stay there," and Bram stopped, head tipping again in that childlike, curious way he had.

"Christ, this thing is heavy." Cringing, Bram set his pack down on the snow. It landed with a hollow clatter.

He didn't move toward Zach. Didn't speak. Only stared from a little more than twenty-five feet away, eyes a half-lidded squint that made Zach a bug in a jar, Bram giving an impatient *tap-tap-tap* on the glass.

Still with his same odd remove, Zach blinked back. Watched through his throbbing face as Bram's all-eclipsing shadow sprouted long talons that pierced the snow. Grew blackly shining serrated teeth when his father bared his, perfectly white and even and square, in the imitation of a man's smile.

"You obviously want to rest a minute," Bram said. "That's okay. I do, too. Then we'll go."

Human and inhuman overlapped. Tangled.

As Zach's chin lolled toward his chest under the awful weight of Bram's shadow and smile, his headlamp tripped over Bram's backpack. A flash of red from a mesh pocket made him look again.

It was the bottle of lighter fluid.

The clatter sound of Bram's pack—the same noise as when Zach set down a stack of firewood, threw kindling into the hut's stove.

Did his father have wood in his backpack?

Dry wood and lighter fluid. Lighter fluid and wood.

WARNING SIGNS

The attack, the avalanche, had left behind bruises. Brokenness. Proof of harm. And yet those physical, visible signs seemed somehow easier for his mind to cope with than the possibilities that now bent Zach, consumed him, and the base, devouring fear that rose from the reptilian part of his brain. He looked out on the scene, flipped through the events of the last few days, the last few months. All he'd witnessed, heard, overheard, suspicions he'd pushed away when they seeped into consciousness from his darkest edges. It all began to fold together, each fact a playing card riffling into a whole that neatly interlaced into the very worst of everything.

Zach's blood beat thick in his throat yet he sagged, utterly exhausted. The Underself, cruel and slippery, was Bram's true face. He saw that face, saw his father, who had told Pike he couldn't do the thing close up, tying Zach into the sleeping bag with a ski strap to distance himself, to erase Zach's voice as he'd tried to lay claim to his own name, his own humanity, calling out to the predator in the cabin. His father, so incompetent at building a fire, so unprepared for the wilderness, stuffing the ancient blanket onto the coals left in the potbelly stove thinking it would ignite, smoke, suffocate. And when the blanket's tatters only smothered, only steamed and stunk, Bram, gnashing his teeth, grunting that horrible, animal noise as he emptied Zach's backpack, his coat, had found the camping matches Zach's mother had carefully placed in his emergency kit, lit them, once again tried to set fire to the blanket.

But Bram had failed. Too frenzied, too inexperienced to set things alight, to understand the blanket's damp rot kept it from burning. And so the frustrated shadow of the Underself had beaten the thing on the floor it had decided was no longer useful as a living son before charging out to get supplies to set the cabin on fire.

In Zach's head, the GPS map. The timing clicked together. The trip from the miner's cabin to Pantheon to fetch fire starters, dry wood, lighter fluid, would take about fifteen minutes for a grown man as strong as Bram. A little longer to return uphill.

Zach followed the curves of the cruel logic, the story his father would tell. Zach had tried to go down the trail for help but had gotten lost trying to return to the hut. Poor kid must have felt lucky to have found the cabin, not realizing he was making fatal errors. And who could blame him, really. After all, Zach was still only a child! He must have spilled the lighter fluid as he was starting the fire. He didn't understand that when he fell asleep, when he ignorantly left the stove's door cracked, it might cast a spark, ignite the accelerant that he'd let puddle on the floor, drip on the blanket, seep into the dry, old wooden furniture. Of course that would set the cabin instantly ablaze, trapping Zach within its inferno. He probably never even woke up. He'd been found in the melted husk of his sleeping bag, after all. And the poor father, the poor girl, to lose the son and brother so soon after the wife and mother. Poor Bram, who'd lost so much family to addiction and fire. Poor, pitiable Bram, the true victim, the true survivor, as always.

His father jerked his chin in the hut's direction. "Time to go, kid."

Zach shook his head.

Bram hadn't left him for dead in the cabin. He'd only made sure Zach was trapped, neutralized, because Bram knew from experience that to get away with murder he needed Zach alive as the cabin burned.

"That's not a request," Bram ordered. "Let's go."

"It was you."

"What?"

"Was it the same with them? The fire?" Zach gestured limply toward his father's backpack.

Bram glanced down at the red bottle then back at his son, his claylike, pale face juxtaposed jarringly against the shadow behind him.

"Get that light out of my eyes, kid."

Zach turned off his headlamp, plunging them both into gray darkness, the sun beginning to lift the night's velvet.

"That's better," Bram said. Then more quietly, almost to himself, "Isn't it strange how you can see better without a light once the moon's out, or like now, just before first light? It's kind of beautiful."

Zach blinked, not sure what to do with his father's soft musings about moonlight and dawn. "That's why you have the lighter fluid," Zach said. "Because of before. Because you got away with it before."

"You're being ridiculous."

But Bram's voice was thin and his tone unnerved in a way that made Zach's body purge something noxious and parasitic, his dark speculations disgorging into words beyond his control.

"The articles—they said Serena and Abraham Junior had smoke in their lungs." Zach couldn't be sure given the semidarkness, but Bram seemed to flinch at the sound of the names. "They'd inhaled smoke, so the police knew they were alive during the fire, that they hadn't died before. Been killed before. But Abraham Jr., he couldn't get out of bed by himself. And your wife. She had problems. She was unconscious, the articles said. That's how you did it. Made sure she was asleep, lit a fire with one of her cigarettes where you knew it would catch, and left the little boy behind. So you could have all her money. Have whatever money you got for killing my brother. That's why you trapped me. But left me alive. To get away with it again. To get money."

His father cocked his head to the side, voice gone thin. "You're not supposed to be reading that kind of garbage, Zakky."

This time his father using the nickname didn't disassemble Zach, but returned him firmly to the present, grounded him so deep into himself that he understood the horrific vulnerability of his situation. Because he might be right about all his father had done and planned to do, but he still had no way to fight him off. At any moment Bram would shake away his surprise, his hesitation, and grab Zach, hurt him, steal him away from Bonnie for a thing as stupid as money, as insatiable as greed, as endless as Bram's desire for control. A furious ball of long-swallowed loathing tore open within Zach at the injustice of it all, and his voice was something else then, a spitting disdain in it as he said, "You don't call me that! Only Mommy does."

Bram scoffed. "'Mommy.' Can't just call her 'Mom,' like a normal kid. She made you such a baby." The outline of Bram's head gave a disapproving shake. "I told her you wouldn't be able to survive the real world the way she spoiled you, but she didn't listen. She had to make you into her little mama's boy."

His father's words made his mother's absence so present that Zach found his balled fists wiping away cold tears and painful strings of bloodied snot.

Bram flung a hand in Zach's direction. "Do you see yourself? You don't even understand who she was! She's not worth crying over."

Zach felt his next words as a betrayal despite knowing they were no secret. "I knew her. And I knew about her drinking."

"She didn't just drink. She was an alcoholic. And a terrible mother. Always turning you two against me, lying, babying you, disrespectful. Always sneaking behind my back."

"No! She was good. A good mom. She tried."

"She didn't try anything. Never tried to toughen you up. Never tried a program. She got what she deserved."

How many times had Zach heard his father's opinions on who deserved what? An endless list spooled out in memory, Bram worthy of respect, success, adoration, instant obedience while his family, the world, deserved only ridicule and correction.

The night she died his mother had threatened to leave Bram. Had revealed that she'd discovered his business was a fraud. Which Zach knew in his father's eyes meant she hadn't just fallen short of giving him what he thought he deserved, she'd threatened to destroy the things he thought were already his.

Zach reeled back in time to all he'd overheard that awful night after their last fight. The sound of his father stalking down the hall. The rumble of the garage door. But had Zach actually heard Bram's car drive away? He pictured his mother in a hot bath, trying to soothe herself after the explosion caused by the word "separation." Saw her quickly growing drowsy and loose because she'd had too much to drink at dinner, and then more to drink as she lay in the tub. He saw his father, only pretending to leave. A shadow creeping up from the garage, spindling silently down the hall and past the room where Zach and Bonnie slept. His father, turned inside-out to his full Underself, slipping into the bathroom where Grace lay with her body submerged, eyes closed, head resting against the edge of the tub.

When I see an opportunity, I take it, Bram had said to Pike.

It wouldn't have required much effort, not when she was like that. Not given his father's strength. A little pressure. A little patience. But there'd been that report. The one that blamed alcohol and pills. The one ruling his mother's death an accident. The report Bram had sent Aunt Felicity, smug over the way it shattered her. Didn't a report mean tests, exams, a search for evidence of a struggle if his mother fought back, tried to escape?

But how hard could his mother have tried, really, when she was like that. How hard would she have even been capable of fighting, incapacitated in that way.

And Bram hadn't hesitated to drug Russ, Dave, and Zach to serve his own ends. Serena, too, had died with some kind of sleeping medication in her bloodstream.

His mother might not even have run the bath herself. Zach pictured Bram carrying her in his arms, helpless, unconscious. Saw the smooth, merciless face of the Underself watch her slip under the water. Wait until it was satisfied.

The idea of it, that all this time his anger toward his mother had been unjustified, that she hadn't left him and Bonnie willingly but had been violently forced from the world, pulled from existence by a vicious hand that was supposed to protect her . . .

Zach bit down on the inside of his cheek. "She was leaving you."

Bram released an unamused laugh. "Always eavesdropping. Always sneaking around like your mother instead of coming at things straight, like a man." He paused, as if waiting for Zach to deny it, before adding, "If you heard that, then you know that even with all I did for her, she wanted to destroy my life." Zach saw the anger that radiated from the Underself at these words as red ripples in the semidarkness. "Even though she could barely function, even though I was the one who gave her her whole life, she still tried to destroy me. A drunken mess. That's what your mom was."

His father's cruel assessments glanced off Zach, gone insignificant.

"She loved me. And Bonnie."

The shadow-creature that was his father half laughed, half scoffed. "She ruined you."

"You did it," Zach said. "You took her from us."

"You're just a kid. A stupid kid lost in the woods."

A hard, condensed bile of outrage rose in Zach's throat. "I'm not."

"Not what?"

"I'm not stupid. Or lost."

Dawn was brighter now, the light losing its gray. The wind spun snow around Bram where he stood exposed in the clearing, and the furious tension of his face, the dark glower of his eyes, made Zach unconsciously lean back.

"What are you dancing around here, Zach?"

A deep swallow before Zach could answer, "You killed all of them."

The accusation seemed to raise the dead, because in Zach's eyes the swirling white of the snow became dead souls. Serena, the brother Zach had never known, his mother, even Pike, encircled Bram, made manifest, all sacrificed for the anointing his father thought their deaths would bring him.

"You make everything so difficult, you know that?"

Bram lurched into motion, flinging himself in his son's direction. Zach turned and fled.

CHAPTER 39

"Stop!"

Zach followed his tracks back toward the sign, focused on the possible refuge of the cliffs beyond. He would try to climb there, to pop out of his skis and scramble away from his father, who might not expect the steepness, who might fall or at least be too wary to pursue him along those cliffs.

His ribs burned. The cold, high-altitude air charred his throat.

"Goddamn it, stop!"

The shadow that was his father traveled at an angle across the snowy meadow, clearly aiming to intercept Zach as he moved along the tree line, but unlike Zach, Bram was slowed by having to break trail.

Zach had been so stupid. He'd done the opposite of what prey should do, poking and prodding instead of soothing and backing slowly away.

He reached the sign and glanced over his shoulder. Bram had gained ground but was still a little less than twenty feet from him, crossing the clearing.

Zach's mouth went dry and his muscles rigid as a dark potential licked at his brain. He froze where he stood and turned toward his father.

At seeing his son pause his flight and face him, Bram slowed, top lip hitching in a way that made Zach imagine the sibilant hiss of a satisfied exhale. The vivid, bestial monsters that had stalked Zach's imagination deflated, instantly tame in contrast.

Zach forced away the acrid convergence of terror and pain that filled him and tried to focus, tried to make himself a creature that was something worse than animal now, too. He'd mimic the mother anglerfish, holding out his stillness, his body, as a glowing lure, ruthless because like his father he, too, had made a decision.

Bram had worked so hard, weaving his webs of insurance, trusts, wills. Bram had waited so patiently for each of his opportunities, fostering weaknesses, addictions, justifications, just-right circumstances. Why was his son so selfish, so uncompliant? Bram deserved this. He was entitled. Zach was his son, his. And now Bram was so close that as he moved toward the promise of Zach's annihilation, his eyes seemed to take in nothing at all but the boy.

The air felt brittle around Zach as his father grew nearer. Everything would change. Was this who Zach really was? It would be easy to prevent it all. To call out. To warn.

His father was less than ten feet from him now across the clearing. If Zach was going to stop it, this would be his last chance.

"She ruined you," his father seethed to himself, to Zach, to an invisible judge and jury. "She ruined you both."

Bonnie. Bonnie without him. Bonnie, whose body, Zach knew now, with a sureness that was bone-deep and undeniable, his father would in time exchange, sacrifice, for money, prestige, success.

Zach stayed quiet, resolved to let it happen.

But no, it wouldn't simply "happen." That was the kind of lie

Bram told himself, and Zach refused to. His silence was action. Zach nodded to himself, and accepted a measure of sin to preserve Bonnie. To save himself. To avenge everyone his father had hurt. His decision to stay quiet brought a peace tinged with rancid satisfaction that spread, merged with his blood, his skin.

"That's right," his father hummed, growing ever closer, and his voice slowing, everything slowing. "Stay there."

If it worked, Bonnie would be safe. If it didn't? Well, Zach had still done all he could do. He'd done all he could think of.

Bram yelped. Floundered. A leg, ski still attached, had been sucked into the snow, leaving Bram sitting stunned on the powder, his other leg bent against his chest, and his arms flung wide.

The mouth of the mine was even less visible than it had been the evening before, now almost completely disguised by snowdrifts. Zach stared, his mind gone utterly blank, every bit of him waiting.

He hadn't expected a halfway result. Had been ready for his father to simply vanish.

Bram looked down at his body, at the snow, at the hole where his leg and ski were caught; the small, dark mouth of the mine's opening. He leaned away from where his leg was trapped in an attempt to free it. But this motion only resulted in him jolting down slightly, eyes wide with panicked incomprehension.

"What is it?" Bram's voice came out broken, choked. "What is this?"

"An old mine," Zach said.

Confusion tripped across his father's face. "In the middle of a field? No. Mines—they're in rock, they're in—"

Bram interrupted himself with a gasp, hands bracing against the snow as though something had taken hold of his foot. Zach pictured the miner's ghost wrapping itself around his father's ankle, saw the filminess of the lost soul lightly, longingly, pulling at it.

"You think you know things. But you don't. It's a mine shaft. Mommy and I found it."

"Don't just stand there, help me!" Bram commanded. Zach moved toward him, a trained response, his body's obedience and the way his mind was still leashed to Bram's orders a surprise.

He stopped and slid back a few paces on his skis, shaking his head. "I can't. It's too dangerous."

"There's got to be something, there's—"

"No," Zach said, the word a thrill, evidence of new strength. "If I go near you, we'll both fall."

His father's face snapped up. "The blanket! Get that blanket, I can hold on to one end, push while you pull. Or the sleeping bag, do you have it? Or—pass me your skis. I can brace myself on your skis. Distribute my weight. Pull myself out. Now, kid! Take off your skis, we have to—"

A shrill, desperate laugh from Zach.

"What's wrong with you? Help me!"

The laugh transformed into a retching; a gasping.

Because he had been right. Bram's words extinguished the last flicker of doubt Zach hadn't realized he'd still been sheltering.

"It was you," he said. "It was. In the cabin. You tied me up. Hurt me. Tried to burn it down and kill me."

"This isn't funny. This is—this could be bad, this could be—"

"You just admitted it."

"What? No, I'd never—"

"You said 'blanket.' To get the blanket. You know about the cabin. You tried to light the blanket on fire. It was you."

Bram stilled, his features seeming to shrink as he tried to recall his words. As his understanding of his confession, his vulnerability, coalesced, the tension in his face fell away. He looked melted, absent, staring blankly out at no one and nothing.

After finding his mother, after trying and failing to extract her body from the cold bathwater that morning, Zach had sat on the bathroom's tile floor, pajama bottoms soggy from the water that had sloshed over the tub's edge as he'd pulled at her, and had seen his reflection in the full-length mirror on the back of the bathroom door.

He'd looked just like his father did now. A person who for the first time truly saw that some things were irrevocable, beyond his control, watching the world uncouple even as you tried to spool time backward to undo mistakes.

"You killed Mommy."

Bram stared up at him.

"Your other wife. You gave us sleeping pills in the hut without us knowing. You gave her pills. And Abraham Junior. You burned him up. For money! I know you did. You knew he wouldn't be able to get out on his own. You don't care about anyone but you."

Bram shook himself, a dog's full-body tremble. His face warped with indignation.

"No," Bram spat, "no. None of that was my fault."

"You never said his name. Abraham Junior. Why not?"

"It's *my* name. He wasn't—" Bram cut himself off, as if seeing that whatever he was about to say wouldn't encourage Zach to help him. "You have to get me out of here! If you don't, you're responsible, you can't live with that, not helping—"

"Was he not good enough? To keep your name?"

Bram said nothing, arms scrabbling, trying to find purchase in the snow.

"You don't say my name, either. Does that make it easier? To do all this? For money. For nothing. And what you did to Mommy. She knew you were a liar."

"You're a child. You don't understand."

A sob welled up in Zach and came out in a wobbling, keening scream. "Just admit it!"

"Help me! Stop pretending to be so high and mighty when you aren't even helping me, when you're just standing there, letting your own father—" Bram blanched. "I can feel it, my leg, it's swinging, there's nothing down—how deep is it? Do you know how deep it is?"

"It was all Serena's money, and you lost it. You needed more. And you got more when Mommy died."

Bram flung his arms out wide to distribute his weight. "I didn't get anything but what I was owed." The words seemed to prompt a thought in Bram, and he stilled. "If that's—is that what you're trying to do? I can—I can understand that. We can make a deal, okay? If you help me, I won't be angry." Bram's eyes narrowed, examining Zach as if the boy hadn't been there before, not really, and was only now coming into focus. "If that's it, if that's what you're thinking? Maybe—maybe we're alike. And I'll find another way. For us to succeed."

All Zach had ever wanted, his father's admiration, his acknowledgment that Zach was an entirely separate person of his own, was written across Bram's face as he waited for his son's answer.

"There's no other way," Zach said, "except Bonnie."

Bram's surprise at the breadth of what Zach knew flitted briefly across him. But then he regained himself, eyes a cold smolder. "Yes. Now help me."

Zach looked down at the ever-ravenous, unfillable emptiness that was his father.

"I'd never."

Bram's handsome face twisted with spite. "You think you're so much better than me? You're a—a—parasite, feeding off what I provide. You're evil, tricking your own father into get—getting—stuck here, wanting me to what? Die?" A harsh laugh. "You're not better than me. Don't you know who I am?"

As if this influx of righteousness had injected him with new energy, Bram strained, all his strength channeled into his arms, his hands, his one free leg.

Zach, immobilized by his awe at the sheer will of it, the desperate strength on display, watched as his father called on every reserve of brute force in his enormous frame to push and thrash.

Bram rose from the snow, huge and dark and swift as the awful shadow that had unfurled behind him in the meadow. He fell to the side, kicked his legs and skis from the mine's opening, and pushed himself backward and away to safety. Briefly, he took stock of his condition, of the way the mine gaped wider now that he had somehow forced it to disgorge him. Then he stood, chest rising and falling as he inhaled deep, relieved breaths.

A vicious, victorious grin spread over his face.

CHAPTER 40

Whip-whip-whip.

For a moment Zach thought the sound was indicating some new brokenness in him, that his complete and abject fear had ruptured something.

But his father's eyes searched the sky, too. Together, father and son caught a glimpse of the distant, shining red beetle of a rescue helicopter before its path dropped below the line of trees around the clearing.

Their eyes met in a bizarrely mutual instant of panic. What was next, what would come now? Bram broke the moment, frowning down at the mine's opening before sliding a few more feet away from it.

Already Zach felt himself falling, understanding before his father seemed to that he would toss Zach into the mine, throw him into blackness to snap apart next to the miner's bones and join his ghost. And yes, when Bram looked at him again, Zach saw only the hard, cruel, and resolved expression of an Underself that had chosen its weapon.

"They'll know," Zach said. "Mommy, and your other family,

and Pike, and—and me? All gone? That many—they'll know. They'll figure it out."

"No," Bram said, calm now, the act already in his past, because once he decided a thing it was as good as done. "They'll blame Pike. He killed Ginny. He tried to kill me. He knew you had evidence. He found you. Attacked you in that cabin. I'll toss his glove in with you. I kept it. Where's the earring?"

"I—I don't know."

"Hm. Keep it to yourself, then. It doesn't matter. They'll find plenty of evidence on Ginny that points to Pike without it."

"I saved your life. After the avalanche."

"That was Dave."

Bram said this with such conviction Zach knew he fully believed it, had edited his memory to make it true and absolve himself of any debt.

Maybe all gifted liars were gifted because they believed their own lies.

A flat smile, Bram elsewhere, already cleaning up any evidence left behind in the miner's cabin, heading downhill toward rescue, alone.

"But you did do it, you killed Mommy, you—"

A dismissive shrug from Bram before he said, "Your mother was killing herself. I didn't do anything but expedite the process."

"Was she awake? When you did it?"

Bram looked almost puzzled by the question, the answer so obvious to him it wasn't worth asking at all. "When it actually happened? Of course. Otherwise she wouldn't have understood what she'd done wrong. Wouldn't have understood it was her fault."

A new kind of devastation cleaved Zach apart, the canyon of it filled to brimming with a cold river of shame, regret, horror, and fury.

"Her fault?"

Bram frowned. "She tried to destroy me."

"How could you," Zach choked out.

His father nodded as if the question wasn't rhetorical, as if it was a thing he'd considered and was willing, even eager, to explain; one final, fatherly lesson. "You believe a lie, kid. Your mother, the world, told you some things are bad, immoral, or whatever. But these things— I've only been rewarded for them. Because the truth is, the rules don't apply to everyone. Anyone successful, if you dig deep enough, you'll see they got that way by breaking rules. And once you understand that, really understand that truth? These things get easier."

"The fire," Zach breathed out. "Abraham Junior."

Bram swept a hand gently through the air as if sweeping away the ashes of his first wife, his first son. "If you're weak as she was, but tried to keep away everything your husband had earned, that he was owed, no logical person would expect him to sit there and just take it. It'd be unnatural. I thought maybe this time . . . but they're all the same. And I tried to toughen you up. Tried to teach you how things are. You never listened. But maybe now you get it." Bram gestured toward the mine. "Some part of you must have heard me. Because you tried to break rules, too."

"Monster," Zach said.

"No." His father's eyes had gone spider dark, his gaze utterly focused on his son. "The only difference between us is that you failed."

At this Bram lunged toward him and Zach's shocked, instinctive recoil caused him to fall sideways into the snow.

So stupid. So uncoordinated. He clawed wildly to right himself, thinking only of Bonnie, her tiny form asleep beside him. Bonnie laughing, Bonnie sticking out her tongue annoyed at him, Bonnie serious over her homework.

At least the note Zach had written was in the hut, hidden, saying something was wrong with Bram's business, that there was something to do with insurance. At least there was a chance someone would find it, report it, ask questions that might keep Bonnie safe.

Zach managed to sit up, sure his father's hands were about to bash his skull, fold over his throat, wrench him from the snow to fling him under the earth.

But Bram stood still, eyes staring to Zach's left, mouth agape. "What is that?" he breathed, barely hearable.

A creature loped across the clearing, clearly fleeing from the approaching sound of the helicopter. The thing stopped some ten feet away, arrested by the unexpected sight of the two humans.

About two feet tall, it was flat-bodied and wide. Four feet long from nose to tail. An amalgamation of dog, bear, fox, yet none of those, the bits and pieces of recognizable things making it unlike anything at all. It stood atop the powder without sinking, its back legs oddly bent as if it had not one but two ankle joints there. Heavy, thick fur went brown, then gold, then black as it shifted slightly.

It was an animal. Not some blue-skinned alien or supernatural, ravening monster, yet equally unidentifiable. Were it not for the intense black beads of the thing's hooded eyes, its part-dog, part-bear face would have seemed friendly; the kind of creature a prehistoric human might have lured into a ring of firelight with meat, and bred to tame.

"What the—"

At the sound of Bram's voice, the creature's head swung away from Zach and it fixed on his father, who went to an open-mouthed silence as if the thing had devoured his ability to speak.

The creature drew back a lip to reveal a long canine tooth.

Zach, not daring to draw its attention, said nothing, and didn't move. Though the thing was familiar, somehow, from a show, a book? He couldn't grasp it.

But he knew that this was his monster. The animal appeared

smaller than it had when Zach had seen it in the woods beneath the circling crows. More compact than when it had frightened him out of his hiding spot and up the mountain the day before. But it had the same shifting coloring. The same gliding, lightweight way of moving that made it seem to hover over the snow. And while the sight of it made Zach go still, the thing was so distant from his monstrous imaginings, had so effectively interrupted his father's attack, that he felt strangely calm even as Bram's hulking mass still loomed close by with its promises of pain and an infinite fall through darkness.

Bram switched on his headlamp, as if that might scare the animal, or clarify it. But all the light did was cause the creature's eyes to flash an otherworldly green in the morning's half-light.

A braiding together in Zach's mind. The vague whisper of a memory: the family watching a superhero movie years before. His mother had thought it might be too violent, but this concern had only encouraged his father to say they should all watch it. Seeing Zach averting his eyes from a scene, his mother had snuggled him close and whispered, "You know that character's named after a real animal? I've always wanted to see one. Supposedly they don't live in Colorado, but I don't believe it! I know people who have seen them, way up high. They look like a small bear. I hope I'm lucky enough to see one someday."

Ginny's ribs. The elk's leg. They were carrion feeders, weren't they? Hunted small game but otherwise consumed the already dead with jaws that broke bone. Elusive. Long-pawed. Able to quickly vanish up trees.

A wolverine.

Bram's eyes flicked to his frozen, silent son, then back to the animal. His lips narrowed into a decisive line.

The air went quiet in a way that made Zach's ears ring. The rescue helicopter must have landed somewhere and cut its engine.

A wolverine explained the tracks in the snow where the crows had circled what Zach was now sure had been Ginny's body, dumped by Pike in the woods before he'd been forced to move her due to Russ's curiosity, his insistence they investigate later. It explained the leg of the elk, yes, but those precise cuts, the elk's bones stripped bare? Dave's words swam back, and Zach saw swarming flies neatly digesting meat before the freeze, elkskin splitting in the sun.

It was all so simple, really. One thing died, or was killed, and others ate it. The result looked different from anything you could have predicted, because you didn't have the right knowledge to understand what to expect. Soon the wolverine would move on and his father would do the same as any other predator. Kill Zach, consume him, feed himself in a way Zach had never expected but logically always should have.

Bram squared his feet, his shoulders. He leaned forward and stared dead into the wolverine's small, flat eyes.

"Rah!" he yelled, Zach yelping in surprise at the volume of it, the threat in that single syllable. "Yah! Get out of here!" Bram's chest puffed forward, whole body taut with aggression, as he swung a ski pole in the wolverine's direction.

A low rumble as the creature peeled its lips back. Its snout wrinkled to retract the nose toward the green mirror of the eyes. It split its jaws to roar, a noise primordial, and yes, monstrous, a sound dripping with saliva, blood, one that came ripping out from somewhere deep.

The little round ears that had given Zach the sense the animal might have a friendly potential flattened to its head. It doubled in size as its fur stiffened outward. Its fangs extended, disproportionately long for its head. The wolverine's whole jaw, raw with blackish gums, bristling with those teeth, protruded from its skin in an otherworldly sneer. And the never-ending sound that whipped from it, tore from its wet mouth, was a horror that promised gulped blood and cracking bone.

"Yah!" Bram yelled again, but the wolverine's cry had siphoned the power from his voice, turned his skin sallow, rounded his shoulders.

The animal slowly lifted a front paw from the snow. Long, curved claws, thick and yellow in the dawn light, splayed from that foot. The imagined sound of these bird-of-prey talons click-clacked over a hard surface in Zach's brain as it took one step, then another, toward Bram.

Zach watched his father retreat from the creature, saw the terror turn Bram's handsome face to a contorted rictus of fear as he stared at those teeth and claws.

For what might be the first time in a very long time, Bram had unknowingly picked a fight with something stronger; something ready for him.

Bram stilled. His head tipped to the side, as if listening to a frequency Zach couldn't hear, and his eyes locked on Zach's, betraying a plaintive confusion.

A rushing sound—that's what his father must have already heard. Around Bram the snow, the ground, was falling, disintegrating, disappearing.

"No." His father shook his head, as though he could make the cave-in untrue. "No."

Zach saw his father's disbelief. None of this could happen. He wasn't like other people. He was precious, special, chosen. The destroyer, never the destroyed.

The beam of his father's headlamp flung up to the white dawn sky. Bram was there, then not there, devoured by the jaw snap of the man-made nothingness below. Only his scream stayed, backgrounded by the soft rip of falling snow and earth. The hole opened wider and wider again until it stopped two feet from where Zach lay.

Zach looked toward the wolverine, the only other witness, then back to the mine. Together they heard the scream fall, heard it fade down the mine shaft. Listened to it cut off, and heard the utter silence in its wake. They watched as little piles of snow, little rocks and chunks of dirt, released along the chasm's edges. Watched them delicately tumble into the void, until the ground seemed to, at last, fully settle.

The creature retracted its teeth. Shrunk down in size. It moved a few steps away from the cave-in before it paused to stare at Zach. Now that it wasn't being threatened, the wolverine appeared tentative, even frightened. Zach broke eye contact with the animal. Lifted his arms slowly above his head.

Out of the corner of his eye, he could only see the wolverine as an indistinct blot against the snow. They both waited, the sun rising to spread light through the trees.

"I am a person," Zach said low, voice quavering. "I am not prey. My name is Zach."

He remembered his mother saying those same words. Remembered her worried but proud expression the year before as she'd let Zach and Bonnie move forward across the open space in the trail alone, without her.

When he spoke again his voice rumbled from him even and soothing. "I am a person. My name is Zach. You don't need to be afraid. He's gone now. It'll all be okay."

The creature stood for one, two, three more seconds. And then it padded quietly into the forest.

ACKNOWLEDGMENTS

From the top of an inbounds Colorado ski mountain at age twelve, I watched an avalanche strip a three-hundred-acre mountain bowl bare in twenty seconds. My fifth-grade class was there that day to take an outdoor safety course, so the timing of that avalanche, our perfect view of it across a mile-wide valley, the way its air-shattering sound interrupted the Ski Patrol demonstration of how to use avalanche beacons, was a coincidence too unbelievable to ever include in a work of fiction. But my deep respect for the latent power of nature was born that day, and so was the idea for a story that might capture the way I felt watching that mountain slide. I'm so grateful I was lucky enough to grow up in a place like the Elk Mountains, where it's possible to witness nature at its most beautiful and terrifying.

Being raised as the fourth generation of my family born in a boomtown of the American West often described as a "playground of the rich and famous" also meant a childhood spent observing the extraordinarily wealthy and those who desperately want to stand among their number. So to the many fathers (and one specific mother) of childhood friends, classmates, and acquaintances whose

ACKNOWLEDGMENTS

relentless entitlement and self-aggrandization harmed others financially, spiritually, and all too often, physically—if you think you recognize some part of yourself here, you're probably correct. And if you're one of the children who grew to understand that sometimes those who claim to love you are truly only capable of loving themselves through no fault of your own, I hope you see your resilience and courage reflected in Zach.

Of course you can only lift a curtain to expose the bad if you see examples of the good. I would therefore like to thank my dad, Robert, whose love of wild places and lifelong work to preserve them has helped keep the destruction and privatization of the wilderness at bay around my hometown. Thanks also to my dad for being the sounding board for the likeliest of unlikely creatures that might stalk high altitude peaks. I have been so lucky to learn not just from my father but also from my grandfathers and now my own husband about what being a father, outdoorsman, protector, advocate, and all-around gentleman can look like.

This appreciation extends to my stepfather, Kent, who I would like to thank not only for caring so ably for my mother during her long terminal illness so many years ago but also for sharing his firsthand accounts of the cattle eviscerated on his Colorado ranch growing up. These true stories were the genesis of Zach's monster.

If you're a ski patroller who rode up a chairlift in the last several years in Vermont, New Hampshire, or Colorado and were interrogated by a nosy blonde with disturbingly specific questions about mountain survival and tech . . . Hello! Thank you for being so generous with your stories and advice.

Thanks also to the innumerable instructors and teachers of all types who taught me, like they teach so many others, to navigate, enjoy, and survive the backcountry. A special thank-you to the volunteers at Mountain Rescue Aspen who not only share these skills

ACKNOWLEDGMENTS

but risk their lives to aid those in danger. I'm confident you would have arrived far sooner than I allowed you to in this story. Many thanks also to Art Burrows for his backcountry expertise; this book is more believable for it. All mistakes with regard to mountaineering are, of course, my own.

While Pantheon Hut is fictional, it wouldn't have been possible to imagine it without the work of the 10th Mountain Division Hut Association, which has created an unparalleled system of backcountry huts I've had the pleasure of experiencing over so many years. Thank you for all you do.

A few resources were invaluable to the creation of this novel. The Colorado Avalanche Information Center proved to be an unparalleled source for accurate and detailed information regarding all things avalanche. John Branch's *New York Times* article "Snow Fall: The Avalanche at Tunnel Creek" expertly examines an avalanche disaster from every angle. This book would not have been the same without the candor of the survivors he interviewed, or Branch's exploration of how group dynamics, human desires, and everyday insecurities can contribute to catastrophe as easily as the very worst conditions. In a similar vein, thank you to mountaineering legend and writer Lou Dawson not just for agreeing to chat but for his incredible first person account of surviving an avalanche in an article titled "The Closest Call" published in *The Aspen Times*, a clipping of which I've carried around since 2004 in a folder vaguely labeled "Creative Inspo(?)." Zach's and Russ's harrowing experiences find their roots in this piece. Finally, Lundy Bancroft's *Why Does He Do That?: Inside the Minds of Angry and Controlling Men* was a constant companion as I wrote *Warning Signs*. It is because of Lundy's absolutely brilliant work and psychological insights that Bram has "learned his society's lessons too well, swallowing them whole."

ACKNOWLEDGMENTS

My inimitable agent, Helen Heller, has made every bit of living this writing dream possible, and I will be forever grateful.

I couldn't ask for better editors than Jeramie Orton, Harriet Bourton, and Lara Hinchberger. Their attention to detail and immersion in both plot and character has made all aspects of this book better. Thanks also to the teams at Pamela Dorman Books/Viking in the US, Penguin Random House in the UK, and Penguin Random House Canada, and thank you especially to Pamela Dorman, Brian Tart, Andrea Schulz, Patrick Nolan, Kate Stark, Kristin Cochrane, Marion Garner, Jane Cavolina, Kristina Fazzalaro, Kayla Fuller, Mary Stone, Catherine Knowles, Georgia Taylor, Roseanna Battle, Natalie Grant, Josie Staveley Taylor, Tricia Conley, Tess Espinoza, Diandra Abernathy, Mike Brown, Jason Ramirez, Dave Litman, Claire Vaccaro, Rebecca Marsh, Andy Dudley, Rachel Obenschain, and Bonnie Maitland for their hard work bringing this novel to shelves.

Thank you to Jemma McDonagh at the Jemma McDonagh Agency for allowing me to see my books in so many different countries, and to the team at WME for all their efforts to bring my work to film.

To my early readers, Nachel Mathoda, Liz Frigola, Ashley Tate, and K. T. Nguyen, I so appreciate you, your support, and your input. And thank you to my sister Rye, a constant source of kindness, advocacy, and advice as one of my very first readers for each project, and whose love of mountain creatures great and small inspired Bonnie's.

I've been absolutely blown away by the generous authors, many of whom I've admired for years, who took the time to read and recommend my work as a new writer. In no particular order, thank you to Shari Lapena, Ashley Audrain, Karin Slaughter, Sophie Hannah, Linwood Barclay, Abigail Dean, Sarah Pekkanen, Alafair

ACKNOWLEDGMENTS

Burke, Nikki Smith, Katie Gutierrez, Gilly Macmillan, Lisa Jewell, Lauren North, Jane Corry, Araminta Hall, Jennie Godfrey, and Chris Whitaker. And a very special thank you to Gillian McAllister, who truly took every opportunity to advocate for my work in a way I could never have dreamed of. You have all shown me what it means to be part of a community.

I cannot thank Jimmy Fallon and his team at *The Tonight Show* enough. They are consummate professionals who made me feel welcome and comfortable on television despite my nerves. And I remain, as always, the biggest fan of *The Tonight Show*'s fans who voted my debut, *Nightwatching*, as a Fallon Book Club pick. Thank you, thank you!

To all the readers, reviewers, and book clubs who give my work a chance, to the bookstores and booksellers who stock and recommend it, my ability to continue writing is all because of you, and I appreciate you every day. I specifically want to mention Buttonwood Books in Cohasset, Massachusetts, The Best Bookstore in Palm Springs, California, and Meagan Briggs of @meagansbookclub for being the very first members of the reading and book community to support my work. Thank you!

Thomas and Eleanor, you show me daily how caring, intuitive, perceptive, and capable children can be. I love you, and am so grateful to know you.

And as always, Jason. I will never stop marveling over how I got lucky enough to find you. I love you, and hope you know none of this would have been possible without you.